They're in Your Mind

THEY'RE
IN YOUR MIND

Susan Adair Harris

Personal Journeys Media, LLC
Trinidad, Colorado

Printed in the United States of America
First Printing: March, 2020.
Published by Personal Journeys Media, LLC
Paperback ISBN: 978-1-7344250-0-0
ePub ISBN: 978-1-7344250-1-7
MOBI ISBN: 978-1-7344250-2-4

THEY'RE IN YOUR MIND is available for purchase in print or e-book from Amazon.com, Barnes and Noble, and other outlets.

Also by Susan Adair Harris:

Death Lost Dominion

The Woman Who Saw Souls

To All Who Struggle to Grow Toward the Light

"Your theory is crazy, but it's not crazy enough to be true."
Niels Bohr

"If everyone helps to hold up the sky then one person
does not become tired."
Askhari Johnson Hodari

"Most of us want a dictator—albeit a benevolent one—
so we can pass the buck... You made me do that... A good defini-
tion of being a victim is when you keep the focus outside yourself
for someone to blame for your present circumstances..."

Edith Eva Eger, <u>The Choice: Embrace the Possible</u>

Contents

Acknowledgments

THIS BOOK BEGAN during years crowded with real-life social trauma and natural disasters. If I needed an emotional sandbar on which to gain perspective and rest from the flood of despair, I figured others did, too. A friend loaned me *The Bowl of Light*.* Within, I discovered the concept of the *'e'epa* as described by shaman Hale Kealohalani Makua. Whether or not you accept the *'e'epa* as deceptive psychic entities--an explanation I transplanted as a possibility--or prefer to use them as a metaphor for degrading social forces, they provide an anchor point in my novel for trying to comprehend how good people can condone and even commit bad behavior. We are all comprised of bits of good and evil. The trick is to incline the mix toward the positive as consistently as we can manage.

---

*(Wesselman, Hank. *The Bowl of Light: Ancestral Wisdom from a Hawaiian Shaman*. Boulder, CO: Sounds True, 2011.)

With Thanks...

MANY PEOPLE CONTRIBUTED to the completion of the novel. Judy Veris-Decker was always ready to help. Without Meghan Russell and Sharon Qualls, it wouldn't have been published. Others who assisted include Esra Beyatli, Kay Evans, and the Trinidad Writers' Group. Jeffrey M. Pill, Mary Miller Johnson, and Heather Carey continue to be my most ardent supporters. As always, my beloved husband David Harris provided reference information, a voice of perpetual encouragement, and chocolate.

Ben Boyd, a faithful reader and author, died before he could tell all the stories that danced in his head. I thank him for his gracious reviews and honor him for his beautiful spirit he shared so generously.

Finally, I am forever grateful to my fans who are able to peer through the morass of words I present to find thought provoking gems worthy of the hunt. I love hearing their feedback, because it is for them that I publish.

Chapter 1

Wildfire

RICHARD TELLER DIDN'T mean to die. Or maybe he did, without knowing. His life was wobbling like a top losing momentum, but he was too far inside to see. He stood staring stupidly at the wall of flame surging toward him. The savage, panting hunger of the beast overwhelmed his senses. In that moment he lost his ability to move or even think. He could see his neighbor Brad's house screaming as the monster swallowed it whole, belching flames from the holes where Brad's bedroom should have been. Rich thought he heard a laugh in the roaring crackle. The monster was amused because humans had believed in houses, in safety.

Movement beside him caught Rich's attention. Julie was on her knees, clawing through the grass he had meant to mow. The light glistened from her wedding rings—the ones he had yet to pay for. The wedding had been a big pain, but the two of them were supposed to live happily ever after here in his house by the lake, his inheritance from his dad.

Nothing was as it was supposed to be. Sparks fell around Julie like tiny discarded stars—she who had been the anchor of his universe, the glory of his bed. The wildfire would be the end of it all.

I've killed us both! The thought flashed into his mind as he slapped away an ember that had begun blackening his shirt. Smoke was searing his lungs. The wildfire was racing toward them fast… too fast. He coughed as he realized he really had waited too long to leave. The monster vomiting digested pieces of Brad's house would be their death. But death had never felt real to him. He had mocked it many times, always confident he held the aces. He'd been injured and sickened, but he couldn't be defeated. Surely. Like Dad said, you just had to decide to make it through.

"Get in the truck!" he shouted, but Julie wasn't paying attention. She was still frantically searching the ground.

What the hell are you doing? he muttered in his mind, but before he could give his question voice, she had found the tubing he bought to fix the fuel line the wood rats had eaten off his tractor--two long lines of black tubing—the wrong sizes. He'd thrown them aside when he realized. He had been so sure... so sure he could use the tractor to make a fire break, to be the one who didn't have to evacuate, to be able to show Brad that education doesn't make a man. He was still certain his plan could've worked...if only the tubing hadn't been the wrong sizes.

Julie rose to face him. Her eyes seemed to reflect the fierce burning as she glared at him. She shoved one of the tubes into his hand.

"Into the lake!" she commanded as she ran toward the dock. She didn't bother to glance back to see if Rich was coming. He was.

He didn't know if he was glad or angry to have her giving him orders. *Maybe she doesn't care if I'm following*, he thought bitterly. *She blames me. She wanted to evacuate yesterday.* He hated it when she made him feel like this—foolish and submissive. But at least she had a plan.

She stopped and pivoted so quickly that her auburn braid slapped her arm. She was shouting at him. "We'll swim out before it gets here—only far enough so we can stay underwater and these tubes will reach the surface. Expel as much air as you dare to help you stay down and suck up only what you have to through the tube. Breathe in slowly and exhale slowly. Be calm."

"The truck..." he repeated, knowing she couldn't hear and not caring. He knew she was right. They had been married just long enough for him to know she thought she was always right. There was no time for them to drive the winding road to the highway. The lake was their only escape.

Rich gawked as Julie reached the end of the dock and performed a lifesaving leap to avoid fully submerging, flinging herself as far out into the water as she could. He dived after her, proud of his college form. He glided some distance before he surfaced, choking on both water and smoke. He could see her already swimming with quick, desperate strokes, so he increased his pace. He was tall and strong and had always been a better swimmer so they reached the drop-off together. She threw him a hasty half-smile as she expelled the extra oxygen in her lungs and sank from sight. She didn't need to sink as far, she was that short.

He did his best to copy her, fighting the panic he felt as he lost more and more air. He sucked a long drag from the tube and choked, realizing he hadn't situated it above the water. What a dumb mistake. Nothing she would do. She was a professional mermaid—the entertainment kind. He had first seen her swimming up and down in front of a picture window in a fancy Vegas restaurant, blowing kisses to the guys at the bar. They used to bribe the bartender for her name. She was everything he ever wanted then, with her long red hair writhing around her head and her boobs bulging from the top of her glittery costume. She was a fantasy. He used to call her his wet dream. She always made a face when he did.

He resurfaced, coughed, and tried to sink again. He needed to use his hands to force himself down, treading water in reverse...too much effort for tiny gulps of thick, hot air. He thanked himself for wearing heavy boots—the ones Julie scorned for being stupid in the summer. They might help him stay deeper, and he could tell staying deeper was becoming more imperative by the minute. Why hadn't she insisted on their evacuating yesterday? Was she testing him?

His feet touched the bottom, raising a cloud of silt, and then he had to struggle not to bob up. Julie was only a vague shape. He wanted to grab hold of her. He wanted to clutch her survival.

A chunk of burning debris zipped into the water beside him. A part of Brad's house? Served Brad right. *Burn that mansion of his to the ground. He likes to invite us over—a barbeque with nasty imported beer and bragging. Enough to make you hurl. The latest, the best, of everything. Look, Rich, our new outdoor kitchen the size of your whole back yard. Sonuvabitch.*

Rich felt himself slowly rising. *Why is it so hard to stay down? Don't bodies sink?* He exhaled more air, hating himself for doing it because it intensified his panic. This staying at level was Julie's thing, not his. He was a big man. He needed big air. *There's no way this is going to work,* he thought, feeling Death gradually sliding coils around him…anticipating a meal. *People are naturally buoyant. They're supposed to float.* This was Julie's fault. Why the hell did he listen to her, anyway? At least in the truck they would've had a running chance.

* * *

Just beyond his reach, Julie was searching for him. His flailing had roiled the water into the consistency of overcooked lentil soup, but she thought she could feel him nearby. To keep herself from weeping with fear for him, she fed her anger.

He can't take my advice. Oh no. He knows better. He always knows better. He's probably trying to tread water and he's sucking up soot.

What would she do if she found him? She couldn't breathe for him like the scuba people do. She didn't dare hold enough air. In reality, she was already sucking in too much smoke herself even though she was barely moving at all. Her lungs felt like the gunk in the bottom of Rich's grill—the nasty caustic goo that never seemed to burn away. Was this what emphysema felt like? Her mom had died of emphysema. Julie thought ruefully she should've pitied her mother more.

Rich was thrashing again. If he kept it up, he'd run out of energy before the fire passed. And then… the probabilities were ugly. Drowning? Burning up? Her stomach knotted. *Damn him! I'd be scared for him—I AM scared for him--but I'm furious, too. He asked for this! He told me he knew the fire was going to miss us. He knew. And I listened. I asked for this! I did what he said! I knew better and I still did what he said.*

So this was marriage. This was love. Keeping him happy. Letting him think he was smarter than he was. Never letting herself realize that believing she couldn't function without him was his turn-on.

She might have been crying. In the water, it was hard to tell. She wanted to let go and sob. Being slightly hypoxic was flushing all sorts of crap out of her cells. What kind of relationship did she have with Rich? Were they in love or merely stuck together like bare-naked old candies in the bottom of her purse? Had she married out of abject loneliness?

Her thinking halted abruptly as awareness that she was rising zapped an alarm through her body. Rich wasn't the only one in jeopardy. If she didn't calm down, she'd pop to the surface like so much dry wood. She had to relax, slow her respiration, exhale a little more, ignore the voice screaming she wasn't getting enough oxygen. Draw only tiny half-breaths through the tube. Keep the tube above water.

Routine. Staying down should be routine. She had to make it feel routine. In beginning mermaid training, she and Lani had been taught to use visualized meditation to keep their respiration under conscious control. Think of a safe, soothing scene. And after many hours at work, they could stop visualizing and use a key word.

Peace. Kind of a corny, obvious key word, but it worked. Julie repeated *peace* in her mind and her body relaxed. She had learned to use *peace* when the unexpected happened—like the time Lani accidentally crimped the air tube. *Peace* when the tubes were tangled. *Peace* when the set collapsed and pinned her down.

Her heart was still pounding. A word wasn't enough. She was too frightened—for her, for Rich. She needed to create a mental scene— a place for escape. She needed to return to a time when water was her friend and she felt empowered surrounded by it. She needed to remember her childhood when water was her invisibility cloak—her favorite refuge:

* * *

I was about ten years old.

"DAMMIT, WHERE'S JULIE?" bellowed my dad.

I could hear him even below the waves. I loved it down there, peering through the yellow plastic of my facemask, watching fish and people's legs as they swam by. My dad's legs were a funny, hairy green. The leg holes of his swim trunks ballooned in the water as he swam by me. He wanted

5

to teach me to swim, but I wouldn't let him. I hated his impatience. I hated his swearing.

I moved away—not actually swimming but walking on the bottom—no, not walking. Gliding. I felt graceful and beautiful—no longer the dumpy adolescent my sister liked to mock. I wished I didn't have to surface.

"DAMMIT, JULIE. I CAN SEE YOU."

I knew he was bluffing because he was facing the wrong way. Somewhere my mom was laughing through the smoke rings of her cigarette. "She's right behind you, Ernie."

I stood up. "Yes, Dad?"

"Didn't you hear me call you? Are you going to spend the whole day underwater?"

"I watch people swim. I learn things."

"Well, you sure as hell aren't learning anything from me. You're still dog paddling like a baby."

Mom took a long drag on her cigarette. "Oh, leave her alone, Ernie," she said through her exhale. "She's doing fine."

I tried to look repentant, although I couldn't imagine what I was sorry for. Dad liked his kids to be sorry.

I waded closer to shore so I could lift the cracked white rubber rim of my facemask to release the tiny pond sloshing beneath my nose.

"What the hell kind of life are you going to have when all you want to do is spy on people underwater?"

"She probably watches people pee," interjected my sister Barbara from the shore where she was sunbathing...as usual.

I wanted to tell Barbara you can't see pee in the water—not in lake water—but I didn't. You can feel the warm spot. It's nasty.

"At least she isn't getting sunburned," offered Mom, and I could guess she was glaring at my sister.

I dipped below the waves again, grateful for the silence washing away the muffled sounds.

Julie felt braver filled with the illusion of invulnerability that drove the little girl inside her. Her eyes were closed. She was detaching from her situation beneath the fire. She thought of her dad scoffing when she told him she was going to have a job as a professional mermaid, as though she had said she was going to make a living playing with dolls. He told her mother he was certain his youngest daughter was secretly a prostitute because the only occupations he knew about in Vegas had to do with gambling, sex, or both.

Julie remembered the time her mother brought Dad to see her show. Even Ray the bartender said her performance that day was poetry. Dad wasn't impressed.

"You want me to say I think it's great that my daughter is a display in a goddam aquarium?" he asked his wife. "Do you have any idea what those men at the bar are thinking when they watch her in that outfit she wears? She might as well be a prostitute. They're undressing her in their minds every day."

If Julie had been on dry land, she might have sighed with the memory. Trying to please her father was a hopeless task. He didn't like her and he didn't like Rich. But all that was long ago. Her mother was gone and her father was cursing at the caretakers in the retirement home. Today being a mermaid wasn't a job...nor was it a fantasy.

She began a chant in her mind, a chant of survival:

I need to relax. I can command my breath. I have enough air to live.

I need to relax. I can command my breath. I have enough air to live.

* * *

Not far away, Richard clawed the water, grasping for the shape he couldn't see. The lake mocked him, turning liquid to clouds so the only one who could save him had disappeared. Everything was wrong.

Julie, help! He could feel the heat above him—no, not above him. On him! His hair was on fire! He spat out air, sinking low enough for the cool water to surge over his head. He couldn't be hysterical. Men didn't get hysterical. But his vulnerability had become physical pain. It was real. His head was burned. It hurt like hell. Death laughed. Rich could hear the voice: *You're losing, Rich. You're a loser.*

He sucked hard on his tube, but instead of oxygen he sucked smoke. His chest ached with longing. He wanted to cry. Where was the happy ending? Where was Julie? He never should have listened to her. He was too big for this goddam mermaid thing. He was suffocating.

His mind screamed. *OH GOD, I'VE LOST HOLD OF THE TUBE! WHERE IS IT? WHERE THE HELL IS THE GODDAM TUBE!*

He had no reserves—no more air. *Dammit, where's Julie? Why doesn't she help me? Julie! Julie! If you love me, help me! Julie! JULIE!*

* * *

Just beyond his reach Julie was holding fast to her lifeline, concentrating on keeping it vertical. Her eyes were fixed on the light above her that wasn't sun—light that writhed in undulating yellows, oranges, and reds—the beast smelling cowering life beneath it, waiting for a chance to strike, to consume. She struggled to contain her fear.

She could feel Rich thrashing. Hopeless desperation short-circuited her nerves making them sizzle and pop like the fire. What could she do? What in God's green earth could she do? How could she tell him he had to calm himself or he wouldn't be able to control his breathing? She squeezed her eyes closed to concentrate, realizing she was absorbing his panic.

Without warning, his fingers found her, gripping her neck, choking away the precious air she was holding. He dragged her closer, accidentally allowing water to fill her tube.

She didn't let go of it. Her mind was racing. In lifesaving she had learned to back off and let a panicked victim lose consciousness so she could tow him to shore. But if Rich lost consciousness it wouldn't help. She couldn't surface. She couldn't tow him.

He's going to kill us both! Oh, Rich. I love you. Why did you have to do this? Why couldn't you act like an adult for once? We could've made it. We could've survived.

Survival was a chill, a concrete thing that gradually encased her heart. Only one could live, and it wouldn't be Rich. *I can hold my breath...a long time. I practiced. I can't overpower him, but I can outlast him. I simply have to...hold on...relax...know I can do this.*

His grip loosened. He was drowning...or burning. *And there's not a damn thing I can do about it. Not a damn thing. NOT A DAMN THING!*

Rich, I'm sorry. I'm so, so sorry. You could've shared my tube. I could've helped you, but you had to stay calm—trust me. You had to work with me.

She pushed his unconscious bulk off her and snaked her tube back to the surface so she could blow it out. She had to risk sucking in air now. She couldn't wait any longer. There wasn't much oxygen in the smoke...but enough. Surely it was enough. She tried not to take the caustic gas into her lungs. Just sip. She sipped at it like it was an expensive single malt scotch whiskey. Sipping—that was the key. Sip and exhale...just enough. Her world was blurry, threatening to float away and leave her behind, but it didn't.

It's still here. I'm still here.

Forgive me, Rich. Forgive me, God.

I'm still here.

Chapter 2

The Mermaid on a Rock

DARKNESS DISGUISED THE line between water and sky so that all appeared to be blackness from below. Was it safe to emerge? Julie tried to imagine the scene that might lie waiting for her in the stinking night air, but her thinking had congealed thick and cumbersome as her body temperature dipped. She couldn't concentrate. What was it she was deciding? Breathing. Yes, breathing. Of course. Seizing more than a sip of air…finally…after all these hours. Her lungs ached to feel a rush of oxygen. Worse…she felt so very sleepy. Red flag. Too much chill. Sleepy plus water. Even without thinking, she knew the equation. If she lost consciousness, she would die. The water would win. There could be no more deciding. She had to warm herself.

She rose slowly toward the surface, unsure if she should trust the illusion of grace that swept through her. The water reflected conflicted heavens where the blood orange moon struggled to find a slot between dark clouds. When her face was above the waterline, she gulped a tentative breath and choked on the soot still rioting in the air. Even so, the luxury of a long inhalation was worthwhile. No mermaid show had ever kept her down this long.

Around the lake the land lay beneath smoldering ash, as though it had suffered a surge of lava and not fire at all. The homes that had once elbowed one another for space along the shores were represented by only an occasional naked chimney thrusting third finger defiance into the sky. Disfigured black skeletons of boats and trucks lay as though strewn among the ruins of metal sheds and boatlifts. Here and there, bricks tumbled out of order, prostrating themselves before the destruction.

"Focus!" Julie ordered herself, hearing her voice as an alien growl in the snapping, hissing landscape. Bright spots of crimson and gold flickered through the gray ash. Like hangers-on after a party, partially hidden bits of flame refused to leave. If she tried to escape, they would singe the plastic of the soles of her sneakers before she could reach...where? Where could she go, anyway?

Yet there had to be some refuge between the deadly chill of the water and the searing heat of the land. She scanned the shoreline for a rock formation she remembered. The neighbors had fought over whether it should be bulldozed away to make more beach. With no vegetation there to burn, surely the stone would be cool enough by now to be safe. At least she could pull herself out of the water that seemed to suck away more warmth with her every heartbeat. She had stopped shaking. That was bad. She had battled the cold for these many hours by envisioning times when she was miserably hot, but her body would tolerate no more illusions. She was sliding into hypothermia.

She struck out toward the rocks, purposely avoiding seeing the bulk that was Rich's body bobbing gently near the shore with the evening waves. She couldn't think about him now. The fact of him was too soggy, too heavy with recriminations. Her instincts for survival shoved him into the blackness.

Swimming felt oddly difficult, as though the water had somehow thickened into black oatmeal. Scrambling with soft fingers that scraped their flesh onto the coarse rocks sapped the last of her strength. The stone retained warmth from the fire that had passed nearby, and she hugged herself to it as she curled into a fetal position on the tiny ledge. Sleep soothed her before she was aware.

Chapter 3

Waking to the Nightmare

WATER SPLASHED INTO her face, a spray of cool wetness. *That Rich and his stupid jokes.* Julie opened her eyes to tell Rich to leave her alone and saw a helicopter gleaming against the morning light. Her mind came whimpering back to consciousness. How had she not heard the deafening roar? The sound crushed against her now as the wind from the blades threw up more water. Beneath the orange-and-white body of the helicopter hung a huge orange bucket, dipping into the lake, creating rings upon rings of tiny waves.

Rescue! She tore off her still damp white shirt as she struggled to her feet and waved it.

"Help me!" she whispered, thinking a whisper was as good as a shout against the thunderous sound.

The helicopter whooshed away, sucking her hopes along with it.

"Damn," she muttered, pulling her shirt back on.

The clouds of smoke had parted somewhat, leaving a gap for a scarlet-stained sun to beam light over the scene. She tried not to look for Rich, but she couldn't stop herself. His body pulled her eyes to the side of the lake where his bulk bumped against someone's metal dock. The fabric of the bright red t-shirt she had bought him—the one that said "BOSS" on the front--swayed slightly in the tentative morning waves. A tiny strip of his back shone pink and wet above his belt line. She felt sick and defeated. Her last insane hope that he might have survived, that she might have been wrong to dismiss him, disintegrated. He was definitely dead.

Now what? She hugged her knees to her chest and wondered why she wasn't crying. The fire, the lake, his death—it was all too much. She who cried over old dogs and injured children and muti-lated butterflies had no tears for her dead husband. Her chest felt paper-thin, as though she had been run over by a steamroller. No blood could circulate through her crushed heart. Her mind wasn't certain she hadn't fallen out of dimension into a nightmare.

The increasing roar of a helicopter made her turn toward the sound. This one was smaller and headed straight for her. Someone leaned out the side, waving at her, so she stood and waved back. The helicopter inched closer. A person in a helmet seemed to be settled in some kind of strap seat that was being lowered by someone else in a similar uniform. Somehow, the helicopter managed to deliver the person to the spot where Julie was standing.

"Are you injured?" shouted the helmeted person, who turned out to be a woman. "Do you hurt anywhere?"

"No. Just cold. I was in the water and then here on the rock."

The woman slipped straps over Julie. "I'm going to signal Jose to take us up. I've connected you to me, so you're perfectly safe. Don't look down if it bothers you. Is there anyone else we need to pick up?"

Julie strained to see the dark eyes behind the helmet. "My husband is dead. That's his body floating by the dock there."

"We'll send people back for him. We're a rescue crew, and we have plenty to do." The woman's voice slapped the air like waves against the side of a metal dingy. This wasn't her first rescue or her most dramatic. The line went taut and soon both women were in the air where the scent of burning swirled with them.

Julie wanted to cry, to sob, as she clung to the rescue lady. But she didn't. Mermaids don't lose their composure. *Stay in character.*

Arms from within the helicopter hauled her in, fastening her into a seat as the helicopter tilted into a turn. They were leaving the lake...and Rich...behind. The man who had pulled them in squatted beside her, slipping headphones over her ears.

"My name is Randy," he told her through the headphones. "We're taking you to a staging area a safe distance from Eden where paramedics will check you out and see to your needs. Are you having any trouble breathing?"

Julie stared at him. He wore a white beard—like Santa Claus. Breathing. He had asked about breathing. She vaguely remembered coughing. Air was fickle. She nodded.

He slipped a cannula into her nostrils and she felt cool oxygen irritating her nose. She coughed, harder than she had before because she realized she could. Her lungs hurt.

"Just take it easy and breathe as naturally as possible," Santa Claus directed her. "What's your name?" He leaned close to hear her reply.

"Julie, Julia Scott Teller, Mrs. Julia Scott Teller."

"Are you burned?"

She shook her head. "I hid in the water. I'm a mermaid."

He was smiling slightly as he held her wrist in his hand. "Good for you. Let's see your temp." He held a small device to her temple. "A little cool. I'll wrap you in a warm blanket and you can relax until we reach the staging area. Just signal me or tap my arm if you need anything."

She nodded. In spite of the horrible noise, she felt sleepy. She didn't want to live in this world. She wanted to go home to Rich. She abandoned consciousness and Rich held her close.

When she woke, she was lying in a hospital bed, surrounded by diaphanous turquoise curtains. A drip was delivering liquid into her hand and a cannula exhaled gentle oxygen into her nose. It itched something fierce. Would anyone notice if she pulled it out? She did. She was rubbing the spots where her nostrils were irritated when a male nurse came bustling in.

"What happened to your oxygen," he said rather than asked. He didn't pay attention to her as he tucked the two prongs back in place, but he had to notice she was conscious because he spoke to her. "Doctor's orders. Your lungs are recuperating." His face flushed red and sad pockets hung beneath his eyes although his body bulged with muscles beneath his scrubs. If he had planned to be a hero, he hadn't planned on being on call for so many hours. He didn't need to tell her she wasn't his only patient. "Well, good morning,

Bright Eyes. You're looking much, much better. I'm Bryan. I've been checking in on you."

"How long have I been here?"

"Since yesterday. The doc gave you something to help you rest because you were pretty agitated when you arrived—which made sense because you were both hypothermic and hypoxic—cold and half-suffocated." Hair that might once have been auburn lay mown to a stubble in a ritual circle around his bald crown. In defiance, gray hairs sprouted from his ears.

Julie lay back against the avalanche of pillows beneath her head. "I apologize if I said anything rude to you. I appreciate your help."

He smiled. "Thanks but you didn't say anything unkind. You did keep muttering about being a mermaid, though. I think that was the reason the doc gave you something to help you sleep."

"He thought I was delusional."

"I guess."

She struggled to sit and he automatically leaned over to assist. When she was settled again, her bed readjusted, she touched his arm. "I wasn't delusional, Bryan. I *am* a mermaid. A professional. I worked a bar in Las Vegas—the pool behind the bar—you know, swimming around in a sequined tail."

His laugh was loud and long. "Well, that's a new one on me! On the doc, too, I guess. I can't wait to tell her."

"I was trained to stay submerged for a long time with only a little tube to provide air. The lake saved me from the fire... My husband died." The last sentence slid out with a plop like a slug set free.

Bryan's face fell. "Oh, honey, I'm sorry."

"He wasn't the only one who died, I'm sure."

"No. Not the only one." His sympathy softened the air and made her want to cry, until a quiet buzz interrupted. He glanced down at his beeper. "I gotta run, but I'm glad you made it. You're my first mermaid." He patted her hand before he hurried away.

She tried to smile but the image of Rich's body expanded to crowd out all other thought. Rich was dead. Her husband. The man she had trusted to make her life more predictable and less insecure.

The man who had made her into a wife. She closed her eyes, wishing her drip were poison. Her unloved consciousness slid away.

She woke to the sounds of the hospital—business-like plastic sounds of soft dings, erratic voices, and doors opening and closing—lives coming and going—an encapsulated world where tightly made beds signaled adjustments in population. When she opened her eyes a crack, she could see Belinda sitting beside her, scrolling through emails on her phone.

Julie kept her eyes closed. The last person on Earth she wanted to see was Rich's mother Belinda, self-appointed matriarch. She rested like a blotchy pink sack of pudding, drooping over the edges of the chair beside the bed. Her enormous chest rose and fell with the slightly wheezy breath she pushed in and out through her wrinkled pink mouth. The flowers of her dress seemed to stretch and groan around her, straining in a hopeless attempt to disappear into the night of black background fabric.

Belinda had not approved of Rich marrying Julie. Although Julie's lowly status as a mermaid was particularly odious, Julie doubted Belinda would have approved of Rich marrying anyone. No one was good enough for her boys. She had probably imagined a life with them perpetually orbiting around her—especially Rich, the one she thought most closely resembled a Greek god. When Rich and Julie had first lived together in an apartment not that far away... before his father had escaped from the hospital into death...Belinda felt free to call at any hour of the day or night to request—more like demand—take-out tacos or ice cream or maybe a nice thick steak. Mostly Rich went. He hated discord. But beneath his slavish attention and vows of devotion, he hated his mother as much as he loved her. He couldn't admit it.

Rich. An image of his body floating face down resurfaced in Julie's mind. She felt nauseous and mortally wounded and trapped in a hostile universe. Even Belinda was preferable.

She opened her eyes.

Belinda didn't notice.

"Thank you for coming," said Julie in a voice that was a croak.

Belinda snorted—not on purpose. She was merely breathing. "Oh, Sweetie. You're awake at last. Of course, you know Rich will never wake up." The enormous freckled pillows beneath her double chins heaved. "My poor, poor baby. You threw away a good one when you let him die. The nurse told me about it." Belinda began to cry, or maybe it was a sob strangled by suffocating emotion. The bag of pudding was quivering dangerously, as though it might suddenly burst and smother them both with corpuscles stuffed with self-pity.

Julie waited a polite minute. "I love him, Belinda." The scene needed discordant music in a minor key played on peculiar antique instruments. Nothing about it felt real—except the pain where her heart should have been. Why wouldn't Rich evacuate when she asked?

Belinda dragged a soggy tissue from the pinched chasm between her breasts and dabbed at her eyes. "Of course you cared. Of course."

"Everything's gone, isn't it? The house, Rich, and everything."

Belinda turned toward her with bloodshot blue eyes behind heavy purple glasses, peering at Julie with acid focus. "Everything. Everything Earl and I worked for all our lives. I told him the two of you weren't ready to take it on."

"I'm sorry. We did our best. Rich died trying."

"Nothing left but our home…and the business. Al will have to run it now. Earl would be upset. He always favored Rich. He was never fair to Al. Never forgave him for not being good at sports. I'm sure that was it. Earl loved football. He and Rich went to every home game. Sometimes Al went, too. He wasn't a fan. Well, God has intervened. Al will have his chance, after all."

Stomaching Belinda was enough—too much. Julie couldn't ask herself to add any images of the brother Rich called Fat Al to the collage in her mind--Fat Al who obediently sucked parasites from his mother's hide, retreating to cower within the safety of her razor-toothed mouth when challenges arose. He always felt like a threat—as though he might unhinge his jaw at any moment and devour Julie whole. She remembered him staring at her chest in her wedding dress—not because the dress was especially sexy but because his attention invariably stopped there, at her bust line, whenever he encountered her. He could remove her head by thinking it away. Maybe he had already devoured it.

"You can stay with me." Belinda was talking at her. "I suppose you'll have to." Her words shuffled reluctantly through the air like a child called to naptime. Requirement. No more.

"I couldn't inconvenience you like that." Vomit surged up and down Julie's throat. A couch in someone's apartment. A cardboard box beneath a bridge. Anything, anything but more time with Belinda and Al. "I'll stay with my friend Lani."

Belinda snorted—on purpose this time. "Oh. That slutty girl from your pool job? I remember her. She threw herself at Al at your wedding reception and stuffed herself with the most expensive desserts. I think she stole wine and took it home. She was disgusting."

Julie pushed her call button. Surely she could come up with a reason she couldn't have visitors right now.

"I can't chat any more. I have to rest, Belinda."

Belinda nodded, setting waves of movement into serial action down what should have been her throat. "I need to rest, too. I lost my boy. You made me lose my boy. I'm calling Al to come for me." She was crying again, punctuating her sobs with tiny whooshes as she tugged tissue after tissue from the box beside Julie's bed with one hand while her other pushed tiny clicks on her cell phone, summoning her youngest son. She gestured for the slender nurse who answered Julie's call button to help her shift her gargantuan weight into her wheel chair. "I need to get back in my chair. I'm through here."

When she was settled and had regained her breath, she turned her head toward Julie. "I told him I'd meet him by the nurses' station—now that I've been asked to leave. We'll let you know about the arrangements we make for..." She choked, gagged, and reached out to slurp water out of Julie's glass. "...For poor darling Richard's funeral."

And then she rolled away. Julie thought she spotted sympathy in the eyes of the nurse as she took the glass Belinda had used.

"Mother-in-law," explained Julie. And it was enough.

"I'll get you a clean glass," said the nurse.

Chapter 4

The Grandmother

"Well, damn, Jules! I owe you maybe a zillion times over, but I'm not living alone these days. Do you remember Dean? Or maybe you never met him. I think we hooked up after your wedding. I mean, we aren't actually hooked—not yet. But he is living with me…two people in a crappy little studio. It's tight but he's so damned yummy I could eat him with a spoon. He buys me pizza. Can you believe it? A guy who buys food without being forced! He even contributes to the rent. He's not my typical guy at all. You'll be amazed. He's a drummer…you remember how I love drums…and he has masses of curly black hair. He's ultra-sexy."

Julie sighed, not caring if the sound went out over the phone. In her mind's eye she could see Lani's artificially flushed face, her long waterproof eyelashes, and her tight electric-blue knit top. She usually added a scarf tied around her long cobalt blue hair—something exotic. She never quite removed her mermaid persona.

"Lani, I need a place to stay. I've got nothing. Nothing. Everything burned. If you don't have room, do you think Veronica would take me in?"

"Who? Veronica? Oh, *Veronica.* Oh god, Jules, you can't be that desperate."

"Yes. I'm that desperate. Rich is gone. I can't stay with his mom. She's a monster."

"Oh, yeah. I met her at the wedding. What a bitch. I mean, she's past bitch but I don't know any worse words. I'll have to ask Dean. And Rich's brother…what a loser. At the reception, he kept following me around, staring down my top and drooling on my shoes as though he'd never seen female flesh before…nothing like your Rich who absolutely worshipped you. God, I'm sorry about Rich. I had a feeling something was going to mess that up. I get feelings, you know. It's in our genes. He set off alarms when I saw him—seriously, alarms. I think I told you. Or maybe I didn't. I didn't want to screw up your happy ending, even if it was temporary. Give me a couple minutes, will you, Jules? I got an idea that might work. I'll call you right back."

"Sure." But Julie was talking to dead air. Lani had already disconnected.

Julie leaned her head back against the wrought iron of the park bench. She was probably resting on bird shit. That would be appropriate. She closed her eyes, trying to imagine the weightless limbo of water, that sense of being outside reality. She longed for the familiar images of purple-and-orange plastic coral she had always found comforting. Where were the aquarium fish and spilled doubloons the decorator arranged around the glowing pirates' chest? Julie was a mermaid from a make-believe universe. Everything was perfect there. She was perfect there—beautiful, magical and untouchable. An object of desire...perhaps unreachable desire itself. Until she gave in and accepted Rich. And now nothing. A leftover wife. A damaged survivor trapped in air that reeked of diesel and brake linings and yesterday's cafeteria casserole. Her neck hurt.

She sat up straighter and opened her eyes. A patient was clomping by, his pale blue hospital gown flapping over the baggy gray boxers he had on beneath. Shuffle shuffle clomp, shuffle shuffle clomp, as he moved his walker ahead of him. He paused to see if she might be willing to chat, his gaze hopeful behind his thick glasses, his white hair glorious in the afternoon sun. She closed her eyes again and he got the hint. Shuffle shuffle clomp. Shuffle shuffle clomp. And he moved on, leaving a scent trail of urine and antiseptic behind.

When she was certain he was gone, she reopened her eyes. She supposed it was selfish of her to have claimed the only courtyard bench in the shade of a tree, but she didn't care. Her life lay broken and spoiled around her feet. She was due a portion of self-pity. She had gambled and lost spectacularly—like the chumps who wandered out of the Vegas casinos, bloodless and dazed by the immensity of their ruin.

Her phone rang. She had to think a moment about how to open a line. It was a cheap pay-ahead phone a social worker had loaned her. She didn't know her own number. "Yes?"

"Jules, it's me. I've got you all set up. You can stay with Tutu—that's a Hawaiian nickname for grandmother. She's got a stucco stand-alone she's had forever. She's lived almost forever. She must be close to a hundred. I have it written down somewhere. She needs help once in a while—she falls, but don't you dare tell her I said so. It's a big secret or something. Anyway, she's glad for the company. You don't even have to pay. She likes taking care of people. You can sleep on her daybed in the sewing room and use the clothes I left when I moved to my place here. Really. Have whatever you want. They're kind of ho-hum. A couple muumuus from my Hawaiian period. Not me at all these days. I meant to donate them or something. Did I ever take you to meet Tutu? No, I guess not. That was before we started at the bar. Damn, have I been gone that long? Amazing. We're getting old, Jules! Her neighbor said he'd come get you. He's super quiet and odd, but not dangerous. Tutu likes him. His name is Manson—not that Manson—maybe it's Mansfield. You know me and names. I don't remember. But his first name is Will. He drives a ratty blue pickup and has a nasty girlfriend named Gloria. And my Tutu's name is…oh, god, what is her name? I call her Tutu, you know. Kalani. That's it. Kalani. Common spelling. Get it? Ha ha. I mean it's a foreign name--Hawaiian. Mine is, too, but at least it's easy. My great-gran insisted we honor the old family names. She said she was from Hawaiian royalty. Can you imagine me as royalty? I've never even been to Hawaii that I remember, but Kali says I have. Tutu's a sweetie. You'll love her. Everyone does—well, almost everyone."

An old woman as a roomie. Not exactly ideal…but she wouldn't be Belinda. "Thanks, Lani. I owe you."

"Oh, Jules. It's the least I can do. Oops. Gotta go. Dean will be home shortly and I need to freshen up. Will said he'd meet you in front of the hospital. It'll take him about 45 minutes so you have plenty of time to get ready. Love you, Babe. Hang in there. Call if you need me."

Without a chance to say goodbye, Julie sat staring at the phone. What did she have to get ready? The Red Cross clothes she had on. The bag from the hospital. A bunch of papers to sign to say she'd find a way to pay her astronomical bill. How many years did people get for bank robbery? What a deadening day.

By the time a disreputable blue pickup drove up the circle drive at the entrance to the hospital, Julie had talked herself into a full-blown depression. The crabby guy handling billing had contributed mightily. Where the hell was she supposed to get ID when her life had burned up? He almost threatened to hold her hostage until she came up with something, but Belinda had signed enough papers to keep him at bay. To owe Belinda was enough to turn any day dark.

Julie walked to the cab of the pickup, shielding her eyes from the sun in order to address the shadow at the wheel.

"Are you Will Man-something?"

His voice sounded irritated. "Manning. I'm Will Manning. Lani has never gotten it right. I'm assuming you're Julie Scott."

"Julie Teller. I got married."

"That's close enough. I'm supposed to pick you up. Can you climb in by yourself or would you like a hand?"

"I can manage by myself, thanks." She opened the passenger door, wincing at the piercing squeak of the hinges as she felt a twinge of pain from hauling herself up. "Your door needs oil."

"I don't sit in the passenger seat much." He exhaled heavily. "Do you have luggage?"

She slammed the door closed, a little more forcefully than necessary perhaps, and thrust her plastic hospital bag in his direction. "This is what I have in the world. Everything else is ash."

He maneuvered the truck away from the sidewalk into the driveway lane. "Miss Kalani didn't tell me. She just said you were coming to live with her. Were you injured in the fire? Never mind. Stupid question. You're exiting a hospital. I'm sorry you were hurt."

"No. I'm fine—simply fine." Julie busied herself trying to snap the seatbelt latch that refused to snap. Eventually she noticed there were two receptacles and she had chosen the wrong one...annoying and somehow his fault. She had no use for pity. "I needed a place to live and Lani's grandmother needed an assistant."

"Miss Kalani? Do you know her?"

"Not yet."

He chuckled. The sound made him less forbidding, so she stole a glance at his stubbled cheek beneath his black-rimmed glasses. Graying. Probably balding beneath his sweat-stained baseball cap.

"Miss Kalani doesn't accept much assistance."

"Then I guess I'll be her companion."

He braked for a stoplight. "She may be old—late nineties, I think—but she hasn't lost any marbles. Don't play poker with her. She'll own you."

Julie considered a couple retorts, found them lame, and merely grunted, "I don't gamble." She thought about telling him that nobody who had ever worked in Vegas and had an ounce of sense gambled. But she wanted to discourage conversation. She was none of his business.

He reacted to her tone and fell silent.

They rode without talking most of the way to Lani's grandmother's house, each mentally muttering about the failings of the other. The air between them felt unnatural and prickly. By the time the truck came to a halt in front of a tidy stucco house with cobalt blue trim, Julie had determined she had rushed past being private and screeched into bad manners. "Thanks for the ride, Mr. Manning," she said as sincerely as she could manage.

"Nobody calls me Mr. Manning."

"Will, then. Thanks for the ride, Will. When I find a job I'll reimburse you for the gas."

"Not necessary. I owe Miss Kalani." He approximated a quick smile, folding commas into his face.

She slid down from her seat onto the sidewalk. She could see someone opening the blue front door. "Okay then. Goodbye, Will."

She closed his truck door—harder than necessary on purpose--and wondered if he could be watching her as she walked up the sidewalk to the steps.

Lani's grandmother didn't fill the doorway. She stood like a small, handmade cultural doll designed for tourists to tuck into their luggage and small girls to embrace at night. The white of her embroidered tunic reflected the glare of sunlight as her long skirt grazed her gnarled bare feet. Her dark skin lay in sun-blessed furrows over her prominent cheekbones, tough yet somehow appealing beneath her cascade of fuzzy white hair. She was old—an age that lay past guessing. Her weary brown eyes and wide nose spoke of islands and drumbeats. Her unblinking gaze pierced Julie, taking her measure without apology.

"Miss Julie. Come in." Her voice fell soft and low as it slid smoothly over consonants.

Julie followed the old woman's ambling gait into what she guessed was the living room where a faded threadbare loveseat sprawled before a table stacked with books. Lani's grandmother gestured for Julie to sit as she lowered herself into a scarred wooden rocking chair. Ignoring the silence that felt awkward to Julie, the grandmother peered at her long enough to compile an inventory of details. She wasn't a woman who missed much. Her rocker squeaked a slow steady rhythm.

"Lani told me about you."

"I figured she had." Julie shifted on her seat, feeling the lumps of worn padding beneath her. "She didn't tell me much about you—except that she used to live here. You aren't alike—you and Lani. You seem far more...settled."

The grandmother laughed, a sound that recalled the warbling of contented birds. "More settled than Lani! I hope so! Living can bring wisdom to them as is alert. To others, it bring only aching bones. I got some of both."

Julie sat forward, eager to make a good impression without knowing why. "Thank you so much for letting me stay with you. Lani said you need help, and..."

The grandmother shook her head, pursing her lips into a dark red accordion. "She say the same about you."

Julie nodded, realizing how insensitive her phrasing had been. "Yes, of course. I do need help. I had nowhere to go. What I'm trying to say, albeit badly, is my life hasn't involved much helping, but I'm happy to do whatever I can to be useful.

The grandmother rocked. "You didn't help your family?"

"Not much, no. We lived in different states. We weren't close."

"Few families is when you know the truth of it." The grandmother sniffed, and then dabbed at her nose with a handkerchief she pulled from her bosom. "You gotta have honest emotions to build a family, and not many can handle reality these days. They want a happy ending in 60 minutes minus commercials." She chuckled as she stuffed the handkerchief back inside her blouse and turned her gaze to her guest. "I gotta warn you I ain't lost none of my contrariness. Some die from the inside out. Not me. You might find living with me more of a challenge than you expected."

"I can't imagine that you..."

The grandmother interrupted her. "You ain't gotta imagine. I say what's in my mind, and just now I wanna know about your loss. Lani said your husband died in the fire."

"Yes." Julie could feel a surge of sorrow that lodged itself in her throat instead of her heart. "He did."

The grandmother nodded, staring hard. "I've known many losses. Each echoes the others and none been easy. I don't believe in holding a brave face, Miss Julie. Penning up your sadness only make it sour. In this house you gotta feel free to weep or wail or even cry out if you feel a need. If I see you holding in your sadness as you are now, I'll pick at your wound until you let it flow free."

Julie crossed her arms, gripping herself tightly. "Please don't do that—at least not now. I don't have the strength."

Again the grandmother nodded. "Strength been overrated. Sometimes what you need is a burst of weakness. But I'm gonna honor your wishes for the moment. You been through lots of changes. As you get to know me, you gonna know I am as you see me—a safe place if not always a gentle one." She pushed herself out of her chair with a small groan. "Come, let me show you your room. Sad to say, the daybed ain't no more comfortable than it looks, but I don't make the beds in the attic no more—too many stairs. Only my grand-daughters stay there when they visit. Don't mind if your sleep ain't peaceful. From what I know of grieving, and I know plenty, it won't be—not for a long time, never the same as before. Accept whatever rest you can find. I'll wake you up for dinner. Tonight I gonna cook you one of my spicy recipes—enough heat to remind you you're alive."

Julie stood to follow her. "I like spicy food."

"As everybody should. It keep the blood clean." The grandmother shoved a dented plywood door open. "This here's the bathroom. The only one down here. We share it, so please don't hold me up too long in the morning or after meals. I ain't got time to wait these days." She continued down the short hall to the next plywood door, this one decorated with childlike paintings of huge tropical fish.

The grandmother paused. "Lani painted the door. You probably guessed." She pushed the door open, revealing a space submerged in shades of aqua and teal—the wall color, the daybed cover, even the furniture. The grandmother shrugged. "I know, so much blue! I told her swimming in the pool was natural for her because she been liv-ing underwater for years. It used to be my sewing room. These days I sew only when I gotta do it—something about bending forward so long. My back don't like it. You're welcome to toss the shiny fish pillows in the closet. I doubt they're your taste."

Julie smiled, thinking of Lani's cobalt blue hair. "You haven't told me what you'd like me to call you."

"Will call me Miss Kalani cuz I'm old. I suppose he mean respect. He old-fashioned in his way. But you call me Tutu. It's a nickname from the islands. I'm used to Tutu."

"If you'll call me Julie—just Julie. Drop the miss."

The old woman nodded. "Fair enough. Rest well, Julie. Later, you can wash dishes. Making messes be more satisfying to me than cleaning them up."

Julie felt sick as she shut the door. Nothing sounded worse than spicy food or having this old woman poke at her sorrow—nothing except spending time with Belinda. At least the grandmother meant well. Didn't she?

Chapter 5

Bathrobe on a Motorcycle

MAUREEN CREPT DOWN the stairs on tiptoe as she had done automatically for the past months, acutely conscious of the tiny crunch of her slippers on the carpeting. Mother hated noise. But, of course, Mother was dead now. People had come to the parlor to see her off...distant family mostly. They brought a confusing cloud of feelings and noise. They asked Maureen all sorts of inane, intrusive questions. And then they were gone...off to some cemetery where a stone would eventually record Mother's dates of birth and death, and she would lie forever beside the bones of the only man who had ever been worth her time. Maureen declined to go to the cemetery—at least not then. She would go another time, all alone, when she could sit on a bench and feel the sun and wind and not be asked any questions.

Teeny, the cat whose name hadn't suited his body for years, meowed at her from the kitchen. Time for him to eat. Maureen sighed as she recalled the pantry shelf that held the cat food—a stack dwindling to a very few cans. Soon she would need to drive to the grocery for more—more of everything. The crowd of people had brought food and eaten more than they brought. People were like that. They took. Her ex-husband Gage had taught her that much. Thank God he hadn't come to see her mother off. Mother might have sat up and slapped his traitorous face.

Downstairs the smoke was thick enough to make her eyes burn. And someone was pounding on the door. Maureen paused. She had a rule never to answer the door—especially when she wasn't dressed, but now that Mother was gone, she would have to break some of her rules. She would have to be a caregiver for herself again. It felt like growing up...a second time. Hopefully she would do better this time. She checked to be certain the baseball bat was behind the door before she opened it.

"Yes?" she ventured to the sooty fireman outside.

"You have to get out!" he ordered. And when she didn't move, he added, "NOW! Go south or you'll die!" He hurried back down the steps.

Maureen hadn't known fear for several years—back in the old days in court when the case was going down the toilet and a life was at stake—a different brand of fear, but she recognized the surge of electricity through her heart. The fire. She had heard there was a fire outside Eden. But there was technology to tame wildfires these days—chemicals and trucks and planes. Fires didn't intrude on towns...into neighborhoods. It was all wrong. Still, the flames were here. NOW. Dear God. She could sense the oppressive imminence of death.

The fireman had already moved on, pounding on another door. Maureen clumsily struggled to slip on the loafers she kept by the front entrance and ran to grasp Teeny. His long body flopped over her arm, and he complained bitterly that he hadn't finished his breakfast. That couldn't matter any longer. Maureen could see the fierce red storm charging up the hill that led to town. Why hadn't someone told her it was coming? Had she ignored a warning? How could a fire storm that big be a surprise?

She slipped the strap of her purse that she kept in a drawer behind the door over her head and shoulder and rushed down the steps. There was no time to get the car out of the garage even if there had been space for it on the street. She would have to take the monster motorcycle her brother Pat had left in the side yard, promising to pick it up when he returned from his job in Hawaii. She couldn't worry that she had never driven a motorcycle by herself for more than a few feet. The street was clogged with cars.

She shoved Teeny into the bag Pat used for his gear, zipped it nearly all the way, and made sure it was securely fastened to the bike. She climbed on, baring her legs as she pushed her housecoat out of her way. Teeny yowled and Maureen took off—wavering at first, unsure if she was going to be killed by the bike before she could burn up—but then with more confidence. Life was turning a page for her. She could hear Pat's voice in her head: *"You have to live again some time, Rini."* She smirked. She was doing her best. She wove through the traffic as well as she could, ignoring the people who yelled at her until there was a woman, a dark-skinned mother hugging a small child to her chest, waving madly with one arm. Decent people didn't ignore the plights of children.

"PLEASE! HELP!" screamed the mother, and Maureen slowed. Could she drive the bike with them on board? Maybe not, but she had to try. She stopped after some difficulty and the woman climbed on with the child still gripping her like a newborn sloth.

"Hang on!" yelled Maureen, as though they wouldn't think of it. "And watch out for my cat in the bag." She could feel the woman's arms firm around her and the child. Squishing three people onto the seat was probably illegal. The weight made starting up scary and balancing terrifying, but Maureen decided not to think about it. They'd survive or they wouldn't. No point in worrying. If they dawdled any longer, the smoke would kill them.

The huge bike wobbled as she navigated up and down the side-walks...perhaps it was reacting to her knees shaking. Her hands ached from her frantic grip. She leaned forward, hearing an echo of dialogue about the think method from *The Music Man* as she forcefully imagined herself in command of the metal beast between her legs. Who was it who rode motorcycles in the movies? Keanu Reeves? Channel Keanu Reeves. The bike wasn't fooled by her bravado, but it stayed upright, anyway—perhaps by the grace of God.

She wasn't sure where to go. Fire didn't care a fig for the best laid routes of men—the beautifully landscaped roundabouts and curving boulevards. If she stayed on the street, the fire would win. She remembered an alleyway she and Pat had used as kids on their bicycles—mostly blocked now by the homeowners who used it only to move their riding lawnmowers to well-hidden sheds but perhaps wide enough for the motorcycle. She could cut across the neighbor-hood and head...where? To the highways, to Sacramento...away. Not much of a plan but good enough. Away was an excellent plan.

They bounced along the alley, zooming too close to garbage cans. The woman riding in back deftly kicked one aside as it tipped toward the bike. Garbage tumbled after them in a smelly flow. The roar of the bike echoed and grew deafening between buildings. Ahead the passage narrowed, partially blocked by a wheelbarrow of yard clippings. Maureen swore beneath her breath. The woman behind her gasped. They'd make it or they wouldn't. She aimed for the gap and prayed. Somehow they squeezed through. Had the bike held its breath as she did?

She could hear screams in the distance…or maybe she felt them. She always felt too much. She didn't dare wonder what was happening behind them. She didn't want to know. The bike vaulted from the alley onto pavement. The car behind her leaned on his horn. She concentrated on the road ahead. She could zoom past the cars if she used the shoulder—a foolish move but so was burning up. She felt the curses hurled at her. It couldn't matter. She had enough trouble controlling the bike on the gravel. She couldn't split her attention. It swayed, fighting the stones. It wanted to fishtail. That would be bad. She forced it forward by sheer will. She was going to have bruises where her passenger was clinging to her, but who could blame her? They were one sloppy move from disaster.

Finally they were on a highway where the traffic wasn't as dense. She swerved around cars that braked unexpectedly. The spirit of Pat must be driving. She was operating far past her skill level. There was no choice. She had two other lives depending on her, and Maureen wasn't the kind to let anyone down.

She drove for what registered in her mind as hours, passing strip malls that didn't seem to have any connection to the firestorm behind them. Oddly, she thought of the tired joke about the man from North Dakota walking south carrying a snow shovel, determined to continue until someone stopped him to ask what that thing was. She wanted to be far enough from the fire to feel safe—to be around people who looked bored or pissed off instead of terrified. Her buttocks and back were complaining bitterly. Pat must get a huge surge of macho from riding around this way for him to ignore the discomfort. Or maybe he had tougher buttocks. She pulled into a gas station. "Let's stretch and regroup for a moment," she told her passenger, shouting above the roar before she realized she could shut the motor off. She worked to lower the kickstand.

"I gotta pee," came a small voice from behind her. The woman climbed down and lifted her child to join her.

"We'll be right back," she promised, her plea to find Maureen still there when she returned plaintive in her eyes.

Maureen nodded, conscious for the first time that she was wearing only her bathrobe and a ragged nightie. Mother always said to wear good underwear when you went out...just in case, and here she was in faded panties with stretched-out elastic and a nightie she wore only when she was feeling very sorry for herself. Even her housecoat was a dirty, tattered disgrace.

A middle-aged man wearing a fishing hat stood at the next pump. He gestured with the nozzle, "You need gas?"

She had to search for the gauge. "Yes, I do." Naturally Pat wouldn't have filled the tank before leaving his bike to sit idle. She was lucky she had made it this far, since she had never thought to check. She swiped her credit card, and the man pulled the hose taut so it would reach the bike. He stared at her as the gas gushed. His glazed, sunken eyes looked like he had been roused from a deep sleep that left him caught in the tendrils of dark dreams.

"Running from the fire in Eden?" His voice quavered.

She nodded.

"Where else, huh? You got ash all over you. Guess we all do. Damn scary. Who could've thought it would be so bad. We weren't sure we'd make it out. I think some didn't. I think people burned. Houses are going up like kindling. It looks like Hell. The main escape routes are parking lots. Bad planning, I'd say--having only one main way in and out. Maybe picturesque but real bad planning." The nozzle clicked and he turned to replace it in its cradle. "I'm afraid this place won't be safe long. No place is safe. Depends on the wind. Don't think I'll ever feel safe again. I didn't know if the pumps would work. You and your friend better move on."

Maureen thought she should smile, but it wouldn't happen. Too much fear and wind had frozen her face. "Thanks for the help. I appreciate it. I never filled a bike before. I wasn't sure how."

The man shrugged. "Good to be able to help somebody. Not as hopeless."

He opened his car door and Maureen could see a plump middle-aged woman in a baseball cap and diamond earrings sitting in the passenger seat. She couldn't smile, either, but she and Maureen exchanged little waves that were more like jerks of the hand—automatic obligatory courtesy. And then the man slammed the door and drove his soot-covered car out into traffic.

"I peed in the bushes," declared the little voice, and Maureen turned. The child was a little girl maybe five years old, her hair carefully plaited in tiny braids, a pink teddy bear tucked into the straps of her denim coveralls. Her huge brown eyes stared without blinking. She had already seen too much. "The potty door was locked. Mommy helped me."

Her mother extended a hand. "Kalia Ramirez. My friends call me Kali. This is my daughter Lila. I don't know how I can ever thank you. I couldn't get our car out. Somebody abandoned a truck right in front of our driveway. I thought we...," she paused and glanced at her little girl. "I thought we'd have trouble finding a ride."

Maureen accepted the handshake, feeling strength in the trembling fingers. This was a woman who was used to handling crises. Accepting help was difficult for her. "Maureen Reynolds. Call me Rini." Kali was slightly taller than she was and probably younger. She was wearing red sneakers, tight blue jeans, and a maroon t-shirt. Deep furrows hung under her eyes, as though she didn't sleep much or maybe from stress. Her hair was secured in tiny braids like those of her daughter.

"I was afraid I was going to kill you both," confessed Maureen gravely. "It's my brother's bike. I don't ride it. I'm sure you could tell."

"You did fine. We're here, after all."

They stood for a moment, staring at one another. There were too many words to say.

At last Maureen broke the silence, forcing her voice to sound even, the way she used to do in court. "That guy who just left told me we won't be safe here long. I think he's panicked. Do you have a choice of where we should go from here? I haven't been out of the house much this past year. I was caring for my mother who had cancer and died last week. I lived in DC before that."

"I'm really sorry." Kali looked like she might cry. Her fear had become grief. But she wasn't the type to cry. She drew a ragged breath and exhaled it with a sigh. "My husband is working a job down in Texas—living in a company RV. My grandmother lives south of here—outside Sacramento. I told Daniel we'd stay with her, if that's okay with you. You're welcome to join us. Tutu will have some of my sister's clothes we can wear. Lani leaves clothes wherever she goes. I can direct you. If that works for you, I'll text Tutu and let her know we're coming. What do you think?"

"Are you sure she'll have room for me...and my cat?"

Kali almost smiled. "She'll make room. Tutu can handle anything."

Maureen met Lila's gaze. The little girl had no doubt these women were going to take care of her. Maureen remembered feeling the same confidence in her parents. It had been misplaced, but that wasn't their fault. They had done their best to protect her, to keep her separated from all threats, from the vagaries of life itself. And her naivete had been her downfall. She climbed onto the bike, waiting for Kali to settle herself. "Then it's off to Tutu's we go," she said cheerily as she silently prayed they'd make it.

Chapter 6

The Wrong Side of Existence

RICH'S MOTHER BELINDA glowered up at Julie from her seat in her wheelchair as Julie walked beside her down the hall toward the funeral home office. Belinda's eyes were red slits in her puffy cottage cheese face. Mucus drooped from her nose before she swiped at it with a tissue. "I told them Al and I could handle things, but they insisted, INSISTED you had to be here as the widow. I tried to tell them you were hardly married before…," she began snuffling again, "…before you got my poor baby drowned with your underwater nonsense. I warned Rich you'd be trouble. I told him…but no, he was under your spell. Sex, that's what it was, raw sex—shaking your sequined tail at my poor lonely boy. You're a Delilah." The hum of her wheelchair motor underscored her soggy sobbing.

Julie drew a long, deep breath—as though she were about to submerge. "What are we doing here? I don't see how we can plan a funeral when they haven't recovered his body yet."

Belinda's glare was acid. "From what you've told me, I have to assume we won't be worrying about an open casket. Other than that, there are plenty of choices to be made. Some of us don't wait until the last minute when the duty is really important. Dolly said it was okay and even prudent for us to make the major decisions now."

The funeral director rose from behind her mahogany desk as they entered. As she approached them, Julie could see she was a short, stout woman with oddly black hair and a taut, shiny face that bragged of multiple plastic surgeries. She was made taller by three-inch heels suitable as weapons with their pointed toes and metal insets. Her dark, stiff pantsuit whooshed menacingly with her movement…armor against true emotion, perhaps…as she flashed a scarlet-lipstick smile beneath the frames of her trendy glasses. Rows of golden beads hung from golden snake chains around her neck, threatening to snare Belinda as she leaned over to embrace her.

"Oh, I'm *so* sorry, Belinda! What a tragedy you're forced to endure—so soon after Earl." The woman's unctuous words seemed to seep from beneath a manhole cover, slimy and transparent. She shook Al's hand as she spoke, recoiling a little from the touch of him. Belinda didn't notice.

"You're sweet, Dolly," murmured Belinda, dabbing at her eyes with her soggy tissue. "I knew I could count on you...once again. You did such a beautiful job with Earl. Everyone said it was one of the nicest, most tasteful funerals they had ever seen—the live music, that gorgeous coffin, so many flowers...beautiful. Earl would have been proud." Belinda started snuffling again, so Dolly pivoted to extend a hand to Julie.

"And you would be Richard's widow. Please accept my sincerest condolences."

Julie took Dolly's cool, soft, pudgy hand. It felt like bloated death. It gave her chills. "Thank you." And because Dolly was staring at her, Julie began talking as she drew her hand back. "Have you known Belinda long?"

Belinda interjected an answer. "Dolly and her family have handled every Teller funeral for ages—back to the grandparents. Her father was a saint. We wouldn't trust anyone else."

Dolly cooed appreciatively. "It's a privilege to work for people like you."

Belinda rolled forward, motioning for Al to push the other chairs aside to accommodate her. Once she was situated, Al dragged an armless chair beside his mother and seated himself. The chair groaned impolitely.

Julie didn't bother trying to claim a spot at the desk's edge. She was happy to sit in a corner. She would have been happier still if she had been able to wish herself away, to scatter her molecules across an emotionless universe. Tears lay behind her eyes, begging to be released. But this was no time to cry.

Dolly rolled her maroon leather office chair into place behind the desk and opened a large black leather folder. "Now then, before we go into the showroom to select a coffin that will embrace Richard and keep him safe into eternity—one that tells everyone how very much you loved your son, we'll..."

"...No."

Dolly paused, shocked to have her recitation of her script interrupted. She looked at Julie as though the landscape painting behind her had spoken. "What? Did you say something, Dear?"

"I said no. Rich will not lie in a gorgeous coffin for eternity. He'll be cremated."

Belinda's thick neck seemed to flare, and Julie could sense venom shooting toward her eyes. Belinda's voice had become a hiss. "We do not believe in cremation. After the funeral, Rich will be buried in the family plot alongside his father as we planned." She turned her chair to face Dolly, dismissing further discussion. "You really don't have to be here, Julie. Al and I can handle these troublesome details. We have experience. Dolly will give you a form to sign."

Julie straightened. "I'm not signing anything except a cremation order. Rich and I talked about our deaths, and that was what he wanted. This is *his* funeral...or it will be when they recover him."

"He's dead!" exclaimed Al in his nasal wheeze. "These choices belong to the family. Don't upset Mom. She's suffered enough."

Julie's knuckles strained white in her lap. As much as she had been struggling to restrain her grief before, she had to work far harder to restrain her sudden fury. "Yes, I realize he's dead. I saw him. But I'm his wife, and I say we'll do as he wished regardless of family tradition. You can make his funeral into any kind of show you like, Belinda. Funerals are for survivors. But you will not bury his body."

A sickly silence clotted around them. Belinda turned her wheelchair far enough to be able to face her adversary. "And how do we know you're telling the truth, *Julie*?" She spat the name, her spittle defiling the tidy air of the office. "When did you have time to discuss death with Richard? You weren't married that long. On your honeymoon? In your bed?"

Julie drew three long breaths, mentally counting as she did so. One thousand one. One thousand two. One thousand three. She imagined Rich beside her, reminding her of his hatred for coffins that pretended bodies would never decay. He didn't want to rot or to end up as a mummy on some future scientist's bench. "*When* we had the discussion doesn't matter. Whether I'm telling the truth doesn't matter. What does matter is that I am the widow and the decision is mine." She was shaking all over and her heart felt like it might explode, so she folded her hands tightly.

Dolly nodded, glancing nervously from Belinda to Al. "Yes. It is."

"Hateful girl," muttered Belinda.

"Bitch," added Al beneath his breath.

Julie sat silent through the rest of the proceedings. Once she had chosen a plain stainless-steel urn that made Belinda snort and Al glare, she retreated into recesses deep within her mind. Rich would want his mother to be happy; she could guess that. He wouldn't argue with the ostentatious, actually gaudy ceremony. He had given in on their wedding, although it was supposed to be Julie's choice, and he would give in on his funeral if he were present. As usual, Julie's assignment would be to survive the day.

While she sat, staring at nothing until her awareness left the room, her wedding day replayed in her mind.

*   *   *

The sky bubbled with gray and black clouds, threatening rain or worse. The sides of the tent Belinda had rented especially for the reception puffed in and out like the cheeks of someone about to hurl. Julie stood in the dressing room of the lodge beside an open window. Even the wind tearing at the curtains couldn't help her breathe. Perhaps it would sweep away the seats and the ridiculous ornate arch under which Rich and she were supposed to exchange vows—archaic pseudo-religious vows about obeying.

If she mumbled the words, would they still be binding? Not that she believed any of Rich's people took vows seriously. Thank goodness he was different.

Of the line of bridesmaids, only Lani remained beside her. The other bridesmaids had gone seeking the open bar. They were Rich's friends—old girlfriends, cousins--anyone Belinda thought would look better than Julie. Lani sighed loudly.

"Dang, Jules. That's some dress. Too high on top and too much everyplace else. If you dyed it green, you could pass for a Christmas tree. Belinda must hate you a lot."

Julie nodded as she glanced down at the rows upon rows of white lace ruffles decorated with pink roses that surrounded her like a stiff layered hurricane. "She paid for everything. So Rich said the choices were hers."

"I guess. But pink? This pink?" Lani tugged at the neckline of her bridesmaid dress that dipped dangerously close to revealing the dark summits of her breasts. "I'm not the pink type, and this is the only dress I could find that was the right color. Her instructions said we all had to have the very same shade. Against my blue hair, it's a party, not a wedding. Stripper pink. Somebody she likes must look good in it, or else she's telling everybody this is your taste."

"Rich's old girlfriend Amanda is brunette. She looks good in it. She's downstairs getting shit-faced."

Lani examined herself in the full-length mirror. "It looks like frosting on a kid's cake."

Julie made a face. "No kidding." She shifted her weight on her painful strappy high heels, wondering if she could lift her feet and let her dress support her. "At least I won't have to worry about Al leering at me."

"Sexy it ain't. A guy could be wearing it, and no one would know. But it's only for the day, and Rich won't care. He adores you no matter what."

"I suppose. When I tried to tell him how bad the dress is, he said that'll make it more fun to take off."

Lani shrugged. "That's men for you."

"Yeah."

"Belinda didn't pick out your trousseau, did she?"

"Yeah."

"Oh, Jules. How could you let her? What did she choose... sweatshirts?"

"She paid for it."

Lani made a scoffing sound in her throat. "It cost you too much, if you ask me. I'd rather be married in a swimming pool or the ocean."

Julie commanded herself not to cry. Runny mascara would only delight Belinda. "I love him, Lani. He's worth it."

Lani hugged her tightly...as tightly as she could around the solidified wedding dress. "Of course he is, Jules. You're gonna be wildly happy."

* * *

Julie took a cab from the funeral home. She wanted to distance herself from humanity. Tears began coursing down her face as soon as she was closed inside. She didn't try to stop them. Released at last, her crying swelled into a formless being that absorbed her into violent, quivering sobs and made her gasp for air. The driver glanced back at her.

"You okay, Sweetheart?"

"No, but that's okay." She was thinking Rich was gone and nothing would ever be okay again. She should be dead with him.

The driver was quiet for a few blocks. "Can I call somebody for ya or buy ya a drink or somethin'?"

She shook her head, assuming he could see in the rear-view mirror. For the first time in her life, she was wondering what suicide would feel like.

Perhaps the cabbie could sense the depth of her despair, because he started talking again. "I lost lots of family before. It sucks, but ya keep goin'—to honor them, ya know? There's another side and ya get there. Was it a parent?"

"My husband."

"Oh sh… I mean that really sucks. But yer young; ya got a bunch of life left. Trust me. There's another side."

She glared at the back of the seat. Another side. That was precisely the problem. There were two sides to existence, and she was on the wrong one.

Chapter 7

Bed One Guy

THE MAN WITH no name lay in Room 112, a turquoise curtain away from someone moaning. He opened his eyes with effort. Dizziness. Blurry shapes. Nothing looked familiar. He wanted to moan, too, but any movement hurt. His head was swathed in bandages. Where was Mom? Where was Julie? What the fuck was going on? A stocky nurse wearing a mask leaned over him. She smelled of antiseptic and made him feel sick.

"Where am I?" he muttered, ignoring the pain.

"You're in a hospital in San Francisco," she told him in a nasal voice that instantly irritated him nearly as much as having her touch him. "Now that you're awake, I'll need to ask you a few questions." She retrieved a clipboard she had left on the counter beside the sink and fingered the pen. "First, what's your name? We've been waiting to get an identity for you. We've been calling you Bed One Guy."

He ignored her. He hated hospitals and now he was pretty sure he hated this broad, too. How could she pretend to be cheerful when he was hurting? What kind of caregiver does such a thing? He'd file a complaint. As soon as he could.

"San Francisco! That's miles and miles from my house. How did I get here? I was in the lake…with Julie. We were doing her mermaid thing."

Her voice softened. "The lake?" Her forehead crinkled and he knew she didn't believe him. "I'm sorry, Honey. We don't have a Julie. Maybe she was taken somewhere else. You were in the fire—or nearly. You have a few burns—on the top of your head for the most part, some on your face, and some on your back. Pretty much second degree. Nothing next to what some are suffering. We specialize in treating burn victims here. Rescuers found you. It looked like you might have crawled to safety and the wind took the flames another way. You're a miracle, really. You should be thankful you're alive."

His mind churned up bitter mental vomit. *Should be thankful? Who gave her the right to dictate? Who's thankful for being burned to a crisp? Where do they get people like her? What am I doing here? And where the hell is Julie?*

"I'm Richard Teller," he said in his coldest business voice. "I have plenty of insurance. You won't get stiffed. Call my mother Belinda Teller of Teller Real Estate. She'll handle this. You'll need to answer to her for the care you give me."

* * *

Maureen's motorcycle passenger Kali didn't bother knocking on the door of a house that felt more like home than the house she had abandoned to the fire. She remembered turning this doorknob when she had to reach up to grip it. Here was safety and sanity and Tutu's warm hugs. A memory flashed through her mind of hiding deep beneath the bed in the attic, trying to disappear into the shadow so no one could ever find her, no one could ever make her go home again—back when Mama was sick and took too much medicine and forgot to fix meals. The echo of Lani's crying stuck to her memory like old oatmeal to a dirty dish.

The bellowing noise of the motorcycle had announced them as they arrived. Tutu would be waiting—hopefully with food. Tutu's cooking could cure any problem, and Kali had plenty—a distant husband, a hungry child, and no home or car or job. Kali opened the door and Lila ran in, leaping into Tutu's welcoming arms.

"Tutu!" Lila snuggled into the old woman's sinewy embrace. "There was a big scary fire that made me cough but Mommy said we'd be okay and I got to ride a motorcycle! I need to go pee." She tugged at the crotch of her coveralls to emphasize the urgency.

Tutu nodded and took Lila's hand. "This way, Precious One. You remember." She twisted to acknowledge Maureen with a nod as she left. "Welcome to my home. Everybody call me Tutu. I hope you gonna do it, too."

Kali smiled at an unfamiliar white woman standing in the doorway to the kitchen. At first, she couldn't think of what to say. The woman was striking with her long red hair and old-fashioned pinup figure. Kali thought she was wearing a dress she recognized from Lani's flamboyant collection. This woman had the chest for it. "I'm Kali. Lani's sister. Tutu said you know her."

"Julie Scott...Teller...Scott." Julie's eyes were bloodshot and parts of her hair were singed. She had no smile. Another fire victim. Her voice arrived as though from a distance—weak and uncertain. "Lani and I are friends. She sent me here. We worked together."

"...In Las Vegas. I remember. I saw you doing your mermaid thing once. You were good." Kali suddenly realized Maureen was still standing behind her. "Oh, and this is Maureen Reynolds—Rini. She rescued me and Lila. If she hadn't picked us up on her motorcycle, I doubt we would have made it away from the fire. I couldn't get out of our driveway. She's our hero."

Maureen shook her head, realizing she still wore curlers; they always worked better for her than a curling iron. "No big deal. I was glad for the company and a place to go. I had no clue which way to head." She shifted her shoulder bag behind her, closed the door, and tried to pull her soiled housecoat closer over her nightie. "I hope somebody has clothes I can borrow. I can't go shopping like this. I look like hell." The immense black bag hanging on her back meowed. "Oh, and is it okay if I let my cat out?"

Tutu had returned with Lila in hand. The elderly woman came to embrace Kali as only a grandmother can and then hugged Maureen who seemed to withdraw slightly. "I like cats," Tutu told her. "A purr be the best calmative we got. A good cat work better than a therapist. Maybe that cat wanna relieve herself in our backyard? We gotta make up a litter box. I'm sure I got something that'll do. Kali tells me I save too much."

The huge feline wriggled free of his prison as soon as Maureen held it next to the floor and then stood, trying to make sense of his strange surroundings.

"He's a boy," corrected Lila. "Maureen told me. His name is Teeny."

Tutu patted Lila's braids. "Of course, Precious One. I can see that now." She turned toward Maureen. "Would he mind if Lila take him outside? I guarantee she ain't gonna let him out of her sight, and my yard be well fenced."

Maureen nodded and Lila struggled to enfold the mass of meowing fur.

"I'll be careful with him. I promise." The little girl staggered into the kitchen under Teeny's weight. Squished between Lila's arms, the cat glared guilt at Maureen.

Tutu surveyed her newest guests as one assesses a fresh garden. "Kali and Lila can share the double bed upstairs. Maureen's gonna have to take the single bed in the store room. You find the stairs to the attic behind the house outside the kitchen door. Kali can show you where I keep the door key for up there. Once she dust, the attic ain't bad. There's a bath Kali and Daniel installed a few years back. Made it handy when Kali was pregnant. I got plenty of sheets and blankets in the dresser up there and the windows open. Of course, depending on the smoke in the wind, you might wanna leave them closed."

She smiled at Maureen. "I imagine you'd like a nice hot soak, and Julie here can help you find something to wear—nothing you'd choose, most like, but it'll be clean. Then we gonna sit down and have a good dinner. I got a pot on now." She started toward the kitchen but stopped herself. "I'll ask Will next door if he can take you all shopping tomorrow. He got a collectible car that's a darned sight better ride than his truck...if I can talk him into using it." Julie's grimace made her chuckle. "He's more patient than he seem to be. Just don't scratch the paint or upholstery in his pride and joy. Them's killing offenses."

"I'LL PAY!" Maureen's voice was so unexpected and loud, everyone startled. She looked sheepish. "Sorry. Mother was nearly deaf before she died—last week. It'll take me some time to stop shouting. And now I have her inheritance plus my savings. I'll provide the clothes and the groceries. Please, let me contribute what I can since I'm not family or even a friend."

Tutu pursed her lips. "Nonsense! The fire made us family and family we gonna be. You're all welcome here as long as you wanna stay. A house need people to be a home. It ain't been glad to have nobody but me rattling around. I got a feeling we was meant to meet."

"Me, too," mumbled Maureen quietly without looking at anyone.

Unsure if she intended to speak aloud, no one commented.

An old-style landline phone on a side table rang into the pause, and Tutu moved to answer it. She held the receiver toward Julie. "It's the sheriff's department. They wanna talk to you, Dear."

The others pretended to be occupied with their own concerns as Julie listened to the voice on the other end of the line, but they couldn't help trying to piece together the bits of words they could hear.

"Yes, thank you. I understand." Julie didn't seem to notice everyone was watching as she hung up, perhaps planning how to catch her if she collapsed to the floor. Her face had gone pale and her hands were visibly trembling.

"They can't find Rich. They're dragging the lake." She drew an audible breath ragged with horror and grief. "My husband. I saw him drowned in the lake and now the recovery crew can't find him."

Chapter 8

Dormant Emotions

MAUREEN SANK HER body deeper into the bath. Julie's tearful grief at dinner had rekindled her own and she wanted nothing more than to slip beneath the water and stop living. Both her father and mother had shone on her life with warmth and nourishment, loving her beyond all reason until Maureen grew to womanhood thinking she was favored by God. Now her mother's face wavered in the steam. She was wearing her "Honey, it'll be alright" face, the one that made Maureen's eyes fill because it was the expression she missed most, had depended on most—way too much. After all, her problems had been her own design, due to her own failings. She had let herself down even more than the dreams of her parents—and all due to trusting too much. Her bedroom shelf had been crowded with trophies—swimming and tennis and debate, the wall plastered with awards. School never posed any particular challenge, and law school was no different. Finding a lucrative position based on her reputation had almost been a matter of choosing her favorite firm. And then she met Gage.

She would never forgive herself for being fodder for his voracious ego. He dined on her as savagely as any wild creature might, tearing away her heart, weakening her muscles, and—in the end—destroying her fine connections with her mind. Her parents fell prey to his practiced charm. He seemed to be the perfect partner for their golden child. He was handsome, witty, and roguish. They spent lavishly on the wedding, quietly gleeful over the prospect of grandchildren from such a glorious union. But there were no grandchildren.

The final scene of Maureen's relationship with Gage ran in its perpetual loop in her mind.

Rock and roll music pounded against the walls of the party room of Gage's favorite night spot, a sharply pretentious trend-setter. Couples were already dancing and anyone who wasn't was liberally indulging in the best of the open bar. Maureen wasn't fond of either the place or the music. They charged too much for everything. Gage thought that made the oddly shaped food taste better. But she couldn't wait to see the wide smile on his face when he arrived. He was so damned handsome when he smiled. He could excite her with a single touch. She grinned as she thought slyly she would've preferred for them to celebrate alone, but there would be time enough for that later if they didn't drink too much.

"Isn't this going to be awfully expensive?" asked her father as he perused a menu he had insisted on being given. "You could buy a condo for what this is costing. I hope you got a good deal."

Maureen laughed. Gage wouldn't be happy to see her parents, but they were an integral part of her successes, and they adored him. Of course they had to be here. So did her adorable brother Patrick who was dancing with a gorgeous blonde—the legal aide who kept showing up whenever he was around even after Maureen told her he wasn't interested. Gage would definitely not be thrilled to see Pat. They didn't hit it off.

Maureen planted a light kiss on her father's cheek. "Oh, Dad. We don't need a condo and, besides, we can afford to splurge now. We both make good money. Extravagant celebration is in order— just this once. Gage has been hired by Simpson, Epstein, and Brandywine—his first job! He's set!"

Her mother sipped at her martini. "But you got him a foot in the door, didn't you, Honey? You look stunning, by the way—absolutely stunning. I hope you have a good photographer. Is that a new dress?"

"Of course! Special occasion. And yes, the photographer is excellent. Speak of the devil..." She smiled as the photographer snapped a couple shots of her with her parents. She would want copies of them. "I helped Gage study for the bar and opened the door, but he earned his way through. He's talented and amazing."

Her father took a long drink of his Irish whiskey. "I think you're amazing. You paid for his law school and I'd bet good money you helped him with his briefs and exams."

Maureen laughed, a little harder than was necessary. Her father was old school, which created all sorts of difficult situations.

The waiter signaled her and she raised a hand. "Here he comes!"

Gage looked better than she had imagined...and so did the nearly naked young brunette draped on his arm. Gage waved to the crowd. "Hello, everyone! Thanks for coming to my little party. Kudos go to the lovely Rini who organized all this."

People applauded awkwardly. Everyone was watching the brunette.

"And this is Tanya, a cherished old friend and moral support." He leaned over to kiss her. "She's my reward for a job well done. Unfortunately, we have a previous engagement, so I'll leave you in Rini's capable hands."

He and his consort passed close enough to Maureen for her to be enveloped in the brunette's perfume. "I tried to warn you, Rini," her husband told her quietly as he paused. "Really I did. I figured you'd use your spooky sense to see it coming. I'm a cad. You're better off without me."

"He's right about that," growled her father. "Take him for everything you can."

* * *

Even more than having been used, Maureen hated the idea that she had played a part in a tired old story—a role that should have belonged to an empty-headed clerk or dowdy librarian. Perhaps it was hubris. Extremely successful attorneys often fell prey to hubris. She didn't believe she could fail. So when she fell, her descent was spectacular. And so was her recovery.

George Bentley—G.B. He wasn't a rebound; he was a cyclone sucking up everything normal and spitting it out bent. Her only barely legal courtroom machinations saved him from a prison sentence he secretly deserved, but he wasn't evil, simply careless and unfettered.

She had no ethical license to become personally involved with him, yet she couldn't resist his power, his intelligence, his raw sensuality. He was passion that seduced her against her better instincts. He was danger and indulgence and lust—the temporary flare of a match in the night. But with her he walked on the safe black of ground that had already burned. She pulled away from him deliberately, painfully, wisely, knowing she could never retrieve the bit of her he owned. It would stay with him forever. She punished herself for her transgression with solitary confinement.

She retreated into her loneliness.

Father suffered a stroke, lost his speech, and was gone.

Mother gradually declined, inviting this disease and then that to relieve her grief until, at last, cancer did.

Her brother Patrick was the only person who gripped Maureen so tightly she couldn't be entirely lost. He had always been the cheerful one, chuckling at the fuss when his grades dipped precipitously, shrugging when Father exploded into one of his lectures. Pat had no ambition to be extraordinary. In fact, as he watched Maureen fencing with their father through marriage, divorce, and decline, he relished the fact that no one carried heavy expectations for him. He was free. He had stored enough brightness to sustain both siblings. But he was currently on a research vessel outside Hawaii, not knowing his mother's lovely home lay in burned rubble and his motorcycle had rescued his sister in his stead.

Maureen gazed down at her pale, slightly paunchy belly she could force to protrude from the bath like a bloated white walrus. Humiliation was fattening. She had eaten her despair, not caring how bitter it was. Food was energy and energy approximated life. Mother had tried to warn her. Now she would have to decide if she wanted to go back to an earlier incarnation of herself or create a new one—someone cannier this time. The women downstairs were going to need her, even if they didn't know it yet. She could feel it as she often felt the inevitable.

She rose in a whoosh from the bath and pulled the towel around her. The clothes she and Julie had chosen from the sad array in the sewing room lay on the ladderback chair beside the tub. They were ridiculous but clean. Who wore muumuus these days—particularly an electric blue one with a riot of unlikely flowers in neon hues hanging onto one another with bright purple vines? She dragged the curlers from her hair and sighed. Wispy brown. Probably one day going bald like Mom. What difference would it make? Being attractive wasn't important—not any more. She wasn't sure if anything was important.

The sun was setting. Its vibrant banners of color unfurled across the smoky skies caught her attention so she didn't notice Kali sitting on the bottom steps until she had nearly stepped on her. Kali seemed to find their near-miss amusing.

"Feeling better?"

Maureen nodded. "Sorry. I didn't mean to grow maudlin and make dinner any sadder than it was. Julie's grief was a trigger of sorts, I guess, for emotions I hadn't permitted myself. My mother died in her proper time. I need to catch hold of myself. I'm not fit company. I should go to a motel."

Kali made a disgusted sound with her lips. "Do you want to be all alone in a motel? Be honest."

Maureen's voice shrank. "No."

"You wouldn't find one, anyway. On the news they said everything's full." Kali patted the step beside her, and Maureen accepted the invitation to sit down, feeling the fabric of her muumuu billowing with the motion and the soft wind. To anchor the skirt, she shoved her hands deep into the pockets, disappointed to find them empty. She had fantasized sea shells.

Kali's voice was a gentle alto, the kind of soothing tone you imagine all mothers should have. "We've each come through a trauma. You need us as much as we need you. When we spread the shock around, it doesn't seem as overwhelming. The fire took the only home Lila has ever known, a house Daniel and I worked hard to afford. At the risk of sounding like my tutu, don't second guess fate."

Maureen attempted a smile that failed miserably. She shrugged, instead. "I know you're right." She adjusted her skirt, forcing it to create a tent across her knees. "I hadn't cried over my mother. It took her so long to die, and the experience was wrenching—sadistic. I thought I'd be glad when it was over. I thought I'd feel blissful relief. But I don't. I still feel stricken—as though I hadn't expected it. Those months watching her deteriorate inch by inch didn't change anything. I miss her."

Kali pulled her knees close to her chest, straining the denim fabric of her worn jeans. "We should all cry more. We hold too much in. I do…out of habit and for Lila, but it's a bad example. She needs to know you can be strong and emotional, too."

"I don't like being emotional. It makes me look weak."

Kali shook her head. "That's a male myth. You can cry and still kick somebody's butt." She grinned. "I've done it. In fact, when you release your emotion, you can be better focused, more dangerous."

"Dangerous?" Maureen turned to see her companion more clearly. "Do I want to be dangerous?"

Kali's teak-colored eyes had hardened. "Sorry. Habit. I taught combat in the Army. I don't talk about it in front of Lila, because it's the last place I want her to consider going, but I wanted to prove something to myself. I don't remember why, exactly. Once I was in a real battle, I knew what a dumb mistake I'd made. But I accomplished my goal. I proved I can be as badass and cold-hearted as anybody, and I hope I never do it again. I didn't like myself. I hated what I'd done. I got out as soon as I could."

Maureen nodded as though she understood. Was combat analogous in any way to courtroom battles? Probably not. "I'm sure you already know Kali is the Hindu goddess of creation and destruction." It was a random recollection that probably shouldn't have found voice. She avoided the other's gaze. "I feel like I should apologize to you for something, but I'm not sure what—your service to the country, maybe…my ignorance of foreign affairs, certainly. I was reading classics while you were risking your life."

"No apology necessary…or thanks, either," replied Kali matter-of-factly. "I made my own choices."

Maureen nodded again. She never shared like this—especially with strangers. Maybe it was the house that felt so much like a summer camp dormitory or Julie's contagious sorrow or maybe the fire—knowing all the artifacts of her previous life that had been stored in her mother's home were ash. Perhaps it was the realization that actual war lay low in the back of Kali's mind and refused to die, an immortal dragon twisting and belching flames—a greater curse than she herself had ever faced. Whatever the cause, Maureen felt oddly at home for once. She sighed as she pulled her hands out of her pockets into the light. "Is this dress as ugly as I think it is?"

Kali's laugh changed her looks entirely. Her skin glowed in the final rays of the day—the deep dark tan only God could give. Maureen, whose pale complexion inevitably went directly from alabaster to scarlet in the sun, always noticed beautiful skin.

"My little sister Lani has always had colorful taste," Kali told her. "I call it bizarre. It would look better in Hawaii—but not much better."

Maureen wanted to tell her how much she envied her skin color, but it didn't sound right in her head—patronizing, perhaps, so she kept the comment to herself. "Did you grow up there?"

"No. We visited once, but we couldn't afford to stay. Tutu was broken-hearted. She wanted to walk in the footsteps of the ancestors. Our family was close to royalty or shamans or something. She tried to explain, but I was never much for history or what I perceived as fantasy. She didn't want to talk about it after we had to leave. She said maybe it's better to let the past lie dormant."

Maureen sighed. "That word *dormant* bothers me. *Dormant* isn't permanent, is it?"

Kali stood and stretched. "Nothing is."

"I'm hoping my past stays dead." Maureen wasn't anxious to go back into the house. "So you're married—to Daniel in Texas?"

"Yes. How about you?"

Maureen didn't look up. "Divorced, no children."

"I'm sorry."

Maureen used the railing to pull herself to her feet. "Don't be. The divorce was the balm—not very effective, but balm nonetheless. The pain came first."

Kali met her gaze and they understood something in the silence between them. Maureen was thinking she had found an unlikely friend as they went through the door to the kitchen.

* * *

Next door, Will Manning stripped off the last of his clothing and stepped into the shower. He let the hot water gush over his head.

"Who was that on the phone?" called Gloria from the doorway.

"Miss Kalani."

As usual, Gloria sensed a gap into which she needed to intrude. She stepped into the bathroom, no longer caring that the steam would turn her hair into a frizzy mess. "What does she want you to do now?"

"I'm driving Kali and the two other women shopping tomorrow."

"So…they can't drive themselves?"

"They don't have a car and I'm not about to loan them the GTO. They need funeral clothes. Their houses burned."

"Sounds like Miss Kalani's fixing you up to me. She never liked me." When Will didn't comment, she continued. "I saw one of the *roommates*—long red hair, big boobs. Some hot stuff, or so she thinks. I guess this will be a painful assignment—you and a carload of women."

"It's for a funeral, Glor."

"Yeah. I heard. The old woman told me. The redhead's man is dead. Sounds like she needs a replacement."

He stepped out of the shower, wrapping the towel around himself as he squeezed drops from his hair. "Try not to sound shrewish, Glor. It doesn't suit you."

She looked away, automatically smoothing her hair with her hand. "I didn't mean it like that. I was kidding. Do you like her?"

"Are we still talking about the redhead? I told you about her. I met her once—gave her a ride from the hospital. Not a sexy occasion. I haven't even met the other woman who came with Kali and Lila on the motorcycle. Pull back the claws, okay? I'm the chauffeur. The end. Don't make a war out of a drill."

60

"I'm not the jealous type."

"The hell you aren't."

Will took his time preparing to shave. He wanted Gloria to leave him alone. He had wanted that for several months now, but he didn't know how to ask for it without inviting a dramatic scene. And revenge. Gloria fed on drama—something he hadn't guessed at first. The fact that their relationship wasn't remotely honest any longer didn't matter to her. He was a possession, and she never gave up anything while it was still viable. God help her children, if she ever had any—certainly not with him, if he could prevent it.

He dared a sideways glance and was relieved to see she had left the doorway. He was ambiance to her, a convenience, a guy—an artist--she could brag about to her friends, a ticket away from being alone. She'd be gone in a millisecond if she could find a better offer. If she didn't try so hard, it would probably happen. She was an attractive woman. For lots of guys that would be enough.

He drew the razor down his cheek, slowly, inspecting the cleared path through the shaving cream it left behind. He didn't have to ask himself how he had gotten into this mess. An uncomfortable cocktail party celebrating a book he had illustrated. Too much hard liquor. Donny, his agent who wanted him to look less single. To Donny anyone over thirty who wasn't attached had to be gay. He often said children's writers shouldn't be gay, although he never gave a reason. Maybe because he imagined he was still in the closet.

And then there was Gloria smelling fabulous. Pliant. Agreeable. Sexy. She knew how to make a few dynamite seduction dinners. Plus, Donny had primed her with appropriate opinions. He could guess what Will wanted to hear.

For his part, Will had allowed his solitude to bubble over into loneliness—a sticky mess he had worked all his life to avoid. Just him, the old drawing table, the computer, the ideas. He shouldn't crave more. He spent his time pleasing the little boy he held inside, the one who would let himself giggle if the image was funny enough. Other people were hazardous—people like Gloria who could fake a giggle. She never really liked his work. She simply wanted him. And while he was under the influence of toxic loneliness, he thought he wanted her, too.

Maybe some of the women next door would spring him from his trap. Gloria wasn't good at manipulating women. She was already intimidated by the redhead and she hadn't even met her. Maybe he'd need to make friends with whomever was over there—just friends. He knew enough to stop there now. Miss Kalani was the only woman he truly trusted. She was a damned good substitute for family.

Chapter 9

Drying Tears from Within

Richard's aftershave. He always uses too much.

Rich?

Sun falls around me—heavy and warm. It blurs my sight as though I'm looking through a waterfall or maybe a dirty shower stall. I squint.

Rich?

The edges of his being are fuzzy and faded, as though someone has been trying to erase him with one of those soft pink erasers, but I see his eyes. Those deep blue eyes. I know his eyes.

Rich?

He nods, smiling. Of course it's Rich. He holds me. I missed his touch. I melt against him, his muscles, the scent of him.

I'm sorry, Rich. I am so sorry.

He strokes my hair as he likes to do. His fingers get caught in the long strands and he tugs them free. It hurts. "Don't worry, Baby. I won't leave you."

But you did. You died.

And then he isn't there. I can't feel him any longer.

Rich?

They sat around Tutu's kitchen table, Kali on a rickety chair, Maureen and Julie on resin lawn furniture dragged in from outside.

"It was just a dream." Kali sounded certain, as she seemed to be certain about so much. In the morning light, her skin glowed bronze. She was an ancient Egyptian stone bust—shiny-hard, missing a headdress. She'd make a striking mermaid. "You wanted to see him, so you did." Kali's voice fell low and rich, brewed strong from a life of difficult experiences and a need to take command. Julie stared at her, thinking that the powerful dark woman operated by holding the world away from her as one holds a baby with a dripping diaper. Stay out of striking distance; that was Kali's way.

"It felt real." Julie stared down at her hands as they held her cup, thinking she never should have said anything about the dream. She didn't know the women sitting around the table. What in the world had possessed her? It was something Lani would've done. The intimacy of Tutu's house seemed to demand it—perhaps because Tutu did—hominess magnified by the morning sun. Vintage kitchen fabric crowded with yellow and red flowers and images of old-fashioned coffee pots. A round oak table, its blemishes mostly covered by a mended yellow tablecloth. Wooden chairs that didn't match, squeaking and groaning threats that they might collapse, set beside stained white resin lawn chairs that were molded to force you to sit back. The smell of toast and coffee and freshly scrubbed bodies.

Soon we'll be strangers again, Julie thought with some relief. *They're thinking I'm a fool, and I'm not convinced they're wrong.*

Maureen was drinking tea that smelled like a field in summer. Everyone could hear her swallow in the quiet of the kitchen. Lani's scoop-necked dress hung lifelessly on her, gapping where Lani's large chest used to fit. The bright rose color reflected up onto Maureen's chin, shadowing her abnormally pale skin until it resembled a section of a watercolor painting. Her light brown hair curled into wisps around her somber face. She was very attractive in her way—if she hadn't been wearing that dreadful rose dress. Rose wasn't her color. "Some dreams are real," she said, staring at Julie who could feel an open door behind Maureen's gaze. The draft chilled her. Life was careening into weird again. Maureen belonged near Tutu. What was she allowing in?

"You think he was really here?" Julie asked her in a whisper.

Kali wasn't as tolerant. "Sometimes we see what we want to see," she re-emphasized, looking at Julie as a mother might discipline a child in church. "But what we want and what we get don't necessarily match."

Lila staggered into the room then, with Teeny draped clumsily over her arms like a huge gray hairy worm. He was almost more than she could carry. "He likes me," she announced to Maureen. "He kisses me."

For his part, Teeny seemed dazed. He had sent his spirit elsewhere so he could endure endless little girl affection. It was the first sign of sainthood Maureen had seen in him. Mother would've been proud. His fur stood at electric attention from Lila's petting, a suitable halo above his green eyes.

"He doesn't like everyone." Maureen caught Lila's attention with the intensity of her gaze. "If he's unhappy, he claws you. Pay attention. He'll tell you when he's had enough. Please believe him when he says so."

Lila made a face that crinkled her dimples. "He wouldn't hurt me. He likes me. We're going to play house in the living room." And she plodded off, the temporarily selfless cat still imprisoned within her pudgy brown arms.

"You have to be careful of fantasizing too much," Kali warned Julie once Lila was gone. "It makes you weak…saps the strength you need to deal with reality."

Tutu emitted a disgusted sound from her position at the stove. "And you gotta beware of dreaming too little. Just because you ain't found a way clear of trouble yet, Kali, don't mean there ain't a way."

Kali rolled her eyes and Maureen and Julie could tell they were witnessing dialogue from a script begun long ago.

Tutu brought a fresh pot of tea and poured a cupful for Maureen. "You two buy clothes so you can go with Julie to the funeral whenever it is. I got a notion Julie's mother-in-law got evil in her fingernails. I'll tend Lila and the cat. Julie's gonna need backup."

"No." Julie looked around the table, thinking the women there— strangers, really--had no idea how to visualize her world. They couldn't imagine the predator mother-in-law she knew and the glee with which she could torture Julie, blistering her self-respect, stoning her soul. In private Belinda had no qualms, no scruples. Julie couldn't protect herself, much less anyone else. She pictured Belinda stuffing Kali's stomach with hot coals while Maureen was drawn and quartered—images she remembered from a high school history class. Belinda wouldn't discriminate between Julie herself and anyone who might be her friend. She had done her best to shred Lani at the wedding. Luckily, Lani was made of tear-resistant, nonstick material. These women didn't deserve such a fate. No one did. "This is my problem," she told them flatly.

Kali shrugged. "That woman isn't *my* mother-in-law. There's nothing she can say that I haven't heard from fouler mouths. Maybe when she sees you've got friends, she'll go easier. You got enough to handle without her shit."

"Kali!" Tutu scowled.

"When that's what it is, I say it—as long as Lila's outside."

Julie gaped at Kali, seeing her underlying warrior for the first time. She could imagine there was nothing Kali wouldn't do to protect her little girl—no violence that would be too far. Nothing. But why would she be willing to defend someone she barely knew? Was she paying Lani back for something? It didn't make sense. All these women talking about how to reinforce a stranger. None of it made sense.

She thought of the scene at dinner, how she had broken down in exhausted tears trying to tell about her experience in the lake with Rich, about the corpse bumping, bumping, bumping into the dock. Maureen had nearly joined her weeping. No one could mistake the welling in Maureen's blue eyes. She was a special kind of sensitive to feelings, it seemed, which was logical if you remembered she had sat by her mother as she died only days earlier. What kind of hell was it to watch a mother you loved deteriorate inch by inch? Maureen hadn't had time to process the horror of death and loss any more than she had. Yet here she sat, pale and silent. "It's not fair to ask Maureen to go through another funeral so soon," Julie told the group.

Maureen looked up from the table surface, magically able to dry her tears from within as though she had done it many times before. "I tried not to be emotionally present for my mother's funeral," she explained. "I did my best to disappear. I can't say I'm anxious to endure another one." She gulped down her tea, apparently not noticing how hot it had to be, before she continued. "I cheated. I wimped out. I hid inside myself. I let my little brother handle the social necessities." She sucked in a long breath and exhaled it through her nose. "I owe my mother better, and it's time I paid my debt. We'll flank you, Julie. Kali on one side, me on the other. We'll stand beside you at the funeral. If anyone mocks you, I'll *hurt* them."

The ferocity of her tone sizzled in the air in odd contrast with her soft white African-violet face. No one said anything for a moment.

"Not physically," she added, with a self-conscious twinkle. "But I can have a mean tongue."

Kali laughed outright and so did Julie and, finally, Maureen. For a moment, the women had been certain Maureen had lost her senses. They were all ready to see madness in someone else.

Chapter 10

Darkness Rising

THE MALE NURSE raised the back of the bed so Richard was seated nearly upright. Richard didn't like the nurse. He didn't want him touching him. Men didn't belong in nursing unless they were...less than, as Dad would've said. They probably got off on stuff like catheters—especially on other men. There should be a law.

Rich snarled at him when he suggested Rich move to the wide upholstered chair. Was he crazy? He was still in pain, which that damned nurse should know perfectly well since he was the one who was so stingy with pain medication. Rich was glad to see him leave. There would be a female in the next shift if he remembered right. She was cute, too.

He scowled at the TV. Stupid, stupid, and more stupid. Weren't patients depressed enough?

And then his mother appeared. Thank God. About time. The mass of her Kelly-green track suit only barely covered by a hospital gown filled the doorway. "Oh, Baby!" she cried and rushed forward as quickly as she could manage with a cane to steady her jiggly progress.

"Oh, my poor darling!" She pulled off her mask and leaned over him, weeping onto his face. The tears hurt, but he was so glad to have someone truly care at last that he remained stoic. She kissed his cheek and the scent of her perfume molded around him like poured plastic. "What has that bitch done to you!" she muttered into his ear.

She was weeping more copiously now. He hated it when she got this emotional, but he was too relieved to see a friendly face to say anything. Finally, his world would start making sense. His mother would make certain he got enough pain meds. She always got her way.

She squeezed her bulk into the chair, scowling at its creaking. "You'd think they'd provide decent chairs at these prices. Oh, your poor head! And you had such beautiful hair! How long before it grows back? Did they tell you?"

When he saw himself in her pupils, he knew that was one place where he would never fail to be all he had hoped to be in life. His success was guaranteed. With her, he was always home. She was German chocolate cakes and sunscreen at the pool and a new car every year.

"Mom, the doctor didn't have time for many questions. They have a lot of patients from the fire here. He said it would take as much time as it takes—a few weeks, maybe, but as long as I don't get any infections, it'll all be fine."

She snorted disgust. "These doctors these days! As if they aren't paid enough. What about your face? Your beautiful face!"

He had anticipated this. His burns were miserable and worse when he considered he might have to plan plastic surgery to retrieve the profile that had made him so popular with women. He didn't want to tell his mother the truth of it. She would be too upset, and when she was upset she gushed—like a toilet overflowing. It wasn't pretty. Better to change the subject.

"Where's Julie?" he asked. "No one here can tell me anything about Julie. Was she killed? Did she make it out? Tell me the truth."

Belinda glowered—her face blotchy red and pink and white. "Oh yes. She made it out, alright. Not a scratch on her. I saw her myself—haughty as ever. Baby, she left you to die! She told everyone you were dead. We all believed her! I nearly fainted when the hospital called me. Al had to fetch my pills."

His mind struggled to understand. "She left me? Julie left me?"

Belinda leaned closer over him. "She told everybody you drowned. Of course, she was the one who wanted you in the lake, doing her mermaid act with her. She admitted it. I suppose she thought she was going to inherit what your daddy meant for you. She said she was sure you were dead. Dead! Baby, we planned your funeral!" Belinda began sobbing, gasping and whining at once. "Oh, it was awful! It was so awful! She didn't care what we planned for you. She said so! She wanted us to hurry up and incinerate you so she could get on with life."

He felt his stomach lurch. "Did she say that?"

Belinda pursed her lips into a pink funnel. "Not in those words, exactly, but that was what she meant."

His head hurt—the burns and now a terrific throbbing. Better to change the subject until his mind stopped whirling. He couldn't risk a recurrence of the nightmares. "Where's Al?"

"Downstairs. Waiting. He's been such a peach. He didn't think you'd want to see him. I told him the bad feelings are just brother stuff. Of course you love one another."

Richard nodded. He didn't feel like loving anybody anymore. "Tell me more about Julie. Where is she now? Is she here?"

"No, thank God. She isn't here. Baby, I didn't tell her you're alive yet. I didn't want to hear the disappointment in her voice. That murderer! We'll get you home where we can make sure you're comfortable with a decent home care nurse and then I'll call her."

He stared at the line going into his hand. His mother had always hated Julie. He knew that. And maybe she was right, after all. "Where is she?"

"Staying with some friends, I guess. I hear the beautiful lake house your daddy gave you is nothing but ashes. Oh, I'm so glad Earl will never have to see it gone! He loved that house. I'll never forget the wonderful times we had there. Remember the poker games? Daddy taught you…"

"…Mom, you were telling me about Julie."

Belinda made a face like a baby with a full diaper. "Oh. Julia. I have a phone number for her someplace. She wouldn't stay with your family. She never liked us. You know she never liked us."

"Mom, you have to tell her now. Or give me her number and I'll call. I need to see her. I need to hear what happened—how I came to be so far away. Why she left me. I don't remember what happened." Flashes of his nightmares exploded like paintballs in his brain. Hallucinations. In place of memories he had hallucinations. Reality would be the best antidote.

His mother snorted again. "As if she'll tell you the truth..."

He swallowed. "Mom, she's my wife."

"More's the pity!" She was quiet for a moment, then leaned very far forward to speak in a near whisper. "Richie, they said a man picked her up from the hospital. She's already got a man. I warned you. She took the first man who came along as soon as you were gone."

* * *

Everyone was waiting in Tutu's living room for their shopping trip—everyone except Julie. Maureen stood in the kitchen doorway, wearing the ungodly rose dress that didn't benefit much from the belt she had used to subdue it. Kali stood near her in her same old jeans, hugging Lila against her knees. Tutu sat on the sofa, cradling the gigantic Teeny in her lap. They had anticipated seeing red puffy rings around Julie's eyes after hearing her soft sobs in the night, but the erotic décolletage of her dress commanded their attention, instead.

Julie could sense the silent intake of breath circling the room. She knew Lani's push-up bra—the only clean one in the drawer--was pushing too much. Lani gravitated toward the dramatic. Nature's work had become two large, soft orbs that were only barely restrained. The effect was worse than her mermaid costume. Maybe she should have opted for protruding nipples.

"You look nice in that mossy green." Tutu's comment made everyone laugh.

"It's a good thing we're going shopping," Julie said with an attempt at a smile and an upward tug at her plunging neckline. "I'm afraid to turn sideways." Her words reminded her of something her mother would've said, a comment that would've been paired with furrowed brows. Mom never approved of advertising your wares, as she called it. Only Rich would've given her an enthusiastic thumbs-up.

"Lani has never been shy about having a big chest," offered Kali with a grin. "She got my share."

Julie was about to tell an anecdote about Kali's sister when she noticed Will standing near the door, looking uncomfortable or maybe just hot.

"I brought the GTO," he said, an odd sort of pain lining his voice. "A 1966 Pontiac GTO...I restored it myself. It's cherry now. Miss Kalani said we couldn't all fit in my truck."

Kali laughed outright. "Oh my gosh, Will, what a sacrifice!" She turned to Julie. "No wonder he's driving us! He's extremely picky about who sits in his treasure. Nobody--and I mean *nobody*--besides him can drive it. Ever! He's been working on it for years. Lani and I were allowed to watch him work...from a distance, but when I asked to drive, he nearly passed out. Isn't that just like a self-appointed big brother? It's his greatest work of art."

"It's very nice," affirmed Tutu.

"I can wait in the car while you shop and make sure nobody steals it," muttered Will. "It's quite valuable. Some people would prize it. If I park way out in the lot, it'll be safer from scratches. I can move close when you're ready to leave."

Kali was still grinning. "I think that's a wonderful idea. Now that Jules is here, we can get going."

"I hope I haven't kept you waiting too long." Julie said it to Will without thinking. It was what she repeated nearly every time she went out with Rich. She was never ready fast enough for him, even when she was early. He called her the ultimate fusser, but he never complained about her appearance once she appeared. Rich invariably liked her appearance.

The phone rang then, and Tutu answered. "Yes?" Her eyes widened. "It's for you, Julie." Her expression crushed the air into silence.

It had to be about Rich. Had they found his corpse? Was he burned up? Had the wild animals found him first? Would she have to identify his bloated body? All the ugly possibilities that had kept her awake all night replayed themselves across her mind in a gruesome montage. Julie crossed the room which had stretched into the length of a football field. The phone receiver felt dangerous in that moment. She didn't want to touch it. She held it away from herself until she could summon the courage to answer. "Yes?"

"Jules, it's me."

"Me?"

Me? She stopped breathing. It couldn't be his voice. *It couldn't be.*

"Jules, say something. Goddammit, it's Rich, your husband. Surely you recall."

Her knees buckled. Tutu must have signaled Will, because he was there, his arms around her. He lowered her gently to sit on the sofa beside Tutu.

Rich was yelling into the phone. "Julie, answer me! Julie!"

Will picked up the phone. "Just one second. She needs a second." He squatted before Julie. "Are you okay? Can you talk now?"

Julie nodded and took the phone. Her hands were shaking so hard Kali could see the motion from the kitchen doorway. Her voice was nearly a whisper. *"Rich. Dear God, Rich, is that really you?"*

"Yes, it's me. Who the hell is the guy?"

* * *

The conversation didn't go well. Julie's breathing was quick and shallow by the time she hung up the receiver—as though she might explode at any moment. Kali brought her a shot glass of whiskey which she downed without pause.

Will stood by the sofa. No one could've missed hearing Rich shouting on the other end of the line. "Damn, I'm sorry," Will apologized. "I shouldn't have answered the phone. Of course it confused him. I didn't mean to make trouble for you. Do you want me to call him back and explain?"

Julie shook her head, struggling to calm her breathing. "He wouldn't believe you. He's upset, he's on drugs, and he's with his mother. He's in a hospital in San Francisco."

Maureen made a sound. "Dang. They must be farming burn patients out all over the place...or did she take him there?"

Julie was staring into space, her face flushed, her eyes moist. "No. He doesn't know how or why he got to San Francisco. He thinks

I'm hiding something from him. Belinda told him I tried to kill him." She turned to face the others. "*She told him I tried to kill him!*"

"You're nice. You wouldn't try to kill anybody," assured Lila.

"No, of course she wouldn't," agreed Tutu, struggling to rise with the cat in her arms. "Why don't you and me take Teeny out to play? I think he look like he need a break."

As soon as the back door banged closed, Will joined Julie on the sofa so he could be level with her eyes. "Listen, you need some time here. We can plan this shopping thing tomorrow. Is that okay with everybody?" He looked around the room.

"NO!" Julie pivoted to look directly at him. "I can't just sit still after that. My nerves are shorting out. This is too much—way too much. I need to walk around. I need to do something normal. I need to see shoppers and racks of clothes and price tags. I need to set this aside until I can stand to think about it. One more shot of whiskey, and I'll be ready to go. We have to buy clothes."

Kali nodded and headed for the kitchen. "I got you covered."

Julie took several deep breaths, exhaling them shallowly as though she were preparing for a dive. "He's alive. I saw him floating like a dead fish and he's alive. I don't know whether to laugh or cry."

Maureen came to take the phone from Julie's hands. She placed it on the side table. "My ex used to yell at me like that during the divorce. It takes a lot out of you."

Julie accepted the whiskey Kali brought. "Yeah. He never used to yell. Honestly. It's his mother. I could hear her in the background. She can whip her boys into a frenzy. But he's alive. Thank God, he's alive!"

"Do you need a ride to San Francisco to see him?" Will's lips twisted into something like a smile. "I don't mean with me. I don't want to make things worse, but I could loan you my truck. Or maybe Gloria could take you when she gets back from New York. She likes San Francisco. Or you could rent a car…"

Julie seemed to sink into the sofa. "How could he think I tried to kill him?" Tears pooled beneath her pupils. "How could he believe her?" She downed her second whiskey.

Kali's voice was low and kind. "He's injured and he's scared. He isn't himself."

Julie stared at her hands that were still quaking. "He sounds like his dad." She stood up and then put a hand out to Maureen to steady herself. "He prefers his mommy right now, and that's fine with me. I can't be with him while he's like this. What could I say? He's listening to his mother! He's not himself. He's crazy. He thinks I'd kill him. I'm his new wife—the one who loves him--and he thinks I'd kill him!"

Maureen placed her hand over Julie's. "Maybe you should take a little time by yourself. Or we can sit with you. Whatever you want."

Julie shook her head. "No, no. As long as I don't have to drive, let's go get some clothes. I don't want to think. I don't want to think a single serious thought. Let's go buy clothes—lots and lots of clothes." She turned to Kali. "Only please make sure I don't pick out anything Lani would like."

Kali took her elbow. "You're safe with me."

* * *

Julie slept fitfully that night. At last she rose and padded through the darkness to the kitchen, out of habit rather than hunger. The smells reminded her of her family kitchen when she was growing up. The most profound family moments seemed to happen there— cookies and chili and conversation. Julie had been standing beside the stove when her mother told her she was going to die. Something of her mother had seemed to linger over the cookie jar.

Tutu was sitting at the table, playing solitaire with a worn deck of cards. Polyester threads poked free from the seams of her quilted blue bathrobe which was cinched around her waist with pillow cording. Her steel gray hairs danced with wild abandon around her head from static electricity, swaying with the breeze from the open window. She appeared older and frailer in the yellow light from the vent hood above the stove. "I could make you a cup of tea," she offered without looking up.

"I'd do better with a stiff drink."

"A time and place for everything." Tutu rose with a little difficulty and headed for the stove. "I got a tea gonna do more for you than whiskey at this point."

"I don't like tea."

"You won't like this, either, but it might take the edge off so you can sleep. It's valerian."

"Am I supposed to know what that is?"

"Just a tea, Dear. Just a tea."

Julie watched the old woman set her teakettle to boil. "If this tea is so good, what are you doing up? It has to be late."

"I like the night—walking around in the dark as if there ain't no death."

"That's creepy."

Tutu chuckled. "When you at my age, death be just another shadow. Anyways, whiskey can get you to sleep, but it ain't gonna keep you there."

"I wouldn't mind experimenting."

Tutu turned to face her. "Are you a drinker?"

Julie dragged a chair out from under the edge of the table to mask the tears she was fighting. "Rich says I'm one of the worst drinkers he ever met—a cheap date. I'm asleep after two beers."

Tutu dropped loose tea into a painted ceramic cup and filled the cup with steaming water. "I wanna hear more about this mother-in-law of yours. You want milk or honey?"

"Neither...thank you."

Tutu pulled a bottle of Jamison's from under the sink and poured herself a glass, then grinned as she added a generous portion to Julie's tea. "My doctor say this be safer than drugs. He knows I don't pay him no mind, anyway. I didn't get this old listening to him." She lowered herself back onto the chair she had occupied earlier and turned toward Julie. "Okay. Tell me about that family you married."

Julie stared into her tea, inhaling the steam up her nose. It smelled like dirty socks. She couldn't think of a single reason why she should trust this decrepit old lady with her story except it squirmed inside her, way past its due date to be told. She took a deep breath and began. "They were repulsed by me from the first time we met. As soon as Rich told them I was a mermaid, they decided I was an empty-headed slut—pardon my language. I guess it was the costume or maybe my pay, which wasn't great. Lani probably told you. But no one could have been good enough to please Rich's mother Belinda. I think the idea of defying the family made Rich want me more."

Tutu turned her glass in her hand, staring at the liquid within. "Forbidden fruit taste sweet."

"I mean, it was love at first sight for Rich, or so he said. He and his family were in Vegas for a conference when he first came into the bar. He didn't go home with them. He fussed over me so much it was embarrassing—sending flowers, filling the bar stools with his friends, protecting me from the guys who tried to meet me at the dressing room door. He said he was my guardian angel."

"I bet his mama didn't like that."

"Right in front of me she said he was acting the fool."

"And his daddy?"

Julie squirmed on her chair. "Being around him made my stomach hurt. He was a self-centered bully and a pervert. He didn't do anything that wasn't a gift to himself. Rich adored his dad for his success and feared him at the same time. His father ran a string of real estate offices—his own little corporation. I think he figured my marriage to Rich was a temporary inconvenience. He made some lame joke about me being a trophy catch—you know, because of my fish tail, but it wasn't all joke. I think he envied Rich. He would've been happy to find a trophy wife for himself, but Belinda would've destroyed him if he even mentioned divorce. I'm sure he cheated on her during his trips...and he took plenty of trips. Belinda had to know. She was careful to ignore a few unnamed women at his funeral, and she watched the budget very carefully. Rich and I were married not long after he died when Rich inherited the lake house."

"So did your mama stick up for you at your wedding?"

"My mother had died long before then. Emphysema. She would have been no match for Belinda, anyway. Belinda ran the wedding since we didn't have the funds. My dad's in a retirement village that soaks up money."

"You wasn't happy with your wedding then?"

"I've never seen a more bizarre ceremony—and one of my high school friends was married in the concession stand of a Walmart."

"Sound like somebody sentimental."

"They were, actually. Even the reception was a lot warmer than mine."

Tutu made a face into her drink as she slowly swirled it around in her glass. "I gonna tell you something that sound crazy, but I want that you heed my words."

Julie's cheeks puffed up before she released a frustrated exhale. "How can anything sound crazy after this past week?"

Tutu didn't smile. "I won't explain now, but I know things. You be careful around your in-laws tomorrow and from now on—very careful."

"Careful in what way?"

"I understand Maureen gotta drive you to the hospital tomorrow because the rental in her name, but I want Kali to go, too. She been trained in the Army, you know. Got real good." Tutu's eyes seemed to darken in the yellow light. Julie suddenly felt the chills she had as a child when her uncle told her ghost stories in the campground.

"Army! What are you expecting to happen?"

Tutu shook her head slowly. "I don't know yet, but there's a darkness. Maureen gonna sense it, but she ain't ready to understand."

Julie nodded an affirmation she didn't feel. Tutu had seemed so wise and kind. Watching her take herself seriously while she was acting like a carnival fortuneteller was extremely bad news. It meant Julie might have to move in with Rich sooner than she thought—judging from today, far sooner than she wanted. If he had to stay in rehab, she might even end up living with Belinda for a while. Nothing could be less appealing. She gulped the end of her tea and rose. "I think I'll go back to bed now." She took her cup to the sink, rinsed it, and set it carefully onto the dark red rubber dish mat. "Thanks for caring, Tutu. I'll watch out."

Chapter 11

The Bile Mother Spews

MAUREEN LOOKED LIKE a different woman in her newly purchased navy silk shirt and khaki slacks—more professional and younger. She asked the others to keep the car quiet so she could concentrate on driving the unfamiliar rental and hear the electronic map directions from her cell phone, but Kali suspected she was avoiding conversation. Perhaps she was wary of where the talk might lead. Julie sat in the passenger seat, staring out the side window at the houses and yards and strip malls they passed. She had chosen to wear what she called her new anti-in-law clothes—an earthy brown boatneck tunic with loose black pants—nothing overtly sexy. She had pulled her hair into a knot at the nape of her neck and wore only minimum makeup. The effect was more striking than ever—classy and timeless.

Kali took her place behind Maureen, saying she wanted to be able to extend her legs. But she actually wanted to observe Julie—to see what Tutu had warned her about. Not that she could ever see all that Tutu described. But when hard times rubbed a child raw, that sensitive spot would forever be on alert, and her warning system was blinking red lights. If only she understood what she was watching for. Was Julie the danger or the victim? For the shopping trip, Kali had replaced her jeans with new workout pants that could double as slacks, topped with a scarlet top. Red always seemed to deliver a sensation of heat and power into her skin. She didn't believe in mysticism, but sometimes it seemed to believe in her.

They stopped for Maureen to use the restroom at a convenience store that reeked of fried food and diesel fuel, even through the closed car windows. "I'll just be a minute" Maureen told her passengers. "Anybody else?"

The others shook their heads, and she left.

Julie twisted in her seat. "Kalia…"

"Kali will do."

"Kali, then. Tutu said she wanted you to come…I guess to defend me? Did she tell you she warned me?"

"Yes."

"What does she mean 'there's darkness'?"

Kali shrugged. How could she answer without validating Tutu's brand of spirituality, which she was loathe to do? There were already too many people running around spouting woo-woo advice they couldn't back up. "She learned old beliefs from her grandmother. The elders talk about darkness versus light a lot. And she has a way of knowing how you feel. She watches and listens. When she heard your husband yell at you, she took the threat seriously."

Julie shifted in her seat. "Rich wouldn't hurt me."

Kali nodded, not agreeing. "I worked for social services for a while. There's plenty of research. The yelling is first. Then hitting. Then violence…if no one intervenes."

"I don't believe it. Not Rich."

"Suit yourself."

Julie clicked the latch on the console open and closed and then open and closed again. "I know Tutu means well," she said at last. "Rich did sound bad. Being with Belinda is always bad. She smothers me as completely as though she sat on me."

Kali didn't laugh.

"She told me I could come to live with her, but you'll notice I'm not carrying a bag with any clothes. I know not to step on poisonous snakes." Again Kali didn't react. The silence scraped against Julie's nerves, irritating her. Tutu and Kali didn't know Rich or his mother at all. How could they predict what might happen when Julie confronted them? How could they conclude Julie wouldn't be able to handle the situation alone? The idea was mildly insulting. "You don't have to come in with me," Julie told the woman in the back seat. "It'll be ugly, but I'm used to it by now."

"Used to it?" Kali pursed her lips. With her hair wound high on her head, she looked like a modern version of tribal royalty—determined and smug. "That's the point of my being here, isn't it?"

Julie wasn't sure what she meant. "Yeah, I guess so."

Maureen had returned, so Julie straightened in her seat. "I don't mean to be ungrateful. I'm glad you're with me," she told Kali. "I'm glad to know you care."

Maureen started the engine, not realizing she wasn't yet part of the conversation. "You're welcome. With the backlog of requests after the fires, you'll have to wait quite a while before you can replace your driver's license. Funny, because the credit card companies can't replace those cards fast enough. They don't want to miss a nickel in interest! I wonder if they'd let you rent a self-driving car? Not that I'd recommend it. I've worked with enough computers that I wouldn't trust them with my life...or yours, either, as it happens."

Julie threw a little smile toward Kali. "Thanks."

St. Francis Memorial Hospital was a multi-storied concrete building in the city, imposing and professional. Maureen dropped off Julie and Kali and promised to wait with the car for as long as the visit might take. "I've had my fill of hospitals," she told them. "I had to fight her caretakers to let my mother die at home. They were positive she needed more than a visiting hospice nurse and me—as though nonmedical people can't learn how to administer drugs. They should know better, considering the epidemic of addicts." She flourished a thick book she had purchased the day before. "750 pages of political intrigue. I'm set for a few hours. Text me when you're ready, and I'll pull around to pick you up."

As Kali and Julie entered the hospital, their shoes clacked across the gleaming marble floor inside the front entrance. A pleasant older gentleman at the reception desk gave the women a practiced smile as they approached him. "Welcome to St. Francis Memorial. How may I help you?"

When Julie gave him Rich's name, he took only a moment to locate him on the computer. "He's not in the burn unit. Apparently, his injuries weren't that extensive. The Bothin Burn Center is a sealed unit to prevent contamination. We have only 16 beds. Richard Teller is in a private room on another floor. He was moved to private yesterday." He jotted the number on a small sheet of paper that he handed across the counter to Julie. "The elevator is down the hall to your right."

As soon as the elevator doors had swished closed, Julie looked at Kali. Oddly, they were the only occupants.

"Dread. I feel dread," she told her.

Kali reached out to touch her arm. "Then it's a good thing you didn't plan to stay with your mother-in-law. You made her son happy. You don't owe her anything."

Julie's heart dropped with the ping that warned the doors were about to open. "Oh God," she moaned quietly.

Belinda greeted her at the door to the room. She was wearing a disposable mask, paper booties, and purple plastic gloves. A gigantic hospital gown stretched over her dress. "You have some nerve showing up here." She glared at Kali. "Your taste in friends hasn't improved."

A small blonde nurse wearing large brown-framed glasses hurried to supply the new guests with gowns, masks, slippers, and gloves. "Please, ladies. Before you enter, cover your shoes, hands, mouths, and outerwear. It's a precaution until the patient's burns are better healed." She helped Kali with her gown.

Hearing the voices, Al came out of Rich's room, straining to gain a glimpse down Julie's shirt as she bent to cover her shoes. He, too, wore a gown that could have tented a small family. He looked Kali over, smirking at her small chest. "She doesn't need to come in. Rich doesn't want to see any more of her kind than he has to. Dad did his best to keep them out of our lives. You give them an inch, and they take over, whining about how unfair everything is."

"*Her kind* is my friend." Julie slipped into the gown the nurse was holding for her. "You need to leave, Al. You spread infection every time you open your mouth." She stepped back protectively so Kali could precede her through the door. "I'm sorry you had to hear that, Kali. Rich has relatives who are lower life forms."

The nurse pretended she wasn't following the conversation. "Only two visitors at a time, please." She turned to Belinda. "I can help you take off those things."

Belinda snorted. "I should be one of the two visitors I'm his mother. I don't know who the hell that other girl is."

Julie ignored her and followed Kali into Rich's room. She could hear Belinda hissing behind her.

"You wait, Missy. You're gonna get yours one day."

The nurse quietly closed the door behind Julie.

Julie moved directly to the bed where Rich was sitting upright. His face was partially bandaged and partially deep red with blotches of white.

"Oh, Sweetheart!" She leaned over and lifted her mask enough to kiss a healthy patch near his lips. "I'm so glad to see you! I can't tell you how glad!" Her tears begged to fall as she wondered how she could embrace him.

His gaze was glacial. "Took you long enough to come."

She perched on the chair beside his bed, telling herself she didn't feel the emotional chill he was emanating. "I'm sorry. I came as soon as I could. I'm staying outside Sacramento and I didn't have transportation. Our cars burned along with everything else."

"So *she* drove you?" He was staring at Kali who stood near his feet.

Julie forced a smile that lay on her face like suffocating plastic wrap. "Rich, this is my friend Kali. She's Lani's sister. You remember Lani from Vegas—the one with the blue hair? We swam together. She was my maid of honor. I'm staying with their grandmother."

He nodded toward Kali. "Thanks for bringing my wife." With his facial expression, he could've been saying, "Make sure you empty the wastebaskets."

"My pleasure." Kali's tone matched his.

He was only superficially polite, which wasn't like him. Kali looked stunning in the sunshine beaming in from his window—her skin contrasting with the light turquoise of the hospital gown, and Julie knew he noticed. Rich appreciated attractive women—even black women he would never acknowledge publicly. He had that in common with his father.

He returned his attention to Julie. "So does that guy on the phone live there with you, too?"

Julie ignored the twisting in her stomach. "No, he's a neighbor with a car...and a girlfriend."

"I'll bet she doesn't look as good as you."

Julie reached out to hold his hand, relaxing a little. "Thank you, Sweetheart."

He didn't return her soft pressure. She had misread him. His voice remained crisp. "Kali can go now. I have some things to discuss with you."

Julie hesitated. "She can hear anything we say."

"You make close friends pretty fast, don't you?" He exhaled hard and Julie wondered if one day it would sound like the snort Belinda made so often. "I seem to be in no position to argue. I want you to tell me what happened to me. You have to know. Don't bullshit me. Tell me now."

Julie didn't realize she had retracted her hand until she felt her fingers gripping one another in her lap. "Rich, I thought you were drowned. When the fire passed, I swam to the rocks by Richter's place—or where Richter's place used to be. Everything was burned. A rescue helicopter came in the morning and took me up in a basket and flew me away. You were still in the water. I saw your body half floating."

"And you never checked to see if I survived? You didn't insist the rescuers check?"

"You looked drowned. Your head was submerged."

He shifted in the bed. "Nice to know your bride doesn't bother to see if you're dead or alive."

"You were mostly under water."

His stare burned. "You used to live under water...in that damned tank."

"Rich, I'm sorry. If I had seen any sign you might have survived, I would have gone to you. But I had hypothermia and you looked dead. The rescuers thought you were dead, too. They said they had to prioritize their time to get to everybody."

"So is Mom right? When I told her I had hallucinations of insect people carrying me, she said I was dreaming of you as you are to me—you know, how praying mantises eat their mates. Is she right? Did you *mean* to kill me?"

She stood up. Her vision was clouded with tears. "How can you ask me that? I love you, Rich. I married you!"

"And I'm a fool."

"Yes, you are. You're listening to that bile your mother spews. You used to know better."

"I used to believe you cared."

She stood for a moment, fingering the ring she wanted so badly to throw at him. She deliberately slowed her breathing. "You're in pain right now and on drugs. You're listening to a woman who has hated me from the first moment she saw me. She's so jealous of me she radiates green. This is no time for us to make life decisions."

"Then tell me how I got here. Tell me why you lured me into the lake instead of evacuating."

"Lured you!" Her blood rushed to her face as her heart raced. Words she struggled to hold back rioted in the depths of her mind. The rising heat of their violence forced her filtered speech to emerge in a rush. "You can tell your mother we didn't evacuate because you thought you knew better. You thought you could stop the fire all by yourself. If we hadn't gone into the lake, you wouldn't be in a bed right now; you'd be in a morgue...or a canister. You're welcome! And I don't know what happened to you. I wasn't there. If you don't know, I have no idea who does."

His voice was a snarl. "That's convenient, isn't it? You're innocent because you weren't there when I was carted off by God knows who. Did you think I was dead or did you wish I were?" His eyes narrowed. "You wanted the money from our property. You know you're on the papers. You watched me change my will. Did you lust after my inheritance? Tell me the truth."

She folded her arms over her chest, restraining most of the assassin words from escaping. "No, I don't want your inheritance. The truth is I don't even know if I want *you*." She walked toward the door where Kali stood waiting. She didn't bother to turn to talk to him. "Call me if you recover the man I married."

"Do me a favor and hold your breath until I call!" he shouted after her.

Kali held the door for her. She was half smiling as she whispered, "You didn't need defending."

Belinda sat in the hallway, her body draped over a stool that had been provided for her, her face scarlet with rage. "You bitch! How dare you upset my poor burned baby! I never should have let you take this... *person* in with you. *I* should've been there!"

Julie paused only briefly to reply. "Trust me. You were."

* * *

Julie didn't begin to cry until they were well on their way home. She claimed Kali's former place in the back seat so she would have enough space to explode, and she needed every inch. "Tell me it was his meds!" she pleaded at last through her sobs. All her recent trauma flooded through her, washing the tangled debris of her life ahead of it. "Tell me there's some excuse."

Kali twisted in her seatbelt. She had done her best to try to convey the essence of the meeting to Maureen in as few words as possible, and they had all ridden in silence ever since. "I'm sure drugs didn't help the situation."

Maureen shook her head. "Men can be assholes. It's an incontrovertible fact. Sometimes it's temporary and sometimes it's a permanent condition."

Julie blew her nose into the tissue Kali had provided. "How do I know which this is?"

Maureen shrugged. "See if it goes away. But personally, I'd say if a man believes you tried to murder him, your marriage is in serious jeopardy."

Kali made a face. "Rini went through an ugly divorce, so she has a jaundiced view. Your guy may think differently when he feels better."

"I almost threw my wedding ring at him."

Maureen shot a disdainful glance at Kali. "Go with your instincts, that's what I say. But think about what you're doing. You can pawn a wedding ring."

Kali faked a moan. "Oh, you're a big help."

"I tried to stay out of it." Maureen cursed at a car that swerved into her lane to cut her off. "Men have had several millennia to get their acts together and most of them are still charging around scratching their balls and picking fights. When scholars say women are the civilizing force, they aren't exaggerating."

Kali sighed. "Some women."

Julie wiped her nose a final time. "Yes, some women. Others are deceitful and mean."

"'When they're good, they're very, very good...'" recited Kali.

Maureen finished her misquotation. "'And when they're bad, they're horrid.'"

Chapter 12

Out of a Rat Hole

HE LUMBERED UP the stairs to his room—not much of a room, a hole in a building, like the kind rats find only bigger. When you turned the lights on fast, you'd see the centipedes and cockroaches scatter—like the brown people in the villages when they knew the guns were coming. He had a hot plate the super suspected but hadn't seen, a miserable little TV he swiped from the community center, and a bed that smelled of urine and who knew what else. He deserved better. He had earned better. He pulled his gun out of his waistband beneath his tattered sweatshirt and laid it on the table.

Little Paulie, that was what the guys had called him, back in the war. Little Paulie, because he was big, like a pro wrestler only not a fake. He was good at killing, and over there people had appreciated his talent. "You saved our butts today, Paulie. You're a one-man firing squad." Over there he was somebody. He liked war. He liked that rush of adrenalin he got when he went on patrol. Life was exciting when you didn't know when you might lose it. Living mattered. He would've stayed for as many tours as they'd give him. They should've wanted him. He fit in there. It was home. But they sent him back here. Sent him to counseling—as if he'd go to some bleeding-heart liberal bastard therapist. Sent him into this hell of nothingness. And what was he supposed to do now?

Ma wouldn't give him his room back. Said he was a bad influence on the kids—like they couldn't get in trouble all by themselves. Said he didn't have no place there anymore. More likely she was afraid she couldn't beat on him now he was a trained soldier. He'd show her where to put that wooden spoon. He'd wrap her leather belt around her worthless neck. Nobody would hear a sound. Just a quiet pop. Pop. And she wouldn't be able to beat on anybody. Doing it would be real satisfying, too, but he couldn't afford to make the news. Not in his current business.

On the street he met a guy who knew a guy who knew another guy who needed somebody like him, and that was his job now. Stay invisible. Take out people who had overstayed their welcome. Clean up. That was his job. People janitor. Take the garbage out. He chuckled into his beer. Pretty soon he'd be able to get a better room—maybe an apartment with air conditioning. He'd buy back the stuff he'd hocked to get his guns—the stuff he'd swiped right under Ma's nose. People janitors got paid real nice money. Prospects were good.

Chapter 13

Too Much Wind to See

ONCE LILA WAS safely in bed asleep with Teeny, the women gathered around the kitchen table. Outside, the wind intensified. Tree branches scraped their frightened fingernails against the house. The house creaked as though the joints were abandoning their assigned positions and would soon release the roof to sail off into the night. It was a time for shadow people to command their minions. Wisps of cool air scurried through the kitchen, sneaking in through secret passages, acting as spies for the mad wind.

Tutu poured each woman a little whiskey in a juice glass. "We need to loosen up!" she announced.

"Time to tell what happened in that hospital room today," Maureen concluded. "I can't do it. My version is secondhand. Not admissible. Tell Tutu what you saw, Kali. You're our eye witness. Julie's too involved. And don't skip any details. We're here to back up Julie, but we need to assess what we're up against."

As Kali recounted what she had seen, Julie sat silent, staring at the table. How had her life become a public concern? It felt good and bad at once.

"He's not himself," Kali repeated for the third time that day. "Men are really just oversized boys who get overwhelmed now and again. He's been through a lot and he isn't sure what. Trust me; people who are recuperating aren't at their best. They're angry and confused. Give him some time to think. Not knowing what's going on can get on your nerves. He may come around. You can walk out on him later if he doesn't."

Tutu nodded. "When he feel better, his mama ain't gonna make his world bright. He gonna remember being happy, and he gonna want that again. He gonna want you." She reached out to lay a boney hand over Julie's. "Don't give up too soon. Things got a way of working out if you want them to bad enough."

"I don't know." Julie sipped at her drink, wishing she dared grab the bottle. "He's not at all like he was before. His mother told him the insect people he saw in his dream represented me in his mind, and I'm not sure he didn't agree with her. You didn't see his face. He looked at me like I truly was a praying mantis come to eat him. He was vile."

Tutu straightened in her chair. "Insect people? Did you say he saw insect people?"

"It was a hallucination or nightmare or something—from being nearly drowned."

Kali poured herself a second drink. "With the stuff they've probably got him on, it's a wonder he didn't see worse than that."

Maureen was staring at Tutu. "What's the matter, Tutu? You look upset."

Tutu waved a dismissive hand. "Nothing. Just surprised is all. I heard talk of insect people before. There was stories when I was little. Crazy stuff, I guess." She glanced at Kali who scowled. "But I want you ladies to be careful."

Kali shook her head. "You're not going to talk about darkness again, are you? You're scaring Julie. There's no such thing as insect people, Tutu. You're watching too much TV."

Tutu slid her glass across the table, making it collide with the salt shaker. "We don't know all there is. That's a fact." She sighed heavily. "I ain't saying I believe in insect people and I ain't saying I don't. I got to think on all this, that's what I'm saying. And ask the ancestors. I don't talk to them enough. Just do me a favor and watch out. That's all. Watch out."

Kali rolled her eyes for Julie's benefit. "Sure."

Tutu rose abruptly, her face red. "Don't you disrespect me or the ancestors, Kalia!"

Kali lowered her gaze. "I apologize. I don't mean to disrespect you, Tutu, or the ancestors, either. I truly don't. I'll watch out. I swear."

Tutu nodded. "Okay then."

Kali turned to Julie. "I could use some air. How about you, Jules? Care to come with me to check on Lila? If this wind wakes her up, she may be spooked."

Julie pushed herself away from the table. "Yeah, I think a horrendous wind may be exactly what I need. Coming, Rini?"

Maureen shook her head. "In a minute. I haven't finished my drink yet." She stayed in place until she and Tutu were alone. Then she downed the remainder of her whiskey and took the empty glasses to the sink. Her movements as she washed the glasses were deliberate, as though she were working in a different universe in which gravity and time operated more slowly. At last she set the final glass to drain, but she didn't turn around. "I feel darkness, too," she said in a near-whisper. "What does it mean?"

Tutu finished the last of her drink before answering. "You know how sometimes there's a disease and seems like everybody got it but nobody knows why some got it and some don't?"

"Yes."

"Something like that. Some kind of danger. That's all I know right now."

* * *

Outside, Kali and Julie sat on the steps, huddled against the side of the house, letting it shield them from the worst of the wind.

Kali spoke first. "Tutu isn't demented. It's what she was taught."

Julie twisted her hair into a long knot to keep it from lashing her face. "By who?"

"A kahuna, as I heard it. A wise man—kind of a shaman and chief combined. They often talk in metaphors."

Julie gave up and laid back against the higher step, letting her whipping hair obliterate her face. "I guess it wouldn't sound as weird if we were in a tropical setting. California doesn't feel very mystical."

Kali laughed. "Oh, I don't know. I've met guru types out here. And wasn't San Francisco the original home of hippies with flowers in their hair?"

Julie nodded. "I remember hearing the song."

Kali paused, considering a change of topic. "Is there any way you can find a time to visit Rich when his mother won't be around?"

Julie pulled hair out of her mouth. "Not for a while. She has him trapped and she isn't going to miss her chance to indoctrinate him."

"And he believes her?"

"Not usually. Not completely." She sat up straight before continuing. "When his dad was here, Rich could see the dysfunctional relationship for what it was. But now, I don't know. I figure he came so close to dying that it's going to take him a while to adjust to being alive. Maybe he never will. He's back to depending on Mom. He can't even see me." She sighed and stood up. "With this wind, I can't see anything."

Kali nodded thoughtfully as she rose. "I can attest to the fact that being near death does change your perspective. Usually it highlights what's important. Sometimes the adrenalin of veering so close becomes addictive. And sometimes you sink so deep in fear that everyone becomes an enemy—especially yourself. They call it depression."

The wind abruptly paused as though to lend dramatic emphasis. "You were there?" asked Julie.

"Yeah. I was one of the ones who returned to living."

Julie smiled. "That must have taken guts and willpower. You can be my role model." She plodded up the steps to the door, letting Kali precede her.

"I'm no role model. I'm never finished coming back, but if I give you hope, I'm glad." And Kali led her inside before the next gust of wind smashed its face against the door.

Chapter 14

Broken Down

"RICH WANTS ME to come to him in the hospital," Julie told Maureen over breakfast a few days later. Her face was pink with anticipation. "He just called. He promises Belinda won't be there. He asked her to stay away."

Maureen sipped at her smoothie, swallowing the response that arrived in her mind unbidden. "How did he sound?"

"Not as belligerent."

"That's a start, I suppose. Do you want to go?"

Julie stirred her coffee, as though she had added cream. "I think I have to. He deserves a chance. He's my husband."

Maureen nodded her head, measuring what she had to say and discarding the words she didn't think were appropriate. "That doesn't make you property, you know."

"I know." Julie sighed heavily and looked up into her friend's eyes. "He says he wants to talk about property, as a matter of fact. We owned the house in Eden together. He changed the paperwork before the fire. He wanted to show me he wasn't like his dad. He trusted me. It was really sweet."

The yellow of Maureen's new blouse reflected the morning sunshine. She wanted to look especially bright today. She pushed back her hair, thinking she needed to tread lightly if she were to keep herself out of Julie's decision-making. After her experience with Gage, she was hardly an unbiased source. "My advice would be don't relinquish your share—at least not without compensation. That land around Eden will be worth a small fortune soon. Real estate agents were always bugging Mother to sell because of the proximity to the lake and the magnificent views of the mountains. Once they clean up the fire debris, it'll be ready for new construction. The change won't take long. It never does if there are profits to be had. The money would give you a decent fresh start if you need one. Don't let your heart cloud your head, Jules."

"No. I suppose not." Julie looked like she might cry. "Maybe he wants to apologize, to start over. We hardly had a chance to begin. He used to tell me I was his world."

Maureen made a weird little sound without realizing it. "Oh, Honey, I know you'd like to think this is all a bad dream, but be prepared in case it isn't. You're more vulnerable than he is right now, because you've got guilt going against you."

"I did my best to save him," Julie told her as tears blurred her eyes. "And failed. But I didn't try to kill him." She swiped a hand across her cheek.

"Only his mother would believe you did." Maureen exhaled as her expression grew more somber. "I get a bad feeling about her, Jules—a really bad feeling. Don't underestimate her."

"No. I don't and I won't. But she won't be there in Rich's room. He promised." Julie rose to dump her uneaten toast into the trash. "So will you drive me? I haven't replaced my license yet, so I can't rent a car, and Kali has an appointment for Lila."

"I'm sorry, Jules, not this time. I'm on my way to pick up my brother Pat at the airport in Oakland." Maureen's smile spread into a happy glow as she stood up to clear the table. "He finally managed to get away from work to come to the aid of his big sister in distress...better late than never! And, thank goodness, he's going to handle the paperwork and prep to have his motorcycle shipped to his place in Hawaii. I wasn't looking forward to doing that, and I told him so. I'm pretty much done with motorcycles. But I'm going to brag like crazy about my bike riding skills. He won't believe it! To tell you the truth, I don't believe it. He couldn't get me to ride with him—too scary! I can't wait to see him, but I won't tell him how much I've missed him or he'll tease me unmercifully. He always makes life shinier—a perfect balance for dark old me. You'll like him." She paused, remembering suddenly that she was supposed to be answering a request. "Can you call Will for a ride?"

Julie rolled her eyes. "All I need is for Rich to see me with Will again."

"Was Rich always that possessive?"

Julie pulled her hair back into a ponytail and knotted it. "I guess he was. I didn't notice—probably because I didn't want to."

Maureen chuckled. "That's my girl. Eyes wide open. Will knows enough to stay out of sight. Go ahead and call."

* * *

Julie wondered if she should've called a cab as she sat on the front seat of Will's battered truck. His shocks left much to be desired. "Thanks for doing this," she told him to fill the silence. "I'll reimburse you for the gas, and I'll be happy to buy lunch."

"No need for all that," he answered without looking toward her. He was wearing clean jeans and a v-neck t-shirt—dressed up for him. "I was bored, anyway. I was hoping I could find one of those speedy lube places to cheer this tub of bolts up. It's not sounding good."

She made a face. "You totally restored the GTO and you can't bother to change your own oil?"

He laughed. She hadn't been sure he would. "Yeah. Dumb, huh? But it's not fun to work on this monster anymore. Too depressing. The problems only get worse. I've even thought of replacing it—maybe with something little that doesn't gulp gas; I'm mending my evil ways."

"Electric?"

"God, no. I'm not ready to go that far."

Their conversation settled comfortably on the mundane and inconsequential. Julie was relieved and surprised that he would chat at all. He was an odd combination of surly and nice. She wondered what Gloria was like.

By the time they reached the hospital, the truck had developed the automotive version of degenerative muscle failure. The prognosis was dire. Will's face twisted into a scowl.

"Shit. I never should've trusted the beast this far. You go ahead and have your visit. I'll find someplace to resuscitate the monster and meet you back here."

Julie felt oddly exposed as the truck sputtered and jerked away. Shouldn't she be excited to be alone with her husband at last? She wasn't. She was scared and she wasn't sure why.

No one suggested protective gear this time. A tall, elderly female nurse asked that Julie refrain from touching any of the healing skin and waved her into the room. Rich was sitting on the bed. The burns on his face distorted the tissue enough to create the impression of a permanent scowl. He looked more like an unfortunate cage fighter than the clean-cut college football player he had been. He could frighten small children.

"Oh, Rich, that looks painful. I'm so sorry you're injured."

He nodded acknowledgment. "You aren't the only one."

"I meant to save you, you know. Surely you know that."

He shrugged. "I'm here, so I guess it worked. After the doc visits, I'm going home today."

She nodded automatically, then caught herself. "Home? How can you go home? There's nothing left but a chimney."

"To Mom's."

"You're going to go live with your mother? Really?" Julie perched on the edge of the chair beside the bed. "You don't have to do that. We could rent an apartment or something. I could take care of you. You told me I was a good nurse when you had the flu."

He fingered the papers on his tray table. "There aren't any rentals available. Even the hotels are full. Eden was nearly wiped out. People are moving out of state to find places to live."

She reached out to take his hand. "We don't have to stay here. We could go back to Vegas. They have good medical facilities. We could be newlyweds all over again. Rich, you'll heal. Everything will be okay."

He shook his head and slowly withdrew his hand. "…And you could get your old job back? I could be the husband of a mermaid? No, thanks."

She did her best to smile. "I don't have to be a mermaid. I can do other things. I was accepted to go back to college, you know. I did well on the tests. I can do more than swim."

He smirked. "Like we could live on the income you can make? I don't think so. No, I have my job at the business, and I'm ready to move up. It'll be all mine soon. We just have to decide what to do with Al. Mom's giving me Dad's office with new furniture and carpeting, but I'll work from home until my face is fixed. I don't want to scare the clients."

She dropped her gaze. "…Home being your mother's house."

"Yeah."

Her voice crouched small and young. "Rich, I don't want to live there."

"No one invited you to."

Her heart squeezed. "Exactly what are you saying?"

"I'm saying you can stay with your friends, and I'll stay with Mom. She can afford a visiting nurse, and she has plenty of space. Meanwhile, I want you to sign over your half of the Eden property to me. You can't develop it and I can. It's part of my family and always has been. I'll have the attorney meet us somewhere away from Mom's house to sign the papers—maybe in the bank. You should feel more comfortable there. Their conference rooms are nice."

She stood. "I can stay with friends and sign over my half of the property to you—for your family?" She swallowed the tears that wanted to fall, her stomach lurching with their bitterness. "Rich, why would I want to do that? What about our marriage? What about our plans together? What about 'Jules, I love you and I want to prove it?' Were you lying? Did you stop? What happened to this being *our* property? You keep saying *you* and *I*. Where's the *we*? Are you suggesting a divorce? Really? A divorce? A *divorce,* Rich? We haven't even been married a year yet and you're ready to give up?"

His eyes narrowed. "Stop being melodramatic. I'm suggesting you sign over that property until we figure things out. Who knows how long that might take and this opportunity won't last forever. Be practical."

She kept her voice even. "What, exactly, are we trying to figure out?"

He ignored her question as he reached for his water glass. "Who drove you here? That black woman with the weird hair?" He slurped as he drank.

"Her hair isn't weird. But, no, this time the neighbor did."

"The guy."

"Yes. I needed a ride. I asked him."

Rich waggled his head slowly, like a snake sniffing the air with its darting tongue. "And you want to know what we have to figure out?"

Julie was quiet for a few moments, pacing to the window, knowing who had sent most of the flowers and even a teddy bear without looking at the tags. "Mommy's taking good care of you, is that it? At first I believed jealousy was an issue between us. But I think you're using my friendship with Will as an excuse to push me away." She pivoted to face him. "No. I won't sign over the property and disappear. You can tell Mommy getting rid of me isn't going to be tidy, if that's where you're headed. I trusted you, Richard. I let myself love you, and I married you. I put up with that tasteless wedding because you asked. I wore the ugliest wedding dress in the history of mankind. I moved away from my friends and my job. I trusted you! Well, now I have new friends, and I'll tell you which things need to be figured out. You need to figure out if you love me—if you ever loved me. If not, why did you marry me? Think it over. I'll wait."

She grabbed up her shoulder bag and left before he could reply. She could feel his fury tumbling after her like a searing gray pyroclastic cloud--something immediately lethal if it caught up to you.

* * *

Will was nowhere to be seen when she came down, which was a good thing. She could feel the color in her face and her quick breathing. Tears slipped down beside her nose. If she let go, she might dissolve. She didn't want Will to see her like this—soggy and emotional. He was the practical type. She didn't want to let herself feel defeated and crushed. Belinda couldn't win. She couldn't. Let her take her baby boy back; she still wouldn't win. Julie dried her face with a tissue from her bag and texted Will: *I'm ready to go when you are.*

He answered almost immediately: *I'm at a nearby garage. Not looking good. Want to wait at the hospital where it's comfortable?*

No. Give me directions. I'll walk over.

The walk was longer than she had guessed it would be, but she didn't care. Walking felt good. Pain would feel good to her. She needed the reality of her body to counter the sun-storm of her emotions.

Will was pacing back and forth in the space assigned to be a customer waiting room when she arrived, his face glum. Behind him in the tiny row of nicked and battered plastic chairs allotted for guests, a stout man in a worn blue suit dozed, his freckled bald head bobbing toward passers-by. The air circulating from the bays slid around the space, carrying the heavy smell of tires and automotive fluids and male sweat. Metal tools clanged against concrete and the zooming zipping sound of an air wrench punctuated the noise of traffic passing outside. The garage itself huddled in the midst of the city, a vestige of earlier times humbly aware its days were numbered.

"Everything okay?" asked Will as Julie approached.

"Fine." She adjusted her sunglasses.

He didn't notice her lie. "Well, that's one of us." He sighed. "The truck is permanently dead. It's not worth what it would take to fix it. I guess I saw that coming and ignored it. I apologize for acting stupid and putting you in a bad situation. So now there's no decision left. These guys are going to part it out and dump it. If I'm lucky, I'll break even."

She drew a couple long breaths, exhaling Rich and his mother. "And how do we get home?"

"I called Maureen. She and her brother are going to drive over from the airport to pick us up. They're already on their way, but it'll be a while. Traffic's a bitch from Oakland. Want to find someplace to have a drink?"

She nodded. "Only if it's alcoholic."

Will was quiet until they had settled in a booth in a busy downtown bar and she removed her sunglasses. He was studying her now, and she knew it.

"I don't want to be nosey, but you look like hell."

"Oh, thanks."

He leaned forward on his elbows. "I mean, you look like you've been wrestling dragons."

She nodded. "After a fashion..."

"Was it my fault? You can be honest."

"No."

"Good." He exhaled and placed his folded hands on the table. "Want to talk about it?"

She almost laughed. Usually Will's face had a way of warning off personal disclosures. "I think my marriage needs last rites."

"Meaning it's about dead?"

"Yeah."

"I'm sorry." He paused, waiting for more words to come to him. The waiter arrived. "What'll it be?"

Will pulled out his wallet. "Guinness for me. What would you like, Julie?"

"Double scotch, neat."

Will almost smiled. "You heard the lady. We'll be here a while."

* * *

By the time Maureen and Patrick entered the bar, Julie had long ago surrendered any attempt at conversation. She was glowering at her half-full glass of scotch, her third. She didn't bother to greet the newcomers.

Patrick resembled Maureen only remotely. He was the kind of lean that never changes over the years. He had the look of someone who didn't care about appearances except as an afterthought, yet he still managed to look tanned, fresh, and friendly. The side part of his brown hair gave him a boyish, vintage impression as though he had stepped out of *Boy's Life* fully grown. Smiling as he slid into the booth beside Will, he gestured toward the empty glasses waiting to be cleared. "I'm happy to be the designated driver. Looks like you might need one."

Maureen leaned toward Julie. "He looks innocent, but offering to drive is a ploy to get the steering wheel away from me. Pat can't relax when I'm driving. And after I taught him to drive, too. Will, Julie, this is my little brother Patrick. It's his motorcycle parked at Tutu's house."

Julie forced a smile. "Nice to meet you."

"Pleasure's mine." He flashed a wide grin that seemed to be wasted on the company at hand.

Maureen continued. "...And Pat, this is Will and this is Julie. He's an artist and she's a professional mermaid."

Pat leaned forward. "Mermaid? I've looked for them, but you're the first I've met. I'm a marine biologist. I'd guess we're both permanently waterlogged."

"I suppose so." Julie looked to her friend, her expression wrinkled with pain. "Rini, you were right. Rich tried to get me to sign away the property, but I didn't do it. I think we're getting divorced. He's moving in with his mother and we haven't even been married a year. She's a vampire and he's a miserable sonofabitch." She drew a tissue from her purse and blew her nose.

Will sat back. "*I* think it's time we ordered food."

Maureen nodded. "Good idea."

After they had given the waiter their wish list, the conversation halted. Everyone stared at the table. Maureen played with the salt shaker.

Pat twisted enough to be able to see Will beside him. "Rini tells me you had to junk your truck."

"I should've known better than to drive it over here. Wishful thinking, I guess. I was trying to protect my GTO."

Pat perked up. "A GTO?"

"1966. My treasure. Restored it myself. It's my idea of a bank account."

"I'd like to see that."

Will brightened. "Any time. Where are you staying?"

Pat shrugged. "I'm not sure yet. We need to scope out the motels. Rini and I seem to be short one house. She told me Mom's place was totaled in the fire."

"You can bunk at my house." Will finished his beer and pushed the empty bottle to the edge of the table. "Maureen's been staying with Miss Kalani next door. There isn't anything available nearby these days—too many displaced people. I have an extra bedroom and lots of closet space, as it happens. My girlfriend went to New York and tells me she plans to stay there. We'd been done for a long time, anyway. I shipped most of her stuff out yesterday. So I'd appreciate the company."

Pat considered for a moment. "Okay then. How much do you want to cover expenses?"

"I always make too much food, so we're good there. Buy your own booze."

"Fair enough."

The waiter came with appetizers.

Julie turned toward Maureen. "Is *everything* easier for men?"

Maureen nodded. "Yup. Pretty much."

Chapter 15

A Lower Pay Grade

LITTLE PAULIE SAT at his lopsided table wiping down his best friend—a Glock 9 mm. He loved the way it almost glistened under his tender touch. Take care of your friends and they'll take care of you. A sorry looking metal suitcase lay open on his bed, a suitcase secretly filled with other friends. Each was carefully wrapped. It wouldn't do for them to clatter together when he had to relocate in a hurry. His business required him to be mobile and wary.

From the TV on top of the dresser a talk show host raised his voice to emphasize the stupidity of some snot-nosed environmentalist. Somebody should take out all those tree-huggers before they could breed more. But Paulie didn't do politics. No money in it—unless the big boys wanted to play. They didn't hesitate to make six and even seven figure deals. They had their own ways of taking out garbage and they used specialists. He didn't work on that pay grade, but maybe he'd learn.

He was between jobs with The Organization at the moment, so he had taken an assignment from an amateur—several amateurs, if his guess was right. Risky. He'd have to cover his tracks really well after this one. Beginners weren't good at being anonymous. Dumb shits. He didn't like working for amateurs because they could fuck up a wet dream, but the job wasn't hard. A simple clean-up. A little surveillance, careful planning, and just the right moment. Nice and easy. Not much challenge for his kind of expertise, but the money would cover his ass—his debt to a guy with no sense of humor about such things.

His next big assignment had been delayed—the stupid jerk mark had broken his ankle during a vacation on the greens in Scotland, and he was lazing around in a castle drinking Glenlivet like he belonged there. Asshole. Not readily accessible anymore. So the timeline was changed, and his payment to The Boss was going to be short. No one messed with The Boss if they wanted to live longer, and Paulie intended to live longer. Life was just getting interesting again. The amateurs were paying him way too much for the nothing job they had in mind—enough to cover what was left of his debt and then some. Not that he'd tell them. Dumb shits. Their money was as good as anybody's. They were a little gift from Fate.

Chapter 16

The Heap on the Porch

"Tutu, I have soap in my eyes!" wailed Lila from the bathroom. "Help! Help!"

Tutu held up her hand to tell Kali she could handle the crisis. "It's baby bubble bath," she confided. "It probably don't feel good, but it ain't supposed to hurt her."

Kali nodded. "Be my guest, but don't let her get away with whining. It's high time she toughened up a little."

"You and your toughening," muttered Tutu as she ambled down the hall. "There gonna be plenty of time for toughening. Let her be a little girl."

Kali dropped onto the sofa beside Julie, ignoring the poof of dust. "What a pain, trying to walk the line between being too lenient and too strict. Daniel's good at it, but I guess my military training doesn't help. I just don't want to raise a wimp. Girls need to be more resilient than ever these days."

Julie smiled. "Somehow I don't think any child of yours will ever be a wimp." She leaned toward her conspiratorially. "Grannies are supposed to spoil kids. It's in the grandma manual. My grandma made me into a glorious brat every time I visited her, and I loved every minute. A few times I thought my mother was going to come to blows with her. It's a wonderful gift to have a champion. She made me feel important."

Kali made a face. "It just seems so counterproductive—like Tutu and I are working against one another."

"No. You're in separate lanes, that's all. Kids need both." Julie sighed and checked her cell phone. "It's really helpful of Rini to hurry up and buy a car. Now I don't have to ride with Will. She's lucky she has her brother here to help her shop. Those car places are really aggravating when they're dealing with single women. When I bought my little used Honda, they treated me like I was mentally deficient and kept asking what color I like when I had questions about reliability or resale value. You have no idea what a liability a big chest is when you want to be taken seriously. But you'd think Rini's process would go faster with Pat there—especially since Rini's buying something new. She texted they were ready to leave a while ago. Shouldn't they be here by now?"

Kali picked up a paperback from the side table and started leafing through it. "When was the last time you bought a car? Even if your financing's in place, it takes forever. I'm not sure, but I suspect the sales people do it on purpose. When you're exhausted enough, you sign all sorts of crap you shouldn't just to escape. And you're talking about a brother/sister act doing this. They probably have to argue every detail. Rini said she won awards in debate in school, and you can tell. She could persuade anybody."

Julie laughed. "I'd never buy a car with my sister. I'd never buy anything with her. I love her, but we belong in distant universes. Hers is all black and white. Mine shimmers in living colors. We can't live far enough apart. She drives me crazy." She checked her cell again. "What in the world is holding them up? Do you think it's just traffic?"

"Oh, for pity sake!" Kali threw her head back and exhaled her frustration. "You're as impatient as Lila! Go outside and wait. Then you can see them coming. You're bound to hear Pat's motorcycle, unless he took a side trip on the way home. That thing is really loud." She returned her attention to her book. "I don't know why you're so excited, anyway. It's just a car and it's not even yours. You should join me and try reading one of Tutu's mystery novels. She has some good ones."

Julie shrugged as she rose. "But it's new and electric and Rini said I could try it out. I've heard they're almost silent. It'll have all the latest gadgets. It's something happy for a change. I need happy." She headed for the door.

Across the street in a nondescript used Ford, Little Paulie prepared for his perfect moment. Nice boring, working neighborhood where almost no one was home during the day. No one to care about a regular guy with long hair (he'd chosen a brown wig this time) and a baseball cap in a piece-of-shit car. He was chuckling. The hit was wearing a t-shirt with a heart emblazoned on the front. How thoughtful—not that it was precisely over her heart. She had been out on the porch once already, but she was watching for someone. She'd be back. And he'd be ready. Slam. Bam. Thank you, Ma'am. Before whoever she was expecting arrived. Quick and easy.

She stepped out. He chose his shot and squeezed the trigger. *Ffft.* The satisfying sound of a silencer. Love that. Nothing to alert anyone. He unscrewed the silencer and respectfully placed it in his lunch pack. He trusted his aim after all these years, but he looked over to check, anyway. She was down. Job done.

He zipped the gun into his lunch pack and pulled away, nonchalantly turning down a side street before anyone would have time to realize there was a connection between the car and the woman falling down.

Well done, he told himself. *Another job well done.* All he had to do now was dump the stolen car and collect the money—just in time. The Boss was waiting.

* * *

"NO-O!" yelled Kali abruptly, leaping up from the sofa. "You can't go outside naked!"

She caught Lila's arm as she attempted to run past.

"But Tutu said Maureen is bringing a new car! I wanna see!"

Kali turned to Tutu, who was bustling from the bathroom, a bath towel in hand. "Tutu! This isn't the islands! Tell her in California young ladies are expected to have modesty!"

Tutu laughed. "Girls shouldn't be ashamed of their bodies, but I told her she could go before I seen she wasn't dressed yet. My fault." She reached Lila and wrapped the towel around her. "Come on, Dear One. Get some clothes on so you're ready when Maureen and Pat get here or you gonna miss all the excitement."

Kali opened the door, smiling as she anticipated telling Jules what had just happened. It was the perfect dose of happy Jules said she needed. But the screen door didn't open all the way. It bumped into a heap on the porch. She looked down to see what the obstruction was.

Julie.

"JULES!" Kali knelt beside her friend, realizing with a start that she was lying in a rapidly expanding pool of bright red blood. "Oh god." She ducked low behind the brick porch railing as she pulled off her shirt and held it against the wound. Stop the bleeding. She searched for the source. Behind her consciousness, beyond the sweet smell of blood, an image of an Afghani boy—he was no more than a child—lying before her, the gunshot hole in his abdomen resulting in the whole of his digestive tract blasted out in gory bits behind him. The laugh that had been on his lips blown away. His eyes, staring at her, not in fear or hatred or even pain, but confusion as his life seeped away into the dirt. Bombs crashed. Military weapons fired—so fast, so hard. She stared at the blood on her hands. Yes, the ghost of his blood was there, as it always would be, but this blood belonged in the now, to Julie, and zapped her mind back to the present.

Bullet hole. It was a gunshot wound. Kali knew gunshot wounds. This one went all the way through the shoulder—small caliber. Who uses that? "TUTU!" she shouted as she tore her shirt in half. "CALL 9-1-1! JULES IS SHOT! CALL 9-1-1! TUTU!" She automatically scanned the neighborhood for a shooter while pressing against both sides of the wound. She couldn't see any movement. Who was out there? *What was happening?*

Julie tried to focus on the face bending over her. Her mind wasn't functioning well. She began to shake, and she couldn't get a decent breath. Was she cold or sweaty? "Shot? Kali, what's going on? Why are you yelling?"

"Mommy, is she alive?" asked Lila anxiously from behind her mother. "Is there a school shooter? We have to get in a closet or a cupboard or a toilet. Teacher said so. Mommy, you're outside in your bra."

Kali kept her voice steady. "No school shooter, Lila. Probably an accident. She's fine. Get back in the bathroom and stay there. Tutu, keep her inside away from here!"

Lila backed into the living room. "I'll stand on the toilet. I know how." She turned and ran down the hall.

Kali could hear Tutu's voice on the phone. "Please, send an ambulance right away!"

Kali's voice fell low and calm. She had played this scene many times before, but never at home, never in a place that should have been safe. "It's okay, Jules. You're hurt but you'll be fine. Just relax. Breathe. Keep breathing nice and slow. Everything's okay now." But Kali was still searching the area for any sign of the shooter.

* * *

"Julie, you're on the news!" announced Lila that night after dinner. "And there's Tutu's house!"

"Use your inside voice." Kali tucked the blanket more tightly around Julie who was lying on the sofa, her shoulder swathed in bandages beneath one of Lani's over-sized t-shirts. She spoke quietly in Julie's ear. "A lot of the pain is from the doctors digging the scraps of your shirt out of your shoulder. It'll get better as the drugs really kick in. I'll be right here if you want anything. Don't hesitate to ask." She dropped to the floor to sit cross-legged beside the sofa to watch the TV where an anchor newsman was explaining Julie's *incident*.

"Do they know who did it?" asked Maureen from the hallway, unable to discriminate words in the soft volume.

"Not yet. It's too soon. The police are still interviewing the neighbors. So far, no one saw anything."

Pat joined Kali on the floor. "Do they think it's a random drive-by?"

Kali shrugged. "Too soon to guess, but I don't know if we've ever had a shooting in this neighborhood. I don't remember hearing of one. Our demographic is generally a little too…mature." She glanced at Julie who seemed to be dozing and dropped her voice. "The cops said it looks like Jules was the target, so they asked her if she could think of anyone who'd want to hurt her. She said she didn't know of anybody in California who even knows who she is—except for her in-laws. I met her mother-in-law and brother-in-law. I'm no investigator, but they didn't seem like the type to me. Nasty but not violent. Otherwise, who holds a grudge against a mermaid?"

"You never know," muttered Will from his position in the chair beside the sofa.

Tutu emerged from the kitchen. Her age hung on her face, weighed down by all the cares and disappointments she had seen in her years. "Turn off that news. We got enough trouble to fret us. Time we focus on helping Julie feel what's good in this world. We tole the doctors we'd tend her, and that's what we gonna do. Give her a couple days. Then I gotta tell you all something my tutu tole me. Don't matter if you think it's foolish. It's gotta be said."

Kali shut down the TV, avoiding Tutu's gaze. "Tutu's right. You can see too much news."

Pat rose and started for the door. "I think we've had all the excitement we're going to have for today—too much, if you ask me. It's time for everyone to settle down." He turned toward Maureen. "Don't hesitate to call if you feel uncomfortable about anything and want reinforcements. We'll come running."

Will didn't move. "Pat, I don't feel good about leaving...until we have a better idea of what's going on." He glanced at Kali.

She exhaled her irritation. "Will Manning, you've known me for years, so there's no excuse. I don't know what you could do that I couldn't."

Will chuckled. "I should've guessed you'd say that." He turned toward Pat. "She's ex-military."

Kali sighed. "There isn't much to do against a sniper but be on guard. I can handle that—probably better than either of you. I have experience. Besides, we have police surveillance out there tonight." She glanced at her daughter whose eyes were wide. "Today, I think Lila is the hero."

Lila perked up. "Me? I'm a hero?" She ran over to plop onto her mother's lap.

Kali hugged her close. "When you ran out…bare butt in the air… and I yelled at you, Jules turned. The doctor said that saved her life."

Lila leaned forward to whisper to Will behind her pudgy fingers. "I was naked."

Will nodded with exaggerated solemnity as he stood up. "Sure sounds like you were a hero to me." He leaned over to give Lila a high-five and headed for the door where Pat was waiting with his hand on the doorknob.

Pat wasn't smiling. "I wonder if the shooter knows he didn't kill her yet."

Will gestured for Pat to leave. "Goodnight, everybody. See you tomorrow."

Chapter 17

Trouble with the Help

LITTLE PAULIE SNARLED into the phone. "Where's my money? It wasn't at the drop site. Where is it?"

Al Teller did his best to sound intimidating...to impress both his mother and the hit man. "You don't get paid when you don't do the job. You're a fuckup. Julie Teller is still alive."

"She was on the news. We saw her," added a woman's voice in the background.

Al repeated what the woman said.

Little Paulie shifted the phone in his hand as though his rage could slither through it. "Listen, you little shit. I did the job. If she isn't dead, I hit her again, but first you pay me. You give me the money or I come and hurt you. I hurt you real bad. I blast your knees and cut your face. Maybe I make you a soprano. This isn't a game."

Al lowered his voice to disguise the fear that was rising behind his thoughts. "You won't be able to find me. I'm throwing away this phone. We'll use some other way of taking care of our problem. You're fired." He disconnected.

Paulie stood for a moment, letting his fury feed his heartbeat. His temper was a living being that he kept on a tight rein...until now. His payment to The Boss would be late. Not possible. He was a walking dead man. And The Boss would make sure it was a painful, messy exit. He'd be an example.

He rubbed his hand over his shaved head. His temper panted and drooled, hungry for blood. Nothing to lose now. Time to go out in glory. He'd use both the Glock and his MAC-10—cowboy style. He didn't want to grow old, anyway.

Alfred Teller tossed his phone onto the kitchen counter to emphasize his bravado and stood watching it slide across the surface. "Don't worry. I told him, Mom. I said what you wanted me to say. I was tough. You heard me. I think he underestimated who he was dealing with." He opened his beer, chugged most of it, and belched. "He's an employee, like anybody else. You do the work or you don't get paid. That's how we roll at Teller Real Estate. See? I could handle the Rosewood branch by myself."

Belinda folded her arms over her abundant chest. "I'm shocked he couldn't do the job properly. He's a professional! Didn't you tell me he's a professional? How does he stay in business? If we didn't have to stay a clean distance from the whole affair, I'd have words with him myself. I detest incompetence. You can't find good help with anything these days. How hard is it to aim at Julie's big plastic breasts? They stick out far enough."

Al snorted his laugh, and beer came out his nose. "Ow. That didn't feel good."

"Use a napkin. Clean up your mess."

He nodded as he hastily wiped the kitchen counter. "I'm pretty sure her boobs are real, Mom. Rich wouldn't marry a girl with fake boobs. He knows the difference. So do I. They move different. They don't feel the same, either." He finished cleaning and looked up for approval. Belinda ignored him as she stared into space, and he went to throw away his napkin. "I'll drive downtown and dump this phone—after I clean the prints off it. I watch those cop shows. I know what to do. I'll buy a new one someplace far from here and use cash."

His mother drummed her manicured fingernails on her side table. "Well, hurry it up. We need to get to the office. They run amok when no one's there to supervise. Heaven knows what promises they'll make."

"I gotta relax a minute first, Mom. This is stressful." Al pulled another beer from the refrigerator.

Belinda sighed through the wheezing that was her breath. "We should've done this before the wedding. Her name never would've been on the property and she wouldn't have a right to a cent. We could've saved a lot of money and humiliation. But Rich was our problem then."

Al chortled as he opened his second beer. "We did save a bundle, Mom. We didn't pay...except the retainer."

Belinda pointed at him so abruptly the flab beneath her arm waggled. Her voice lashed out, cracking through the air. "Don't be stupid, Alfred! We didn't save anything, and we didn't solve anything. Now we have to pay somebody new to take care of our problem—maybe somebody who'll charge more. And we can't use the channels we used when we found this idiot...too many strings leading to us. We're back at square one. I don't like that. I don't like that one bit. The more we fuss around, the greater the odds we'll make a mistake. And I don't tolerate mistakes."

"You could make Rich find somebody else by himself. It's his mess, after all." Al glanced sideways at her, knowing he was treading on slippery ground.

"No!" Belinda used her fist to squash her empty can of soda. "He's upset and he's injured. I don't want him fuming about her anymore. Knowing she tried to kill him has been hard on him. I've never seen him so angry. He even snaps at me. The idea was to make sure this was over. For him, it needs to be over now. He can't take dragging this out. The doctor says he needs to calm down or he's going to have the same heart condition that killed Daddy. We'll have to clean up this mess ourselves. I can depend on you, can't I, Al? I'd do the same for you, Baby."

Al grinned at her. Finally, she was depending on him...really depending. "Sure, Ma. I can step up. I told you lots of times. I can step up. I got this."

Chapter 18

Prone to Evil?

TUTU HAD INVITED the guys to dinner with everyone else, crowding more lawn chairs around the table with her old wooden ones. Julie was feeling better, although she wasn't happy about the prospect of wearing a sling for two weeks She had refused pain killers today, partially from pride and partially because she had a crazy notion she'd done something to ask for being hurt. She felt oddly embarrassed to have everyone fussing over her. Surely it was all a mistake. Someone had meant to shoot another woman at another address. Surely. In the meantime, she couldn't help being unusually jumpy. Silly.

The conversation at dinner skimmed along like a nondescript stone destined to quickly sink away only to be replaced by another skipping stone that was just as expendable. No progress. No meaning. Everyone was careful to keep their attention on a sunshiny surface.

"Jules, I'm glad I helped save you, even if Mommy was mad at me," opined Lila during the first pause. "She said you turned when she yelled at me. Turning was good." She hopped down from her seat and twirled to demonstrate. Then, because she liked the way her loose top flared when she twirled, she did it again with her arms extended.

Julie smiled, although her forehead remained lined. "Yes, I guess she's right. Nice turning. Thanks, Lila."

"Never mind that now," interrupted Kali, shepherding Lila away from the table. "Why don't you turn in the living room?"

"It's okay." Beneath her smile, Julie felt sick. She didn't need to be reminded how close she had come to being dead, but everyone had done precisely that all day. She pushed her plate away. "I'm not hungry tonight. I talked to the detective again on the phone this afternoon. It's all crazy. Too much excitement."

Maureen reached over to touch her arm. "You have a right to be shaken. Just take it easy for a couple days. Do you like to read? I'd be glad to pick up a few books for you. Or maybe a movie?"

Pat gathered the last of the plates and delivered them to the sink. Will moved to help. "I can bring over my DVD player, if you need one."

Lila was standing in the doorway to the living room. "We can get *Cinderella* to see. I used to have it in our old house. I'd watch it with you, Jules! I love that movie! She has a big blue dress that twirls out and there's a guy who's a lizard and he eats a fly!" She grimaced dramatically.

Julie rose from her seat. "That sounds nice. We'll see how I feel, okay?"

Tutu allowed herself to be nudged aside from the sink by Kali and the two men. She drew off her apron. "While you folks finish up those dishes, I gonna set myself in the living room. Come and sit, Julie. Lila can play outside with Teeny. I got things to say to the big people."

The seriousness of her tone made Kali roll her eyes. "Not the darkness talk, Tutu. Please not the darkness talk."

Tutu pursed her lips but didn't reply.

"Prepare yourselves," muttered Kali beneath her breath. Pat chuckled.

Once all the adults were settled in the living room, Tutu stopped rocking to face them.

"What I got to say is gonna sound strange to you, but I'd take it as a courtesy if you didn't laugh, because what I got to tell don't come from me. My tutu heard it straight from a great kahuna—maybe the highest holy man ever in Hawaii. The kahunas sometimes hear the ancestors in their meditations. They get messages. Maybe other holy people in other places in the world get the same messages. That's how important the messages are. Truly holy people understand each other, because they're connected to the same Source, and all people get a chance to transform to be more than they was before. They get a chance to be more... spiritual."

"More religious?" offered Pat helpfully.

"No, this ain't book religion I'm talking about." She frowned at him before continuing. "Religions might be spiritual and they might not. Some is both. Depends on the people theyselves. Religions rest on rules men made up—some good, some only ego. I don't know if I'm gonna tell all this just right. I don't remember the words my grandmother used, but you gonna get the idea if you ready to hear. Maybe death gonna come knocking on my door one day soon when I ain't looking. I got a lot of years already spent. I gotta make sure I share my tutu's words. Bad times is happening."

Her rheumy eyes peered from one to the next, earnestly searching for a sign of openness.

Will leaned forward, resting his arms on his knees. "Go ahead, Miss Kalani. We're listening."

"Them insect people or the greys with big heads, big eyes, and little bodies that folks talk about..."

"You mean *aliens*?" asked Pat, his skepticism fringing his voice. "Are you talking about aliens, Tutu—as in little spacemen?"

"Yes." Tutu was quiet a moment, waiting for scoffing. The others remained silent, so she resumed. "Aliens. Just those two kinds. They been here a long, long time. They stay out of sight, but they do things. They bring the masters of lies, the *'e'epa.*"

"And who are they?" asked Pat, taking more care with his tone of voice this time.

"They invisible. They climb into your mind and spread poison darkness—make you think negative thoughts. They work to overcome your conscience until doing bad seem okay. They make you mess up until you lose confidence in your truth, make decisions that is hurtful. They tear apart the rules people followed to keep them good. They feed on imagination because that's what them aliens don't have."

"So they're demons?"

Tutu scowled. "You talking religions and myths. I'm talking real beings, here now—parasites of the mind. You heard of parasites, ain't you? I hear tell they got parasites in the ocean and everywhere. These here parasites live in your mind. You look around at the world today and wonder how people can go bad so fast—how people you know can act ignorant when they was smart. How they can talk hate when they was good-hearted. How families can be torn apart from the outside when they thought they was close. That's the *'e'epa.*"

Pat squirmed. Not airing his objections had become almost painful for him. "I'm a scientist, Tutu. If these things are invisible, how do we know they're there? Aren't people just naturally prone to doing evil? Isn't that being human?"

Tutu's brows nearly collided in her wrinkled forehead. Her voice began to quake. "I didn't believe. I didn't pay enough attention. I thought my tutu was talking fairy tales. Kali's mother, my beautiful daughter, was a wise, wonderful woman. Nobody better on this earth. Fine mother, geologist--*scientist.*" She glared at Pat. "But scorned for her skin color—dark because her daddy was black. Made her question maybe she wasn't enough. Made her vulnerable to the *'e'epa.*" The old woman began to hug herself. "Maybe them insect people found her when she was in the field alone. Maybe her no-good husband was infected. Some way they got to her. Drove her to choose drugs over her little girls. Killed her. Real fast. Real fast."

* * *

Kali didn't react to the acidic old memories rising within her like vomit, eating at the carefully smoothed surface of her mind. Mama stood before her as she had been so very long ago, her skin the warm brown of eggs fresh from the hen, her hair a halo of independent blackness, her eyes soft and deep, the impenetrable darkness of infinite love.

"My babies, my beautiful babies," she would say in a voice like thick, sweet cream. And she would pick up Lani, who was a baby, and kiss her all over until Lani gurgled with pleasure. Then Kali would laugh at the overwhelming joy of Mama's love. It was a very old memory, now replaced with other images.

Lani crying, hungry and wet...too heavy for her older sister who struggled to change her. Kali piled the soiled diapers one on another on the back stoop to keep the stench away from the house. Soon there would be no more diapers as there was no more formula. Instead, Kali fed the baby with peanut butter on her finger, wincing when Lani chomped down with her new teeth.

And Mama lay on the sofa, pale and cold, her eyes rolled back. She needed changing, too, but there was no one strong enough to do it. Papa was merely a name for a face that had long since disappeared. Kali kept trying to match the number shapes on the paper by the phone to the buttons, pushing each one carefully. But she reached only the angry voices of strangers. "Hello? Hello? Dammit, who's there? Go to Hell, then, and don't call back!" Until, at last, she heard the music of her tutu.

"Hello? This is Kalani."

"Tutu, Mama's sick on the couch. I can't make her wake up! Lani's crying. I think she's hungry."

And the magical Tutu voice answered her. "Don't cry, Precious One. Everything gonna be alright. I'm coming now, but it's gonna take a little time. Turn on a light and wait until you hear my knock. Don't open the door 'til then. Promise me."

"Okay, Tutu. I'll wait."

The wait lasted forever. And then Tutu was at the door. But Mama never sang the goodnight songs again. Men came and took her away. There was no Mama anymore. Only Tutu.

For years Kali worried that one day Tutu would lie down on the couch and not wake up. So Kali forced herself to grow up very fast inside—faster than her body could grow. And when she was a woman, she joined the military to be absolutely sure she would always be strong enough.

* * *

Shadows of Kali's memories must have registered on her face, because Patrick turned to her. "I'm sorry. Drugs have destroyed many good people."

Tutu slammed the flat of her hands on the arm rests of her rocker. "No! Not just drugs. People got knowing inside. But if they don't look in there to find their light, they can be lost. They ain't bad people. Just poisoned. Some by self-hate or too much ego. Some by the *'e'epa.*"

Pat straightened in his seat. "So is this an ancient religion?"

A frustrated tear slid down Tutu's cheek, and she brushed it away as though it were a fly. "No. Like I said, not a religion! Just a knowing *beneath* religions. You look around. You gonna see trouble burst open like a ripe pod. Folks gonna say the trouble is just natural—something been coming a long time, but maybe not. Maybe it had help getting here. Good people gotta find their light to be safe. They gotta connect to Source some call God. That's all I'm gonna tell." She pushed herself out of her chair.

"Thank you, Tutu," Julie told her softly. "Sharing that took a lot of love."

Tutu laid her hand on Julie's shoulder. "Bad already started happening to you. More is coming. I can feel it—more is coming to all of us. I wanna give you the power to stay safe. You gotta find a way to feed the light inside you."

Julie patted the old, soft leather hand. "I'll do my best."

As Tutu ambled away down the hallway, Maureen leaned close to Kali. "She means well."

Kali nodded. "Yeah. She does."

When the men had gone, Kali and Maureen took Lila upstairs to bed with promises of bedtime stories. Meanwhile, Julie tugged a slip of paper from the pocket of her jeans. On it she had written a number the detective had told her over the phone. She vaguely recognized the area code. Dad. She pictured him in the residential care center, watching TV in the lounge with the buddies who complained about the world with him, cursing the news as they critiqued the appearance of the female anchor. Slow news day. And then he heard her name. *Julia Scott Teller.* And a photo--her in that damned mermaid outfit. His daughter. Someone had tried to kill his daughter.

Since he had no other numbers that worked, he called the police precinct and demanded to talk to the detective. No, he told them, he didn't have any helpful information…except that woman was his daughter. He had to talk to her. If they couldn't give him her number, they had to relay his number to her. Dammit, they had to. He was her father.

The click of the telephone keys seemed unusually loud in the quiet of Tutu's empty living room. Julie paused before the last number. Did she really want to open this door? Wasn't the world kinder, saner with it closed?

"Hello?"

"Dad? It's Julie. I got your message to call."

"Oh, thank God." The words didn't sound like him but the voice did. "I saw you on the news. Are you…okay?"

"Yeah, Dad. I'll be fine. Just a hole in my shoulder. It'll heal." Did she sound casual, way more casual than she felt? In what world do innocent people get shot on the front porch? What became of a country in which shooting wasn't common? Perhaps the shooting was news only because she was white and her old publicity photo was sexy. She braced herself for her father's harangue.

There was a pause made caustic with coughing. "Who was this guy—the guy with the gun? Why did he want to hurt you?"

"Nobody knows, Dad. I think it was mistaken identity. I don't think I was the one he wanted."

"Well goddam!" He coughed again. "What the hell kind of place are we living in? It's fucked up and getting worse; that's what kind. Are you mixed up with shady people, Julie? Tell me the truth. Drugs or money laundering or shit?"

She sighed. "No, Dad. I just survived the fire." She didn't need to add that last bit, but the little girl inside was still hurt he hadn't called. He hadn't checked to see if she lived through it all. He had always loved her older sister Barbara better, but didn't he care at all?

As though he heard her thoughts, he answered her. "I tried to check on you after the fire. They have fucked-up records over there where you are. Nobody knew where you went. They said I should watch Facebook for clues. Fucking Facebook! Like I knew how to do that. Even the orderlies around here didn't know how to find you, and they spend all the time they can sneak free on their fucking cell phones. I looked for you, Julie. I know you don't believe me, but goddammit, I tried."

Somebody in the background standing near her father cautioned him not to swear. He ignored the advice. "I care, Julie. That's the fucking truth. I wanted you to know. It wasn't just your mom that cared. It was me, too."

"Dad, you walked out of my wedding. You weren't there for our dance."

"You married into crude people. What can I say? That guy you married…"

"Richard. His name is Richard, Dad."

"His mother asked me to leave. Said I didn't know how to behave. She found me offensive because I said what I saw."

Julie's laugh was thin and forced. "She's hardly one to talk. Dad, you were right about them. Rich and I aren't doing well. I think we might end up getting divorced."

He started to say something, caught himself, and paused. "I'm sorry, Julie. I'm real sorry. I know you were pretty gone on that guy."

"Thanks, Dad." His sympathy melted her, stripping her down to the little girl who had never been quite what he wanted. Her mind produced a yellowed image of her climbing into his lap. He hadn't held her long. He never held her long. But for one glorious moment, he was big and warm and safe.

"You still doing that thing in the pool with the tail?"

"No, not now. Our house on the lake burned. I'm staying with friends."

He coughed. "That's good. Friends are good. I'm glad you got friends, Julie." He coughed again and she wasn't sure he wasn't crying. "Maybe some time you'll be near here and drop in. Whaddya think? You know, if you're in the neighborhood?"

Her voice quavered. "Sure, Dad. But you're pretty far from here. I'll have to plan a trip like that—after this injury mends and I have a chance to get settled. I can't drive now. I can't even rent a car because I don't have any ID. I'll let you know when. In the meantime, I'll give my number to your caretakers in case you need anything. How are you doing?"

"Oh, you know. Same old. They got more advice for me here than your mother did...and that's a lot. Just do me a favor and watch yourself, will you? And don't be afraid to set your horizons higher. You got brains, you know. You could do anything."

"Thanks, Dad."

"Julie?"

"Yeah, Dad."

"I love you." His voice hung ragged in the air. "I always did."

"I love you, too, Dad."

And he hung up.

Tutu came to slip an arm around her shoulder. "It's okay to cry," she whispered in Julie's ear. "When something's beautiful, you gotta cry."

Chapter 19

Destined for Infamy

LITTLE PAULIE CHECKED his MAC-10. Ready. He knew what it would do, and the thought made his heart race. He'd missed this—the spray, the blood, the screams. Today would erase any awareness of his creeping arthritis or eyesight crowded with floaters or bad teeth. Today he was the young warrior again—mighty, fearsome. He patted his Glock. People would talk of this day with dread, with awe.

The Boss wouldn't have a chance to smash his knees. No humiliation. The Boss would probably laugh. Paulie had found the only escape from him and his boys. Paulie had guts. He deserved respect. For one terrible moment, he wondered if he might survive. After all, he was that good and so were his weapons. What if he got away and lived? Did real estate offices carry cash, because he needed plenty or surviving would be temporary at best. The Boss had ways of finding people. Did real estate offices have safes? Hell if he knew. He'd stopped by in one of his disguises to check out the layout and the schedule, but he hadn't been able to think of an excuse to ask about a safe. They blew him off as another wannabe somebody dreaming about owning property he'd never be able to afford. They barely disguised their disdain, but kept up the patter just in case he had some dough they could grab. They'd steal from anybody, but they did their best work ripping off the hardworking trusting ones. The world would be better off without them. Enter the people janitor. Too bad he wouldn't have a chance to take out a bank or two at the same time.

Somebody destined to be a legend didn't have to survive.

Chapter 20

Opposite Sides of the Table

MAUREEN SETTLED HERSELF on the sofa and turned up the volume on the TV. She had clipped her hair back with barrettes that matched her brown slacks, and she still wore the fuzzy white slippers she had used all day. "They're talking about the Eden fire on TV!" she announced loudly enough to alert everyone. "They think it was arson, but they don't have a suspect yet. I saw the story on my cell. I thought they might have more information on the evening news. So far, not so much."

Pat sat beside her, slipping his arm around her shoulder to reveal wide wet swaths across the blue fabric of his t-shirt beneath his armpits and down his chest. He crossed his long, hairy legs so his dusty cross trainers stuck out into the room. The scent of his sweat permeated the air around him. He had just finished his daily run.

"I hope they find out the fire was an accident," he said, his expression grave, "...even something hugely stupid, just because I don't want to think it wasn't. It's almost inconceivable that anyone could hurt so many people deliberately. I wonder if he...or she...realized people would die. You'd think he'd have to know. Bombings— did all this start with the Oklahoma City bombing or was it 9-11? Mass shootings—adults shooting kids, kids shooting kids, adults shooting anybody nearby. Setting fires, letting children die—who finds satisfaction in murdering strangers? What's wrong with these people? I'm glad Mom didn't have to know the situation would only get worse. She used to get upset by intentional cruelty."

Maureen glanced at him, wrinkling her nose as she picked his arm off her shoulder. "You're naïve. And you need a shower."

Pat answered her by flapping his arm nearest her like a chicken wing, making her groan in mock pain.

Emerging from the kitchen, Tutu wiped her hands on her apron. "Lots of people get infected and get worse. Some was gonna do evil, anyway, because they got dark souls." Her lips squeezed together so that her words had to crawl out one by one. "Watching that negative stuff give it power. Maureen, you better be careful where you put your attention. You got the sensitivity. Somebody like you need to hold onto positive things."

Pat grinned. "Yeah, like appreciating that I'm healthy and I want to be with you and not that I stink."

Maureen gave him a shove. "Tutu, I'm here in your house where life is as positive as it gets—as long as I don't sit too close to Pat when he's sweaty." She turned toward the TV just as Julie entered the room. Pat indicated space beside him on the sofa, and Julie joined them.

On TV a young blonde reporter wearing a royal blue polo shirt with the station logo emblazoned on the pocket was holding a microphone toward a gaunt middle-aged woman in slacks and a t-shirt. "I was going to the dentist's office right down there," the woman said into the microphone, her eyes wide with fear, "I had a four o'clock appointment...when I heard something that sounded like a machine gun. I thought I must be wrong. I mean, I've been coming here for years without any trouble at all. Then police zoomed in from every direction. They told everybody on the street to go inside and stay there. We were scared to death! We did what they said, moving way back from the windows and under the counters. You never know what's going on these days! There was more shooting and then everything got quiet." Beneath the image, a crawl explained: "Breaking News: Real estate office shooting, multiple injuries, probable fatalities."

The reporter held the microphone in front of herself as she elaborated, her back to the building now isolated by yellow crime scene tape. "An unknown assailant entered the Teller Real Estate Office at approximately 4:00 pm and immediately began shooting. Police responded within minutes. The police and the shooter exchanged fire. The police information officer confirms there are numerous fatalities among the office personnel, and two police officers injured. They were transported to the hospital but are not believed to be in critical condition. No names have been released. The shooter was killed on scene by police. They believe he acted alone. No identification or motive yet. A press conference is scheduled for 7:00. We'll stay with this story as it develops. Back to you, Jim."

"That's the main office of Teller Real Estate!" The color drained from Julie's skin. She gripped Pat's arm with white fingers. "What if Rich was there?" In her mind she could see him falling, blood outlining his riddled body on the industrial gray carpet. She wasn't sure her heart hadn't stopped. *That's where the administrative offices are! What if Rich was there? What if somebody tried to kill him, too?"*

Pat didn't answer. He didn't want to say what he was thinking.

There was a knock on the door and for a moment no one moved, as though afraid the tragedy had come to find them. "I'll get it," volunteered Kali who had been standing behind the sofa. Her demeanor had changed to one cautious and taut with anticipation. The others couldn't quite hear the conversation at the door, but they saw her step back to allow a man in a dark suit to enter the room. He was stocky and nearly bald. He held his identification in his hand.

"Detective Jess Rainey. I see you've been watching the news. I need to talk with Mrs. Julie Teller…someplace private would be good."

Pat whistled. "That was fast."

"I remember you," said Julie, struggling to rise from the squishy sofa. Seeing the detective had ripped her consciousness in two. Half of her mind flashed back to the shock of her bullet wound and pumped alarmed adrenalin into her heart. Her shoulder suddenly throbbed. The less reactive part of her remembered him interviewing her at the hospital and the questions she had trouble answering clearly. He wasn't an enemy. He was a neutral pole, a place to rest and unburden yourself. Wasn't he? Was anyone safe? She fought to breathe deeply. Not so different from preparing to dive. She simply had to conquer the trembling. *Be the mermaid.* "Would the kitchen be okay? We could close the door."

"That would be perfect." His breath seemed to wheeze through his nose. Was he disquieted, too?

"Let me know if you want me to be with you as your legal counsel," called Maureen from the sofa, intending to be helpful.

Julie looked from her friend to the detective. Why would she need counsel? Was the situation flipping leaving her as a villain? What did Maureen see that she didn't? "Should I have an attorney with me?"

He shrugged. "It's your right. I have a few questions."

She approximated a smile for Maureen's benefit. In the pool she had been forced to smile. Life wasn't so different. Play the heroine. *Look, Dad, I can feign calm and courage! A mermaid is strong.* "I don't think so, Rini. I haven't done anything. I think I'm good." She commanded her mind to stop suggesting ways in which she could be in jeopardy. In fact, she commanded her mind to shut up. She led Detective Rainey into the kitchen, and Tutu closed the door behind them. They sat at opposite sides of the table. She hadn't noticed before, but his eyes were so dark they didn't seem to have pupils, which loaned him an otherworldly impression. She thought of Tutu's aliens.

"Rich isn't dead...is he?" she asked before he could say anything. She knew she shouldn't have asked. It probably looked bad. But she had to know. She had to know.

He didn't answer her question. "Have you been here all day?"

"Yes."

"Can anyone verify that?"

Verify? A chill skipped through her. He sounded like the guys on TV—the guys who ferreted out evil. "Everybody here. I guess Pat...Patrick... went on a run a while ago...he's the sweaty one on the sofa...but everyone else has been here the whole time."

He nodded thoughtfully. "When we talked before, you told me the only people who could conceivably want to see you harmed would be your in-laws." His eyes seemed to penetrate into her as though he couldn't be bothered with her exterior. The liquid darkness oozed into her mind.

Julie tried to remember exactly what she had said in the hospital. It was impossible. She could barely recall talking. Had she made any accusations that could come back to haunt her? She remembered someone advising her to tell the truth but don't elaborate. Had it been Maureen? "Yes, I said that, but they wouldn't hurt me physically. They're disgusting and mean-spirited, but no one has touched me since Rich's father died."

"Could you be more specific?" The detective jotted notes in a little red spiral-bound notebook he pulled from his pocket. What was he writing? She had said no one, but of course she didn't mean it. Surely he knew Rich touched her. He was her lover. He was her husband. But maybe she should've said *except Rich*. "Rich's father tried to feel me up under my skirt one time, but I pulled his hand away and then Rich came into the room. So I never gave him a chance to assault me, if he would've done such a thing. He was a lecherous, sexist man, but he's deceased now, so it's a dead subject." Why had she said *dead subject*? Did he think she was trying to be funny?

The bottomless eyes looked up at her. "Did you tell your husband about the incident?"

"Yes. He said it showed his father had good taste in women." That sounded terrible, didn't it? Was she maligning Richard? "But I didn't need Rich to stand up for me," she added hastily. "I can do that myself."

The detective held his gaze and his voice steady. He was watching her. "Your in-laws were among the victims of the shooter today. They didn't survive."

She couldn't piece together an image. Smears of deep scarlet filled her mind, slowly whirling to the sounds of sirens—the collage that had painted itself when she heard the news report. The fear for Richard. Belinda and Al hiding, screaming, collapsing...bleeding their hate, their love, whatever made their lives meaningful to them into stains on the carpet. "Oh my god. Nobody deserves that. Not even them." In that moment, she meant it. She felt something akin to pity. "What about Rich?"

"Did you believe they might have had anything to do with your shooting?"

The detective's voice didn't change, as though what he had told her was of no consequence. She felt offended by his callousness. All those people in the office. She couldn't quite recall their faces—some white-haired man who sat at a desk by the door. He had smiled at her once. Was he still there? And a girl...Amy Something...who wore weird pink lipstick and too much eyeliner. Why them? And how could a mass shooting possibly relate to her? Was he going to tell her Richard was there? Richard was dead? Her heartbeat grew erratic. "I told you last time, no. I still think I wasn't the right target. I think it was a mistake. What good would it do my in-laws to have me shot? I don't have anything they want."

His gaze seeped inside her. "Did you ever consider hiring a hit man to eliminate them?"

She sat up straight, her muscles electrified. "Good god, no! A hit man? Like the mob? That's movie stuff, isn't it? Reasonable people don't have people they don't like killed. I wouldn't do a thing like that. I wouldn't even have a clue *how* to do a thing like that. I assume you can't just Google 'hitman' to find somebody. And I have no money to pay anybody until I get a job. I'm staying here because I don't have anywhere to go." She told herself she was babbling—saying way too much--and clutched her hands together in her lap to stop. Babbling made people look guilty. Her stomach churned.

His attention didn't waver. "You might have your husband's money."

Have Richard's money? What was this guy saying? Her breath caught. "Was he killed? Richard? You didn't tell me. *Please.* I love him." She exhaled heavily. "I already told him I don't want his money if we get divorced—just my half of the property sale to get me started again. I don't want his money if he was killed, either. I don't want his money, period. Is he okay? *Please tell me.*"

The detective jotted more notes. "So you and he have been having problems?"

She had been elaborating. She should've brought Maureen in. "I guess you could say that. I told you last time he thinks I tried to kill him in the fire. I didn't. I saved his life as far as I can see—even though I thought he died. But if he's sure I wanted to kill him, then the trust of our marriage is gone. And trust is the same as love, isn't it? *Please, is he alright?*"

The detective grimaced without realizing as he rose. He stretched his back before he trained his featureless eyes on her. "I'm authorized to tell you your husband wasn't at the office, Mrs. Teller."

"Oh, thank God!" She wiped tears from her cheek. "No matter what, I don't wish him dead. I married him because I love him. I just don't like him right now."

The detective didn't comment. "Have a nice day, Mrs. Teller."

When he had gone, Julie approached Maureen, who was standing by the TV, now turned off. She could hear the others going into the kitchen. She dropped her voice, as though only Maureen would hear. "Belinda and Al are dead, but Rich is alive. He's alive! I'm so glad. He must have stayed home. Maybe he's working from home. He's vain about people seeing his burned face. He's used to being handsome and healing is going to take a while. But, Rini, the detective asked me if I ever considered hiring a hitman to kill my in-laws. Me...hire a hitman! Am I a suspect?"

Maureen lowered her voice. "Did he read you your rights?"

"Um, no."

"Then you aren't a suspect...at least not now. And you probably won't be. You may have a motive...although it's mighty tenuous. How many people don't like their in-laws? They still don't hire a hit on them. Plus, you don't have any means. You need means, motive, and opportunity to murder somebody." She grinned. "Cheer up. Hopefully, the worst is past."

Julie sighed. "Not really. Now I have to call Rich. I have to tell him I'm sorry his whole family is dead."

Maureen touched her arm. "Not his whole family. He still has you."

Julie nodded dumbly as she punched Belinda's house number into her phone. The phone rang several times before Rich answered.

"What the hell do you want?"

"Rich, I'm so sorry. I just heard about your mom and Al and all those people in the office. It's unbelievable. It's horrible. I know we didn't get along well—your mom and me, but I'm still sorry."

"Yeah, I'll bet."

His bitterness confused her. Did he think she was involved? She kept her voice soft and gentle—nothing that could cut or bruise. "This has to be a really difficult time for you. Is there anything I can do to support you?"

His voice was a snarl. "Sign the divorce papers when they arrive."

She was silent for a moment. So it was done...or almost done. Her marriage had slipped away before it had a chance to grow. Their beautiful love had drowned more surely than Richard had. "Divorce? Are you sure? Not a trial separation? This has gone really fast..."

"...I'm sure."

Tears slid down her face. "I wish all this had gone differently, Rich."

He paused. "I wish it had been you killed." And he disconnected.

Chapter 21

A Physical Disagreement

THE NEXT AFTERNOON translated Julie's mood into weather that seemed to be suffering from the flu. Gray clouds paled the sky while sorry little drips soaked the feverish landscape, miserable with humidity. Maureen was in the process of purchasing a condo outside the city, and the prospect of losing her and Pat and Teeny was depressing everyone—especially Lila. So no one was sincere when they smiled as she and Pat returned in Maureen's electric car.

"Only the final closing left!" announced Maureen. Her face seemed younger and brighter than before, as though she were gradually un-aging into the beguiling woman she had been. Light danced in her eyes. The others assumed she was energized with a new beginning.

Pat slid his arm around her. "It's a really nice condo. I approve heartily! Lots of room for guests. I already picked out a space for me when I visit."

"When do we get to see it?" asked Julie in an attempt to seem excited, but she didn't care to know.

Maureen let her fingers trail along the back of the sofa, tracing animated thoughts she wasn't sharing. "Not for some time. It needs all kinds of renovations that I hope will be done while we're gone, but I wouldn't bet on it. Craftsmen are nearly impossible to come by these days. So many fire victims are starting to rebuild."

Kali nodded ruefully. "We'll probably sell our property. Daniel doesn't want us to stay here. He says the States are too violent. He's talked about going back to Mexico. He has family in a little town outside Guadalajara."

"Oh no!" Lila hung on the hem of her mother's tunic top, her expression tragic and her voice a whine. "No, Mommy, no! I don't want to leave here...ever!"

"Nothing is set yet, Baby," Kali told her, caressing her face, but Lila wasn't cheered.

Julie turned to Maureen. "You said you were going to be gone. Where are you going?"

Pat smiled mischievously. "I've been saving a special secret since I arrived, and when I look around the room at your faces, I think this is the perfect day to share it. *I'm getting married!*"

"Married!" Julie laughed as she hugged him. "Congratulations! Way to surprise everybody!" As he hugged her in his guileless *Boy's Life* way, she thought of how lucky some girl was going to be. She would never lack for affection. Her husband would never turn on her. Pat was unfailing sunshine.

"Does Rini know the bride?" asked Kali.

"Not yet." Pat's grin nearly exceeded the breadth of his face. "I'm marrying my closest friend Norman, an inventor and computer genius. I guess he'd be the bride. He's great—smart, funny, more practical than I am. We've been together for a couple years. He does his best to keep me out of trouble—the patience of Job. You're going to love him. I do. You're all invited!"

Julie's smile drooped into a gape and, without realizing, she backed away from him. Why hadn't Maureen told her Pat was homosexual?

"...And we're flying you to Hawaii for the wedding!" added Maureen, beaming with excitement.

"Hawaii," repeated Tutu reverently. "I never thought I'd see it again." She wiped her eyes with the edge of her apron as she came to wrap Pat in a grandma hug. "You got a bright spirit, Patrick. I honor your love as *mahus* was revered among the people in ancient times. Thank you for including us in your most important day. Thank you for taking me home." He leaned down and she kissed him on his cheek.

Lila looked up at her mother. "Flying? In an airplane? I love airplanes! I never went in an airplane before. Are we going, too?"

"Yes, yes!" Pat took Lila's hands in his and began dancing her around the room. "Everyone! Will and even Daniel if he'll come.

It's next month. You're going to love Hawaii and the fresh fruit and beaches and music. Make sure you bring sunscreen and swim suits. And you're going to love Norman. He's the most honest, caring, intelligent man I've ever met—one of the native islanders. He can't wait to meet you all. I've told him so much about you—even you, Peanut! His aunt is making a grass skirt just for you. You can wear it over your shorts. She'll show you moves from the hula—it's a dance like this." He demonstrated a couple steps with hand motions that made Kali giggle. "Your skirt will sway with you and you'll be great!"

Lila launched into her own energetic version of what he had shown her, resembling a fledgling bird attempting flight more than an islander. "Like this? I can do this! Watch me!"

Her gyrations intensified as Pat applauded.

Meanwhile, Maureen slipped her arm around Julie. "It'll be a perfect antidote to all the negativity we've survived together—a magnificent change of scenery. Just what the doctor ordered."

Julie nodded without speaking, looking around to see if anyone else appeared shaken.

Lila had exhausted the attention of her audience, so she returned to her mother's side. "Can a man marry a man?" she asked, perhaps sensing Julie's discomfort.

Kali smiled. "He can if they're in love."

Lila clapped. "Oh good! I never went to Hawaii before. Tutu told me I wasn't borned. Have I ever been to a wedding, Mommy? I can't remember. I think I love weddings. Can I get a new dress?"

"Yes, of course and no, you've never been to a wedding." Kali turned to Pat. "Daniel won't be able to leave the job site next month—they're completing a final technical phase and he's the phase manager, but I'm sure he'll be glad to hear we're away from here. He's been terribly worried. Still, flying all of us to Hawaii is too costly. We can't accept a gift that big."

"Yes, you can!" Maureen took her hands. "You simply must! This wedding is the best thing to happen to Pat and me in years—probably ever. Look how happy he is! Look how happy I am! I want desperately to share the experience with my beloved disaster family. I need you beside me. I'm the best man...er, person. Aside from a couple friends from D.C., you're all I've got. Please, *please* say you'll come."

Pat laughed at Kali's concerned frown as she pulled away from Maureen. "Don't fret, Lovely Lady," he told her. "We have it all worked out—well, actually, Norman figured it out. Like I said, he takes care of me. Norman and I have a good friend named Nainoa with a gigantic house by the sea. He's a big mucky-muck on the island but a super nice guy. He's qualified to marry us. That's where we're going to have the wedding—at his mansion. It's fricking gorgeous. He uses it for conferences. Nainoa says he'd be happy to have you all stay there—no charge. Everyone will have a separate room. The wedding is his gift. He has a big landscaped pool with a slide and an outdoor shower plus a gourmet chef who's handling the catering—and our food, too. We're having a luau after the wedding with all the traditional dishes and dancers. It'll be incredible. The beach is right out in front."

"Yay!" Lila began dancing around the room by herself. "We're goin' to Hawaii! We're goin' to Hawaii!"

Pat continued over Lila's happy chant. "You're all coming as my family, since Mom and Dad are gone. Norman has dozens of relatives on site and super cool friends. It won't be boring! I promise! This secret has been a real pain to keep, but I wanted to wait until just the right moment to tell you. I nearly gave it away so many times! Tonight we'll go out to celebrate that I finally got to break my surprise—my treat!" He slipped his arms around Maureen from behind, rocking to and fro with her in his arms.

She laughed, twisted far enough to kiss him lightly on the cheek, and patted his face before releasing herself. "I'll drive. Then you can all enjoy how great my new car is!"

Pat perched on the arm of the sofa. "On our way, I have an appointment to meet an old friend—a guy I've known since high school—to give him a gift certificate we set up for him so he can buy his own plane tickets. His family has to travel to Children's

Hospital to get the doctors to okay their trip before they can go so far away. Their boys were terribly ill when they were adopted. Sammy's sure they'll get the green light, though. The boys have been doing really well. Anyway, after I contact him, we're off to celebrate with good food and adult beverages. Meanwhile, I've pre-ordered delivery for Tutu and Lila—Indian, their favorite."

"Indian! Yummy!" exclaimed Lila, hopping up and down. "I love Indian, don't I, Mommy?"

"Of course, Darling," Kali assured her.

"Come, Precious One," urged Tutu. "We gotta put away the table settings. We won't need so many tonight. We gonna have a special meal just for us." Lila padded after her into the kitchen, singing a tuneless song in a flamboyant, melodramatic style she had seen on TV.

"We'd better get changed," Maureen warned Julie and Kali. "With Pat in charge, we're bound to have quite an evening. Totally unpredictable, naturally. After all, we're talking about Pat's choices here."

Julie opened her mouth to decline the invitation, but the force of Maureen's happiness and Pat's glee quashed her reluctance. She could feel his buoyancy lifting her above a darkness deep inside. She did her best to smile over the queasiness in her stomach. First, she was going to spend this evening with a homosexual...at least she'd be in a group...then, she'd attend a marriage of two men. Her universe was vibrating again, softening borders and blending dimensions. She was a meteor hurtling through space never guessing where she might land. "I'll wear my best sling," she said, thinking ahead to the ceremony and hoping she wouldn't look aghast. Would the couple have to kiss? Wouldn't that be sickening?

* * *

The atmosphere in the car as Maureen drove to the bar where Pat was to meet his friend crackled with happy energy. Under the streetlights her sequined silver dress reflected in the windshield giving the impression they were driving into starlight. As she drove, Pat was dashing through an impromptu monologue so filled with excited adrenalin that it was nearly devoid of spaces.

"Sammy has worked hard to make his nightclub something special. He's sorry he can't entertain us tonight, but a private party reserved the place—paid big bucks. I guess you'll meet him at the wedding. He and his partner Joe adopted two of the most adorable kids you could imagine. Their parents abandoned them because they had so many medical issues. I don't think you can fool kids when they aren't wanted. They know. But they've blossomed with Sammy and Joe loving on them. Wait 'til you meet the youngest. He's a pistol. The older one is more serious. He had to be a parent for his brother for so long. He writes wonderful poetry for his little girl-friend—at least I think it's wonderful. How should I know? Lila will have a ball with them at Nainoa's house. They're funny and smart and too cute for words. Like her, they never stop."

"Speaking of not stopping, take a breath, Pat!" ordered Maureen glancing sideways at her brother in the passenger seat. "You're talking so fast, you're going to pass out. Tell me where to turn up here."

"It's nice to hear someone really happy." Kali was staring out the side window in the backseat, thinking of her husband who was living so far away and so close to concentrations of bigotry. "I have to take breaks from the news these days because it wears me out. I was hopeful about the future of humankind for a while, but now people seem to be devolving."

Julie nodded, not caring that no one was looking. Her nightmares twisted in a kaleidoscope of disturbing images from the fire and the shooting. Happiness seemed distant from her. She sighed. "I suppose I'd feel cheerier if I could stop almost dying."

Will, who was seated in the middle, grinned at her. "It's a bad habit you have there."

She wasn't smiling. "Yeah, I guess it is."

Kali was reading the names of nightclubs on the signs they were passing. She thought of her free time in the war, how she had been open to doing anything entertaining, anything to dull the sharpness. "Maybe we can find someplace that has good music after we eat. I like to dance. Tutu says it's in my blood. I don't take her too seriously, though. She says it's in Lila's blood, too, and you've seen her coordination."

Pat made a disapproving noise. "Hey, the peanut is only five. Dancing shouldn't come with criticism. It's supposed to be fun." He demonstrated a few exaggerated moves in his seat that made everyone chuckle. "We'll have to do some fast talking to get Rini out on the floor, though. She thinks she has to look choreographed or she can't move. Over-achiever syndrome. Oh, the bar is just up here."

Maureen shook her head in mock dismay. "Sometimes I can't believe you and I are siblings. How could we be more different?"

"There it is!" Pat pointed toward the bright rainbow neon sign for The Happy Traveler. "It's about being content with your journey through life. Get it?"

"Yeah, we get it, Pat." Maureen pulled into a parking space across the street. "We'll wait here. I don't want to embarrass you by making you toddle along beside your big sister. You used to hate it."

He laughed. "I'm proud of you; you know that. And I haven't toddled in years. Have you ever been in a gay nightclub?"

She cocked her head. "Oh sure...not. D.C. lawyers try not to frequent places where they'll make copy for tabloids. The closest I've come was watching *The Bird Cage* with Robin Williams and Nathan Lane. That place of theirs was a hoot. I adored those guys."

He searched the other faces in the car for answers.

"I don't think we'd fit in." Julie didn't look at him.

Pat chuckled. "The place I'm thinking of has all sorts of patrons—plenty of straights. You won't be the only ones. It's just a fun evening."

"Haven't had the experience," said Will. Kali simply shook her head.

"We can go straight tonight, if you prefer, and fix the gap in your education in Hawaii. Norm and I know a club with great entertainment and a killer band. "He opened the door and leaned toward his sister before he exited. "I remember when you and the ex-jerk used to dance. I thought you looked good. You're hot, Sis, and that's a fact."

Maureen made a face. "There are many reasons he's an ex. Get going. Your friend will be waiting."

Pat's departure deflated the air in the car somewhat, and everyone remained quiet for a few moments. Julie was the first to break the silence. For her the prospect of being inside a gay bar loomed as a threat. Rich would have a fit if he knew. "I had no idea Pat was gay."

Maureen turned in her seat. "Does it make you uncomfortable? I forget to tell people because Pat wears it so naturally. This wedding isn't mandatory, you know. We'll still love you if you decide not to come. Or you can come to Hawaii and skip the ceremony. Pat would never want to make you uneasy—especially after all you've been through lately."

Julie could feel her face flushing. Was she the only one in the group who was having qualms? Suddenly she felt awkward. She really did like Patrick—or had liked him before she knew. It was all so strange and unnatural. "I'm glad to see him happy. And I'm honored to be included in a family event. It's just that I thought I'd be able to tell. Rich said it was always obvious."

Will made a sound that was a derisive cousin to a laugh. "And you believed Rich?"

Julie ignored his question. "How do you feel about finding out like this, Will, after he's been living with you?"

"Finding out? As if he's been secretive? The topic never came up." Will shrugged. "Fine. I feel fine. He's a good guy."

Julie dropped her voice as though that might lend her more privacy. "I don't mean to be intrusive, but are *you* gay?"

Will laughed outright. "No, Jules. I'll admit I felt a little weird about being around people of alternative sexual orientations when I first encountered them. My birth family stayed inside the lines. But I got over it. In some ways we're the same. In other ways we're different. The end. In art, you need to be open to fresh perspectives. You don't have to agree with them." He leaned back in his seat. "Honestly, Pat's been a much better housemate than Gloria. He doesn't leave a mess in the bathroom and he's funny. I like him. His bike is a monster."

Irritated by his condescending tone, Julie turned toward him, effectively moving herself farther away from him on the seat. "So you'd go waltzing in there with him if the bar were open?" She gestured broadly toward the nightclub.

Will's expression evolved into a smirk. "Well, I wouldn't *waltz...*"

Julie shoved his arm with her good hand as Maureen came to her defense. "Give her a break, Will. You can know only what you've had an opportunity to learn. I get the impression our Jules had a sheltered childhood."

Julie nodded. In her mind she remembered her father's disapproving scowl when he discovered her lab partner in high school was Jewish. He said Rachel should pay both their fees for the lab specimen, because she could afford it. Julie sneaked the money for her half out of her mother's purse. She had almost forgotten. "My family didn't mingle with Catholics or liberal Protestants, much less Muslims or Jews or gays. Lani was the first person of color I ever really talked to. My dad convinced me everyone unlike our family was scary and probably dangerous. He meant well, but Las Vegas was a shock. I was terrified for weeks."

Kali made a huffing noise. "Your family would have been appalled to meet me. I'm darker than Lani. I hear insults from white strangers almost daily and did even when I was in uniform. I figure it's their problem, not mine."

Maureen was staring straight ahead, perhaps glimpsing the past. "Dad wanted to kill Patrick when he found out. Literally. He never believed Pat didn't have a choice. He couldn't forgive him. He threw him out of the house. Mother was furious. She sent him the money for college."

"Rich's family never believed it wasn't a choice, either." Julie sighed. "They did their best to block gays from buying property, and seeing gay families set them off. They were convinced all gays are pedophiles, and they nearly persuaded me. I'm still a little creeped out by gay couples, to tell you the truth. Sorry, Rini. I guess it's ironic Belinda and Al would come to a violent end since they were stuffed with hate. I was never sure they didn't have Klan robes in the back of some closet."

Kali shifted uncomfortably. "Tutu always says what you send out comes back to you, but since the military, I don't like to think about that too much."

"You're nothing like the Tellers, Kali," said Julie, looking around Will to make eye contact. "They were quick to condemn, and seeing innocent people hurt didn't bother them. I thought Rich was different. He said he was."

Will opened his mouth to comment, but Kali interrupted, deliberately changing the subject before he could say anything. "I won't lie. I'm excited to be going to Hawaii. I haven't been there for years. I wonder if it'll feel like home."

"Do you believe in ancestral memory, or whatever they call it?" asked Julie, relieved to be on a cheerful topic.

"I don't know," replied Kali. "Sometimes when Tutu's talking, I get a weird sensation that I've heard what she's saying before. Knowing Tutu, I probably have."

"GOOD GOD!" exclaimed Maureen suddenly, leaning on the horn and startling everyone. *"Those guys are beating up Pat! They're going to kill him!"* She pulled her cell phone out of the console and began clicking buttons.

Julie leaned forward to see four burly men in dark t-shirts and jeans restraining Patrick while they pummeled him into an agonized lump. Kali and Will were already jumping out of the car.

"CALL 9-1-1!" Kali ordered Maureen as she ran toward the fight.

Julie was never sure exactly what happened next because it all moved so fast, but she could see Kali kicking and boxing and twirling as if she belonged in a martial arts movie and might levitate at any time. Although her quick responses couldn't evade all the blows directed at her, she didn't go down. Her face had become fierce and hard. Julie could imagine her armed with a military weapon. She'd be frightening.

With a grunt Julie could hear from the car, Will yanked a man who outweighed him by half off Pat as he lay on the pavement in a defensive curl. The man threw a fistful of gravel into Will's face, but Will wasn't deterred. He kept coming back to re-engage over and over.

Pat was suffering vicious kicks to his stomach—one kick and then another—by the only man not yet fighting either Kali or Will. Julie climbed out of the car, slipping her arm out of her sling.

"*What the hell do you think you're doing?*" Maureen demanded to know, interrupting her phone conversation with a police dispatcher.

"I can hit somebody with something…"

"No. You can't. Kali and Will don't need you in the way. You'll get them hurt. Here." Maureen climbed out of the car and shoved her cell into Julie's hand. "Stay on the line in case dispatch has a question." With that Maureen ran into the melee, pulling her skirt up to her hips. She leaped onto the back of Pat's attacker, wrapping her arms around his throat and her legs around his body as he struggled to throw her free.

Reluctantly, Julie stood beside the car. A woman was talking in her ear. "Are you still there?" the dispatcher asked from a distant reality.

"I'm here."

By the time the police sirens approached, Kali had two men disabled on the ground and was working on the third. Maureen was lying, winded, where the man had flipped her over his head. Pat struggled to regain his feet and Will landed his last best punch.

Julie rushed over to join the group as soon as the assailants were restrained by the officers. Blood was dripping from Pat's torn face, but he did his best to grin at Maureen. "It's good to have a big sister."

Maureen nodded, although her brows were knit together. "I learned how to do that from you, remember. But I never did get the chokehold right." She brushed broken sequins from her torn skirt. "Damn, that pavement is hard! I'm going to hurt tomorrow."

Julie recounted what she had seen to the police sergeant who seemed hugely unimpressed, except by the multiple casualties around Kali. "You did that? Holy shit."

Kali shrugged as she wiped a sleeve across her bloodied chin. Her sleek black silk pantsuit had split. She didn't seem to notice. "I taught martial arts in the military and competed a little."

The sergeant emitted a soundless whistle. "Nice work..." Maureen thought he was lucky he didn't add "for a woman," although his pause seemed to voice it for him. "As soon as the paramedics have checked everybody out, I'm going to need you to come down to the station to give statements, and somebody—I'm assuming you..." he indicated Pat who was slumping against Will, "...will need to sign a complaint."

Pat hesitated, leaving space for Will to speak.

Will touched a hand to his swelling lip. Blood dripped purple onto his shirt. "Sign the damn complaint, Pat. You play nice guy, then these dirtballs walk so they can ambush somebody else. Four on one, you know they're cowards."

An attacker whose hateful tattoos bragged about his opinions sniffed up the blood that was escaping from his nose. "Are you his boyfriend?" he asked Will. "We could beat your ass, too. You're useless. If it hadn't been for this black dike here, we'd have been long gone by now."

Kali glared at him. "You're lucky I don't believe in murder. It would be easy to make you dead, and I'm not sure I wouldn't enjoy it."

Grinning, Maureen folded her arms in front of her chest, ignoring the rips in the armholes of her dress and the blood oozing from the scrape on her leg. "Watch yourself. She's the Hindu goddess of destruction." No one got the reference but Kali, who smirked.

One of the arresting officers approached the sergeant and opened his hand to reveal a couple socks full of quarters. He gestured toward the attackers. The sergeant frowned. "Looks like you gentlemen are going to have some extra questions to answer downtown," he told them. "Get them out of here."

Several men had exited the nightclub when they heard the sirens and now stood just outside the doorway. Pat glanced over at them, waving with his best hand that he was okay. "I'll sign," he told the sergeant, "as long as I won't be stuck in court and can't make it to my wedding next month."

An officer beside the sergeant snickered. "Like anything in court works that fast."

The paramedics arrived. Their lights flashed across the scene lending it an almost festive air in counterpoint to the lights of the police vehicles. A young woman in uniform signaled for Pat to join her partner and her in the back of the ambulance. The sergeant turned to the officer beside him. "Mickey, give this guy a complaint to sign and advise him you'll take him to the station when he's through at the hospital."

The officer retreated to his patrol car for the paperwork.

Maureen helped Pat limp to the open ambulance doors, assisted his step up inside as he groaned, and then stood waiting for a progress report. She looked up at the freckled paramedic closest to the door when he seemed to be finished with the exam. "That's my brother. How is he?"

The paramedic shrugged. "He probably has cracked ribs—I don't think any are actually broken. We can't say for sure until he has an x-ray. Lots of deep bruises. I don't hear the wheezing that goes with a lung puncture, but that's a guess. He needs a diagnosis. We're cleaning up the cuts and abrasions to make sure we didn't miss anything. He needs us to run him to the hospital to be properly x-rayed and wrapped, but he's refusing."

Pat was sitting on the bench seat along the right side of the vehicle while the other paramedic hovered beside him. He smiled as best he could at Maureen with his blotchy, swelling face. "I'll be fine. See? I knew to sit on the bench and not the cot. If you sit on the cot, it's more expensive. I've been in ambulances before. I'm used to being beat up...remember in school? I've even had cracked ribs. I'm not going to a hospital. I'm coming with you all. Just don't tell me any jokes. Laughing really hurts."

Chapter 22

Cold-blooded

WHEN DETECTIVE JESS Rainey dropped by Tutu's house the following afternoon, he couldn't help commenting on the patched-up people playing cards around the kitchen table. Kali, Will, and Maureen were marked with swelling purple and black bruises and multiple Band-aids, while Pat still wore smears of dried blood in the creases of those portions of his face not covered by bandages. His right eye was no more than a slit beneath the grotesque violet puff surrounding it. Beside the others, Julie appeared to be relatively healthy wearing her sling.

"If there was a fight, it looks like you guys lost," Rainey said, suppressing a smile.

Pat shrugged. He had to squeeze his voice out of the crack that was his mouth. "The next line is, 'You should see the other guys,' although I'd guess they look better."

"We had a disagreement with a few men in the street last night," provided Kali. "They thought they should beat Patrick to death, and we thought they shouldn't."

Maureen nodded. "We were the good guys. We held them off until the cops got there. But then it ended up we had to go to the station."

"We spent the evening giving police statements," added Julie. "We nearly starved."

Rainey echoed Will's nod. "I'm glad that's not my jurisdiction. Assaults are too common these days. The assault dicks never clear their files. Give me an attempted homicide anytime. Of course, we never clear our files, either. I was in the general neighborhood, so I thought I'd update you, Mrs. Teller. I hope you don't mind me dropping in. I figured you'd want to know as much as possible about your case."

She looked up at him. "Yes?" The detective seemed less intimidating to her now. After all, she had challenged the stares of thugs at the fight, refusing to look away when they glowered at her. She'd been ready to join the melee. She had never been as bold before. Rainey wasn't half as frightening as they had been. And he smelled better.

He stuck his hands in his pockets. "I can't go into details about the evidence, but after a warrant to search his belongings, it looks like the shooter—this guy known on the street as Little Paulie--who killed your in-laws--was probably the same man who shot you. We'll be certain shortly."

Maureen, who had escorted the detective into the house and was now standing in the kitchen doorway, smiled. "Which means you aren't a suspect, Jules. Not many people put out a hit on themselves, although I've known a few I wished would."

"I don't understand." Julie scowled at the cards still in her hand, trying to think clearly. "What's the connection between me and the people he murdered in the office? Somebody wanted to kill Teller family members? But then why did he kill all those other people, too? Because they were there? Just a grudge?" She looked to the detective.

He drew a breath mint out of his pocket and squeezed it out of its crackling plastic wrapper into his mouth. "I'm not authorized to share conclusions," he said around the mint that clacked against his teeth. "And I have to get going."

Limping slightly, Maureen led him out of the room. "Thanks for letting us know," she told him on the way to the front door. "We've had enough to worry about lately."

He glanced back toward the kitchen before he exited. "Apparently."

When he was gone, Julie laid her cards face down on the table and exhaled. "It doesn't make sense. I'm sure lots of people wanted to hurt Belinda and Al...I often fantasized about doing it myself... but then why attack me? I mean, Belinda and Al could have been killed, you know, almost accidentally...as innocent people who happened to be there in the office...the way guys kill indiscriminately in schools or concerts. But the gunman was pretty specific about trying to murder me. Why? Why would this guy I never heard of try to kill me?"

"This sounds like a crime novel," began Will laying his cards down as Julie had, "but maybe somebody had been ripped off or insulted or fired by Tellers, and you happened to make the hit list as a member of the family."

Julie frowned. "I doubt that. I haven't been a Teller very long. I never worked in the real estate office. I've been there only a handful of times—mostly following along after Rich. And no Tellers have ever been here at Tutu's house. Even if you're right and he wanted to eliminate the family, how did this Paulie guy find *me*? I'm not listed at this address anywhere."

Pat started to lean forward, realized how much it hurt, and leaned back in his chair, instead. "Those kinds are good at finding people—at least in the movies. Maybe he's putting pressure on Rich—you know, like the mob. He wants something, so he starts killing the people Rich loves the most until Rich agrees to cooperate. I've seen movies like that. Norm says I watch too many movies."

Julie rose. "You're assuming Rich still loves me—not a sure thing these days, believe me. And what would Rich possess that anyone would be that desperate to get? He's not really rich, and he doesn't gamble."

Kali tossed her cards onto the table, not caring how they landed. "Paulie sounds dense to me. Brain damaged. Getting yourself killed doesn't seem like an intelligent strategy to achieve anything."

"He probably didn't plan to get dead," replied Pat. "Bad guys never believe they'll be caught...at least they don't in the movies. Of course, I don't hang out with bad guys enough to have firsthand knowledge...except in fights like last night."

Will began gathering the cards from the table top. "Sometimes they do—suicide by cop. And you're guessing this shooter guy was working for himself. Maybe Pat's right about him working for somebody else, Jules--somebody like Richard. Richard had plenty to gain—the inheritance he'd have once all of you were dead. He has motivation to spare."

Julie felt her chest collapse. She had to suck breath through. Her face went white. "That's not possible," she said in what came out as a whisper. "Richard cared more about his family than about money. Especially lately. He cared."

The heat of Maureen's rebuking glare caught Will on the side of his face. He had ventured too far. He tried to cover his faux pas. "Or the Mob. Paulie could've been working for the Mob. Maybe he thought all the Tellers were going to be there that day and he was supposed to wipe them out. They were good at making enemies."

Julie took a few moments to recover. Yes, of course. Someone else. Paulie was working for someone else. The Mob. It didn't have to be Rich at all. *It couldn't be.* She pushed her hair back from her face with both hands, pulling it into an unfettered ponytail that she released down her back. "The Tellers were too egotistical to get involved in anything that would put them under someone else's control," she said miserably. She stopped there. This guessing was making her want to scream. What was happening wasn't a book or a movie. This was her life. This was her marriage, her love. Her shoulder throbbed.

"And maybe the shooter was simply bat-shit crazy," offered Maureen kindly. "Normal people can't follow the reasoning of someone who's deranged. You'd be shocked at the weird things that can set a person off. FBI personnel are trained and they still struggle. I've talked to several profilers. We won't get close to the truth, I'm sure. Better leave it to Rainey."

Tutu made a snorting noise as she came in from the sewing room. "No more of this talk! Lila gonna be here in a minute and I won't have you upsetting her. I don't know what this murder been about, but I'm telling you straight, the trouble ain't done. Those *'e'epas* is active, and susceptible folks gonna get worse. Now wash the table and set your minds on what's good, to keep you safe. We got a trip to plan."

Julie went to the bathroom to vomit.

* * *

Richard Teller sat across the desk from Dolly Shoatsky, funeral director. He couldn't imagine how his father had found the woman attractive enough to waste time having an affair with her. Her shiny desk reflected a glow upward onto her double chin, and from his close perspective, Rich could see the gray roots at the base of her ultra-black hair. Dad must have been desperate. Ironic that Belinda had insisted on having Dolly handle her husband's final arrangements. But Richard knew his mother carefully ignored her husband's infidelities. She hated sex, so someone had to handle it. Handle it. That was a kind of joke.

"You know, Mr. Teller," Dolly was saying, "we will certainly do everything in our power to honor your poor mother and brother properly. Luckily, I already have a sense of the colors and styles she preferred. We worked so closely together! How she loved your father! Every detail of his funeral had to be just-so. Belinda was a wonderful woman who was never given the attention she richly deserved. And her dear son, your brother Al. Oh, the loss! If only they had been armed."

"I'm sure they were," he muttered aloud. Inside, his emotions were churning like a stomach planning to disgorge itself. "Like it mattered."

She was staring at him, so Richard nodded which she read as permission to continue her impromptu eulogy.

He had cried more than he would've thought possible that first night he heard he no longer had a mom. He felt hopelessly alone, abandoned, rejected. He felt reduced to being a kid again. He couldn't remember the last time he had cried…certainly not for his dad. Dad had yearned to have a son who would be all that he had hoped to be when he was younger…but he hadn't yearned much. He didn't want his son to outshine him. If he thought there was a danger, he wasn't too proud to batter his oldest, dearest boy until that boy grew big enough to make the outcome uncertain. Then he switched to emotional sticks. What did they call it…extortion? They had been foes as much as family.

But Rich's mom had been the frame of her eldest son's life… hovering over all his triumphs and missteps. Bossing…definitely. Fiercely protecting…oh yeah…every time through every age. And Al, well, as tiresome and repulsive as he was, Al was family. You had to love family. Mom insisted. But Al was also a pain in the ass. He was so sure he was the bright one, the misunderstood one. He had tried more than once to turn Mom against the brother he envied. But Rich and Al both knew which brother both parents loved best, which brother was designated as the primary beneficiary. If Al had known the extent of their favoritism, he would've shit. He would do anything for his mother.

"And your lovely wife, will she be a participant in the proceedings?" asked Dolly in her unctuous voice.

"My lovely wife?"

"Yes, I had the good fortune of meeting her—Julie, isn't it? What a stunningly beautiful woman! Represented what she saw as your interests with such gusto—you know, before we had the miraculous news of your rescue. I hope you have a chance to thank her."

"We're getting a divorce."

Dolly's expression transformed immediately…good trick. "Oh, I *am* sorry! But she was quite cold-blooded, wasn't she?"

He nodded. "Like she had sea water in her veins." He stood up. "Don't worry. I'll still find a way to thank her for everything she did for me. I won't forget."

Chapter 23

The Wedding of a Go-To Guy-Friend

THE FLIGHT TO Hawaii was long, but Lila's exuberance made it seem less so as she exclaimed over the birds, the view of the Pacific, even the clouds. She had Kali read to her from the industry magazine and she played checkers with Pat. She had to tell Maureen and then Julie about the marvels in the restroom, which she visited as frequently as Kali would allow, and she delighted in the delivery of drinks. She spent her extra time drawing multiple crayon pictures to give to Pat and Norman to celebrate the wedding. She was the expression of curiosity and wonder the others had long forgotten.

"You have to share the pictures with Norman," she warned Pat in a whisper. "They're for both of you. See the names?" She pointed to her scribble across the top of the sheet.

"I promise." As he folded the artwork into his carry-on, Pat was relieved to observe that Norman's legs in the drawing were as long and fleshless as his and neither had a detectable torso.

"That's her trademark style," advised Kali. "You're lucky you get a happy head."

Pat smiled. "They're great. Norm will probably frame them. I needed to lose a couple pounds since I've been lazing around waiting for my ribs to heal. Looks like I might have overdone it."

Nainoa, their host, was waiting to greet them in baggage claim. He was a sharply rectangular man who looked like he could stand strong against any wind. His rugged native face gave the impression of jutting out beneath his thick black and gray hair, delivering a wide, disarming smile that could sell anything. The tailoring and fabrics of his traditional clothing declared his wealth, but his welcome was warm and unaffected. He enthusiastically embraced Pat and anyone else in their party who seemed to be open to a hug and an extra lei.

"*Aloha*! How was your flight?"

Tutu sighed. "*Aloha*. I feel good to be home. My legs ache...so much sitting!...but I wouldn't miss this for anything."

The large Hawaiian extended his arm to her. "I can get a motorized chair for you, if you wish, and I can have a massage therapist ready to ease the distress in your muscles when we get in."

Tutu folded her thin lips. "I ain't using a wheelchair, thank you very much. I been waiting to be here for most of my life, and my feet need to feel the ground. I can't wait to stand barefoot in the sand. But a good leg rub sound fine."

Nainoa threw a look to Patrick and patted Tutu's hand. "Hawaii has been waiting for your return. Our transportation is just outside, people. I hope you'll enjoy the ride. We'll take the scenic route, if that's okay with you, Grandmother."

Tutu nodded. Her whole face smiled.

The ride—a stretch limo with a bar and soft Hawaiian music—was as comfortable as their ultimate destination, his home—a rustic mansion lying across a lookout, lounging in the afternoon sun. Each person was assigned a private suite on the second floor with an astounding view of the ocean and access to both the deck and an interior hallway with an elevator. Servants moved soundlessly to accommodate their needs. Everything was designed to delight visitors and make them amenable to business or pleasure. It was a tourist's conception of perfect Hawaii lying above the beaches of the ancient land.

"I'm flying Norm in from his job site in the morning," Nainoa told them at dinner in his capacious dining room. "He insisted on finishing his project before he takes time off. Patrick can tell you that's Norman for you."

"How do you know Patrick?" Kali asked him across the long, beautifully appointed table. She couldn't help recalling banquets with the military top brass during which she had been expected to be charming. She was, after all, a woman and in charge of charm by default. She wondered what this man of authority was thinking and how he would react to Daniel.

"I work with Norm now and again," he told her. "He's the genius behind some of my most successful products. He introduced me to Patrick. Pat's well known around here for his research. We treasure the ocean, and his research will help us preserve it. The truth is, Norman and Patrick are family to me. Norm and I have been best buddies since we were small. He stood up for me at my wedding. We attended school together. He's still my most valuable advisor. I'm delighted to be able to help them out."

"Nainoa's from an old Hawaiian family," interjected Pat as he raised his glass of wine in tribute. "To one of the best friends anyone could ever have."

Julie raised her glass. What had happened to Nainoa's wife, she wondered. She had seen a lovely native woman beside him in a photograph in the hallway. Had he divorced her? At least he hadn't killed her...or had her killed. The thought took her back to her own unanswerable questions about Rich—a place she was loathe to visit. She drank her wine a little too quickly. Here in Hawaii, in order to relax it was best not to think at all.

* * *

The next day, she was surprised to see how diverse the people attending the wedding seemed to be as they arrived to the traditional sounds of ukulele music. She had expected to feel out of place, but instead she felt inadequate as she met accomplished artists, musicians, and scientists among the more and less ordinary guests. This was no place for a Las Vegas mermaid. She fell silent. What could she add to the conversation? She didn't read enough. She didn't understand enough. How could she open her mouth and look shallow and foolish in front of homosexual people?

It was like a party you might see in a film about someone very sophisticated. Perhaps she had misjudged Patrick, who reminded her of a high school guy who would've been the go-to guy-friend prom-substitute for girls who were left without a date—before they knew he was gay, of course. Or maybe not. A nice gay guy was a safe companion for a girl out late. Even Mom had said that. Yet here he was mingling happily and more successfully than she was.

Some of the wedding guests were with partners of the opposite sex. Some not. Julie seemed to be the only one who cared who belonged with whom or what anyone had chosen to wear. She drew a long breath. The atmosphere felt soft and warm. She could pretend to be at ease. She was good at pretend. Her wedding had been a model of pretend. She had pretended she enjoyed it, when the only part she liked was when she and Rich left. At least she needn't have worried about her dress this time. Her long deep-blue shift was perfect. It looked great with her lei. She wondered if one of the lesbians might hit on her. No one did—probably because of her wedding ring? Or maybe there were no lesbians present? Or maybe she didn't understand lesbians at all.

When she finally met Norman, he radiated intelligence beneath his large dark-rimmed glasses and intense brown eyes. His black hair had been carefully combed into obedience—a fruitless effort in the warm tropical wind. His white slacks held a precise crease beneath his white shirt embroidered with white flowers, and his warmth glowed quietly in his smile. He was a perfect counterpart to the flamboyance of Patrick as he embraced him gently and kissed him lightly on the lips. Wearing a slightly less pressed version of Norman's white outfit belted by a red sash, Patrick hugged him in an embrace that might have been heartier if his ribs had been fully healed.

A young native man stood by, ready with more leis, while another snapped photographs.

Pat stepped away from his partner to perform the introductions. "Norm, I want you to meet my big sister Maureen. We call her Rini."

Maureen reflected the tropical sunshine in her pale-yellow tuxedo-style full-skirted dress. The soft fabric swayed slightly in the breeze, emphasizing the curves of her body as pale strands of her sienna hair curled around her face. Today, onlookers could easily spot her relationship to Patrick in her broad smile.

Norman draped a lei over her head with a soft-spoken *"Aloha"* and offered her his hand to shake, but she leaned forward to hug him, instead. To Julie's eye, she wasn't pretending.

"I can't tell you how thrilled I am to have you in the family," she told him. "It'll be wonderful having two brothers." A twinkle in her eyes forewarned that she was about to tease Patrick. "Maybe then somebody will remember my birthday on time!"

"I was at sea!" protested Pat.

Norman chuckled. "I'll make a note of it."

"And this is Julie Teller," continued Pat going through the small group, "the first professional mermaid I've ever met."

Julie stepped forward, standing an awkward distance from Norman.

"Aloha," he told her. "I've heard you aren't a siren *mo'o* who lures men to drown, but a sea goddess." Norman adorned her with a lei and accepted her self-conscious handshake. "Pat told me how you rescued yourself and your husband with your mermaid skills. Quick thinking. I applaud you."

Was she blending in? Julie worried. "Thank you," she said in her best soft mermaid-on-a-radio-ad voice. Meeting people was so much easier with Rich by her side to do the talking—if Rich would talk to a gay guy. He probably would if he saw a sale to be had. For him, money was the great equalizer.

"And this is Kalani," continued Pat, "grandmother to Kalia and her daughter Lila. They come from a long line of Hawaiians. You may know of them."

Norman gave her a smile that melted through his carefully groomed exterior, revealing the boy within. "We'll have to sit by the sea with Nainoa who is a *kahuna pule* and talk about the ancient ones before you leave," Norman told her. "I would be honored."

Tutu sighed deep happiness into the Hawaiian air. "Everybody call me Tutu." She seemed pale but natural among the islanders, like a butterfly first set free from a cocoon, stretching wet wings to the sun. Someone in the house had plaited her wiry hair with flowers.

"Of course." Norman respectfully draped a lei over her head. "*Aloha* and welcome home, *kuku wahine.*"

Tutu beamed. "*Aloha*—which mean love, peace, and compassion," she translated glancing at her companions.

Kali was next, resplendent in a coral-colored dress that complimented her skin and made her gold jewelry glow. She accepted Norman's lei graciously, giving him a gentle hug. "*Aloha*! I'm so glad to see Patrick happy. You make a perfect pair. And these leis are gorgeous! Thank you. Aren't they beautiful, Lila?"

"This is the prettiest lei I ever saw!" exclaimed Lila hopping on one foot. "I like Hawaii." She was wearing a grass skirt that she swished with her hand as it swung over her flowered dress. She sniffed the flowers of her lei and launched herself into an original interpretive dance that required quantities of twirling. "Thank you, Mr. Norman! I look beautiful! I can dance better now."

Patrick laughed as he turned to Will, the next to be introduced. "Norm, this is my now good friend Will. He gave me a place to live, and he and Kali and Rini fought—literally fought--to protect me. I told you about it on the phone. If it hadn't been for these good hearts, I might not be here."

Norman's expression grew solemn as he placed a lei over Will's head. "*Aloha.*" He touched each guest in turn with his grateful attention. "I'm deeply in your debt—all of you. Pat means more than life to me."

Will shrugged. "We had to help. Maureen was watching." When Norman didn't laugh, he continued in a more serious tone. "We were glad we were there. Kali showed them what a woman with martial arts training can do."

Kali demurred. "Maureen and Will were fierce, and Pat did all he could against terrible odds. It was my privilege to help."

Norman's forehead wrinkled into lines between his eyes as he gazed at his love. "I'm concerned that Pat has to return to the mainland for court. People there are not as kind as most native Hawaiians, it seems to me. Forgive me if I think many people are losing their brightness—poisoned by selfishness, hate, and greed. Or maybe they never had quite enough."

Tutu nodded, dropping her voice as though sharing a confidence. "The *'e'epa* been doing their work. Many have fallen to low vibrations."

Pat took Norman's hand. "Oh, it's not as bad as all that," he assured her. "Haters have always lurked in the shadows and run in cowardly packs. But I'll be careful. No more bars while I'm on the mainland going to court." He reached out to touch Norman's hand. "I'll be in a hurry to come home to you."

Tutu placed her hand over theirs. "Tomorrow I gonna ask you to take me to *Puuhonua o Honauna* Historical Park, the place of refuge, where I gonna pray to block the *'e'epa*. And I gonna ask the ancestors what I can teach you all to keep you safe."

Norman smiled. "I can take you to a private place more sacred than that."

"But in the meantime," interrupted Kali a little hastily even though the mention of *'e'epa* didn't seem to faze Norman, "this may be the most spectacular setting for a wedding I've ever seen." She didn't want to know if Norman believed in insect people.

He led them forward then gestured toward the rows of chairs. "I've reserved seats in front for all of you as Pat's family. I hope you don't mind that we've adopted friends to stand in for your family, Maureen."

"Call me Rini and these make great relatives to adopt. I'm all for it."

The ceremony began shortly thereafter. As the *kahuna pule* or holy man, Nainoa used his sonorous voice to sing a chant as he walked Patrick to the circle of flowers where the ceremony would be performed. He was followed by Norman's sister as maid of honor, Maureen as best man, Lila with her basket of flowers, and Norman's young nephew carrying a ring box. A tall Hawaiian man stepped forward to blow a startlingly loud blast on a conch shell to quiet the guests and announce the approach of a smiling Norman, who now wore a crown of *haku* flowers and greenery. Patrick turned to watch him, his expression soft and joyful.

When Norman reached Patrick, he lifted a long *maile*-style *ti* leaf lei over Patrick's head that Nainoa used to bind the hands of the couple together after Patrick adorned Norman with a pink *pikake* lei. Then Maureen bestowed a lei on Norman's sister and Norman's sister placed a lei over Maureen's head. At last the musician on the ukulele joined others on guitars to play the Hawaiian Wedding Song while hula dancers interpreted the words and Nainoa led the vows. When they had finished, Nainoa went to dip a *koa* wood bowl into the sea, added a *ti* leaf to the water, then sprinkled the rings Norman's nephew had brought three times as he recited a final chant before the couple exchanged rings. He presented Norman and Patrick with jars of colored sand—each with a different color—for them to pour into a single glass container, mixing the colors together. Finally, the couple wrapped a *ti* leaf around a lava rock and deposited it in a rock formation by the sea.

"I've never seen Pat as happy," Maureen told Julie as she joined her in the seats. Tears pooled in her eyes making them glisten. "I love him so much. He's excited and obviously respected in his profession. Mother would be absolutely thrilled. She never expected him to be successful...I suppose because Dad never did. Pat's right; Norm is special. I'm so pleased! Pat did better at choosing both a career and a partner than I did."

"Better than I did, too, I guess." Julie glanced at the people around her, noting their rapt attention. "My wedding was miserable next to this. The decorations were garish and I felt like I was in the way. Rich got drunk and I wished I were. And now I have to ask myself if he could be trying to kill me. Where did I get off thinking a gay wedding would be more offensive than mine? These people feel like they came because they truly care."

Sitting on the other side of her, Will whispered, "I'm honored to be here. Thanks, Rini."

The celebration following the ceremony matched the ebullient good feelings of all that had gone before. The luau unfolded like a huge tropical flower, revealing tables crowded with quantities of food and drink, native dancers who performed hulas and a fire dance with flaming torches, and finally, a Hawaiian musical group playing music to suit varied tastes. Pat and Norman had danced, and now guests were enjoying their chance to kick aside their shoes and enjoy the sensation of sand between their toes. Kali agreed to dance with Lila, who was twirling at every opportunity, and Maureen accepted a gracious invitation from the widower Nainoa. Will watched her moving in Nainoa's arms for a moment before he stood up and turned to Julie. "Would you like to dance?"

Julie looked up at him. "Will, I'm married."

He smiled. "It's only a dance, Jules, not a proposal."

Tutu poked Julie's arm. "You ain't very much married. Have a little fun."

Julie accepted Will's hand, alarmed at the sensations she felt from his touch. She would have to be very careful with this friendship.

Chapter 24

Still in Danger

EVERYONE WAS QUIET on the plane trip back to the mainland, except for Tutu who snored as she slept in the seat beside Lila. Her days in the sun had toasted Lila to a deeper brown that tied her to the land she had left. She curled against her mother as a puppy might, secure in her place. Kali wore ear buds but kept the sound so low no one could guess what she was hearing. Her head bobbed slightly with her private beat. She didn't want anyone to know she was listening to Hawaiian music. She didn't want to admit how much she longed to call the islands home.

Will was playing chess on a small board with the white-haired man in the seat beside him. He wasn't sure who had made the first overture after his checkers game with Lila, but he was delighted to have discovered a worthy opponent. Neither spoke so only chess aficionados could determine how the game was progressing between their small exclamations of delight or dismay.

Maureen sat beside Julie, idly flipping the pages of a magazine she had purchased in the airport. "This is going to sound silly," she said in a conspiratorial tone, "but I feel like an orphan without Pat. He held me up through my divorce, and…believe me…it wasn't easy. I lost my confidence, my sense of self. I took careless chances, did things that weren't at all like me. I still can't believe I was so foolish. I started questioning my every decision—even stupid ones like what to have for lunch."

Julie stared ahead. "Rich always chose what we had for lunch."

"You're kidding."

"No."

"Why did you let him?"

Julie shrugged. "I guess I thought he was taking care of me. We didn't disagree."

"Not ever?"

"Not that I remember…until the fire. We weren't together all that long."

Maureen grimaced. "How can two individuals never disagree? Honestly, how can that happen? You don't have to argue, but you must disagree sometimes. When two people become one in marriage, somebody disappears—the woman, most of the time. It's not romantic; it's pathetic. Didn't you have any opinions of your own?"

Julie leaned forward to look out the window past the woman beside her, watching the play of light on the wing beyond. Metallic silver glided over wispy clouds through a slice of brilliant blue… over the rainbow? If only she could escape to a place where trouble melted like lemon drops. "Before the fire? I don't know. I think so. I don't know. I was in love. Rich said he was trying to make me happy. It wasn't his fault. I wasn't decisive."

Maureen slapped her magazine closed. "Oh for pity sake! You can't make someone else happy. Before Gage and I married…and it was an over-the-top grand ceremony choreographed by my parents…he swore he'd make me happy. It turned out he didn't know me at all and didn't care to. He couldn't begin to guess where I needed support in my bid to fulfill myself. He let me serve his needs until he didn't need me anymore. Rich doesn't seem to be too different. He didn't marry you; he swallowed you whole. No wonder you were indecisive. How would you know what would make you happy when you stopped knowing yourself?"

Julie shifted her posture toward the window. "I didn't really care. Letting him choose pleased him. It wasn't a battle, Rini."

Maureen shook her head. "Being a dictator fed his ego, most likely. You know, Jules, a wife used to be on a level with livestock. Lots of people think they still are. But there are decent men out there—men who'd be fun to share life with. You can do better."

Julie swallowed a lump of tears before it could escape. She closed her eyes. "Maybe I can't. Maybe I don't want to."

Maureen scowled at the seatback in front of her. "That's indoctrinated bullshit. Of course you can. And I'll help you. I can still practice law in California. I'm a little rusty, but I can kick butt in a courtroom—or in negotiations, depending on what happens. I'll work on your divorce. Pro bono. I need the practice."

The middle-aged woman sitting on the other side of Julie cleared her throat. She leaned forward far enough that Maureen could see the graying, permed hair enclosing her chubby white face. "A wife is meant to serve her husband," she hissed. "Don't you dare wreck this poor dear's marriage! A marriage is blessed by God."

"Then she wasn't married," replied Maureen sharply, "because what she had was bondage. God doesn't bless bondage."

The woman's face turned red and she pursed her lips, but before she could say more, Julie interrupted her. "I appreciate your concern, but my good friend and I are just chatting. I'm sorry if we disturbed you. These seats are crammed together too much for privacy, but we'll try to be quieter."

The woman couldn't see Maureen's face beyond Julie, but Maureen scowled, nonetheless. "Just beware, Dear," the woman said, patting Julie's hand. "Satan's minions are everywhere, trying to destroy what's good in this world."

"I'll be careful," Julie promised, thinking this woman was the second person to warn her of danger. Tutu's warning had been prescient. Could Satan's minions be the same as *'e'epa*? This pudgy pasty-faced woman reminded her of her older sister, the self-appointed Keeper of All Wisdom and Truth—not much like kindly old Tutu. Julie drew a long breath and reoriented her body more toward Maureen. She was sick of people weighing in with advice about her marriage. No one—no one knew better than she—and she didn't have a clue what to do next. She held her magazine open for Maureen. "Did you see the article in this magazine about the benefits of blueberries? I love blueberries."

Maureen rolled her eyes. "Really? You want to talk about blueberries? I should've ordered a scotch."

They didn't see the woman again until they were all waiting for luggage at the baggage claim area. The woman was buxom enough to make her lavender muumuu hang like a circus big top around her. Her forehead was creased with indelible worry lines, and her mouth dipped in a permanent downward arc. She glared at Maureen as she tugged her suitcase off the carousel. "There's a good reason why you're divorced," she told her before she padded away in her flat-bottomed sandals. "Think about it."

Maureen looked at Julie and they both laughed. "She's probably a marriage counselor," suggested Julie.

"Or a prison matron."

Lila came dancing over to them with a monkey doll, a gift from Patrick. "I really, really, really like Hawaii. Mr. Nainoa said I could come back anytime."

Kali walked behind her, her face glowing blue from the light of her cell phone. Her lips spread into a wide smile. "Oh, thank God! Thank God! We have a good reason to be in California instead of Hawaii, Lila. *Daddy's coming!*"

"Daddy!" Lila's squeal caught the attention of the people nearby. "Daddy, Daddy, Daddy!" She began twirling in circles. "When? Is he here?"

"He's on his way. In a couple days!" Kali's joy radiated, lifting her posture and lighting her face. She looked to Julie and Maureen. "You'll have a chance to meet my Daniel. He's the finest man I've ever known. Being at a wedding made me miss him worse than ever. I almost wept. I couldn't help remembering our wedding day. After a civil ceremony here, we went to his hometown in Mexico and were treated to a huge potluck and then a celebration with crowds of his family and people from his town dancing in the streets. I think the entire population partied. Either Daniel is one of the most beloved men in the city or everyone there seizes any chance to celebrate— maybe a combination of both. I found out I don't have a limitless capacity for tequila. God, we danced and drank all night!"

"I'm so jealous!" Maureen sighed. "I can't wait to see what kind of man appealed to the Goddess Kali. He must be something.

It's time for me to move out of Tutu's place, anyway. Lila can have my bed. My condo reno will need on-site supervision here on out if I want to be happy with the outcome." She turned toward Julie. "Besides, I need to set up meetings for my new client, don't I?"

"Do we have to act so fast?" Julie jerked her suitcase onto the floor in a physical expression of her annoyance. "Maybe we should wait to see…" Her voice trailed off.

"…To see if Rich turns into somebody else?" supplied Maureen.

Kali scowled at Maureen who squeezed her lips together for a moment then sighed. "Sure. Of course. There's no rush. You need to be confident in a decision like this. No pressure."

Julie smiled a maybe-there-really-is-a-Santa-Claus smile that gave her face a middle school aspect. "Thanks."

"No problem." But when Julie preceded them, Maureen rolled her eyes for Kali's benefit.

* * *

Maureen hadn't had a chance to move out yet when Detective Jess Rainey called to ask if he could stop by. When he arrived, he said he had information to share. This time he didn't isolate Julie. He didn't even ask Will to leave…Will, who had come from next door to give Lila the monkey she had tucked into his luggage strap. Rainey gathered the adults in the kitchen and agreed Kali should send Lila to the backyard. He tried to act casual, but his expression was grave.

Julie could feel a surge of icy emotion scraping itself down through her esophagus. Something was wrong. She tried to keep her voice calm. "Please, get right to the point. What do you have to tell me?"

The detective glanced around the table, as though assessing his audience. "The officers on the site of the mass shooting had a chance to question the gunman before he died. We call it a dying declaration, and it carries a lot of weight. He said the point of his being there was to kill the Tellers because they stiffed him after a hit job they ordered. They wrecked his cred with the mob and set him up to be murdered. He said if he ruined their business, that was all to the good because they ruined his." Detective Rainey drew a slow breath. "Julie, the job the Tellers had refused to pay him for was killing you."

"Killing me?" Shudders worked their way down her spine in waves. "The Tellers hired him to kill *me*? Are you sure he wasn't lying? Surely someone else..."

Rainey shook his head. "We checked his story. Little Paulie confided in a couple guys in his favorite bar. They were willing to talk now that he's dead and they could make a few bucks."

Tears slid down her face, not cold, not hot—colorless tepid tears escaping the turmoil within, quietly screaming. "What about..." she couldn't push the name out. It stuck in her throat.

"Rich," supplied Maureen. "What about Richard Teller? Was he in on it?"

"We brought him in for questioning. He denied any knowledge of either hit. He was belligerent. He might have been telling the truth..."

"...And he might not," finished Will.

"That's why I wanted to talk to you all." Rainey fell into his professional voice. "Richard Teller had the most to gain from the two shootings if they had both succeeded. He's the sole heir. I'm not saying he was definitely involved, of course. So far, we don't have enough evidence one way or the other. He could be innocent in both cases, but if he's not, you could still be in danger, Mrs. Teller.

"Of course, if Paulie's story about taking revenge for being stiffed is factual, that probably exonerates your husband for the real estate killings, at least—unless there's a payment or connection somewhere we don't know about. Your husband seemed pretty upset by his mother's death. She might have been collateral damage and not part of the plan.

"As far as your attempted homicide goes, we can't say what your husband knew or how he feels at this point. Maybe he blames you now more than ever—for his near-drowning plus the murders of his family members. People don't have to make sense where revenge is concerned. We don't know how far he might go to get to you."

The detective shoved his hands into his pockets. "Finally, Richard's responsibility in both or either hit—if any—might have been a strictly financial decision, as I suggested before. We aren't sure how the mob figures in—except that they were stiffed at least once by the shooter. They take that kind of thing seriously, and they're not real fussy about who they punish. We aren't talking about forgiving people here. If your husband was involved with them, everyone living here could be in danger, and so could he. Julie, I want you to take precautions, just in case. I know you got your license back, but don't go driving by yourself."

"Trouble," muttered Tutu, staring down at her hands. "Darkness."

This time Kali didn't change the subject. Instead, she asked, "What kind of precautions can she take?"

Rainey shrugged. "I'm afraid that's up to you."

"We could move you to my new condo," suggested Maureen. "He can't hurt you if he can't find you."

Rainey looked skeptical. "Your husband knows about your friends here, doesn't he? Do you have anybody in another city who'd let you crash with them for a while—somebody your husband wouldn't know or remember? We might be able to clear the confusion if we have more time. We probably missed details."

Julie's voice fell small. A twisted, ugly reality sat on her lap and refused to go away. "How can I run from my husband?" She raised her eyes to her friend. "He's my husband, Rini. He's still my husband."

Maureen tilted her head slightly. "That's curable."

Kali stood up, her expression hard. "For the time being, stay close to me, Jules. I can be your bodyguard."

Will cracked a grin. "Believe me, Detective, I've seen Kali in action. She makes Jackie Chan look inept."

Rainey didn't smile. "Depending on who's after you, Julie, you may need all the protection you can muster." He nodded a perfunctory farewell and headed for the front door.

"And have a nice day," muttered Maureen.

Chapter 25

Building Defenses of the Heart

DANIEL RAMIREZ EASILY filled the height of the doorway, but he was taut—strung with the kind of lean stamina muscles that deliver but never boast. He wore a smile white enough for toothpaste commercials that contrasted with the deep tan of his skin. His shining black hair was tightly restrained in a knot behind his head, and he walked with the dignity of ancient times when his ancestors built pyramids across Mexico. He was wearing a newly purchased denim shirt tucked into his jeans as well as worn canvas shoes and a dark leather belt tooled with Mayan symbols. He easily caught Lila as she leapt into his arms, shifting her to one side so he could embrace Kali at the same time.

"This is my daddy!" proclaimed Lila proudly. "I missed you SO much, Daddy! To the universe and behind!"

Tutu hurried forward to add her kisses. She held his face in her age-spotted hands. "We all missed you, Daniel." She patted his cheek before backing away.

"Thank you, Tutu." He kissed Kali soundly and, without releasing her from his one-armed embrace, he turned his attention to Julie who stood in the entry to the hall. "And who is this?"

"I'm Julie…" She didn't want to choose a surname, so she didn't.

Kali had settled against him, looking more pliant and content than Julie had ever seen her. "Julie's house was burned just like ours. I told you about her on the phone. She's the one who hid in the lake."

His smile faded. "Yes. I remember." He spoke with a tinge of Mexican-Spanish accent, but his English flowed easily. "I am so sorry for all you have endured, *Señora.*"

Julie felt suddenly awkward. She wished Rich were beside her. He would know what to say. "Thank you. It's a pleasure to meet you." She tried to command her high school Spanish to come to her aid to no avail. It skittered away into the recesses of her memory as soon as she called for it. She wouldn't have dared air it, anyway. Would it be patronizing? She hated to sound stupid.

Daniel leaned over to set Lila on the ground. "I have a gift for you, *hija.*" He released Kali so he could pull a soft package from his backpack. "It's a big girl dress."

"Oh, thank you, Daddy! Thank you, thank you, thank you!" Lila turned to Tutu, who anticipated what was coming next.

"Come, Precious One. I'll help you try it on."

Lila danced beside her great-grandmother as they went up the hallway.

"I'll see if I can help," offered Julie, exiting hastily.

Kali and Daniel enjoyed a lingering kiss that left Kali with a pounding heart. "I'm so glad to have you near," she whispered into his ear. "You make the world feel kinder."

He kissed her a second time. "I should have been here for the fire and the shooting and to go with you to Hawaii. You've been alone through so much. Please forgive me."

Kali dismissed his concern. "We were fine, but I can breathe better with you here. How long can you stay this time?"

He kissed her nose. "I have no time to be back. I quit my job."

She pulled away far enough to see his face. "You quit?"

"*Sí.* Kal, this country is going mad. Too much has happened here near Tutu's house. There is no safety. As I told you on the phone, I want Lila to grow up where children are treasured—in the cradle of my family. We'll go to live with my mother on her ranch until we can build our own house. You remember Mama bought land for each of her children when we were born. I know there are problems in Mexico, too, but we have family to help watch over Lila there. I won't make so much money, but I'll find work. I can even work online if I have an office in the city. We don't have to stay here. Do you have our passports?"

Kali led him to the sofa, where they both sat. Kali's voice was low. "Yes. I stuffed them in my bag with other papers before we evacuated. But I can't go now, Daniel. Julie's in danger. I promised to protect her."

"She can come, too." He leaned forward, taking her hands in his, his earnestness filling the space between them. "We can't risk staying here, *mi linda.* We would both be forever injured if anything happened to our baby. Our house is already gone. God has destroyed our ties, our plans for this country. With the hate against immigrants rising, I am not welcome here. Soon a naturalized citizen may be no citizen at all. My skills are not enough to protect us. We need to seize the hint. We have been warned. We can bring Tutu with us. Or she can go to Hawaii to be with her ancestors. We have no other reasons to stay."

Kali stood up, pacing to the front window with unhappy staccato steps. "Lani lives here in the States. She's in love and wants to get married. I'm her big sister, the only functional mother she had for years. Even now there's only Tutu and me. I have to be in her wedding. And Tutu has no passport. The process is long. I don't know how many days she has left in her life. Can I ask her to die in a foreign land? I doubt Jules has traveled at all, so she probably has no papers, either, and she's horribly unprepared to live in a strange country—offensively naïve and already stressed. She's likely facing an ugly divorce. We can't just haul Tutu and Jules off to Mexico. They need to make that choice and prepare themselves, if that's the option they want. Tutu doesn't speak Spanish, and I doubt Jules does, either. To be honest, maybe Lila and I would rather go to Hawaii with Tutu than to Mexico, anyway. Tutu's roots in the islands are mine and Lila's, as well. I could feel them when we went for the wedding. Hawaii is beautiful and modern and we have friends there already--powerful friends."

"We can't afford to live in Hawaii." He was frowning now, his great dark brows clouding his face. "We can't wait to sell the burned property or to save my paychecks to finance relocation there. The danger is here, today. Your friend nearly died in this house. What if Lila had been on the porch with her? What if Maureen hadn't taken you both on her motorcycle? If later you find a way for us to thrive in Hawaii, you know I would go anywhere with you. We can travel there another day. But now we must leave this place."

Kali turned to face him, and he could see her angst in her tears. They stared into one another for long moments. When she spoke, her voice trembled. "You're probably right. You go. Take Lila. Keep her safe. I'll come join you as soon as I can—when Julie's safe."

He stood to embrace her, his tears blending with hers on her chest. "*Por favor,* think hard about your choice. How long will our separation be? Suppose Julie is never safe. What then? How long can I live without blood in my heart? To leave you behind wounds my soul. We have had so little time together. I quit my job to be near you. I need you."

Lila came skipping into the room, twirling periodically to demonstrate the glory of her colorful embroidered peasant skirt. "Look, Daddy! Look, Mommy! I'm beautiful! Tutu says so!"

Daniel knelt down to Lila's level. "Tutu is perfectly right. You are dazzling, Lily Pad!"

"Why are you and Mommy crying?"

Kali squatted beside them, throwing a brief glance toward her husband. "We're very happy to be together, my darling. We're crying for the joy of loving you so much."

* * *

After Lila had been put to bed that night, Kali and Daniel met with Julie and Tutu in the living room.

"No!" Julie stood, pacing angrily. "I will not permit you to do this, Kali. You're a mom, not a bodyguard. Your war is over. I won't tolerate the division of your family because of me. Remember, the existence of the threat may be nothing but a bad guess by a bunch of cops who see bad guys behind every bush. It has almost certainly been exaggerated. Or it might not be true at all! Whatever it is, it's my problem, not yours. You barely know me."

Daniel sat with his arm around his wife. He sighed. "You've heard the news about the hatred in this country—the wickedness. Even if I could change the way I talk…if I wanted to…I cannot change my skin. I cannot choose different ancestors. Neither can Lila. We are targets—perhaps more than you. We have no idea who our enemies are. They blend into the population. Just as your friend Pat was attacked by strangers, anyone can suddenly choose to act against someone they see as a threat. The asylum seekers at the border came here fleeing such conditions only to find heartache. We are fleeing the other way."

Julie's face was turning a blotchy crimson. "If you feel the need to go, I understand completely, but Kali has to be with her family. Take her with you."

Tutu began rocking more vigorously. "There ain't no mind where the ʻeʻepa can't exist. Only defenses of the heart can defeat them. We give power to each other when we stay together."

Kali exhaled in exasperation. "That's my point. I've chosen to stay for a while. You didn't ask me to do it, Jules, and neither did Tutu. She isn't afraid of anything. She raised Lani and me. Tutu's personal power is limitless. That doesn't mean she doesn't need me."

Tutu stopped rocking. "Your mother listened to the negative voices. Inside she believed the bad things people said about her. She died for her fear of herself, not because she was attacked. Her darkness wasn't in her skin; it was in her damaged heart. I got more power than that. I earned it. You ain't staying for my sake."

Kali rose and walked to Julie. She took her friend's hands in her own. "Jules, I'm not asking your permission for me to stay. I'm simply informing you. I'm not surrendering my family for you. I'm defending their country—my country...this time without killing, I hope. If I can protect you, it's like defending Pat. I'm part of the change I wish to see in this world, as they say. I'm contributing to the positive. This obligation is greater than you."

There was a silence that seemed to tick like a clock in the space, and then Daniel rose. "Come on, everyone. I brought good tequila. I think it's time we shared a drink."

Chapter 26

Waiting for the Call

"BUT, MOMMY, I don't want to go to Abuela Maria's house without you! You promised you'd stay with me! When you came back from the war, you promised! You said forever! I remember!" Lila hung on Kali's pants. Her tears rushed down her cheeks and a strangled wailing gurgled from her throat.

Kali's stomach visibly retracted, as though she had been punched. "I know, my darling, but I have to help Tutu and Julie. It won't be as long as last time. Daddy will be with you, and you love Abuela Maria. You'll be able to play with the chicks and eat *gorditas*."

"No, Mommy! No!" Lila collapsed to the floor in sobs. "I want you!"

Kali looked to Daniel as he stood at the door. His expression said he wanted to cry, too, but he sucked in a long breath. "Please come as soon as you can, *mi amor*." He drew Kali into a kiss that might once have been reserved for the bedroom. "I am never whole without you." He shouldered his bag as well as Lila's pink one. "I have to drive to Texas to pick up my final paycheck. We'll need it. I'll call you when we're through the border at El Paso."

Tutu brought Lila's monkey. She bent to wrap Lila in her arms, kissing her all the while. "Here, Precious One. I filled your monkey with my love, so any time you need more love, you squeeze him and the love gonna be there for you." Tears slipped silently down her wrinkled cheeks. "Love stretches. We gonna always be connected."

Kali lifted Lila into her arms and held her face in her hand. "Be brave and strong, my darling." She kissed Lila's cheek and released her. "We'll find a better answer. There has to be a better answer."

No one spoke as Daniel's car drove away. Lila's sobs faded into the distance. Tutu took Kali into her embrace as she might a child, and Kali released her sorrow in tears.

"How will we know when your guard duties are over?" asked Julie bitterly. "How do any of us know this sacrifice of yours isn't a terrible waste?"

"That done out of love ain't never a waste," replied Tutu quietly. "What we do from love for others keep us safe from the *'e'epa.*"

Julie wanted to lash out against the absurdity, but the pain in the old woman's face stopped her. Tutu might not live to see her great-granddaughter again. Her sacrifice might be the most dramatic of all.

"We'll make a plan," Julie said at last. "When we've recovered enough from this pain, we'll set up parameters for the situation— the circumstances we can use to judge whether the threat is over. Maureen and I can visit Rich. There'll be ways to figure out where we stand. I can tell when he's lying."

Tutu nodded, not in agreement but to silence Julie. "I gonna call Will to drive us to the ocean tomorrow. The waves gonna wash away some of our hurting."

* * *

The next day, Will didn't say much as they drove. "So, Kali," he said at last, "why couldn't you let me watch out for Jules and Miss Kalani so you could stay with your family? You've known me for years. You know I'd do it."

"You're not around all the time."

"I could be." He scowled at the highway. "Jules' ex isn't going to be stupid enough to try the same thing again."

Julie slumped in her seat. "He's not my ex. He's my husband. And nobody knows for sure he's going to try anything at all."

Will made a disgusted sound deep in his throat. "Loyalty to someone who's worth it is admirable, Jules." He prevented himself from completing his thought. "We'll stop at the animal shelter on the way back. I took it upon myself to do some research. You ladies need a dog. They say a dog is better protection than an alarm system."

Kali crossed her arms over her chest. "Tutu can't care for a dog big enough to be any protection."

"Jules can handle him."

Julie started to protest and decided against it. She didn't want to say she had been thinking of going off on her own. It sounded too much like abandoning ship when she meant to remove the bait from the trap. "I haven't had a dog since I was a girl."

"You see?" Will braked suddenly for traffic, pitching everyone forward. "I knew you must have spent time with animals. I could tell by the way you approached Maureen's cat. A dog will be company and protection."

Kali remained skeptical. "How do you know the shelter will have an appropriate dog—you know, one that's house trained and safe with…?" She caught herself before she said *safe with kids*. She hastily removed her attention to the view out the window and swallowed several times.

Will smiled. "I did some online research and already called. They're expecting us."

Kali frowned. "Aren't you presuming quite a lot?"

"I like dogs," said Tutu from the back seat. "They got good energy."

Julie sighed. "If a dog helps reunite Kali with her family sooner, I'm all for it."

Kali nodded, feigning a smile. "Besides, Will allowing a dog into his precious GTO has to be an occasion. I want to shoot a pic of that. Lani will never believe it."

Both Kali and Julie looked to Will for his reaction. He grinned. "I brought an extendable collar and a couple old stadium blankets with rubberized backs. I told you I'd do my part."

As they hoped, the crash of the waves against the shore touched a primal need—a rhythm of relentless life. By the time they had splurged on a good dinner, they were ready to confront the emotional demands of the shelter. Will had the attendants bring out the multi-colored shepherd-mix dog he had selected. She stood tall and sturdy, over fifty pounds. Her eyes, that were like translucent slices of glazed oak, studied them before she approached Julie, who was squatting before her.

The attendant, an oval-faced teenage girl with quick brown eyes and long black hair woven into a braid, smiled her approval. "Her name is Hermione—you know, after the feisty girl in Harry Potter. Her owner gave her up, and she knows it. They didn't want the bother. She's very smart. She's already spayed and current on shots. Her owner did that much for her. Don't take her if there's any chance you won't be her forever home. She deserves better."

Julie laid a hand beside the dog's face. "Does she like swimming?"

"Her foster home said she seems to have some lab in her. She liked playing in their pool. She'll go anywhere with her people."

Hermione licked Julie's hand in one small, soft stroke.

"I can feel her." Julie's voice was almost a whisper. "I mean, she seems like an old friend." She looked up to Will. "I don't know how you could have found her online, but she's perfect. I want to sign the papers."

"My idea, my treat."

"I'll pay you back." Julie and the dog had both brightened. Hermione wiggled all over in her excitement. "She knows!"

The teenage attendant made a face. "Of course."

Kali bent down to massage the dog's neck. "I like her."

Even Tutu took a turn stroking Hermione's soft fur. "She got a good spirit. She gonna stand by you. She's welcome in my home."

Will spread a stadium blanket over his precious car seat, and Hermione settled herself between Julie and Tutu, her head on Julie's lap.

"Lila and Daniel would love her," said Kali quietly. She checked her cell as she had periodically ever since they left home.

"Have you heard from them yet?" asked Julie.

"No, but it's a long drive. Daniel may have stopped more often for Lila than he does when he travels alone. He'll call when they're across the border. He doesn't text when he's driving." Her voice sounded oddly strained, as though her throat had constricted.

"Good practice," commented Will, turning on the radio. "And now for some music. I find music balms almost anything."

They stopped at a pet store for a leash and dog dishes, leaving Tutu and Hermione in the car. Hermione seemed to understand that Tutu was in her care for the moment. She stood up, turned around, and laid her chin on Tutu's leg. Tutu rested her freckled hands on the dog's head, and they both fell asleep.

Chapter 27

A Civilized Reason to be Afraid

THE MESSAGE LIGHT on Tutu's old-fashioned answering machine was flashing as they entered the house. Kali went to tap it on. The voice was scratchy.

"Mrs. Ramirez, my name is Kathy Conners. I'm an aid worker at the El Paso Border Processing Center. Your husband has been detained as an illegal alien and your daughter was taken into children's detention. Your husband asked me to call to let you know. He needs their documentation. You'll have to contact the administrators. I'm only an aid worker. I'm not supposed to be involved." The connection went dead and was replaced by the jarring buzz of an open line.

"No!" Kali turned to face Julie and Will, her eyes wide with panic. "He has the passports! I handed them to him. I watched him set them out with his cell phone and his sweatshirt. He left them on the nightstand." She ran to the back door and they could hear her climbing the stairs and then running across the attic floor. In a few moments, she was back, clutching the items in her hand. "I can't believe it! He forgot them! He forgot everything! They were under his sweatshirt, and he left his sweatshirt. We were all so upset..." She sank onto the sofa. "Oh my god, he has no documentation. But why can't the officials check the database? He's in the naturalized citizen database. He's a citizen now! Why didn't they believe him? Why didn't they check? Oh dear god, they're in detention! *My baby's in a cage!*" She leaped to her feet. "I have to go to them! I have to go now! There aren't any direct flights. I need to rent a car!"

"Wait a minute." Will gripped her shoulders, holding her still. "The officials aren't going to be waiting for you to show up. They don't care, and their record-keeping sucks. You're going to need somebody to help you through the red tape—get you in the front door. Maureen. She's an attorney. She'll have the best ideas for where to begin. And she has a new hybrid car with incredible gas mileage. You won't have to rent. I'll call Maureen. I'm guessing she'll do whatever she can to help. Go get a bag together and I'll call."

He was already dialing as Kali slammed out the back door.

Catching the mood, Hermione started whimpering softly, so Julie bent down to hug her neck.

"She knows," Tutu murmured. "She knows we got big trouble."

"Maureen's on it," assured Will, ending his call. "She's going to try to contact somebody there at the center, but in the meantime, she's willing to drop everything to take Kali down there. She says Kali can help drive and they'll do a marathon nonstop."

Tutu nodded her approval. "I'm gonna fill water bottles and make lunches." She exited into the kitchen.

"It's my fault." Julie let her tears drop onto Hermione's neck. "If Kali hadn't stayed here instead of going with him…"

"Stop." Will offered a hand to help Julie rise. "Don't do that to yourself. No what-ifs. They don't help. We have to deal with what is. How it came to be doesn't matter anymore. I can't think of anything you or Miss Kalani or I could do except be in the way down there, so we'll stay here."

"But, Will…" Julie lowered her voice to a whisper. "Children have been molested in border detention. Girls are raped. Adults have been killed. The conditions are horrific—bad food, no showers, no space."

He scowled. "And we pay for detention with taxes. Maybe Miss Kalani's right. People are infected with evil."

"Do you believe that?"

"No, but I'd be glad to have some civilized reason why we have to be afraid."

Julie went to the kitchen to help Tutu. Will kneeled beside Hermione. "It's going to be okay, Girl," he told her. "I don't know how, but it's going to be okay."

Kali entered the kitchen from the back door. Her bulging backpack was slung over one shoulder and she was talking on her cell phone. "Okay... I'm ready." She clicked off the call.

"Did Maureen have any luck?" asked Julie, handing the last of the cookies to Tutu for her to bag. Will came to stand in the doorway with Hermione in his wake.

"No. It's too late. Nobody's going to do anything today. It's an hour later in El Paso." Kali was wearing her combat face, hard and stoic. "Maureen's phoning a powerful friend who lives down there. According to her, if anyone can cut red tape, he can. She says we're going to need all the help we can find to get Daniel and Lila out. People just disappear into the masses."

"But they're citizens," protested Julie. "They're both American citizens."

"And you have proof," added Will. "You'll get them out."

The lines in Kali's forehead sank deeper. "I'm certain Daniel explained to them. He's a methodical man. I'm sure he showed them his work ID and his driver's license from his wallet. I'm sure he asked them to phone me, but you don't see any messages on the phone. And I doubt they called his work numbers, either. Apparently, Immigration isn't going to go to any trouble to verify his story. The only reason I can guess is Daniel is Mexican-American. And they don't listen to children at all—except when they send them to court unattended. We're going to have a job getting them to listen to us." She turned to Tutu. "Ask the ancestors to protect Lila, *please, Tutu.* Please have them shelter her from bad people."

Tutu came to hold her granddaughter in her arms. "Yes, Dear One. I gonna ask the ancestors to help you kick some butt."

Will almost laughed. "Go, Miss Kalani."

"But for now, "she continued, "I made a thermos of coffee for you to take in the car."

"Somehow I don't think I'll be sleepy," said Kali with a crooked expression that was supposed to be a cousin to a smile. "I used to be able to sleep anytime, anywhere when I was active duty. But my family wasn't in jeopardy then."

Will and Hermione followed Kali as she carried her backpack into the living room where she dumped it on the sofa. "What are you going to do after they're free?" he asked.

"We'll get the hell out of this country." Her voice was bitter. She sat cross-legged on the floor to pet Hermione. "This isn't what I fought to defend."

Will sighed as he went to the window to watch for Maureen. "We've both traveled, Kali. We both know creeping hatred is everywhere. I was sure the U.S. would be too moral, too civilized for it. So much for ignorant pride."

Tutu hobbled into the room. Julie came behind her, carrying a cardboard box of food. Tutu caressed Kali's hair affectionately. "Bad is everywhere, and good is everywhere. We gotta reinforce the good."

Julie lowered the box onto the sofa beside Kali's backpack. "Like that's easy."

"What's worthwhile ain't often easy," Tutu told her in her annoying grandmother tone.

Kali rose from the floor, swallowing whatever retort to Tutu her mind had produced. "I hope Rini hurries."

Maureen looked freshly showered and groomed when she arrived, the sign of someone used to making public appearances with little notice. A suit hung in the back seat of her car with a bag of high heeled shoes. She wore a nondescript expression ready to transform from pleasant to arch villain in a nanosecond. Even her voice seemed more carefully modulated than usual. "I'm ready," she announced in a tone that would command a jury's attention, and no one doubted her.

"You must be one helluva lawyer," commented Will.

Maureen nodded. "Yes. I am."

"Were you able to contact your friend in Texas?" asked Kali, situating her backpack in the car.

"He'll meet us there tomorrow." Maureen softened perceptibly as she watched Kali place the box of food on the floor of the back seat. "He'll make this happen. You can never mention his name or what he's about to do—any of you. Everything he does is news in Texas and lots of other places, besides. We don't want his name connected to us if we can avoid it."

Will allowed himself a smirk. "Mention it? How could we? You haven't said his name or what he's going to do."

"His anonymity is his condition for helping."

Julie held more tightly to Hermione's leash. "Why is he secret? Is he a big-time politician?"

"He owns politicians. He's stinking rich." Maureen shrugged at her nod to ruthless reality. "He knows how to manipulate systems... just barely inside the law. Anyone who ignores him does so at his or her personal and professional peril."

"He sounds scary."

"He is, but he's effective and he owes me. Let's leave it at that. No more questions. We have to go."

Kali hurried to hug Tutu and the others in turn. "Thank you so much for your support." She paused in front of Will. "Watch over Jules and Tutu for me."

He nodded. "No problem."

She stooped to hug Hermione. "You, too."

And Hermione sat on Julie's foot.

Chapter 28

The Secret Team

THE HOUSE WAS eerily quiet after Maureen and Kali left. Julie stood staring out the front window while Will collapsed onto the sofa. He tilted his head back and exhaled heavily. "A few years ago, who could have imagined we would have so much trouble around us? This country has lost its Yankee Doodle."

Julie turned to face him. "You don't have to babysit me, you know. I have Hermione to let me know if anyone's around."

Will straightened. "I'm not babysitting, and I don't know what Hermione could do to deter a shooter."

"What could *you* do?" Her tone was sharp.

"I don't know. Step in the way?"

"Not a viable plan!"

He stood to confront her. "Why not?"

"Because there's no reason I'm more valuable than you, that's why."

Tutu interrupted before Will could answer. "I got a better plan. Clean up and change to clean clothes. I gonna introduce you to my backup team."

Will leaned on his knees. "You have a team?"

"Everybody I know who got a good heart is part of my team, but this group be special. We meet on Wednesday afternoons. Get changed and take Hermione out to do her business. Then she can come, too."

Tutu was wearing an expression that forbade further discussion, so Will shrugged for Julie's benefit and left for his house.

"How dressed up should I be?" asked Julie as she headed for her room.

Tutu patted Hermione's warm head. "Not dressed up. Just clean."

Will returned after several minutes, his hair wet and a smear of shaving cream forgotten beside his ear. Tutu reached up to wipe it away.

"So who is this team, Miss Kalani? Have I met them?" he asked, feeling young and foolish with her grooming him.

She shook her head. "Not yet. They're unexpected. That's what makes them special."

Julie emerged from the bathroom wearing a ponytail, a soft blue t-shirt, and workout pants. "Is this outfit okay?"

Tutu nodded. "I gonna tell you where to drive, Will. And thank you for helping." She hobbled to the front door.

Julie watched Will's pained expression as he let the dog into the back seat of his beloved restoration project again. Julie smiled up at him. "You need to buy practical transportation if you're going to help friends—a car that doesn't break your heart when it's used."

He sighed as he closed the door on her and the dog. "In my experience, loving always opens you up to heartbreak. It's the nature of the beast."

Tutu directed them in a circuitous route until Will asked if she knew where they were going.

"We been confounding the enemy," she told him without smiling. "And here we are."

"This is a church." Will turned into the parking lot of a gray stone Unitarian Universalist Church. Several cars were already parked, one so crazily that it occupied two painted spaces. "Miss Kalani, as much as I love you, I won't join a religious group for you."

The old woman waved a dismissive hand. "This just a place, Will. Not a compound." As he helped her out of the front seat, she smiled sweetly at him. "We meet in different locations. This be one. Smart, huh?"

He glanced at Julie who avoided eye contact. "Can Hermione come in?" she asked Tutu, who nodded.

"Yes, yes. I trust she housebroken or we gonna be doing some cleaning."

Julie made sure she had a firm grip on the leash and followed Tutu into a side entrance and down the stairs to the basement. There Tutu led them through a doorway into a room bright with neon light. Inside sat a long rectangular table surrounded by ladies of various sizes and races, all looking to be well over sixty-five. Their white or gray or lavender heads were all leaning toward the center of the table until Tutu and her friends entered. A wiry white-haired woman wearing jeans and a rock group t-shirt stood up.

"Kalani! We didn't think you were coming."

Tutu grinned and accepted help seating herself at the table. "Hello, Esra. I brought friends. These is good people, and we need help."

The women were instantly serious—including the pink-faced lady who had left her seat to nuzzle Hermione. "What can we do?"

Tutu pointed out each woman at the table. "This is Naomi and Agnes and Lakeisha and Rachel and Sharon and Esra and Mona. We got other members but we come as we can. We play cards, and when we needed, we be a team. And this," she pivoted enough to indicate Julie and Will to her group, "is Julie and Will and their dog Hermione."

The ladies said their hellos all at once, so Julie and Will could only smile and nod. "What are we doing here?" asked Will, abandoning courtesy.

Tutu shook her head and looked to her ladies for empathy. "Too impatient!" The ladies snickered as Tutu continued. "We generate positive energy. Don't bother about how, just believe me. We ain't got time to tell you, and you'd think it was silly, anyways. When we need more than energy, we do whatever gotta be done—protesting, taking people in to hide, donating time or food or money—whatever been needed. You can't just talk to make change; you gotta do something. We work to transform whatever or whoever can be lifted to a higher plane of unconditional love. That's how we help this ole world."

A higher plane of unconditional love! Will did his best not to scowl. He had painted a cartoonish cover for a cozy mystery novel that was not entirely unlike the scene before him.

The thin woman they now knew was named Esra stood up. Her voluminous white hair was pulled back into a single braid. Her brown eyes appeared huge behind her glasses. "We can see that look on your face, Will. You don't think a lot of old ladies can do anything. But the fact that we're old and female makes us nearly invisible, so we can do more than you think. We can do anything we dare. These are dark times. Kalani wouldn't have brought you to us if you didn't have good reason to understand how dark. Friends and neighbors we thought we knew have embraced negative influences. The people who want to be part of the light must stand together—even if we're forced to do it in secret." The other women applauded lightly and Esra sat down.

Will was edging toward the door. "Listen, I appreciate your sincerity and good hearts, but…"

Tutu interrupted. "Just wait, Will. We ain't trying to convince you of nothing. We ain't part of any one religion, and we wouldn't try to convert you if we was. You and Julie and I come here to get help—no strings attached." She turned her back on him to face the group as she went on to describe Julie's situation and the implied threat the detective had outlined. The women listened intently. A heavy very dark-skinned woman named Naomi spoke in a voice that sounded like warm homemade bread. Large white glasses framed the intensity in her gaze.

"As I see it, we need to send someone to learn as much as possible about Richard Teller. I don't know if we can determine if he has violent intentions, but we'll do our best to find out. I think we need someone white."

"I'll do it," volunteered Mona, a tall, curvaceous woman in stretch pants and a stylish blue knit top. Her short white hair had been cunningly designed and her makeup was impeccable, hinting she was a woman of resources. "I know a few things about real estate offices…and men." Several women tittered and Mona flashed a grin. "I may have to include my niece Zoe. She's both clever and gob-smackingly gorgeous." She focused on Julie. "I'll need to find out how committed your man is to loving you—how easily he can be drawn away and how invested he is in the belief that you tried to drown him. That will tell us something about how likely he is to want to hurt you. We'll find out if there's another woman in the background and what he has to gain financially by ending you. Are you sure you're okay with our investigation? You might not like the result."

Julie could feel something like an imaginary hairball forming in her stomach. "Knowing is better than guessing. I can't be afraid forever."

"Perfect!" Naomi jotted something in her notebook. "And we need a safe house for Kalani, Julie, Will and the dog in the meantime. Mona works fast, so it shouldn't take too long. Plan for a few days but don't be surprised if it takes longer."

Rachel, a small, pale woman whose thinning hair had been curled into a bob, raised one hand as she straightened her rimless glasses with the other. "They can use our cottage. It's by the ocean. Bernard liked his privacy, so it's walled in. Security drives by at uneven intervals. I'll tell them I'm sending guests."

Naomi looked satisfied. "Excellent. If anyone has any further suggestions, you know how to reach me. We'll set up a time and place for Rachel to give Kalani the keys and directions, and wait for Mona to reach a conclusion."

Lakeisha, a bronze-colored woman with closely cropped gray hair, had wandered to the window where she peeked out of the cotton curtains. "Is that your car, Will?"

"Yes."

"Honey, that won't do. You driving a classic. Nobody gonna forget seeing that. Even I could follow it through L.A."

Rachel sighed. "I'll loan them Bernard's Buick. It's navy and not showy. I just renewed the license. I'll keep Will's car closed in my garage."

"Thank you, Rach," said Naomi, making more notes.

"Does the cottage have cell service?" asked Julie, feeling conspicuous. "We have friends in trouble down at the border. I'd like to be able to check on them."

The women turned toward Tutu for elaboration. "It's my grand-daughter and her family done walked into a hornet's nest down there," she said, her pain in her expression, "but I think we already got a person who might help. They're citizens, you see, but evil and corruption hang out together. I ain't sure what anybody else could do. I'll let you know if we need another plan."

Naomi nodded solemn acknowledgement. "Turn your cells all the way off...especially the location...as much as possible as a precaution. Cells are relatively easy to track. We don't know how sophisticated your bad guys might be."

"Our cell service at the cottage is excellent due to the proximity of the tower," Rachel explained for Julie in her thin, weary voice. "You're welcome to use the desktop computer. The password is in the dictionary under 'interactive.' I keep the cupboards stocked just in case, but I'll warn you; I'm a vegetarian. The wine cooler is full and there's beer in the fridge. Use whatever you want."

"I'm not comfortable accepting all this," muttered Will at last. "Take care of Julie and Tutu. I can fend for myself."

"No!" Tutu scowled at him. "You promised to watch over us, and we gonna hold you to your promise. You're going with us."

"Then let us pay for what we use," he appealed to Naomi. He looked miserable, his male pride aching. "At least let me pay. I'm just the bodyguard."

Naomi rose to stand before him. "You can join the group of our younger members when this danger's past, if you choose. They'd give you options you could use to make a difference. Their work is unlike ours most of the time, since they must have the courage to make themselves be seen. And you can donate to humanitarian causes. We want you to become light. That's how you pay us. Kalani can explain to you why that's important for everybody. But for now, hurry home and pack a bag."

Will nodded. "It's a sneaky way to recruit members."

Tutu reached out to take his arm, her smile sweet. "All those times you drove me...you been a member of my team for years. You just didn't know it."

Chapter 29

A Dirty White Knight

"THAT'S HIM, UP ahead." Maureen exited the side road they had been following and headed for a turn-out where a sleek white Mercedes van was waiting. As they approached, the driver stepped out, came around to open a side door, and extended steps to the pavement. Maureen quickly checked her face in the mirror and drew a brush through her hair.

"Who the hell are we meeting?" asked Kali, watching Maureen as she pulled off her over-sized t-shirt, revealing a black top that flattered her cleavage.

"His name is George Bentley, but you have to forget that name."

"THE George Bentley, zillionaire buddy to the administration? Rini, he's one of *them*. Rumor is he's as dirty as anyone."

Maureen applied lipstick before she answered. "When you're playing with the kinds of people who'll happily scar innocent children's minds for life, you can't play clean and win. G.B. always wins, but you can't ask him how. Trust me; we don't want to know." She climbed out of the car. Kali followed behind her, the blistering Texas sun sucking moisture from her skin.

The driver of the van, a muscular young Titan wearing jeans and a white t-shirt that showcased his immense chest, offered a hand to assist the women into the interior. Maureen accepted. As soon as Kali had entered, the driver retracted the steps and closed the door, encasing them in the cool shadows of the interior—one not unlike a private jet. Pale tan leather softened all the hard surfaces. Kali tensed.

The shape of a man stood to greet them—a tall man wearing a pale gray short-sleeved open-necked dress shirt and dark slacks. The rugged lines of his carefully tanned face contrasted with the refinement of his clothes, being better suited to a movie hitman or western hero. His light brown hair had been meticulously trimmed. He drew off his designer glasses and extended his arms. "Maureen."

She stepped into his embrace and they shared the kiss of a love long abandoned but never dead. Kali looked down politely.

"This is my…G.B.," supplied Maureen after she took a moment to recompose herself. The blush in her face extended down her cleavage. "G.B., this is Kali Ramirez."

"Please, ladies, have a seat. May I make you a drink?" His voice rumbled low, like the sound of a distant storm threatening either relief or disaster. He was a man who knew how to use his magnetic presence to best advantage in any situation. Kali thought she had never met anyone as perilous to approach.

"Yes, please. I'm dehydrating." Kali situated herself on a plush leather sofa. "But nothing alcoholic. I have to get my daughter and husband back as soon as possible. I may need my wits."

"Iced tea then?"

"Yes, thank you."

"And Maureen?"

"Yes, iced tea, please."

He opened a small refrigerator located in the upholstery and removed an artful blue glass pitcher filled with a liquid that made the glass seem green. He took the glasses from a hidden cupboard. "Maureen has told me your story, Kali—may I call you that?"

"Yes, of course."

"I assume you brought their passports?" He placed the drinks on the table between the women.

"Yes." She pulled the zipper on her backpack and tugged the passports free. "My husband is a naturalized citizen and Lila was born in California. I don't know how they can be legally detained, but the law has been pretty rubbery lately. Daniel's in the database." G.B. took the documents from her, and when she encountered his deep blue eyes up close, she could understand Maureen's kiss. Something about him was disturbingly intimate. She picked up her glass and began to sip, mentally scolding herself that the blue of his eyes was probably from contacts. She was being seduced by staging. Exactly how vulnerable was Maureen?

He seated himself in a large recliner. "I have always enjoyed the people and sights of Hawaii. I find both beautiful."

Kali shifted on her seat. "I was born in California."

He might have chuckled, but Maureen spoke up. "Can you do it, G.B.? Can you make the bastards bring them out?"

He smiled. His teeth were unnaturally white. "I've made…inquiries. It seems your family doesn't go quietly, Kali."

"What do you mean?"

"I'll let them tell you. I access stories no one else will ever hear. I can't afford to be as altruistic as Maureen. I have friends and business contacts no one admires. But that allows me leeway to get jobs done. Maureen tells me you plan to go ahead and cross the border once your family is reunited. May I suggest you reconsider that choice?"

"Why?"

"Let's say the disgruntled, the criminal, and the desperate on the other side have made travel there hazardous at best recently. Activities on this side have enflamed their emotions. You might want to take your daughter as far from the border as you can manage."

Maureen finished her tea and placed the glass back on the table. "Do you need me to step in as the attorney? I brought court clothes."

"I prefer this casual look." He smiled. His meaning was clear. "But no, I don't think we'll need your dazzling lawyer-speak today. I'm playing that game myself and doing all I can to circumvent the courts. If I fail, Kali, you won't see your loved ones for some time. Court dates don't arrive quickly around here—not for anyone who fits in with the immigrants. I've made arrangements to help officials forget the altercation that involved your husband—listed as being initiated by him, regardless of the facts. It took more persuasion to locate your daughter. She's quite as spunky as her military mother and, most likely, just as attractive. I think we've arrived to remove her at a very opportune time. She was very nearly lost in the crowd. The lack of record-keeping here defies comprehension."

Kali shrank back into the softness of the seat, feeling her rising body heat searing the leather. Her imagination was fully as merciless as her occasional flashes of PTSD. Beautiful little Lila was vulnerable to people intoxicated with domination. She tried not to think about what that might mean. She wished she didn't know how inhumane conditions were in detention. What could be more aggravating to parents than a leering enemy you couldn't physically fight? Her frustration simmered next door to rage. For once she was relieved she didn't carry the M16 she had once wielded. She wasn't at all sure she could prevent herself from using it.

G.B. continued. "Zack will give you directions to a nice little eatery in El Paso—nothing gourmet but the food is sufficiently edible and the place doesn't stick out. If all goes well, we'll drop off your husband and daughter there as quickly as possible, and you'd be wise to return to California as directly as you can. My influence has limits."

He rose, a dismissal, and Maureen did the same. "Thank you, G.B."

His lips curved into a smile that might have been suggestive. "Perhaps now we're even?"

"Yes," she offered a hand and he accepted it, holding it a little longer than necessary. "We are," she agreed. "Happy ending. Give my regards to your wife."

He chuckled. "Ah, Maureen. I won't be able to do that. I'm supposedly playing golf at the moment."

"Yes, of course."

He offered his hand to Kali. "Best of luck, Kali. You've earned far better than you've received after your military service, but then, that's the story for most vets, isn't it? Maureen will tell you about my company in Hawaii. I think it'll be the best fit. My head of HR says we have a position there where we could use a person with your husband's skills. I had my staff research his work history, and I want him on my team. He'll be a valuable asset. You may apply to the company, as well, if there's a position that appeals to you. Say I recommended you. HR will make it so. I don't know much beyond your military record, but from what Maureen has told me, I suspect you'd excel at whatever you decide to accomplish."

Kali studied him. She would probably never again be so close to someone with as much raw social clout as she was in this moment, and she was glad. Power was a toxic perfume—a flower if sniffed too deeply, deadly to the soul. If there was an *'e'epa*, power was it. "I'm in your debt."

He released her hand. "You fought for this country. You've paid your way."

When they were back in the normalcy of Maureen's car, Kali released a sigh. "God, that was overwhelming. I've never seen anything like it. He exudes wealth and command from his pores. Is he real? Will he help us? Is he all talk or is this going to happen?"

Maureen nodded. "I don't doubt it will. He's not one hundred percent honest with everyone, but he won't lie to me."

"You were important to one another at one time?"

"At one time."

"You don't want to talk about it?"

"No."

"Okay." They rode in silence for a few minutes. "I can't believe you could walk away from him. He's a force. And a great kisser as far as I could see. He could do a lot of good if he wanted to, couldn't he?"

Maureen kept her eyes on the road. "He does a lot of good. It's just that not everything he does qualifies."

Kali nodded her understanding. "He's pretty full of himself. Was he always seduced by his own influence?"

Irritated lines wrinkled the space between Maureen's eyebrows. "You ask a lot of questions for someone who wasn't going to talk about him."

"I'm distracting myself."

Maureen exhaled a disgusted little sigh. "He had a head start from his mother, then he worked hard to build the networks he has. Mostly he skirts legal trouble. But he can't use publicity about something like this. Too hot politically. It doesn't fit his profile and would cause him untold issues. So I hope you forget him."

Kali's mouth bent into a wicked smile. "But you won't, will you?"

Maureen glanced at her passenger. "Probably not. But that was a finale you just witnessed. No more acts to come. Neither of us can afford it."

The diner/bar was tucked into a strip mall, nestled behind café curtains and neon beer signs. Maureen pulled into a parking space in front and shut the car off. "Are you hungry?"

Kali frowned. "I can't eat until I know Lila's safe. I'd be sick."

Maureen turned in her seat so she could see Kali more clearly. "You might as well put something in your stomach. No matter how powerful G.B. is, getting your family out of that hell hole is going to take some time. Adults and children are kept separately. I've heard they give people numbers..."

"...Like the Nazis, only not that organized." Kali opened the door, allowing a wave of hot air into the car. "I can't eat. I can't sit. I can't even think straight." She wiped a tear from her cheek. "Do you know they don't normally let legislators in to see how those children are being treated? What are they hiding? What are they doing to Lila! Bentley said Daniel was in an altercation. There aren't many reasons a man like Daniel will fight. He's the most pacifist guy I've ever met. What did they do to him or what did he see them do to Lila?"

Maureen's attitude softened. "Take a deep breath. You're getting yourself all worked up about offenses you've imagined when there isn't a damned thing you can do to help right now. Lila's going to need you to be comforting...and Daniel probably will, too...so calm yourself. Be the oasis. They'll know if you're pretending."

Kali drew a breath, felt it shatter in her chest, and exhaled the jagged pieces. "You're right. I need to dump adrenalin. I have to move. Do you think I'd attract too much attention if I went through my *kata* over here on the dead grass?"

"You mean your martial arts stuff?"

"Yes."

Maureen rolled her eyes. "Kali, you know the answer. This is Texas and you're black. For heaven's sake don't look scary. We're trying to be invisible."

Kali exhaled another broken breath. "Then I'll just walk around."

"Oh, that won't look weird—you pacing up and down the sidewalk like a caged lion." Maureen picked up her handbag and opened her door. "I'm starving, I'm sweaty, and I need to unglue myself from this car. Hopefully, Daniel will bring his car, so I'll have to drive this one back home—in which case, I need to use the restroom and super-charge myself with caffeine. I figure Daniel and Lila will be hungry when they get here—I heard the meals in that facility have caused constipation that was medically harmful—nothing but bologna sandwiches morning and night. Daniel won't have had time to get constipated, but I doubt he'll reject a decent meal. If you can guess what he and Lila would like, we can order a to-go bag. I'm sure he'll be anxious to put distance between him and this town. I sure as hell would be! In fact, I am. Are you still going to head into Mexico?"

Kali rubbed a hand across her forehead in an attempt to wipe away images she couldn't prevent forming. "I'll see what Daniel says, but I've had my fill of American family values, so I'm ready to do what he asked. Banditos are nothing next to these thugs. Them I can fight."

Maureen's skepticism played across her mouth, but she didn't argue. "We're going to need supplies regardless of which direction you choose, so how about we go inside, eat something, and pick up some take-out boxes?" She climbed out of the car and closed the door, emitting a melodramatic sigh as Kali followed suit. "Thank God! I have to pee."

Hours passed during which they ordered a series of snacks inside the restaurant to mollify the owner, a stout woman who glared at them from behind the counter. They were sitting staring at a pile of takeout boxes when the white van finally drove up.

"They're here!" announced Maureen, but Kali was already heading out the door. She bolted up the van steps the beefy driver hurried to extend.

"*Mommy!*" shrieked Lila, leaping into Kali's arms. "*Mommy, Mommy, Mommy!*" Tears were streaming down her face. "Oh,

Mommy, I knew you'd come! I knew it! I told the other girls. I knew it!"

Kali held her close, aware of the stench that clung to her daughter. A voice from far away in her brain warned that Lila probably had lice. The thought only fueled her smoldering fury. "It's okay, Sweetheart. You're okay now."

"Mommy, they hurt Daddy and this guy was going to hurt me but I kicked him like you showed me and bit him and hung onto his leg and screamed until somebody came. He made me get a shot. Then I threw up on him."

"Well, it's all over now." Kali was searching the chilly shadows for Daniel. She found him lying nearly prone on a recliner seat. His face was swollen and his eyes glassy. *"Oh my god,"* she whispered.

He tried to respond to her, but his words fell from his mouth, slack and almost unintelligible. "...Love you."

She lowered Lila, noticing the red handprint on the side of her face for the first time. Maureen stepped forward to hug Lila against her as Kali knelt beside her husband. George Bentley was speaking. "They beat him up pretty badly. They're calling it resisting arrest. A couple goons jumped him—probably to kidnap Lila for trafficking. There's a lot of money changing hands that way. By the time Border Patrol was on scene, he couldn't talk well to tell them he was a citizen, and they didn't really care. They aren't famous for applying compassion or justice when it comes to minorities. They believed the goons who said he had entered the country illegally and tried to hide by blending in with people crossing the other way. Even in the detention center no one checked to see if he was telling the truth. He needs a hospital. I've had him added to the employee rolls of my umbrella corporation, and I'll cover his medical costs until the insurance goes into effect. I'm giving a card to Maureen with the name of my head of HR. I told him you'd be calling soon. He'll handle everything at the hospital intake. He's a wizard."

Kali took Daniel's hand in hers. "When they took Lila, I fought." His words were slurred. Kali leaned over to kiss his tortured lips.

Bentley's voice was gentle. "He shouldn't be moved more than necessary until he's been assessed, so we'll transport him to the hospital. Then I have to go, so Maureen, why don't you bring Lila in your car and Kali can stay here with her husband? Daniel's car seems to have disappeared."

"Sure." Kali could hear them kissing again before she heard Maureen's soft tone. "Thanks, G.B. I didn't mean for you to have to do so much."

"I'm sorry I needed to. But it was worthwhile. You're an extraordinary woman, Rini. I never should've let you go."

Maureen bent to Lila. "Come on, cute stuff. We'll drive together in my car and you can tell me all about it, while your mom takes care of your dad."

"You have tears in your eyes, Maureen," observed Lila flatly.

"It happens sometimes."

Chapter 30

Ongoing Therapy

LILA WAS ASLEEP against Maureen on one of the hospital couches when Kali emerged from a hallway. She sat beside Maureen, keeping her voice low.

"They're going to keep Daniel overnight. They say he may need ongoing therapy. They did a cat scan and an MRI. They're treating a small brain bleed in addition to his abrasions. They say it's lucky he was in such good shape." She paused to breathe. "I've never been seen this fast in an ER. You certainly get better treatment when someone powerful is behind you."

Maureen nodded. "Yes, you do."

"One call from G.B.'s HR guy, and they acted like I was donating a wing to the hospital. Maybe G.B. is!" Kali sighed. "I'd like to stay with Daniel tonight, if you don't mind."

Maureen made a face. "Why should I mind? I'll get a hotel for Lila and me. But first I think I'll pick up some new clothes for her. Her backpack is missing with the car. Can she shower by herself?"

"Yes."

"I'll stop at the pharmacy to see what they recommend for lice."

Kali touched Maureen's arm. "Oh, Rini. It's not fair for me to ask so much of you."

"I'm not complaining. I love this little widget. After all the time I spent caring for my mother, caring for an adorable little girl is refreshing. I'm honored you'd trust me with her. Plus, I'm not sorry I'll have a chance to get some rest. This has been an exhausting, emotional day. Tomorrow when they release Daniel, we'll get going. The nurse said we need to keep him as peaceful as possible—probably for a few weeks. Even if your car shows up, I don't think you're going to be able to go to Mexico, if that was still on the table."

Kali shook her head slowly. "No. Not possible. The drive to Guadalajara is too strenuous and I wouldn't be able to tend him and drive at the same time." She sighed again. "I don't really want to live in Mexico. I used to be proud of this country. I was willing to die for it. I don't know how it changed so fast. The conflicts set off my PTSD. Why can't people live with one another without going ballistic?"

Maureen sighed. "Human nature, I guess."

"I hope not." Kali rubbed her hands over her face. "I don't even want to visit in Mexico. Daniel's mother is sweet, but her house is chaos all the time with cousins running in and out, and the ranch is worse. We don't have what it would take to build a new house—physically or emotionally. I need a break from chaos, and so does Daniel—especially now. Hawaii sounds like heaven. The HR guy said there's no rush for us to get there. Daniel's job will wait. I can't believe what godsends you and G.B. are."

Maureen stroked Lila's hair, casually looking for evidence of lice. "We'll go to my condo while Daniel recuperates, if that's okay with you. Julie, Tutu, and Will are staying with one of Tutu's friends until they can determine if Julie's still in danger. It's probably best if we avoid Tutu's house, too—just in case. My condo has security and I have plenty of room. When Daniel's well enough to return to work, we can help you relocate."

Kali squeezed her hand. "Thank you. Rini, I can't believe we've been friends for such a short time. You've saved our lives twice."

Maureen smiled. "Hey, you fought for my brother and went to his wedding. We're bonded—family, like Tutu said. Ties stronger than blood."

Lila stirred and Kali touched her awake.

"Baby, I'm going to stay here in the hospital with Daddy just for tonight. Tomorrow we're going to leave this place forever—you, me, Daddy, and Maureen. So can you be a very good, brave girl and stay in a hotel with Rini tonight?"

Lila pushed her lower lip out. "I want to be with you, Mommy. I'm scared. They might come and get me. They were bad, Mommy. Very bad. All the kids were scared. They were too scared to cry, cuz when they did, they got shots or hit or yelled at. The woman took Monkey and threw him away!"

"I know, Baby, but Daddy is hurt and needs me. Rini won't let anyone get you."

Lila turned a skeptical eye toward Maureen. "Can I sleep in the bed with you? I don't want to be alone."

Maureen nodded. "Yup. And we can buy new clothes and have ice cream and watch TV. And we'll take a shower and get rid of your itches."

"...And buy a new monkey."

"We'll do our best."

Lila sighed heavily. "Okay then. I'll stay with you every minute, Rini. Every, every minute. You can keep the *'e'epas* away, can't you?"

Maureen glanced at Kali who shrugged. "I'll shoo them off."

Lila slid to her feet. "Tutu says you have to love them away."

"Then you'll be safe, because I'll love you super hard."

Kali smiled. "Me, too. I love you, Baby." She stooped down to hug and kiss her daughter. "I'm proud of you. Daddy is, too. You've been a very big girl."

"But I didn't like it." Lila took Maureen's hand. Her eyes were wide with terror bigger than her life was long. "Watch out, Mommy. *Don't let them take you!*"

* * *

Back in California, Julie came to sit beside Tutu and Will on a bench facing the ocean. The feel of the sand beneath her bare feet sent shivers of wildness up her bloodstream along with an urge to dive into the surf. What would it be like to actually be a mermaid, slipping beneath the cool green surface, away from noise and guns and irrational people...kin to dolphins and whales and otters? A part of her yearned for the chance, was desperate for the chance. Hermione seemed to sense her frustration and reacted by chasing the waves and barking at the ones that threatened her space.

"Kali called," Julie told the others, watching them turn toward her, their anxiety in their faces. "Daniel and Lila are safe."

"*Thank God!*" breathed Tutu, closing her eyes. "Thank you, thank you, God!"

"But thugs beat up Daniel. He fought them when they tried to take Lila away from him. He thinks they were sex traffickers. When the border patrol came, they believed the thugs instead of Daniel. They arrested him and took Lila to the children's facility. There was a mix-up of some sort. Kali wasn't real clear."

Will stood up. "How bad is he?"

"Bad. He's in a hospital overnight. He has a severe concussion and other injuries. He, Kali, and Lila are going to live with Maureen for a while when they get back. The good news is Daniel has a job in Hawaii that will wait for him to heal and provide health insurance in the meantime...all through some friend of Maureen's."

Tutu seemed to be humming as she opened her rheumy eyes. "I sense them. He got a good job. But he gonna mend slow." She stared out into the sky above the water. "Lila's spirit got wounded, like his. They're gonna need time and love to be whole again."

Will angrily kicked sand ahead of him and Hermione leaped at it. "Why does this kind of shit have to happen to good people? Why did your 'e'epas have to come from wherever they came from, Miss Kalani?"

The old woman accepted his frustration as an honest question. "In Hawaii when I chanted, I got a vision of the great Kahuna. He told me the Earth going through a transition, and the war between good and evil be at its peak—in this country, everywhere. The evil feed on human misery. Only unconditional love can defeat it. When greed eat men's honor, everybody be weakened. The insect people saw what was and knew they could send the 'e'epas to weaken people more—to set them on one another in jealousy and prejudice."

"What do they have to gain?" asked Julie. "Or are they just mean?"

"My grandmother tole me the insect people got no creativity. They come to steal from humans. I don't know much about that part. She didn't explain. I was a poor student then—too impatient."

Julie stared at the relentless waves, feeling their rhythm and their sound. Her shoulder was aching. She had an idea she needed sea water around her—not chlorinated Vegas pool water but the real thing—the great salt sea that had nurtured first life. "I wonder if I could go swimming," she said aloud, abruptly changing the subject. "Do you think there are rip tides here?"

"God, do you know what's in that water!" sputtered Will. "Nuclear waste from Japan and garbage and whale shit! You don't want that in your wound or anywhere. And, yeah, there sure as hell could be rip tides."

His clumsy attempt to protect her made her smile. "Maybe tomorrow. Maybe I'll try swimming tomorrow. A mermaid can't survive without water."

Tutu nodded solemnly. "Water got power. Being here been feeding me."

Will wasn't pacified by Tutu's calm. "We're hiding out here while your friend and her niece spy on Richard who may or may not be planning to kill us. Kali's husband was beaten to a pulp worse than Patrick was. God knows what happened to Lila in that kiddie prison. And we're talking about insect people and powers in water?" He threw his hands in the air. "I'm going back to the cabin to cook dinner. This is too much for me. Come on, Hermione."

When he was out of earshot, Tutu looked at Julie and smiled. "He a good man."

Julie shrugged. "I suppose so." She shifted uncomfortably on the bench. "Tutu, I don't understand what happened to Richard. He used to be so caring. I was certain he loved me. I was certain I loved him. Now I'm not certain about anything."

Tutu rested her soft, boney hand on Julie's. "I know you don't believe me, but I think your man got infected. When he talk about the insect people in his dream, I think he remembering they was the ones who saved him from the water. You saw he was dead and you had it right, but they could bring him back. They got technologies we don't understand. They made him think his memory been a dream and they sent him back filled with *'e'epas* to infect others.

217

These days the haters try to spread their misery like sickness. Why? Haters don't know why. They know only that they hate. They burn with anger. They sure they right even when they bring darkness to they own families."

"Can Richard be...uninfected? Is there a way to purge their influence?"

Tutu rubbed her eyes. "I know only love—especially when people be brave and share love together. But in some the hate rise so strong it be a barrier. Love bounce off. Come back to the cabin. Rest your mind. Feel the love of your friends. Let yourself reach a higher level. That defense you gonna need one day."

* * *

A burly hospital orderly in green scrubs pushed Daniel's wheelchair down the ramp to Maureen's car. Daniel sat upright, looking appreciably improved since the day before. Kali walked beside him, holding a hospital bag of odds and ends. Dark circles underscored her eyes.

"Mommy! Daddy!" squealed Lila, bounding from the car into her mother's arms. "I have new clothes, car play stuff, a dinosaur that's *better* than a monkey, and Rini got me a car seat! But she didn't know how to fix my braids."

Kali hugged her. "That's fine, Baby. We'll let your hair do what it wants today. But I have a big favor to ask. I need you to sit very quietly in the back seat with Daddy all day and tell me in a whisper if you think he needs anything. It's an important job. Okay?"

Lila nodded, instantly grave. She leaned over the side of the wheelchair to kiss her father delicately on the cheek. "I'm sorry you're hurt, Daddy."

"Is okay, *hija*. I will mend." He did his best to smile as he reached out to stroke her head. "Daddy loves you. I'm sorry you had a scary time."

Tears ran down Lila's face, but she made no sound. "I love you, Daddy," she whispered.

Maureen fastened Lila into her new car seat while the muscular orderly helped Daniel into the back on the other side and clicked his seatbelt for him. Kali lowered the shade Maureen had attached to his window with suction cups.

"Just let me know if the air con is too high or too low," Maureen told him when she came around the car to get in. "And don't be shy about telling me if you need to stop to take a break. Boy, am I glad to see you looking better."

His lips moved in what was meant to be a smile. "I have pain meds now. All is much better."

Kali extended a hand to the orderly as she met his gaze directly. "Thank you, Adolfo. I appreciate your help and kindness."

The huge Hispanic man shook her hand. "My pleasure. Good luck, Mrs. Ramirez. Don't take this wrong, but I hope I never see any of your family here again."

She nodded. "We don't intend to pass this way again...ever."

He stood for a moment, chewing on his thought. "Nobody intends to be in trouble. It lies in wait like a *chupacabra* tracking livestock." He gestured toward Maureen. "Your friend, she knows." He was smiling as he watched until Kali was settled in the front seat. He closed her door and waved as Maureen drove the car away.

"We must attract weird," muttered Kali, but Maureen didn't reply.

Chapter 31

A Worthwhile Experiment

RICHARD STOOD IN front of the mirror in the bathroom, inspecting his damaged face. The plastic surgeon had talked about skin grafts if he didn't finish healing properly. He had suffered some infection from the water that complicated everything. Skin grafts sounded like pain—and sitting in waiting rooms and extra bills and lots more hurting. But it would be worth it to get rid of this angry, ugly guy who was staring at him. Funny--but not ha-ha funny--to not recognize yourself in a mirror. It made you feel replaced, like Burned Guy had taken over and was running the show. Who was he, anyway?

People at the funeral for his mother and Al had stared. Not nice stares. You-look-terrible stares. They expected the same old football hero Richard they were used to, but he was hidden. They said it wasn't so bad, but they were lying. It was so bad. You could tell because they looked away real quick when you caught them staring. Some people who should've didn't even recognize him. Dolly What's-Her-Name was the only woman hitting on him hard. The bottom of Dad's barrel.

His phone rang. He didn't want to talk to anybody, but it could be the branch office in Rosewood. They were trying to juggle the business until the main office was cleared of vestiges of the murders, remodeled, and re-staffed. The phone kept ringing. Unknown name. Unknown number. Probably a robo-call. Get rid of them.

"Hello?" Be sure to answer only once and hang up. Twice and you'll hear from the computer again.

"Richard Teller?" The voice was not salesman-charming.

"Yeah."

"I represent people who were not paid because Little Paulie was killed in your office. But, Mr. Teller, we don't accept nonpayment. He owed us and now you owe us. It's only fair."

Richard felt a chill. "What if I don't know what you're talking about?"

"That would be unfortunate, Mr. Teller. We would have to remind you of your family obligations. Most people don't appreciate our reminders. They make the hurt of your burns feel good in comparison."

"Who's Little Paulie?"

The man on the other end laughed without mirth. "I'm sure Detective Rainey explained that to you, Mr. Teller, as if you didn't already know. Please don't insult our intelligence."

Richard blanched as the man cited the amount he expected and where Richard was to deliver it.

"That's too much. My mother's dead and I don't owe for whatever this Paulie guy borrowed."

"In cash, Mr. Teller. This afternoon. Then we forget about you. If you don't pay your debts, we collect. It's business. You understand." The man clicked off.

"Sonuvabitch!" shouted Rich to the empty house. "Sonuvabitch!"

* * *

Mona and her niece Zoe were waiting at the cabin when Tutu, Julie, and Will returned from their morning walk. Hermione bounced behind them. They crowded into the living room, trying to interpret Mona's expression without being too obvious. Tutu handled the casual greetings. She was interrupted by Julie, her need to know swelling until she could bear the pressure no longer. "Well? What did you learn?"

Mona shrugged. Her chic white hair and white slacks outfit gave her the aspect of a celestial messenger. "Your Richard Teller isn't easy to read, and he wasn't available most of the time. He has plenty of financial reasons to want you dead; I learned that much. He's definitely ambitious. Your property in Eden could be part of an exclusive new development. Owners are negotiating like mad. If he could get your rights, he could make a large profit that would give him leverage with his other projects. But whether his intention is to hurry your demise along, I couldn't say with any confidence."

Zoe nodded, rubbing Hermione's head. "He appreciates attractive women. He was more than open to my flirting. I think he needs to bolster his ego now that his face is temporarily disfigured." She ran her hand through her abundant blonde hair, pushing it behind her shoulder. "We might easily have slipped into a relationship, but what that means for you, I'm not sure. He can be very attractive and even thoughtful. He certainly isn't celibate or hasn't been in the past, but does that mean he doesn't love you or never did? I'm sorry; I don't know. I didn't want to fake a relationship to find out. I have my own life to live."

"Yes, yes, of course." Julie tried with little success to disguise her disappointment. "There's only one person who can determine once and for all what he's thinking, and that's me. I can't spend my life hiding out and making the people around me fear for their lives. I have to face him."

Will dropped onto the sofa. "I don't think that's a good idea, Jules."

"I won't go alone. When Rini gets back, we'll set up a meeting. We have to, anyway, to discuss the divorce, if that's what's going to happen."

Tutu hobbled over to lay a hand on Julie's arm. "I gonna teach you how to surround yourself with light and love, to raise your vibration. Then you can't be infected. You gonna see your choices better."

Will slammed his fist onto the arm of the sofa forcefully enough to send dust motes into the air. "Dammit, Jules, if he wants to hurt you, light isn't going to save you. Neither is Maureen. Let me go with you. I'm not a karate warrior, but I can slow him down."

Julie made a dismissive sound. "You'll set him off. He's already jealous of you."

Will didn't reply, but his brows furrowed.

"I'm sorry we couldn't do more to help," said Mona heading for the door. "Teller isn't dumb enough to be transparent. At least you know you married a man with some smarts. How he's prepared to use them is the mystery."

"Yeah," added Zoe as she slipped on her designer sunglasses. "Good luck."

When they had gone, Julie pulled out her cell phone and tapped in a number. "I'll see how Rini wants to proceed."

Will's expression left his face lined and shadowed. "Let me know when they're back and settled. I want to get Kali's take on all this. She could go with you. Surely the asshole isn't threatened by her the way he's threatened by me."

Julie sighed. "I wouldn't be too confident." She jerked her attention to the phone. "Hi, Rini. How is everyone?"

Will could hear a woman talking on the other end of the connection. Julie nodded periodically as though Maureen would see through the phone and finally replied. "Yes, I understand. Why don't you call me in a few days when you've had a chance to recuperate a little?"

The female voice said something else.

"Okay. Give Kali and Lila big hugs from me. I'll tell Tutu. Take care. Goodbye."

"What you gonna tell Tutu?" asked the elderly woman, currently seated on the sofa.

Julie sat beside her. "They're nearing Maureen's condo. Everyone's exhausted, especially Daniel. The hospital told them it'll be at least six weeks before he'll be strong enough to relocate. Hopefully, that'll give them time to sell their property by Eden or at least finish the paperwork and get Patrick to scout out homes on the big island. They want you to move there with them."

Tutu nodded, as though she had been waiting for the invitation. "Yes, yes, of course yes. I'm sorry, Julie, but I belong with Kali and Lila...in the home of my ancestors. Native peoples hold they honor dear. We gonna be safer there." She smiled a wide smile of relief. "I dreamed of finishing my life in Hawaii, but I never thought it was gonna be possible. I can help Daniel regain his power and Lila drive away the demons that got attached to her."

"Demons?" Julie could feel Will's scowl behind her as she asked.

Tutu chuckled. "Only an expression. But not exactly wrong. Lots of people is infected, like I said. The ones who seem darker. The ones who disappoint you—who can't hear truth even when somebody say it straight to them. Many got infected."

"We need a vaccine," muttered Will insincerely.

Tutu ignored his sarcasm. "The cure gotta come from within. We gotta love them hard and then harder. We gotta do our best to support when they do good. Change is a choice, an act of will. It start with humility. It require empathy. It lean on bravery. That's the reason them as can change deserve respect. "She reached out to touch Julie's hand. "To make support like that be your job. I can't see if it gonna work. Much gonna depend on the character of this man you married."

Will threw up his hands. "And you might get yourself killed, but you'll finally know if the creep can be redeemed. Oh hell yeah. That's a worthwhile experiment."

Tutu struggled to rise so Will offered her a hand that she accepted. When she was vertical, she stared into his eyes. "You, Will Manning, gotta take care. You a good man, but when you spend so much time looking into the shadows, you open yourself to…"

"Yeah, I know, the *'e'epas*."

She didn't release her stare. "Goodness needs fed. When you look around you and all seem hopeless, when you feel deep anger that won't go away, when you ain't got nothing positive to think or do, you'll know you got infected. Then you gonna need your friends to remind you of the man you lost inside you." She hobbled toward the kitchen, paused and turned. "I tell you both these things because once I'm in Hawaii, you gonna need to fend for yourselves. Only when I reach the other side of life will I be able to lend you extra energy and even then the task gonna be your own. Free will come with responsibility."

"We'll be fine," assured Julie, wishing Will wasn't wearing his skepticism so plainly. He kept setting Tutu off.

"I'll make lunch," he mumbled, motioning for Hermione to follow. "Then we'll all feed our goodness."

Tutu didn't react, but Julie shook her head.

* * *

Maureen's condo smelled of paint. The appliances gleamed, throwing vague reflections across the shiny ceramic tile floor. The newness of the renovations subtracted any charm the spaces might once have boasted, replacing it with the kind of trendy all-white style envied in magazine photographs. Only Teeny who came sliding across the tiles to greet them brought the warmth of home.

"Awful, isn't it?" said Maureen, looking around. "I'm glad you're joining me here. My mother used to read a poem to me about a 'heap o' livin' and that's what this place needs to be bearable. I'm not sure the mouse holes and crooked drawers weren't better."

"It's lovely, Rini," assured Kali as she helped Daniel to an upholstered chair in the living room. "Your windows are spectacular."

Maureen stood for a moment, assessing the afternoon light projecting designs across the room. "That was my reason for buying this one. I crave sunshine. And the view isn't great, but it's nicer than most."

Lila had already seized Teeny who had decided even being captive to a little girl was preferable to being alone. He sighed his resignation.

"This way." Maureen led Kali down the hall. "I'm putting you and Daniel in the guest room. It has an en-suite and a queen-sized bed. I'll need to find the sheets for it. I haven't used it yet. Let me know how you like the pillows. I tried a kind with cubed temperature-sensitive stuff inside to mold to your head. They're supposed to be fabulous. I'm glad I insisted on buying three bedrooms. Lila can use the sofa bed in the office. I used it before I had the master set up, and it's not bad."

"We'll pay you," said Kali in a soft voice. "Come up with a figure for rent, and we'll pay it."

Maureen waved a dismissive gesture. "Nonsense. We're family—remember? Tutu adopted me, and I'm not letting you out of it. Help me shop for groceries and cook and we're done."

Kali looked distressed. "We can go to Tutu's house. I'm sure the detective was over-reacting."

Maureen stopped, her hands on her hips. "Really? You're going to drag Daniel up and down those backyard steps? I don't think so. Tutu will understand. She doesn't go up and down those steps, either."

"She's nearly a hundred years old."

Maureen opened a cupboard and pulled out a stack of sheets and a couple blankets. "And I feel like I am. It's okay to take when it makes sense, Kali. It's the least I can do after what you did for Pat. It all works out."

Kali tugged Maureen into the bedroom and closed the door. "What are you going to owe your rich friend for his help?"

"G.B.? Nothing. I helped him stay out of prison—which required my taking massive risks with my career. It wasn't a small favor. He promised to repay me one day. This was it."

"He's spending a lot of money on us."

"He has a lot of money." Maureen tossed the bedding onto the cheerful quilt covering the bed. "Listen, Kali. G.B. and I were in love...or maybe in lust...probably always will be. It was intense. But I'm empathetic and he's pretty much narcissistic. *No bueno.* We're toxic together. Like Jules and her crazy guy, I'm guessing. G.B. offered to finance a running affair—in exotic climes, as they say, but that's not my style. I deserve 100% and he's married now. I helped him dig up his benevolent side so he could like himself again. He'd fallen into emotional disrepair from having too much. In return, he helped me feel like a human being who matters. So he'll always be grateful and so will I and someday we'll get busy living apart and stop yearning for one another. Okay?"

"Okay." Kali hugged her friend. "Thanks, Rini."

Maureen smiled. "I'm not kidding when I say I'm glad for your company. I'm not used to being alone again yet. And I'm going to need good cheer when I come home from negotiating a divorce for Jules. Talk about emotional disrepair..."

"We'll be here."

Chapter 32

Of Course You Believe

"WHAT DO YOU mean you're meeting Rich this afternoon?" Maureen followed Julie up the hallway in Tutu's house to the room with brightly colored fish painted on the door.

"Just what I said. There's only one way to straighten out this sneaking around mess, and I'm it. I'll look him in the eye and ask him what his intentions are. He sounded okay on the phone."

"And if he's trying to get you alone to kill you?"

Julie shrugged. "We won't be alone. We're meeting in an authentic Irish pub—in a closed booth so he doesn't have to endure the stares. His face is still pretty sore-looking."

"You could've let me know your plans." Maureen watched her lay out an outfit on her bed. "What does Will say about this?"

"He thinks I'm nuts to consider a meeting. I wouldn't be surprised if he'd decide to play spy and follow me. I'm not telling him, just in case."

Maureen's voice fell low. "Don't make fun of him for caring about you."

"I'm not making fun of him. But Rich is my husband. I love him. Maybe as he heals, he's seeing the world differently. He was never as hateful as his mother and brother. We used to laugh at them together. I have to give him a chance to recover himself." She turned to face Maureen. "What were we expecting from him, anyway? A fire bomb? Somebody with an uzi? What if he had nothing to do with that hitman? Were all of us going to keep on hiding out and going to little old ladies for intelligence briefings for the rest of our lives? It's been ridiculous and I'm changing direction."

Maureen backed into the hallway. "Whatever you say. Where's Hermione?"

"I sent her to Will's house after we got back from the cottage. I told him she's in the way right now. He takes time to play with her. He adores her."

"Okay, then. If your mind is made up, it's your choice. I'll go see if Kali needs help cleaning the upstairs and closing it up. Tutu needs to start planning her move and packing. Do me a favor. Make sure you have my cell number ready, just in case. I can be there in minutes." She paused. "Jules, something's wrong. I can feel it."

Julie flashed a smile. "I'll be careful. I promise. Now I have to get dressed." And she closed the fish door.

* * *

The interior of the pub lay in dark contrast with the bright day. A waiter led Julie down a narrow corridor to the door of a booth. She stopped to draw a long breath. She had chosen to wear Rich's favorite deep green colors and her auburn hair hung long down one shoulder. She knew her short skirt would catch his eye. It always did. If she had to take a chance, she wanted to stack the deck in her favor as much as possible. She opened the door.

Rich sat at the worn dark wood table, cradling a mug of beer in his hands. The most damaged part of his face lay in shadow so that he looked like the old Rich who could turn women's heads. He stood as she entered, waiting for her to slip onto the bench seat across from him. When she had, they both sat, studying one another.

"Corona Lite," she told the waiter. "I'll order food in a bit."

He nodded and left.

"I hate what's happened to us," she said to Rich in a breathless whisper, as though imparting a secret.

"You look good," he replied, not missing the abundant cleavage her blouse revealed.

"The detective scared me," she told him, getting to the point because she couldn't think of anything else to say. "He said the man who killed your mother and brother was the one who shot me. They think your family hired him and then ripped him off, so the office shooting was revenge. The doctors told me if I hadn't turned when I was the target, I'd be dead."

He held his expression steady. "Are you healed now?"

"Not entirely, but I'm on the way."

"I'll bet it doesn't hurt like burns do."

She stared at him. He hadn't been surprised at anything she said. Was that a good sign or a bad one? "The detective said he thought you might have been in on the plot for the hitman to shoot me."

He looked down at the table. "No. I wasn't. But I got stuck paying the bill. Is that what you wanted to ask?"

"Yes."

"You should've known the answer without asking."

Her eyes were tearing, but she ignored the blur. "Why should I? You haven't been yourself, Rich. You said terrible things to me in the hospital."

"You left me for dead—for dead, Jules," he said, seasoning his words with bitterness. "You never checked on me. After I was rescued, you didn't come to the hospital to see me for days. How was I supposed to react?"

She released her tears. If he saw her crying, it could only help her case. "A friend told me you might have actually been dead and aliens revived you."

He made a face. "Aliens? What kind of crazy people are you hanging out with?"

"She's an old lady descended from Hawaiian holy men. She says the insect people you saw were aliens. They transported you."

He scowled at her. "The insect people I saw were a nightmare. You can have ugly nightmares when you're burned up and half-drowned. I never should have said anything about it. You're losing it, Jules. You never used to believe in aliens."

She pursed her lips. "You can open your mind to all sorts of nonsense when your husband's family has you shot."

He was quiet for a moment. "The detective could've been wrong, you know."

"But he probably wasn't. You know how much your mother and Al hated me."

"I can't prove anything—or disprove it, either," he said slowly. "Mom and Al are dead—along with the rest of the office—even clueless Lucy, the receptionist. But I think you're wrong."

She leaned forward. "Then why did that guy shoot me? I didn't know him at all."

He scowled again. "How the hell should I know? I was home nursing a melted face. Something to do with the Mob, but they didn't tell me what. They aren't the kind of guys you question."

She sipped at her beer, eyeing her husband across the table. Something in his expression had changed. "We're what we have left," she told him. "No other family. You and me. We were doing pretty well before the fire. What if we start over? Could we do that or have we come too far?"

"I don't know."

She cocked her head and gave him a ghost of a smile. "We're even now. My leaving you behind should be balanced out by your mother trying to have me murdered, don't you think?"

His eyes were twinkling just the slightest bit. "Maybe." He pushed his empty mug to the edge of the table. "So who drove you here this time?"

"I called a rideshare service."

"Good choice."

By the time the waiter returned with more beer, Julie was leaning provocatively over the table.

"Fish and chips for both of us," ordered Rich. "One filet for the lady and two for me. And more beers. We have a rideshare."

* * *

Maureen was sitting on Tutu's sofa, pretending to be absorbed in a re-run of a reality show that was on TV when Julie walked in, humming a directionless tune. "So, how did your meeting go?" asked Maureen, doing her best to sound casual.

Julie grinned at her. "He's warming up to me. I think we can stop worrying about being murdered and move forward. I almost went home to bed with him."

"Bed!" Maureen's forehead wrinkled. "Don't you think you're going a little fast for someone who was the victim of a hit?"

Julie shrugged. She could feel her beers urging her to giggle. "He's good in bed, Rini. He's really good. You wouldn't know, but that's persuasive."

Maureen exhaled heavily. "I vaguely recall."

"He said he didn't know about the hit."

"And, of course, you believe him."

"Of course." Julie plopped onto the sofa, sticking her feet out before her. "I know him, Rini, better than he does. I think he's sincere." She twisted her ankles in one direction and then in the other. "His face is a mess, but his body looks good."

Maureen's sarcasm dripped from her mouth. "So you're horny."

Julie laughed. "Duh! But it's more than that, Rini. I'm his wife."

Tutu hobbled in from the kitchen and settled herself in her rocker. "I missed what you said. Please say it again." She trained her spectacled gaze on Julie. "Except for the horny part. You can skip that."

Julie exchanged guilty glances with Maureen and grinned. "I told him about the insect people, and he doesn't believe in aliens. He doesn't believe, Tutu."

Maureen laid a hand on Tutu's shoulder. "Maybe you should tell him there's a brain parasite called toxoplasmosis that's inside a quarter of the population of the United States and half of the world population without our realizing. Reminds you of the 'e'epa, doesn't it? Scientists used to think it was harmless in anyone with a strong immune system, so it didn't rate attention. But now they're discovering it can alter the behavior of the host when the host is out of balance, causing the host to be attracted to predators—like greedy, selfish sons-of-bitches, perhaps? The host may take more risks, and even fall prey to schizophrenia, bipolar disorder, or suicidal tendencies—among other neurodegenerative conditions. In other words, it's a brain parasite that can change the way people act when they're stressed. Might explain the current hateful trends in the world, wouldn't you think? Of course, it's also true that emotions are contagious—including negativity and hate. You pick up emotions from those around you. Depends on what you're prepared to believe, I suppose."

"Belief got nothing to do with it," added Tutu huffing a little sound of dismissal. "For centuries, nobody believe in bacteria or viruses, but they died from them, just the same. Did you tell him you love him, Julie? Did he say love to you?"

Julie lay back against the cushions of the sofa. "I told him I love him. I don't remember if he said it back. Rich isn't the sentimental type. But he kissed me. His kisses speak for him. When he heals, boy, we'll make up for lost time."

"Did you talk about the property?" asked Maureen folding her legs into a sloppy lotus position. "Did he bring it up?"

"Property!" Julie made a face, as though she had tasted something foul. "No, we didn't talk about any stupid property. We talked about getting back together."

Tutu rocked with purpose, forcing the rhythm to elucidate something. "Tell me again why you was caught in the fire and didn't leave before."

"The fire...again? Why do we have to talk about that?" She peered at Tutu who didn't flinch. "Okay, okay. We waited too long!" Julie waved a flourish in the air with her hand. "We waited too, too long."

"And why did you wait too long?" pressed Tutu.

"Rich was going to stop the fire, but it didn't work." Julie pulled her feet in and struggled to remove herself from the soft seat. "A miscalculation."

"That was the reason *Rich* didn't evacuate," ventured Maureen. "What was the reason *you* didn't evacuate?"

Julie blew air through a pout. "All these questions! I stayed with my husband. That's the way it is. I stay with my husband. Just because you two don't have one, don't envy me mine!" She marched, somewhat unsteadily, down the hallway.

Tutu looked at Maureen but didn't say anything. Instead, she rose from her rocker and headed toward the kitchen. "Of course you gonna stay for dinner," she said.

"Sure." Maureen rose to follow her. "I'll text Kali that I won't be home."

After Julie had fallen asleep in her room, Maureen and Tutu sat together at the table in the kitchen. Tutu could see a tumble of thoughts and words churning behind Maureen's eyes, so she waited patiently, nursing a cup of tea.

"I understand what you've been trying to tell us, Tutu," Maureen said at last. "The negativity around the border detention facilities nearly overwhelmed me. I didn't want to say anything to Kali, but for me, it was physical—air so heavy I could barely breathe it, darkness so hopeless and wretched I wanted to cry. If it hadn't been for Lila and G.B., I would've fallen apart."

Tutu nodded sadly. "I knew you was sensitive."

Maureen continued. "I felt suffocated from the inside out, as though blood and air were being crushed out of my organs. I clung to old love with passion that was completely inappropriate because my need demanded it. I felt desperate and helpless and lost. Tutu, I was paper, burning and curling black."

Tutu wiped tears from her gaunt cheeks with a handkerchief she pulled from inside her peasant blouse. "Not just Daniel and Kali, but Lila, too, got injured—that pure, sweet girl. Kali want to believe the war she saw be the worst of humankind, but it was only a symptom. She want to believe all lethal weapons is physical. Deep inside, she know she wrong. Her motherhood gonna make her reconsider. Maybe you gotta tell her about your plasmosis thing. She like science. Then she let me surround my great-granddaughter with love and light, a connection to God-Source—and she gonna want the same for her and Daniel. She gotta help her family and herself rise above bitterness, because there ain't no other way to drive out the *'e'epa*. Kalia a good person. Deep inside, she already know."

Tutu swallowed the last of her tea and replaced the china cup in its saucer with a tiny clink. "A place where innocents is mistreated scrape humanity from a person and leave them raw as meat. That place crusted with fear and hatred. The *'e'epa* rejoice because they got they feast. I can soothe Lila like I can soothe you, but I can't take away the memory. All the children there gotta carry scars to their graves. Many gonna be destroyed. Your exposure gonna stay as a scar in your mind."

Maureen reached across to cover Tutu's soft hands with her own. "I haven't used my sensitivity, as you call it, well. I ignore warnings. I walk off cliffs. I had to develop a shield inside myself when I was working in the courts. I stopped myself from feeling. But this was different. This time I needed to protect people I care about, and I couldn't do it. Like Jules. I know she's near something bad, but she doesn't pay attention to me."

Tutu sighed and nodded. "The curse of higher vibration be the distance between you and them that refuse to know." She placed her hands upon the table and pushed herself vertical. "Come. We gonna meditate—or pray, if that suit you better—together. If Julie ain't about to heed us, we gonna send energy to Kali. I feel her heart opening."

Chapter 33

Who's on the Bottom?

MAUREEN BROUGHT KALI to Tutu's house in the morning, Lila bouncing at her side. Lila hurried to execute obligatory hugs on Tutu and Julie in turn. "Where's the dog?" she wanted to know. "Mommy says you have a dog now. I like dogs—the nice ones. I stay away from the mean ones. Is she a nice one?"

"Yup. Next door," provided Julie. "Her name is Hermione and she's with Will."

As though on cue, there was a knock on the front door. Kali opened it and Hermione rushed in to greet everyone. Will came behind, grinning sheepishly.

"Sorry. She knew you were here, somehow, and couldn't wait."

"Don't get in her face," warned Kali as Lila threw her arms around the dog's neck. "She doesn't know you. Be gentle and give her space."

"She likes me!" exclaimed Lila beneath Hermione's licks. "She's kissing me! We're going to be friends! Can I take her into the backyard?"

Will looked to Julie and they both nodded. "Sure," replied Julie. "I think they'll be fine. Hermione doesn't seem to have a problem with being around little kids."

"Just remember not to squeal," added Will. "Dogs get upset if you're loud. And don't squeeze her. She isn't a toy."

"I promise! Come on, Miny!" Lila skipped to the kitchen with Hermione in her wake and a moment later the back door slammed.

Tutu had already settled herself in her rocker. "How's Daniel?"

Kali sank onto the sofa. "Improving—he doesn't have the outbursts he had at first, but it's going to take time. He's easily confused and gets irritable without warning. Sounds bother him and so does bright light. The doctor told me it'll take at least ten days before he's much better. Some of the changes may be permanent. Brain injuries are like that. But Daniel's a very strong person. He'll heal. I'm sure of it. We left him to have a little peace and quiet." She leaned toward Tutu. "His spirit is more wounded than his brain."

Tutu rocked thoughtfully. "I gonna come see what I can do to help as soon as he got enough energy. For now, your love protect him more than you know."

Kali turned to Julie. "I heard you had a meeting with Rich."

Will, who had been ready to go outside with Lila, stopped where he stood. "Jules, you met with Rich? Alone?"

"In a bar. We had a nice time." Julie's words drifted on an air of defiance that was repeated in her expression. "He's more himself these days."

"Good god," Will muttered, glancing at Maureen. "What if he hadn't been?"

Julie made a face. "But he was." She twirled the end of her long pony tail in her fingers. "We're going to live in his mother's house—at least for the immediate future. I'll change the furniture, of course—after a respectful mourning period. It looks like a 1980s funeral home in there, smells bad, and the seats are huge. She had dreadful taste...and a wide butt."

Will stepped toward Julie. "He tries to kill you and you meet in a bar and now everything's fine?"

"He wasn't the one who tried to kill me."

Will's face was blotchy with red. "And you know this for certain...how?"

She glared at him. "He told me." She glanced around the room but found no support, so she strutted past Will. "I'm going to play with Lila. I give my permission for all of you to discuss my life behind my back, but don't expect me to follow your directions when I get back."

No one spoke for a few minutes after they heard the back door open and close.

"Does anyone else think this is insane?" asked Will.

Kali hugged her knees. "I guess it's her call, but I met the man, and I wouldn't be alone with him—not yet."

Maureen sighed loudly enough for everyone to hear. "She married him. By the old rules of following your godhead, she has to back him. He's in charge. She's his woman. I can just see him dragging her into his cave by that ponytail as he brandishes a club. Me, Richard. You, Jules. God, I hate that kind of thinking. All women pay for it."

Will slumped into the upholstered chair. "She's too young to be living by archaic traditions." He turned his head to address Tutu. "What do you think, Miss Kalani? Be honest."

Tutu pursed her lips. "When ain't I honest?" She rocked a few times, and everyone knew to wait. "I feel a fog around her. I can't see through it. She missed her man and loneliness be persuasive."

"So is lust!" sputtered Maureen. "But women can't afford to be stupid about it. That's a man's game."

"Thanks a lot." Will crossed his arms over his chest. "I thought you were against sexism."

She bit her lip. "Sorry. Present company excluded. You're different."

He shrugged. "That's okay. You're right, of course. Most men think with their..." he glanced toward Tutu," ...privates first. And I'm not sure I should be excluded."

"The question is," interrupted Kali, "what do we do?"

Tutu rocked harder. "Nothing. We do nothing. Free will come with responsibilities and consequences. If she feel safe with him, we gotta stand by. Could be she's right about him."

"This is almost too much for me to absorb on top of Daniel's condition." Kali took a pillow from the sofa and held it over her face as she exhaled her frustration. "I haven't been able to shake off the depression I felt from what I saw at the border. I'm so disappointed in Americans, in humankind—and I thought I couldn't think any worse of people than I already did. How can anyone walk around with so much resentment and so little compassion inside? How can they be hateful enough to abuse children and think that's okay as long as the kids aren't white? And now this business with Julie leaping before she's sure. Insanity is contagious. I swear it is."

"Maybe it's destiny," sighed Maureen. "In India, they believe there are four epochs or world ages that are instances of the cosmic cycles of birth, death, and rebirth. The first is a golden age of righteousness. In the second, a decline begins. The third is marked by lying and quarreling, and in the fourth people are greedy and merciless, get into wars without provocation, and covet 'worldly desires.' That stage eventually leads to a super-cataclysm that wipes out almost everybody before the cycles start over. Three guesses which age we're in." She looked around. "Sorry. That doesn't help much, does it?"

Will made a funny noise in his throat. "Where do you learn this stuff?"

"I read." She walked over to touch him on the shoulder. "Why don't you and I take Julie, Hermione, and Lila to a park and leave Tutu to have time with Kali?"

He nodded. "And what if Jules takes one look at us and decides she'd rather be with her Prince Charming?"

Maureen gave his shoulder a quick tap. "So be it. Then we take Lila without her...Lila and the dog. I'll be damned if Hermione is going to live with that man."

He scowled. "I'm with you."

* * *

Julie went with them, but she was careful to leave as much space as possible between Will and her. Instead, she sat cross-legged in the sandbox with Lila, helping her pretend to make food. Meanwhile, Hermione cheerfully dug sand out of the box and onto the grass and anything else nearby.

Maureen and Will rested on the swings, slowly swaying to and fro. "Look at that," muttered Maureen. "You can't start too early to train girls they belong in the kitchen. It's insidious."

Will chuckled. "I never thought of it that way. I do my own cooking. My mom wouldn't have had it any other way."

"You mean you cooked at home—when you were growing up?"

"Yeah. Mom traveled for her job and Dad never graduated past the grill."

She dug at the dirt with the toe of her shoe. "Pat can't cook at all. He's lucky he found Norman."

"So you did the cooking?"

She laughed. "Mother did. I helped. Sometimes she asked me not to. I was that great."

He studied her for a few moments. "You don't care for men much, do you?"

She twisted her swing. "On the contrary. I care too much. They don't return the favor. Their loss."

"Don't blame all of us for the poor taste of a few." He stood up and let his swing settle into its own small path as he watched Julie and Lila. "A woman like Jules is so used to being admired that she doesn't see anyone who isn't in her spotlight."

"Like you, Will?"

He sighed. "I do my own cooking, remember. Maybe we should move on home. I'm sure Miss Kalani has worked her magic by now."

"Do you believe in her, Will—in Tutu, I mean?"

He lifted his gaze to the bird formation passing overhead. "I believe she's one of the coolest old ladies I've ever met. Have you ever played poker with her? She's a terror. Other than that, I don't worry about what's real. I just ride the bull. What does it matter what I think, anyway? After all the nutty stuff they've learned about quantum physics and the universe, common sense isn't a guideline anymore. But Miss Kalani gives me chills sometimes. How about you?"

"I'm a sensitive—not like she is, but in the same ballpark."

He turned to face her. "You see these *'e'epa* things?"

She grinned. "Will, they're invisible."

"Okay, do you feel them then…or sense them…or whatever?"

She dropped her gaze. "I don't know. They sound bizarre. I'm more the visible-parasite-under-a-microscope type. I never heard of them until I met her. I haven't figured out what they would feel like yet,

241

so I wouldn't realize if they were all around me." She paused to draw squiggles in the dirt with her toe. "We don't all sense the same information. And I don't tell people I'm a sensitive. Too much drama attached."

He cocked his head just slightly, echoing Hermione when she was figuring something out. "Why tell me?"

She hopped off her swing and retrieved his baseball cap that had flown off in a sudden gust of wind. "Because you don't care."

* * *

Tutu sat at the kitchen table with Kali directly across from her. She had burned white sage and spread the smoke around the room and now she held Kali's hands lightly. "I gonna help you remember yourself. You know the routine," she said quietly. "Take yourself down into a peaceful place in your mind. Count backward."

Kali's lips moved but she said nothing aloud. Gradually, her shoulders lowered and her breathing steadied.

"Good. Real good. Let yourself feel the love of Lila deep in your heart. Feel her hugs, her kisses, see her smiles, her dances. Feel the love she hold for you."

After a few moments, a wisp of a smile curved Kali's mouth.

"Let that love run through your body. Pay attention to what it feel like because that be the higher vibration you seek. It be pure and it be real. In many people, it been buried or damaged, but it's there. With you, it ride near the surface because you got Lila and Daniel. You gotta remember that each person, no matter what age, be a child…like Lila is…underneath. Many is confused, unhappy, injured, spoiled, but at the bottom they got they child wishing for love and peace. Think of how different Lila would sound if she grew up living loveless on concrete in a kiddie prison. This you gotta remember when you see the angry faces. Feel love and pity for them that lost a sense of who they was sent here to be. Stretch your tolerance."

Kali opened her eyes and shook her head, "I don't know if I can do that, Tutu. You might be wasting your time tutoring me."

Tutu's voice became firmer. "Yes. You can. Look at the haters and remember Lila."

Kali released Tutu's hands and sighed. "I'll do my best. But you haven't seen what I've seen, Tutu. You haven't seen the raw hate and rage."

It was Tutu's turn to smile. "And you ain't seen what I seen, Granddaughter. Do you imagine the world was kinder to me in my girlhood? Do you imagine your mother lost herself in a time of sunshine? The surface often be ugly. You gotta hold the shining depth in your heart for you to be safe. We all children in need of care. You can't help everybody see the truth—nobody can. Not everybody's ready. Many resist and strike out in fear. They the ones you call disappointing. They often dangerous, always toxic; make no mistake. But you can change you. And that be your responsibility. That's the love you gotta share with Lila--the love of the ancestors."

Kali sighed heavily. "I'll try."

Tutu patted her hands. "You look better now. Build your strength, Kalia, like you done with Lani. You gonna need it."

Chapter 34

Expanding Family

His HAND WAS slipping inside the waistband of her shorts as he kissed her, stroking lower and lower. She began arching toward him. And then stopped.

"Rich, we're in front of Tutu's house."

He probed further. "We're married."

"Rich!" Julie pulled his hand away. "Not here. Lila may be here. I don't want to be a sex ed demonstration."

"Spoil-sport." He sat back and grinned at her. "You were great earlier at the house. Just like old times. Not bad for a disfigured guy, huh?"

She eyed him coquettishly. "The scar makes you look more macho—as though you sailed the world and became the most interesting man."

"And we'll do that together, once we rebuild the business."

She smiled. "I'd like that." She reached out to caress the healed part of his face. "Oh, Rich, are you sure we aren't moving too fast?"

"Moving too fast?" he echoed, making a face. "As I mentioned, we're married, Jules, for nearly a year. We're newlyweds by most measures. We get to act like it."

"But what about the suspicions and accusations—the cruel things that were said? How do you unsay them?"

"I was blind angry. So were you."

She nodded slowly. "Yes, I suppose I was."

"We've lived through more drama in our marriage than most people have in twenty years."

"Yes. Nearly burned. Nearly drowned. Nearly shot dead. I can't believe I was the victim of a hitman. It's so *Godfather.*"

He leaned over to kiss her again—lightly this time. "We're moving beyond all that shit, remember? We're not going to talk about it anymore. Mom and Al are dead and so is the hitman. Just forget it."

She looked down at her hands in her lap. "I don't think I'll ever forget it."

"Then ignore it. It's all we can do."

She drew a long breath and exhaled it. "Come on in and let Tutu see you aren't a monster stealing me away. You don't have a good reputation around here, you know."

He threw up his hands. "How can I say no to such an attractive offer?"

Julie knocked on the door and waited for Tutu's reply. "You don't have to knock," sputtered the old woman hobbling to the door. "You live here." Hermione was barking in the background. Tutu held the door for them to enter.

"Not anymore," volunteered Rich before he noticed Julie's grimace. "She's coming home with me."

Tutu nodded—not an assent but a gradual acceptance. "I see." Hermione came to sniff Richard, found him unremarkable and Julie too distracted to pet properly, and returned to Tutu's side.

"Tutu, this is Richard Teller, my husband."

Tutu offered a hand and Rich took it, shaking it twice firmly...as he had been taught to do with clients.

"I guessed who he is," muttered Tutu, avoiding his gaze. "He be very enthusiastic."

Julie grinned. "He's a wonderful salesman."

"I don't doubt it."

"Tutu, I can never thank you enough for taking me in when I had nowhere to go," began Julie, preparing to gush. Tutu raised a hand, stemming the flow.

"No need for thanks. You was good company—exciting."

There was a brief knock on the door and Will entered. "Miss Kalani, I saw an unfamiliar car out front and came to check on you."

Richard extended a hand. "Richard Teller. Julie's husband."

Will accepted the handshake, staring at the entwined hands between Richard and Julie with a cocked eyebrow as though they were out of place. "William Manning. Nice car."

Richard answered. "It was my father's Mercedes, but we're going to trade it in for one that's only ours."

"We?" asked Will, knowing the answer.

"Julie getting ready to go home with Richard," said Tutu without emotion. "But nobody going nowhere until I show you this letter I got." She hobbled to the table beside her rocker where she picked up a bulging envelope. "This from Lani." She handed the envelope to Julie. "It's partly for you. Lani didn't wanna waste postage. I taught her to take care with money."

Julie stood skimming the letter while the men tried to look like they weren't sizing one another up. "Oh my gosh! I can't believe it! She's finally done it! It's an invitation. Lani's getting married—here, in the park by the ocean. She wanted Tutu to be in her wedding, and she figured Tutu wouldn't travel all the way to Vegas, so she and her fiancé decided to be married here."

"Park?" questioned Rich, using his sour face. "People get married in the park?"

"Oh you know Lani. She has to be by the ocean. Sometimes I think she truly believes in herself." Julie turned toward Will to explain. "She's a mermaid, too."

"And she's lured some poor sucker onto the rocks!" joked Richard. No one laughed.

"We'll have to check to see if she needs a permit," said Julie as though Rich hadn't spoken. "She wouldn't think of something like that. She's marrying a professional drummer—Dean Porter. Nice name." Julie threw back her head and laughed. "She's finally going to do it! Oh, I can't wait to meet him." She grasped Rich's arm. "Of course we'll need to help her with the details. Knowing Lani, neither of them has an extra dime, but she does adore him. She says so multiple times here—hence the many, many pages. She writes like she talks. He sounds sweet."

Tutu lowered herself into her rocker. "She call Kali and ask her to stand up for her...with you, Julie. I'm gonna stand for her mother. It ain't gonna be formal with matching dresses and that nonsense. Lani seem foolish sometimes, but she got a kind of wisdom. We gonna invite Maureen. She be family now; Lani gonna like her. And she want you to give her away, Will."

"Me? I didn't think she liked me."

Tutu's eyes twinkled as she replied. "She love you as a brother—sometimes irritating, but somebody to trust."

Will shrugged. "Okay."

Julie drew her cell phone out of her pocket. "I'll call her as soon as Rich and I get home. We have so much to talk about! And I have so much shopping to do!" She exhaled an excited, harried sigh as she checked the cell. "Look at the time! We'd better get moving! I think Hermione is happiest here with you, Will, if you'll have her—at least for now. Rich and I have all sorts of antiques and Belinda loved Persian rugs. We have a lot to sell."

Will nodded.

She winked at Rich. "I'll just be a minute. I don't have much to pack. I'll use a garbage bag."

As she was hurrying down the hall, Rich faked a smile. "How about if you two join Jules and me for dinner? My treat. Someplace gourmet. We're celebrating."

Will's lips made a line. "No, thanks. I'm making dinner for Tutu tonight and it's already in process."

"You cook?" asked Rich in disbelief.

"Yeah, I do."

Tutu began rocking. "He be a wonderful cook. I depend on him."

"Nice," said Richard insincerely. "It's easier to be single if you can cook."

"It's easier to be single than to be with the wrong person," muttered Will. He bent over to kiss Tutu on the cheek. "I need to get back to dinner. I'll bring it over as soon as it's done. Tell Jules good-bye for me. Interesting meeting you, Richard." And he walked out, letting the door close itself behind him.

Lani arrived in a rush a couple weeks later, like a descending flock of squawking seagulls…her long blue hair broadcasting glitter each time she moved. She was wearing an electric-blue mini dress that shimmered with its own light above bedazzled sandals that lifted her several inches into the air. She seemed to walk in a cloud of cartoon stars signifying magic and dizziness and a tear in the universe. Dean trailed behind her—a tall, husky man who walked slightly stooped in a habit he'd followed since middle school. His curly black hair cascaded down the shoulders of his leather jacket. The navy t-shirt he wore was as torn as his jeans. Both he and Lani smelled vaguely of french fries, fried fish, and travel sweat as Tutu hugged them.

"Tutu, this is my sweetie Dean Porter. Isn't he yummy?"

Dean blushed. "Pleased." He wore black liner around his gray eyes that seemed to hide in the shadows of his craggy face, but he grinned with his whole mouth like a child delighted with a new puppy. "I've been anxious to meet you."

"Pleased to meet you, too." Tutu pulled him into a hug. As she stepped back, she was beaming. "I pray for my precious girl to find a good man, and I think you'll do." She gestured toward Will who was waiting in the doorway to the kitchen restraining Hermione who whimpered with yearning to meet the guests. "This here is Will Manning, my good-hearted neighbor. Later, he gonna drive us to dinner. Lani's sister Kali and her family and our newest friend Maureen say they on the way. They wanna follow us to the restaurant, and Lani's mermaid friend Julie and her husband Rich gonna meet us there. Dinner gonna be their treat. Oh, and this be Hermione."

At her name, Hermione lunged forward throwing Will off balance enough that he felt compelled to release his grip on her collar. Hermione bounded first to Lani and then to Dean, blessing them both with kisses.

"Lila call her Miny," added Tutu.

"She's adorable!" cooed Lani as she kicked off her sandals and plopped on the floor beside the dog. Dean squatted beside her.

"Don't mean to be rude and not hug you, Will," Lani sputtered between dog licks, "because I truly am glad to see you and I'm thrilled you're coming to the wedding…I'll bet you were surprised I wanted you to stand in for my invisible dad!…but I adore dogs. I don't know if you knew that. Or you probably did. I brought home a few strays over the years. You couldn't have forgotten the barking so soon! You used to call to complain, remember, Will? We'll have dogs one day, won't we, Dean…you know, maybe once we aren't touring so much? We tour, you know. Nothing too big yet, but Dean is a fabulous drummer. I can't wait for you to hear him. He has great reviews…could be a contract in the works! I have clippings in a scrapbook. Me! Scrapbooking! Who'd believe it! Remember how Mama used to have scrapbooks for Kali and me, Tutu, when we were little before she got too sick? You showed us. I'm going to do the very same thing for our kids. Tutu, I'm pregnant! Or, I guess I'm supposed to say *we're* pregnant. Dean helped! Oh, I wasn't going to tell you like that…I had a speech I practiced in the car…but we're so excited and I couldn't wait! I can't keep a secret worth a darn. Remember how I told Kali about her Christmas present? You were super annoyed with me for spoiling the surprise. Dean and I planned the wedding before we found out—in case that's important to you, Tutu."

For a moment Tutu looked like she had been hit with a gust of wind, but she recovered quickly and grinned. "You gonna be wonderful parents."

Lani lifted her face away from the dog. "Oh, I hope so! I intend to do all the good mommy things—you know, fixing her hair and buying sweet clothes and reading lots and lots of bedtime stories… but nothing too scary. I don't want my precious to have nightmares. We don't actually know yet if it's a he or she or whatever, but who cares? We're going to wrap this child in so much love he or she or whatever will be happy and well-adjusted and practically perfect… in her own way, of course. No creepy expectations. Don't you hate when parents have a list of things they want a baby to do before they even know who she is? But I hope she's creative. Wouldn't that be wonderful? Maybe an actor or musician or clothing designer! But it's not necessary. As long as the baby doesn't come out spouting hateful stuff, we'll welcome her. If she does, we'll love it out of her. We're pretty fierce lovers!"

"Take a breath!" said Will in the space. "You're going to pass out."

Lani laughed and turned to Dean. "You see? Didn't I tell you he's a natural big brother if ever there was one? He's been scolding decency into me for years!"

Dean stood up and offered a tattooed hand to Will. "Nice to meet you, Will." He glanced around the group. "Nice to meet all the names Lani has been telling me about. Sorry my parents won't be here. Dad really wanted to meet everyone. When she was well, my mom would've insisted on coming. She would've wanted to celebrate the prospect of being a grandma with the rest of the family. But she has Alzheimer's bad and gets upset in unfamiliar places, so my dad stayed home to tend her. We promised we'd email pictures. But they love Lani and send everybody their best."

Will smiled one of his rare, open smiles. "I'm relieved to know Lani chose well. I watched her grow up."

Just then Kali burst through the front door and Lani jumped up to embrace her with characteristic enthusiasm. "Oh my gosh, I can't believe how much I've missed my big sister! I already told Tutu about the baby, Kal. I just couldn't wait."

Kali laughed and hugged her harder.

Lila took Lani's spot on the floor with Hermione while Daniel and Maureen lingered in the background, the soft blue of Maureen's dress contrasting with his red shirt and black slacks.

"Of course you have to be Dean!" exclaimed Kali, catching her sister's flamboyance as she stepped back to survey Lani's boyfriend. "Welcome to the family!" She squeezed him with an energetic hug.

"My privilege," he replied with his easy grin.

"You're right, Lan. He is adorable." Kali slipped a hand around Maureen's arm. "Lan, Dean, this is Maureen Reynolds—Rini, our family hero. She saved Lila and me and then she saved Lila and Daniel."

"She saved me two times!" added Lila from the floor. "One, two! She and G.B. got me out of the cage! I hated it there. And Daddy. Daddy got out of the big people cage. But Daddy was hurt—real bad. Bad people hurt him. We had to be very quiet so he could get better. He's pretty good now. You don't have to whisper unless he's sleeping, but you can't scream."

Lani hugged herself to Maureen who looked overwhelmed as Lani launched into a monologue close to her ear. "Kali called to tell me all about it, and you're my hero, too. I'm so glad you're coming to the wedding. I can't wait to get to know you better. You look smart, but you don't look like a lawyer—except the women lawyers on TV. Kali didn't tell me you're sexy. No wonder this mysterious rich guy would do anything for you."

Maureen demurred. This wasn't the anonymity she had been planning to give the G.B. incident. Hopefully, Kali hadn't shared his actual name. "I was fortunate enough to have access to the resources we needed at the appropriate time, that's all," she told Lani, acutely aware of her automatic attorney-esque vocabulary. She was rustier at juggling roles than she thought.

Lani moved to Daniel, hugging him gently and dropping her voice as though he hadn't been subjected to her previous outbursts. "Oh, Daniel. I'm super glad you're doing better. You're my favorite brother-in-law!"

Daniel smiled, an expression he was using more frequently these days. "I'm glad to see you, too, Lan. It's been too long."

Lani kissed him lightly on his cheek. "We'll give you so much love you'll have to heal!"

Will bent over to talk to Lila. "Want to help me feed Miny? She needs to eat before we leave."

"Yes! I do!" He led both her and the dog into the kitchen.

They were barely out of the room when Lani turned to Kali. "So what's going on with Jules? You can tell me. You said you aren't happy she's back with Rich. Did he really try to have her killed?"

Kali quieted Lani with a finger in front of her lips and lowered her voice just above a whisper. "No one knows for certain—including her, but his mother and brother certainly tried. The hit man shot their whole office because they refused to pay."

Lani made a face. "No shit! Rich's brother was one of the creepiest guys I ever met...and, believe me, I've met more than my share of sleazy guys. His mother had hidden fangs...I'm sure of it. She oozed venom—especially around Jules. But Rich was a gentleman in public. He made a huge fuss over Jules from the night he met her. Almost too much, you know? Flowers and presents and fancy restaurants. Like worship more than love. But he was so much better than the drooling vampires that usually stalked her, we didn't look too close. His family was a freak show. I didn't tell Jules how miserable I was to be around them, because she was, too. I figured she'd have Rich to run interference for her. I got a funny sense around Rich...but not humorous funny. Weird. I knew something was going to go bad...but I thought the fire was it. I wonder if I'll know the truth when I'm near him."

"If you do," warned Kali, "don't say anything in front of Lila. She needs to believe there are good adults out there. She's seen enough losers. And Jules probably won't believe you."

Lani struggled to slip back into her shoes. "Well, this is going to be a challenging dinner. I'm relieved we're meeting Jules and Rich at the restaurant. I'm not prepared to be stuffed into a car with them yet. I'll have to focus on the fact that they're helping with the wedding and block out anything else."

Tutu let Daniel help her rise from her rocker. "Richard picked the restaurant and he gonna pay the bill, so we owe him respect."

"Yes, Tutu," said Kali and Lani in accidental unison, and they laughed.

Chapter 35

What Are We Eating?

"Do they have veggie tacos?" asked Lila in a whisper.

Kali peered at the child's menu Lila was holding. Soothing music fell in a mist from hidden speakers—a pianist playing themes long suited to genteel elevators or overpriced fashion departments. People sat in the hushed crowd, leaning across tables clothed in black linen in front of gently flickering table lamps. Only the green-blue glow of myriad cell phones interrupted the studiously polite, dimmed atmosphere.

"No. Chicken fingers. They say kids can have spaghetti or chicken fingers or a hamburger," Kali advised. "It's what they think kids like."

Lila pushed out her bottom lip. "I guess I'll have spaghetti... please." She added the "please" to counterbalance her pout, knowing her mother was watching. "Chickens don't have fingers, do they, Mommy? I don't wanna eat fingers."

Kali handed the menu back to the waiter hovering over the table. "No, Baby. They don't. It's a joke."

Lila crossed her arms over her chest, mimicking a man at the next table. "Nobody should eat fingers. It's not healthy."

The rest of the people at the table ordered in turn, uneasily noting the exorbitant prices on the menu. Richard smiled beatifically. He ordered an array of appetizers for everyone to share. "Would anyone like wine or a cocktail before dinner? They have an excellent wine list here."

He leaned toward the waiter as though they had a long history together. "I'll have a vodka martini, very dry—Stoli Elit if you have it, please."

"Me, too, please," added Julie smiling at Richard.

"Just water for me," answered Daniel and Kali agreed. "Yes, water will do fine for me and Lila." Tutu nodded, "Water, please."

Maureen glanced sideways at Will. "I'll have a beer—a Guinness. How about you, Will?"

"Sounds good."

The waiter was replaced by a sommelier and Richard continued. "A bottle of Caymus cab sav with dinner, please. Anyone else?"

"We'll stick with water," said Lani. "I'm pregnant, you know. Besides, Dean and I prefer to stay away from hard liquor...we've had some bad experiences and horrible hangovers...and Dean doesn't like wine. I'm not too crazy about it, either, if the truth is told—especially reds. They give me a headache. I've heard it's the tannins."

Richard seemed vaguely annoyed. "I think you'll find the better wines won't do that, but suit yourself. And you, Jules?"

She looked up at the sommelier. "The wine he chose." She glanced down the table at her companions. "Richard's good at selecting wines. He's teaching me."

The steward left and a lull fell over the group. Richard interrupted it. "So, I hear the border guards mistook you for a Mexican, Daniel."

Daniel turned his head to face him. "I am a Mexican, Richard, a Mexican-American. They mistook me for someone without papers."

"Those confounded illegals!" exclaimed Richard vigorously. "Immigrants are like roaches creeping over the border. Dad always said they're the scourge of our economy, sucking up benefits and dropping babies. He joined a group dedicated to correcting the situation."

Daniel's expression remained stoic. "Everyone is an immigrant until he's not. Everyone came from somewhere else—even the indigenous if you go back far enough. I was recruited to come here by my company."

"No one in my family has ever been illegal!" Richard smiled at Julie, who looked discomfited. "My ancestors have been here for generations. Great-grandpa made his fortune in gun powder. We lost money in the Civil War because the Confederacy couldn't afford its bills."

Tutu had pinched her face into a scowl. "Not illegal? You was on the wrong side."

Maureen executed an exaggerated twist in her seat to orient her more directly toward Will. "So, what is it you do for a living, Will? I don't think I ever heard the whole story."

Will fingered his water glass, suppressing a grin at her inelegant change of subject. "I'm an illustrator, Maureen. I illustrate book covers, magazine articles, picture books—whatever pays."

"Will draws me pictures!" declared Lila proudly. "He drew Miny for me and Mommy let me hang it over my bed."

Kali reached over to straighten Lila's hair. "Will's very talented. I had a few of his works framed in our old house. They were among the worst of our losses."

"They burned up," concluded Lila.

"I'll do what I can to replace them," promised Will.

"So are you a naturalized citizen, Daniel?" Richard persisted. "Did you take the test? What kind of work do you do that an American couldn't do?"

Daniel drew an extended breath and released it in a sigh. "Yes, I took the test, so now I am an American. Could we talk about something else now? I don't want to dominate the conversation."

Lani pounced on the opportunity. "Kal, I'm going to need all the advice you can give about parenting. Can you believe *me* as a mother? OMG. Dean and I are so excited! He thinks we should choose Hawaiian names to continue the tradition, but I don't want to saddle this poor kid with a name mainlanders think is weird. I mean, having us as parents is enough of a challenge! Right, Jules?"

Tutu scowled into her water glass. "Hawaiian names is beautiful. And you ain't weird."

Julie laughed self-consciously. "Lani, no child of yours will ever be dull, that's for sure."

Their drinks arrived and Richard took a long draught of his martini as he gestured for a second. "If it's a girl, we can hope she'll be endowed as you are, Lani. Then you never have to worry about her drowning. She'll automatically float."

Julie touched his arm. "We don't float because of our boobs, Rich. I couldn't have been a mermaid if we did. You sound like your brother."

He covered her hand with his. "You wouldn't have been a mermaid at all if we had been married then. What husband wants guys fantasizing over his woman?" He allowed himself a little sneer. "My brother wouldn't have said fantasizing. He wasn't good at being polite."

Dean shifted in his chair. "Lani is a knock-out mermaid. I'm always proud of her and the admiration she draws. But now she's pregnant she's going to travel with the band, handle bookings and stuff. She's really clever."

Rich downed his second martini and laughed. "Yeah, I noticed how clever she is right off. I also noticed that she and Kali are darker than Tutu. An African father, perhaps?"

Tutu sat very straight. "My husband was an African-American black man, and a better man never been born."

"I figured he was black," replied Rich, slurring his words slightly. "So you're a musician, Dean? How are you going to support a family on that?"

"He's good, that's how," spouted Lani, her smile faded into a frown. "His band has a contract with a solid company for a CD and a tour if that goes well. He and Will are creators. What do you create, Rich?"

"Deals. I create deals."

"Okay!" said Maureen a little more forcefully than necessary. "Here come our meals and just in time. I was starving. How about you, Will?"

Will nodded. "I was feeling nauseous for a few moments there, so I'll be glad to eat something."

"Thank you, Richard and Julie, for buying us this real good meal," said Tutu firmly. "We all grateful."

"Thank you, Richard and Julie," echoed Kali, and Lila copied her intonation exactly. "Thank you, Richard and Julie."

No one spoke of anything but the food during the meal. When it was done, Kali rose. "Lila needs to get to bed, so we'll take our leave. We appreciate your bringing us all together. The meal was delicious." Daniel rose to join her.

"But you haven't had dessert," protested Rich.

"I'd like dessert," offered Lila, but her mother took her hand, and she understood she was to say no more.

"We'll be going, too" added Lani patting her stomach. "I have to watch the calories, you know." Dean smiled at her as he held her chair.

"Thanks for dinner, Richard and Julie," repeated Tutu. "Richard, I hope you gonna feel better soon." Will helped her rise.

"The burns are healed. I feel good. There's nothing wrong with me," protested Rich, but the others were already leaving the restaurant.

* * *

"Did you want me to lie to them?" Rich threw a pillow across the bedroom. "Are you too liberal for me now, Jules? Do I embarrass you?"

"No, of course not, Rich. They're a little pie-in-the-sky. I know that. But they took care of me. I owe them…"

"What? You owe them what?"

"I owe them respect."

He flopped onto the bed, waiting for Julie to pull his covers up. "Daniel is a hiccup away from being illegal and Kali and Lani are going-nowhere black housewives. In the future we'll have to distance ourselves from people like that if we want to be top level sales. The new development is going to go for millions."

Julie tugged the covers to his neck and kissed him lightly before she picked up the blankets she had piled on a chair. She had nearly reached the bedroom door when Rich realized she was leaving.

"Where the hell are you going?"

"The living room. I don't want to accidentally hit you in the face while I'm sleeping."

* * *

The fire! It's coming! I hear its voice, rumbling, slithering, laughing. "Richard! I hunger for you! Richard!"

Eyes! It has crimson eyes that flash and pop—here, there, all around. A thousand arms grasping, fingers scratching, crackling, breathing heat. Whirling tornadoes of flame, loud, obscene. Tall! Higher than God. Satan clawing his way into Heaven with long bloody fingers of fire, sucking away the air, replacing it with soot and burning and smoke like smoldering insulation clogging your lungs. And here I am in the water.

Water turned red. Blood? Flame? Searing pain. Water in my chest. No air! Choking, coughing, sinking away from the red into black.

Julie mocking me. It's easy, Rich! Just breathe slowly! What's the matter with you? And she turns away, She leaves. She leaves me. Julie! How do you do it? How do I breathe? How do I live? Jules! Dammit, don't leave me! Where are you?

The fire answers me. Laughing. Laughing. Fool! Foolish Richard!

Insect people floating me, dragging me. Get your claws off me! What do you want? What do you want? Are you going to eat me? Roasted. Burned. Medium rare. Well done. Pain suffocating me. Pain and pain and pain.

* * *

Richard sat up in bed, gasping for air. "Jules!" he cried, not sure if he was still dreaming and had no voice. "The fire! The fire!"

"Rich, wake up. You're dreaming. Everything's okay."

He opened his eyes, not wanting to, loathing the fire, the smoke, the choking water. But there was no fire. Only Julie sitting beside him.

"You were dreaming," she repeated. Her long hair drooped onto his chest, cool and silky. He couldn't see her eyes in the dark, but he knew their blueness, their green depths.

Was he crying? He couldn't tell. He held her to him, feeling her warmth, her heartbeat. But he had really been in the nightmare. He knew he was there, burning and choking and feeling the pain. This time Julie saved him.

"Don't leave me, Jules. Stay by me. Please."

She hesitated, then caressed his cheek. "Of course." And her long soft body slid in beside him--the mermaid come to save him from the rocks.

Chapter 36

You Mean I Could Die?

TUTU HAD HER head wrapped as her mother and her mother's mother before her had done. It wasn't a cultural statement, only a means to protect her hair from the dirt she was raising. Having company in the house was as bothersome as it was enriching. No one was home today. Lani was attending a fitting for the dress she would wear to be married. Dean was sitting in his car somewhere, waiting for Lani. He was the end of her long shadow.

Tutu should have asked Lani to clean for her, but now that Lani was pregnant, Dean treated her as china. Tutu shook her head. She had never been treated like china and was certain she wouldn't like it. In fact, she took pride in the ragged clothing she wore for this kind of everything cleaning. She enjoyed spitting in the face of her age. People could be obsessed with numbers, when it wasn't numbers that sucked life out of them at all. Surrender: that was it. Surrender made you old. Listening to the people who fussed about all the things you shouldn't do. Listening to the voice inside that wanted to fret over every ache and pain. Letting darkness creep into you so all you could see around you was loss. That was how people got old.

The nightstand. She couldn't stop thinking about the little night-stand somebody had left by the road for the trash pickup. It was a perfectly good piece of furniture as far as she had seen from the car when Will took her grocery shopping. People were so wasteful! All it needed was a good coat of paint—and maybe some traditional Hawaiian decoration. Will would help her redo it. It would be a nice present for Lani and Dean, someplace to keep the baby monitor. The trash people came around close to noon. She had a couple hours, but maybe someone else would see it and imagine how cute it could be. She would need to go now. It wasn't that far and it couldn't be too heavy. Nothing to bother Will about. He had a deadline to meet today.

She took great care going down the front steps. She had taken a hard tumble a few years earlier, so now caution was her one concession to the advancing frailty in her body. If you don't fall, you don't have to mind how long it takes to mend. The sun greeted her with a warm embrace. Walking alone felt like freedom and freedom feeds the soul. She began humming to herself as she moved, remembering the admiring looks she had once inspired with her lithe young body. She could feel her young self, laughing inside her. What a joke to be almost a hundred years old. What a grand joke to have so many years on the outside and a happy coquettish girl inside.

The house with the nightstand was farther away than she had thought. Distances stretched when you were on foot. They insisted you connect with the firmness of the Earth. They reminded you that you were merely another creature, stepping along a span of living, leaving footsteps that would wash away with time. They gave you a chance to look, to see. Tutu loved to walk, even if she had to move more slowly now. She imagined how glorious it was going to be to walk in Hawaii where the neighbors didn't peer at you through their blinds and wonder if your car was broken.

She had reached an unfamiliar neighborhood when it happened. She was never sure precisely what. On TV they showed you every tiny movement in slow motion so even slow-witted viewers would know the progression. Then the viewers could cluck their tongues that the character was foolish enough not to notice the danger in time. But there was no TV camera with Tutu. She was walking and then she was lying on the sidewalk, her hand gradually leaking blood onto the concrete while her consciousness left her to go seek the nightstand by itself.

"Leo, there's a homeless person sleeping on our lawn!" The lady in the white house pursed her lips and furrowed her brows. "Leo, do something!"

Leo planted his thick pink hands on the armrests of his chair. Why did someone have to come now—when there were only minutes before the teams would go to their respective locker rooms for a break? Damn homeless! He scowled at the TV and went to the front door. Sure enough, there was a pile of person half on the sidewalk and half on Rita's flowers. He shoved his way out of the door and down Rita's curved stone path. Damned homeless!

He bent over the pile and squinted at the head. "It's an old woman!" he reported back to Rita.

"Well, don't touch her. She probably has fleas," advised Rita from the door. "Call the cops. There must be a law about lying on someone's private lawn."

"Call 9-1-1. I think she's hurt."

Rita already had her cell in hand. Hopefully the ambulance would come before the neighbors saw and wondered if this was someone who belonged. Alice who lived down two doors had a housekeeper who was black, but her housekeeper wore a uniform. Alice was so showy.

The ambulance didn't hurry too much. An unconscious homeless person wasn't a call they wanted to answer. They had done it too many times. But rules were rules and eventually they showed up. A thin be-spectacled paramedic with soft fuzz on his chin that confessed his youth inspected the damage. "Could be a stroke or maybe just a bad fall." He sighed. "Elderly. No ID. Call around to see who's taking indigent patients."

His partner, a blonde girl with weary brown eyes, shook her head. "Everyone's full to bursting, but I'll check."

The skinny guy secured Tutu onto the gurney and prepared to slide her into the ambulance. "Anything?"

The blonde shook her head. "Like I said, all full."

The skinny guy gestured for the girl to help him load the patient. The homeowners had disappeared into the house. "We'll take her to the nearest ER and then she's their problem."

But the nearest ER was full and losing their sense of humor. "Is she stable?" they wanted to know.

The paramedic said she was.

"We have our quota of indigents and then some," growled the ER doc. "She looks like an immigrant—probably illegal. More drain on the budget. She'll have to wait to see if a space opens up. Take her to General and leave her outside. They'll have to take her."

And so it was that Tutu ended up sitting on a park bench near a hospital, wondering how she had accumulated bandages.

* * *

Will added the final stroke to his picture and clicked the button that sent it careening through cyberspace to the editor who was waiting impatiently for its arrival. Hermione had been a pain for the last half hour, whining and barking and making herself as noticeable as possible. As much as he loved her, today he resented her that much.

"Okay, okay!" He went to the back door, but Hermione didn't follow. She stood at the front door. "A walk? You're lobbying for a walk when I'm trying to make deadline? Miny, we're going to have to talk." He grabbed her leash off the floor where he had dropped it yesterday and hooked it to her collar. She wriggled with anticipation, but sat until he was ready to open the door. Will was beginning to get the impression she had a definite end in mind.

Once outside, she pulled to go to Tutu's house, and Will followed. He was aware of a rising feeling of dread. He knocked, but no one answered. Oh god. The door was unlocked, so he went inside feeling worse with each step. Where was she? She was so old! Had she fallen again? Was she dead?

"Miss Kalani? *Miss Kalani?*" He searched the rooms at a lope, even upstairs where Tutu didn't go. Panic isn't practical.

He ran to the back yard, but there was no one there. He was on his cell before he reached the kitchen. "Rini? I can't find Miss Kalani. Tell Kali. We need to start calling around."

None of the hospitals had heard of her. The police reluctantly took the information. Will was beginning to assign city quadrants for Kali and Maureen to search when he got the call.

"Hello? My name is Rachel Bernhart. I'm here on West Main with a lovely lady named Kalani who said to call you. She seems to have had a fall and been tended by paramedics who left her here not far from the hospital."

"Left her? They left her?" Will was incredulous.

The nice lady voice had one question: "Does she have a regular physician?"

* * *

Kali sat in a chair near the examination table. She was wearing the scoop-necked t-shirt and shorts she had chosen a zillion years ago this morning. If the doctor had known her better, he would've noticed how much more agitated her expression was than usual— a sign of the stress she was containing. But he didn't. Instead, he noted she had grown to be very pretty since the last time he'd seen her—or was that her sister?—pretty enough that he wished she were the patient he had permission to examine. He fingered the stethoscope that hung around his neck bouncing with the jelly movement of his oversized abdomen as he talked. His short graying hair was carefully styled so it didn't interfere with his black-framed glasses. "You haven't been in since your last bad fall—months ago," he scolded Tutu. "You need to maintain regular check-ups at your age. I squeezed you in this time, but that won't always be possible. You're playing a dangerous game."

Tutu raised an insincerely innocent gaze. "You mean I could die?"

"Exactly." He didn't catch the irony and Kali would've laughed if she hadn't been so concerned. He pivoted on his stool to face Kali. "She might have had a minor stroke that precipitated the fall. We'll need to do some tests."

"No, we won't," said Tutu behind his back. "I fell. It ain't no stroke. We'll make sure none of my scrapes gonna get infected and then we gonna let me go home."

The doctor was clearly annoyed. "A stroke is not a trivial occurrence. A more severe one could take your speech or disable you altogether—make you into a vegetable."

"Or kill me." Tutu smiled sweetly. "We ain't gonna blame you, Dear."

The doctor returned his attention to Kali. "I'm not overstating the hazards she's facing. If anything, I'm not being dire enough."

267

Kali reverted to her professional voice, the one she used with recruits in the military. "No, of course not, Doctor. We understand. But after nearly a hundred years, my grandmother has earned the right to take risks if she so chooses."

He leaned forward, threatening instead of becoming more intimate. "Perhaps she has passed the age when she makes sound decisions."

Kali exhaled her frustration. "I don't know many people whose decisions are as wise and kind as my grandmother's. I thank you, Doctor, for your care. If we have any problems, we'll contact you immediately."

He stood up with a whoosh, ill prepared for being dismissed in his own examination room. "You may need to locate another physician who takes strokes more lightly."

Tutu offered a handshake which he ignored. "I don't take no strokes, lightly, Doctor. I take death lightly. Life be more difficult."

He fought to maintain the emotionless expression he had spent years perfecting. "Have a nice day," he said flatly. And he left the room.

* * *

Daniel and Lila and Maureen were waiting when Kali and Will helped Tutu enter the front door of her house. Lani and Dean hurried in from the kitchen. Lila rushed forward to wrap her arms around the old woman. "Oh, Tutu! I cried and cried. I was so worried about you!"

Tutu caressed Lila's hair. "Don't waste no worries on me, Dear One. Nothing bad can happen to me. If I die, I go to a place that's beautiful where I can watch over you every minute. Remember that. I've lived past all the bad stuff." She settled herself in her rocker, moving with the slow pace of her exhaustion. "Maybe you could fetch me a glass of water, please?"

Lila raced from the room on her mission.

"I don't want to tell you what to do, but you need to file a complaint about the paramedics leaving her like that," Will told Kali as soon as Lila was gone. "She could've died on that park bench. You could sue."

Kali dropped onto the sofa. "Oh, Will, you're so white. This kind of thing happens to brown people more than you could guess and lots of times to the homeless, too."

Lani sat beside her. "But that doesn't make it okay. I'm with Will. We need to make a big stink—if not for Tutu, for the next poor soul who doesn't seem as important as everybody else."

Tutu raised a weary hand. "I be grateful for the love, for the worries and the caring. But no. No big stink over me. We got Lani's wedding to plan. We been blessed with happiness. We ain't gonna spoil it by focusing on what's wrong in this world. We gonna be what's right."

Kali lowered her forehead into her hands. "Is this your high vibration again, Tutu?"

Tutu smiled. "Exactly." She closed her eyes. "I gonna know when it's time for me to go, and it ain't now."

Will shook his head. "But you may give the rest of us heart attacks in the meantime."

Tutu didn't respond. She was fast asleep.

Chapter 37

A Wedding of Division

THE DAY OF Lani's wedding arrived with a flock of pelicans flying in formation through the rose-colored eastern sky. Lani and Dean overslept and missed it. No one minded except Richard who had risen before dawn to don his white linen suit and now stood shivering in the early light and a stiff night breeze off the ocean.

"Who sleeps through their own wedding!" he muttered as he climbed into his Mercedes and turned on the heat. "Ask Lani when the hell we can expect this thing to happen."

Julie tapped a message into her phone as she replied. "I warned you we had time to stop for coffee. Lani's never early for anything. Lyle nearly fired her for it more than once, except that she was so popular with patrons."

Richard scowled at the expanse of pink beach beyond the parking lot. He could almost feel the sand in the rising wind scouring the finish on his new car, and mentally he cursed himself for bringing it. Who the hell could he impress in this crowd, anyway? The fact that the humidity was folding wrinkles into his suit was entirely inconsequential. He had meant to make a statement about the elevated status he and Julie now enjoyed, but by the time the rest of the wedding party showed up, the only declaration he would want to make was *I hate weddings*.

"They're leaving the house now," reported Julie as she scrolled through the message on her phone. "Daniel's going to follow Dean so they arrive together. Good grief, Lani writes long, wordy texts. She says she would've gone with a sunset wedding, but the park had too many restrictions."

Richard slouched down farther in his seat to emphasize his worsening mood, ignoring the damage he was doing to his suit. "We're going to owe the caterers more money, you know. They've been set up in the boat house for nearly an hour already. Some of the dishes will be ruined." He glanced at his watch. "They're going to hit morning traffic. Dammit to hell! Why do I let you talk me into these things?"

Julie stared out the side window, swallowing a retort that wouldn't improve the morning. A few other cars had joined them in the lot, but none of them held the wedding party. "Should we invite those people into the boathouse?" she asked. "They were on time. Besides, someone might as well enjoy the buffet."

"So they can stuff their faces with the food we're paying for and guzzle our mimosas? I don't think so. They can wait for the reception." Richard corrected his posture and smiled a plastic greeting to the nearest car. "Lani wouldn't have any friends who could afford our properties, would she? That's a nice Porsche."

Julie shrugged. "Not that I know of, but both Lani and Kali have friends I don't know. Vegas was only one of Lani's ventures, and Dean has played gigs all over with name headliners, according to Lani. Add to that, Daniel was some sort of executive in his corporate job. Maureen said their house that burned was really lovely."

"I can't believe anyone who was well heeled could end up living in Tutu's attic." Richard sighed as he looked over at the couple in the Porsche again. "Maybe we should open the bar, at least. We don't want them to think we're cheap."

"They don't know we're paying, Rich." Julie checked her make-up in the mirror in the sun visor to see if the moss tone of her eye shadow was too dark in the morning light. She had chosen to pile her red hair into a loose cascade on the top of her head to balance a long summer gown that was her favorite green. "And for the record, we all ended up in Tutu's attic because she took us in. We were refugees, not vagrants."

Richard opened his door, grunting as a stiff ocean breeze smelling of dead fish and seaweed rushed in. "Let's lead everyone inside out of the wind. We might be able to do some networking for our money. This is costing a bundle. Besides, we're paying for the musicians whether they play or not. Maybe we should've gone with Dean's band, after all. They might've played for booze."

By the time Lani, Dean, and the rest of the wedding party arrived, the small gathering of guests was already feeling mellow and a little blurry. No one cared when or if the wedding would occur, least of all Lani who was still applying her make-up using the passenger side car mirror.

"Whose idea was it to get married in the morning, anyway?" she grumbled.

Dean's dark eye make-up rivaled Lani's as it countered the bargain elegance of his white suit. His hair was pulled back into a neat pony tail secured by a black leather tie; Lani had vetoed a man bun. He turned in his seat and smiled for the benefit of Tutu, who sat patiently beside Will in the back seat. "Yours, Babe. Morning was your idea."

Lani shrugged as she dropped her lipstick into a make-up bag. "Sounds like me." She laughed at herself as she fluffed her blue hair.

Will climbed out of the car to the thump of music coming from the boathouse and opened Tutu's door. His dress shirt moved independently with the wind emphasizing his open collar and the dark hair beneath. "Miss Kalani, may I offer you a hand?"

Tutu smiled. "Thanks." She hadn't regained her strength, and she was having trouble navigating a polite exit from the car in the long, flowered dress Julie had insisted she buy. "It's a good day, but there ain't no bad days by the ocean."

Maureen pulled her car into a nearby space and shut off the engine. She lingered behind the wheel for a few moments, watching the others.

Dean was helping Lani out of the car. His movements were awkward in his oversized rental suit. "You look gorgeous, Babe."

Lani waved a dismissive hand. "Oh, I'll bet you say that to all your brides." Her white gown hugged her in an octopus style while an electric blue neckline framed her abundant décolletage. That part was custom; she had sewn it herself. Appropriately, she looked like a living fertility goddess figurine. She swished down the boardwalk toward the flowered arch that was erected above the water line. The tide was gradually receding, leaving the scent of whatever had been on the bottom to greet her. "Well, damn. I guess we missed high tide."

Will led Tutu to a folding seat in front, letting her lean on his arm. "Yeah. I'd say so."

"It's still beautiful here," interceded Kali. "And the temperature's rising. We'll be hot soon. You need to wait in the tent for your cue, Lan. Jules and I will meet you there. This is your big entrance. I'll let the people in the boathouse know we're ready to start. Everyone who's coming must be here by now. That's Rich's car over there beside Jerry's Porsche."

Lani and Dean hurried back up the beach, Lani's bedazzled flip flops slapping the wooden planks, to a small dressing room tent that had been erected for the occasion. They passed Maureen who was just making her way toward the shore from the parking lot.

"I'll come with you to the boathouse, Kal." Daniel took Kali's hand to steady her as she walked the uneven path in her tall sandals. His dark suit contrasted with Kali's iridescent turquoise gown— selected by Lani-- that complimented her brown skin and stood out against the white sand. Lila skipped after them, pausing now and then to twirl her full-skirted pink dress.

"They're such an ideal couple," said Maureen looking after Kali and Daniel. She adjusted her broad-brimmed hat that cast a pattern of shade onto her coyly fitted black-and-white dress. "They could pose for cake toppers."

"You look great yourself." Will smiled…awkwardly, Maureen thought.

She tried not to make a big thing out of it, although he said nice things so rarely. "Aren't you supposed to be at the tent? You're escorting Lani, aren't you?"

He nodded. "Daniel's standing up for Dean as best man. I guess they wanted to skip using Richard."

Maureen made a face. "I would," she said quietly.

"Me, too." He offered his arm and she accepted. "Allow me to see you to a seat."

The guests flowed out of the boathouse in a small uneven stream, settling themselves wherever they wished. Richard chose to sit beside Maureen, leaving a space beside Tutu for Will. Daniel stood tall and proud next to Dean close to the gray-haired female minister in a tapestry robe who would perform the ceremony.

When everyone had quieted, a saxophone wailed a jazz version of the wedding march. Lila came first, skipping as she tossed flowers wherever she wished. The attendants came next, each holding a blue-and-white bouquet Julie had insisted was necessary tradition. And finally, Lani took small steps as she walked beside Will, imagining herself in a mermaid's tail. Her head was covered by a long white veil embroidered with white fish and she had included a quilted blue octopus in her bouquet of white spider mums and seaweed. She took her place facing Dean, and as he lifted her veil ceremoniously, she grinned and said, "Would you look at us! We're doing it, Dean! We're getting legal!" He nodded and laughed and so did the others.

The reception was less congenial.

"Enough of this stuffy stuff!" announced Lani after the buffet had been largely decimated. "Let's dance! Get down!" she ordered the band and they seemed relieved to comply. The music thrummed into a tribal beat. She led the group down the beach as she kicked her sandals across the sand and then gleefully tore a slit into the hem of her dress to give herself freedom. Dean discarded the tie on his hair, his white jacket, and his shirt as he came together with his bride to improvise movements that expressed their joy and felt good. Lani threw her head back and her laugh bounced along the wind with the swish of the surf.

"They're drunk," concluded Richard.

"No, they're happy," said Daniel, pulling off his shoes and socks. "That's what happy looks like."

"As if I don't know happy?" asked Richard.

"I don't know what you know." Daniel removed his jacket and draped it across the back of a chair.

Richard was scowling. "Why the hell did I pay for a nice wedding when they would've been satisfied with a keg and hot dogs? People don't know how to accept charity graciously. It's never what they want. Jules, do you know what your little fiasco is costing us? You totally misjudged your friends' taste level."

Daniel stepped forward, effectively blocking Richard's access to Julie. "You both did a generous thing, and it was beautiful. This is the part when people are supposed to put their hair down and have fun. Relax and be together with them."

Richard's eyes narrowed. "I've heard somebody always goes to jail at a Mexican wedding, so I guess you're comfortable with all this."

Daniel paused as he met Richard's gaze squarely. "You shouldn't believe everything you hear," he said quietly.

"And you shouldn't lecture your betters," spat Richard.

Kali intervened, taking Daniel's hand in her own. "Come on, Love. Lila's waiting to dance." Before she walked away, she pivoted to face Richard. "You don't recognize a better man when you meet one."

"Black bitch," muttered Richard not exactly beneath his breath. He glowered at Julie. "What are we doing slumming here?"

"Richard!" Julie seized his arm. Her tone was low but fierce. "Don't you dare wreck this wedding for Lani."

"Wreck it! Sonuvabitch, I'm footing the bill!"

"I think you've made that perfectly clear to everyone." Her glare seared the air between them. "This was my gift to my best friend."

"As if you have money."

"As if I own half of your dad's property." She kicked off her shoes. "I'm going to go find someone who'd like to enjoy the reception with me."

His expression darkened as he threatened, "I'll leave you here."

She drew a long, ragged breath. "Suit yourself." And she marched down into the white sand.

Rich spent the remainder of the reception guzzling whatever liquor remained in the bar as Lani led willing party-goers into the waves. The more they laughed, the angrier he felt. One day he'd get even with that self-important Mexican—in spite of Julie. And maybe he'd get even with her, too.

Chapter 38

What's Mine to Know

"Now that was a magnificent reception!" sighed Lani adjusting the muumuu she had substituted for her dripping wedding dress. "Where's Jules? Was she too proper to have fun with us? She gets like that sometimes—taking herself too serious. That's why we're such good friends. I loosen her up and she keeps me out of jail."

"She went home with Richard." Kali avoided looking at anyone, holding her opinions close inside herself. "She said she was the designated driver."

"Well, he turned out to be an old poop!" exclaimed Lani with forced concern, not caring because she was busy kissing Dean's neck. "If anyone here has brain damage, I'd guess it's him. He's way different from what he used to be. We had a good time together in Vegas once his family had gone home. The man can party! I'll tell you about it sometime." She cocked her head not unlike a toddler contemplating mischief. "We do know how to have fun, don't we, Dean? We've outlasted most of the guests!"

Dean grinned at her. "It's about time we left, Babe. We'll have to check into the hotel and then shower and change for dinner."

Her smirk made everyone smile. "Good idea, Handsome! Thanks to Kali and Daniel...who are footing the bill...we have a fabulous suite in a fabulous hotel tonight. The balcony looks over the ocean! Jules helped me pick it out. It's the kind of place where there's a phone beside the toilet and a sexy jacuzzi near the shower in a humongous bathroom—bigger than our apartment back in Vegas. There's a whole living room and at least three TVs...not that we'll be watching any TV. They're going to have rose petals on the bed and chocolates on the pillows—and champagne. They promised champagne and hors d'oeuvres...can you imagine? I'll bet there's caviar!

The king-sized bed is elevated with gauzy curtains all around. I mean, this place is posh with a capital "luxurious." It would be a shame to have to rush around instead of enjoying the ambiance, wouldn't it, Dean?"

He nodded, slipping his hand under her elbow. "I've got the rest of our clothes in the car already—with the suitcase. Thanks, everybody. We had a great wedding."

She wriggled free of him long enough to hug each person goodbye before he reclaimed her elbow and steered her to the parking lot.

Kali sighed heavily as she watched them leave. "I'm delighted she's having the time of her life—and finally has a decent man. The dates she had before made us worry. They were only barely housebroken and had the manners of warthogs. I swear a couple were genetic throwbacks. And now sweet Dean. I can't believe my baby sister is married...and pregnant. I feel old."

Daniel nodded. He was cradling the sleeping form of Lila. "I'll take Lila to the car. Tutu is already asleep in the back seat."

"I'll be along as soon as we tidy up," promised Kali. "I'll try not to be long."

"Why don't you take your family home?" asked Maureen, holding the wet hem of her dress out into the wind. "Will and I can tie up the details here. Nobody's waiting for us. Besides, Tutu looks spent."

Will agreed. "Good idea."

"Are you sure?" asked Kali, hoping they didn't realize how many details remained.

"Positive," affirmed Will.

When the others were out of earshot, Will shook his head. "Jules should be here to supervise—she and Richard. These are the people they hired, after all. How are we supposed to know who cleans what? This place is a mess."

Maureen shrugged. "I'm sure it'll be okay. They have a detailed contract—start to finish, and I'm not above picking up trash if it comes to that. Besides, from the way she and Richard were going at each other, Jules may have more to worry about than cleaning up after a reception."

Will watched Kali's family drive out of the parking lot. "Do you think she's in danger?"

"I don't know." Maureen stepped back to allow a worker carrying folding chairs to pass her. "He didn't force her into the car. She went willingly. She doesn't seem like the abused wife type."

"Is there a type?"

"Not really." The wind tumbled a paper cup past them, and Maureen stooped to pick it up. "You wouldn't believe how many competent, professional women go home to abuse."

"Is that what happened to you?"

Her smile was wry. "Not exactly, but point well taken. Anyone can be duped—especially by someone she trusts. Research has proven women are generally superior to men at detecting lies—unless they come from someone they love. Girls are weaned expecting romance, but nobody teaches us how to identify the kind of love that lasts. Trial and error. I tried and erred."

He took the cup from her. "I apologize. I didn't mean to pry. It's just that I can't picture a guy being dumb enough to dump on someone like you."

She laughed outright. "Nice compliment. You could consider politics."

He exaggerated his frown. "No, I couldn't. I don't like people that well. Give me a dog any time. Which reminds me, we need to hurry this up. Miny is home crossing her paws waiting for me."

* * *

Julie drove the Mercedes into the garage and pushed the button for the door to close. Richard was snoring in the passenger seat. She watched him for a while, thinking he looked dead with his mouth hanging open. But no, not dead. His skin wasn't that terrible pinkish gray. What she couldn't figure out was how she would feel if he were dead—for real this time. The agonizing hurt deep inside her was gone, replaced by a numbing ache. She missed him—the man she had known. She wanted his arms around her. She wanted him to tell her everything was going to be alright. Was he in there somewhere?

She stepped out of the car and slammed the door. Richard stirred and opened his eyes. He fumbled for the door latch and let himself out. His eyes were bloodshot and the scents of rubber and cleansers and other automobile products were making him woozy. He staggered toward the door to the house where Julie was waiting. He nodded thanks as he stumbled past her into the kitchen.

"I need something solid to eat," he mumbled, leaning against the granite counter top of the kitchen island.

"Will a sandwich do?" Julie went to the refrigerator and opened the door. He watched as she retrieved sandwich meat, bread, lettuce, and condiments from the shelves within. She wasn't smiling.

"I thought you left me," he told her.

"Not yet." She pulled a plate from the cupboard and set about constructing a sandwich from the opposite side of the island. She didn't talk as she worked. Her lips were a white line. When she had finished, she handed him the plate. "Do you want a pickle?"

He nodded and regretted the movement. "You still mad at me?"

She stopped to glare at him. "What do you think?"

"Jules, they're not our kind. They're not white. They're not classy. Dad would have a fit."

She turned her back as she took the ingredients back to the refrigerator. "I don't give a shit what your dad would think. He wasn't a good man. He was a letch and an adulterer and as dishonest as they come. You knew that. If your family was an example of classy whiteness, we can only hope future generations aren't white."

He paused to chew his bite of sandwich, then swallowed. "Our children would be white, Jules, if I had my vasectomy reversed."

She closed the refrigerator door with an unnecessary thud. "If we had children, whiteness would be their misfortune to overcome. I'll be in the guest bedroom. Do your best not to hurl in the bed."

* * *

Richard awoke with an argument on his tongue. He had only to find where to deliver it. Julie was exercising in the workout room. He could hear the muted sounds of her music. Normally, he liked to watch her exercise. The sight always made him hard. But today he didn't want to be hard or happy or even content. He wanted to strike out at the world and leave a big blue bruise. His head hurt and his stomach was upset. The world deserved the worst he could give.

"Jules!" he bellowed through the house, although he knew perfectly well where she was. "Jules!" He tugged at his briefs that had shifted in the night.

At last she appeared from the hallway. She was wearing her gray leotard and black tights. She might as well be in an insulated suit— okay, a curvaceous one.

"What about breakfast?" he demanded rather than asked.

"Could you keep one down?" she asked, her eyes challenging him. He didn't like being challenged.

"That's not the point. The point is I'm hungry and you're in there sweating and pumping iron."

She folded her arms over her chest. His argument had arrived. "I don't see the connection between the two."

He reached down to scratch himself. "I'm expecting you to make me breakfast. That's your job."

He didn't notice the splotch of red creeping up her neck. "When I make you breakfast, it's because I want to, not because it's a job. I don't work for you."

"You sure as hell do. You're my wife."

She jerked the towel from around her neck and wiped her face that was now as red as her neck. "I know you don't feel good and it serves you right. No one made you drink too much. That's frat boy stuff. And I know you're itching for a fight, but I'm not. I didn't marry you to be your servant."

He took a couple threatening steps toward her. "You can't talk back to me!"

She held her ground, piercing him with a glare that sizzled through the air. "I love you, Rich, but if you touch me in anger, we're done forever. Please keep that in mind."

He stopped where he was. His hands were forming fists that hung ready at his sides. "That bitch Kali has turned you against me."

"That bitch Kali has a happy marriage to a man who knows how to treat a woman. She and Maureen and Tutu taught me a lot I should've learned long ago. I'm not your mother. She took whatever your dad dished out because she didn't want to lose the money. I don't like money that much."

He drew his right fist up in front of him and cradled it with his left hand. "I could make you respect me," he growled.

"You could make me hate you." She replaced her towel around her neck. "We're on the edge of falling apart. We have been since the fire…and maybe before. I went along with you when you insisted you could divert the fire even though I knew you were wrong, and nearly got us both killed. I can't give you my voice to crush just to flatter you anymore. There have to be three of us in this marriage—you, me, and us. We either figure out how to love each other or we quit. That's where we are." She turned and disappeared into the workout room, leaving him standing alone.

He stared after her, wondering if he should follow and punch some sense into her. Dad would've told him to control his woman. "Just wait, Missy," he muttered to himself. "A time will come when I can knock you off your high horse once and for all."

In the workout room, Julie stood in front of the mirror, fighting back tears. She swallowed an audible sob and felt its leaden weight deforming her heart. She hated conflict—especially with Rich. He was supposed to be her safe harbor, a place where she could remain forever desirable and loved. He was the partner and protector she had always dreamed. And now he was this soulless beast who wanted to pierce her throat and watch her life bleed away. She had seen violence in his eyes. He wanted to hurt her. Maybe he *had* known about the hitman. She could believe it now.

* * *

Tutu wouldn't have been sure she heard a knock if Hermione hadn't been jumping about, barking excitedly. Someone Hermione liked was outside. As she walked, Tutu straightened the apron she was wearing over her long skirt, patted her gray hair as though to restrain it, and pulled the door open, expecting to see Will.

Julie waited there in a dark blue t-shirt and white slacks. "Hello, Tutu. May I come in? If you aren't busy, of course. I can come by later." As Tutu stepped back to accommodate Julie's entry, Hermione bounded forward, lavishing kisses on Julie's hands until she surrendered and squatted down to pet her. "She still likes me," Julie observed with a touch of awe. "I thought she'd resent my leaving her with Will."

"You want some water or tea or something?" Tutu had anticipated the answer, because she was already seating herself in her rocker.

"No. No, I'm good."

"Then please," Tutu gestured toward the sofa, "sit and we'll talk."

Julie did as Tutu directed and Hermione joined her, resting her head on Julie's lap. Julie began to stroke her, gradually aware of the calming effect of her slow, steady rhythm on herself more than the dog. She sighed and turned toward Tutu. "You knew I was coming, didn't you?"

Tutu un-crinkled her lips into a smile and began rocking. "Some time. I knew you was coming some time."

"How did you get to be so wise?"

Tutu's eyes twinkled. "I made lots of mistakes. After a while, you get tired of stepping in shit and you start watching where you going."

Julie laughed. "You surprise me now and then, Tutu."

Tutu continued rocking. "A person should have many sides." The thump, thump of the rocker was the only sound in the room for a few moments.

"You want to know why I've come," said Julie at last.

"You're always welcome. You don't need a reason."

Julie exhaled a rocky sigh. "But you know I have one."

"Yes."

Julie dropped her eyes to Hermione in her lap. "And you know it's about Rich."

"Yes."

"Do you know what I'm going to say?"

"No."

Julie held her hand out and blew away the dog hair that was clinging to her palm. "Do you still think he's infected—Rich, I mean?"

The rocker didn't pause. "Yeah." A couple rocks later Tutu added, "Maureen say the mind parasite come from food and most people carry it inside. Only a few get real damaged when they grow dark and weak. I say food or aliens or bad blood from the family, it's the same infection. Has he hurt you—your Richard? Has he tried?"

"Not yet." Julie quickly brushed a tear from her cheek, as though Tutu wouldn't have noticed. "I'm not sure he won't, Tutu. He has a look that would turn the sun cold. He uses it on me once in a while."

The thumps went on. "Are you gonna leave him?"

The tears Julie had been restraining ran in rapid succession down her face and onto Hermione. "I don't know. I suppose so. Maybe I'm wrong. Maybe he'll heal. Maybe I'm expecting too much too fast." She reached over to the side table where a box of tissues lay and tugged out a few. "Tutu, I love him. I wasn't sure for a while, but when I thought he was shot in the office, I felt a terrible aching inside—like a part of me was withering into crumpled bits. I don't know why I didn't feel it when I thought he drowned. Maybe he's right and deep down I knew he was alive and I left him, anyway. I don't know."

Tutu nodded in time with her rocking. "Could be you was distracted by bad thoughts about his mother."

Julie blew her nose, and Hermione leaned over to lick her arm.

"Do you believe he love you?" asked Tutu.

Julie dragged in a long breath and slowly released it. "I'm not sure, One minute I think so and then he says something horrible and I'm convinced he hates me. You see things, Tutu. Tell me; does he love me? I have to know. Does he love me, Tutu? Or should I walk away for good?"

Tutu continued rocking, staring straight ahead. Thump. Thump. Thump. Finally, she shook her head. "This I can't see." She turned her gaze to Julie. "I'm real sorry, Julie. I see only what's mine to know. I'm afraid you gotta answer your own question in your own time. But make me a promise."

"What?"

Tutu stopped rocking. "If you start feeling afraid for yourself, you move your backside and leave as quick as you can. Go where you got plenty of people and call Maureen or Will or a cab to come—no matter what the time. Don't make no excuses for your husband if you feel scared. Don't wait to be hit or worse. Leave. Do you promise?"

Julie nodded without speaking.

"Only love can heal him, but you can't provide all the love. Some gotta come from him. Without love inside—enough love to shine out and be his light—he's dangerous. Without love, he live in a red hell where even killing look reasonable. These days many get stuck there. They crowd together, chanting loud enough to drown out right and wrong. Your Richard couldn't heal while his family clung to him. Could be he ain't gonna heal now, either. Like in poker, you gotta read the cards and decide how you gonna bet."

Julie nudged Hermione off her lap and stood up. "I guess I knew that. I was hoping there was an easier way."

Tutu grunted slightly as she pushed herself out of her chair. "We ain't born to have an easy way, as far as I seen." She opened her arms for Julie to enter her embrace. Once she had, Tutu stroked her hair as Julie had done for Hermione. "Love to you, Precious One. Let the love of your friends protect you. Dark thoughts is contagious even without the *'e'epa*. Do what you gotta do to tend your light and stay with God-Source. Feel the beauty and power of who you are and let your light shine out to brighten the lives of others. You saved yourself once. You gotta do it again."

Chapter 39

Sifting the Ashes

"CAN I CALL you back?" Kali hung up the phone. "Rini? Daniel? I need to talk to you." She leaned out the front door to call to Will, who was working on Daniel's car that had mysteriously reappeared from Texas. "Will, can you come in for a minute? You might want to hear this."

Maureen came from the kitchen where she had been filling the dishwasher as Daniel carried a box in from the family room. "That's pretty much it for the things we need to ship," he told Kali as he lowered the box to the floor. "We don't have much and that's good when you see the prices of shipping to the islands."

Will was wiping oil off his hands onto a rag as he entered. "What's up?"

Kali drew a long breath. "I was just talking to Richard on the phone."

Will's forehead wrinkled. "Is Jules okay?"

"As far as I know. The predictions are for heavy rains tomorrow in the burn areas around Eden, and all the homeowners who were burned out are being advised to make a run up there to sift through the debris to see if there's anything they want to take away before the rains do it for them. Not many had a chance to search until after the bodies were identified and removed, and that took a lot longer than they thought it would. They're expecting localized flooding. Richard wants to know if we'd like to caravan. He's offering his assessment skills in case you want a good estimate of what your property is worth now. He says assessment is his specialty."

Will bit his lip and looked at the floor. Maureen answered for him. "As much as I hate to lean on Richard for anything, I have a strong feeling we need to go together on this and let him have his say. He's not pleasant, but I think he's honest. At least he's someone we know. We have to act today or not at all. We don't have to agree to anything."

Daniel shrugged. "A guy called us with a preliminary assessment as soon as people were allowed in, but the number was low ball. We hadn't hired him. We didn't sign. It'll be wise to hear another opinion before we choose someone to put our land for sale."

Kali nodded. "Plus, signing papers will be easier if we do it before we leave without trying to handle everything long distance from Hawaii. And I want to have a last chance to see if I can find my mother's ring. I had it in a little metal box—supposedly fireproof. It should've survived. It should still be there. I must have missed it unless a scavenger picked it up. When we first saw the destruction, I was too upset to do a thorough job looking."

Daniel slipped his arm around her. "My darling is not yet convinced she wants this land to be sold. The ring and our home were both treasures to us."

Kali's eyes were moist. "In Hawaii, we'll be far from Lani and Dean. Who will Lani have here for her? Not even Tutu. When she delivers, she'll be among strangers."

Daniel kissed her hair. "You can fly back here—you and Lila… and Tutu, as well, if she wishes."

Maureen nodded. "I'll be here. Okay, I've never given birth myself, but I can read about it and be empathetic as anything. Or, if you come, you can stay here with me as long as you want. You know I have space."

Kali couldn't help but smile at her friend's earnestness. "Thank you. Knowing you're here helps. Maybe we're being hasty. We'll have to think hard before we do anything that isn't reversible." She sighed without realizing she had. "I'll call Richard back and tell him we're all coming. We'll need to change clothes. Ash may not wash out well. You're welcome to ride with us, Rini. You can sit beside Lila in the back seat, if you don't mind. Seeing the wreckage can tear at you. It did me. I felt gutted. You shouldn't go alone."

"I'll take you, Rini, in my new used car," offered Will. "I'll feel better if I'm there with you all. Maybe I can help with something. And, if we're in a separate car, you can visit your house at the same time Kali's visiting hers. Save time. You won't have to wait for me to run home before we leave, either. I'm already wearing expendable clothes—plus a little grease--and Tutu's watching Hermione. I'll just give her a call to let her know I'll be much later than I guessed."

Maureen smiled at him, a smile that made Kali exchange knowing glances with Daniel. "I'd appreciate that, if you can spare the extra time. I'll just go change."

Daniel released his wife. "I'll make sure Lila wears play clothes. She'll find whatever is there to be dirty. And I'll change, too—I have the jeans I wore in El Paso. Then I'll find the work gloves we bought. Is better for you to talk with Richard, Kali. He talks better with you."

"Okay." Kali took a moment to straighten her posture, preparing herself for her conversation. "No problem."

* * *

The trip to Eden passed without incident, except for a few sideways glances at lunch in a roadside restaurant. Daniel took care to seat himself away from Richard at the table--Richard who had insisted on leading the caravan in his Mercedes. Instead, Daniel carefully restricted his attention to Lila. The waitress had provided her with a sheet to color and a few primary crayons.

"Lily Pad, my darling, remember to eat your food," advised her father. "We won't be able to eat again for a long while." Lila glanced up at him and cocked her head.

"Okay, Daddy. But I'm not done coloring the tree."

Will, too, focused his attention away from Julie and Richard. He picked up one of Lila's crayons and began to sketch on the sky of her picture. "You see? You can add whatever you like when you draw. These are birds with little fairies riding on their backs."

Lila giggled and stuffed the rest of her french fry into her mouth. "I like blue fairies," she affirmed, spraying bits of food ahead of her.

"So, how are you doing, Jules?" Kali asked her friend to fill what seemed to her to be a conspicuous conversational void.

Julie shifted uncomfortably. "Oh, I'm fine. Just fine."

"And you, Rich?" asked Kali. "How are you doing?"

"I'm fine. Did you bring your land plat with you?"

Kali nodded.

"Oh good. That will make assessing much easier. What I can provide is only a guesstimate, of course, but I'm pretty dam…darned accurate. I've done enough of them lately! We just need to see how the damage sizes up—the damage to the property--and what kind of cleanup will be necessary. When we near the actual sale, we'll hire a certified assessor. How about you, Maureen? Do you have your property plat?"

Maureen smiled using more teeth than usual. "I anticipated that particular need, Rich. I think of things like that. It's in the car."

He paused, unsure how to process her tone of voice. "Oh. Good."

Julie decided to change the subject. She focused on Kali. "I suppose you're getting ready for your big move. You must be really excited."

"I suppose." Kali sighed. "I don't know if I'm emotionally ready to leave. That's the problem—what with Lani pregnant and everything."

"But this is a great time to sell," interjected Rich with enthusiasm. "The developers are drooling. You'll make out like bandits. The iron's hot! Lani will do fine. We have excellent medical facilities in California, and Jules can be there to give her moral support."

Julie nodded. "Of course I'll be there for her. Lani's been my best friend for years."

Rich grinned his best plastic grin. "Once you go off the deep end with someone, you're bonded for life. They shook their tails together. Right, Jules?" He chuckled.

Julie wadded up her napkin and tossed it on the table. "Are we all ready to go?"

"Can I take my fairies with me?" asked Lila as she slid out of the seat.

"Yes, my darling," replied her father. "You can take your fairies. Mr. Will makes wonderful drawings."

When they were settled in their respective cars, Richard led them out of the parking lot and back into traffic. Will turned toward Maureen as he maneuvered his car behind the Mercedes. "You know, he didn't have a clue what you were saying to him back there. He just assumes women are stupid."

Maureen laughed. "Yes, I know. I'm counting on it if Jules decides to go ahead with a divorce."

"Do you think it's going to happen?"

She exhaled audibly. "I'm not sure. If I were judging from the looks they gave each other in there, I'd say yes. But they're still together and Jules hasn't said anything. I just hope she chooses well. I had one client whose husband killed her while she was hemming and hawing about whether he loved her or not. Every time I'm sure which way a client will go, she goes another, so I stopped guessing."

"Probably wise." He produced a CD from his jacket pocket. "How do you feel about jazz?"

She settled back in her seat and adjusted her sunglasses. "Contemporary or traditional?"

* * *

A single two-lane bridge spanned the debris infested river that marked the boundary of the outlying housing developments of Eden. The gray water roiled and churned beneath them, clawing at the banks as though it were seething with resentment at becoming a garbage dump. Maureen and Will drove over it into what was left of the neighborhoods and began with Maureen's house. Not much survived, but she and Will used gloves, a trowel, and a rake to sift through the ashes.

At last Maureen stood up, tugging the particulate mask off her mouth. "I'm satisfied I'm not going to find anything else worth saving. As my grandmother would say, it serves me right to lose the mess I should've sorted before Mom died. Burning everything up is one way to prevent overactive sentimentality." She tossed aside a lump that was once a length of wrought iron railing and turned to Will. "Let's go help Kali. I'd be thrilled if we could find that jewelry box for her."

Will agreed. They set their tools in the trunk and drove to Kali's house.

"This is the corner where I met Kali and Lila," Maureen told him as they passed it. "That we weren't killed on Pat's bike had to be an example of divine intervention. I was a lousy driver. We were weaving all over the place, and Pat told me there's a law about too many people on a bike. I don't know why no one stopped us—maybe because I looked like a crazy woman roaring down the highway in my ratty bathrobe."

"I'm sure you didn't look like you were out for a joy ride." Will paused while he parked and turned off the car. "You should be proud," he told her as he opened his door. "With or without divine intervention, what you did took guts."

Kali and Daniel were doing much the same work Maureen had already abandoned at her house, as Richard began to pace out their property lines, clicking away on his cell. "Just wait here," he ordered Julie when she asked if they should help Kali search. "We can't sit in our new car if we're covered in soot. Besides, Kali knows what she's looking for. You don't. Just stay put for a while." She glowered, but she obeyed. He clicked photographs of the devastation. "People died here," he announced loudly as though no one knew. "Looks like they moved the burned-out cars. They'd have to remove the bodies. That's what took so long."

No one responded to him.

In the distance, huge cumulous clouds played surly one-upsmanship, daring one another to billow wider and blacker as they rose higher and higher in the sky until they obscured the sun. Julie climbed out of the car to stand beside it holding her cell phone in one trembling hand. "THERE'S AN ALERT! THEY'RE SAYING IT'S RAINING HIGHER UP!" she called out to anyone who could hear. "THEY SAY WE NEED TO WATCH FOR FLASH FLOODS! WE'RE IN A WARNING AREA!" When no one responded, she mumbled to herself. "Good grief! It wasn't supposed to rain until tomorrow!"

Kali was frantically scratching through the ashes with her gloved hands, tears escaping down her blackened cheeks beneath her mask. "We worked so hard for this, Daniel, and everything's gone. Everything. We worked so hard!"

Lila squatted over the spot that had held her swing set as though she might find a miniatured version hidden in the soot. "My seesaw is burned up!" she moaned. "And my princess perch! It's all nasty!"

Daniel was digging through debris close by. "We'll have another house and another swing set, Lily Pad. Things are just things. We're okay and that's what's important. As long as we're alive, we can start over. As long as we have each other, we're rich."

"You ain't shit, you Mexican dirtball!" muttered a man across the street who was shoving salvageable metals into a long bag that bulged with his finds. He had his black baseball cap turned backward so he could take what he wanted more easily. "Go back where you came from! We don't need your kind here. This is a white neighborhood."

Will took a few menacing steps toward him. "Why don't you mind your own business? Do you have any proof you belong here or are you scavenging things that aren't yours?"

The man scurried away to his big red truck, dragging his bag behind him.

"What balls," muttered Will as he pulled a couple shovels out of his trunk and handed one to Maureen.

"The pious, superior ones are the worst," agreed Maureen. "He has no clue he's a common thief."

Maureen and Will joined Kali, overturning large shovel loads filled with ash from deep within the piles, hurrying because the rumbling, raging sky was approaching. "What does the box look like?" shouted Will as he lifted a lumpy mass of debris.

"That's it!" screamed Kali, rushing to him. "That's the box!" She pulled the scorched box out of his shovel and dusted it off with her gloved fingers. Then she held it before her like a precious religious offering—gold, frankincense, and myrrh--afraid to do more. Daniel and Lila hurried to stand beside her.

"Open it!" urged Daniel quietly. "Let's see what's inside."

"The jewelry is probably melted," commented Richard, joining the group with Julie close behind him. "But even if it's melted, gold is still worth something. You'll need to see a respectable assessor."

Kali fussed with the disfigured latch on the box until the top fell off. There inside lay the gold ring. "It's here! It's okay! I was so upset that I didn't think to take it with me, and here it is!" Her tears were flowing freely now, creating pale streaks down her cheeks. "It's all I have of my mother, and it's here—the one thing she didn't pawn. The gold didn't melt. It's okay."

Daniel reached an arm around to embrace her as Lila wrapped her arms around her mother's knees. Kali was sobbing in reaction to all she had endured and suppressed before and since the fire, sobbing through her own prohibitions, sobbing with relief that life could go on. Daniel kissed the top of her head.

Maureen wiped her own eyes. Her voice was a hoarse whisper. "We'd better go. I can sense the water coming." Will slipped a comforting arm around her shoulder.

"Come on!" Richard pressed his hand into Julie's back. "Let's get out of here. Flood water really depreciates a car. Might be totaled. We need to get across the bridge to higher ground." He grabbed Julie's hand, pulling her into a run. They sprinted to his Mercedes and climbed inside. The hulking red pick-up behind them on what had been the street blew its horn. The driver, a squat man in a black cap, rolled down his window. A scraggly blonde beard hung where his chin should have been.

"Get the hell out of the way!" He looked around the group that was now scrambling to return to their cars. "What are you doing with these low-life apes, anyway? Have some pride, man!" The platinum blonde woman beside him yelled something that was muffled by his closing window, and the truck roared up over the curb and on down the street ahead of them.

"Trailer trash," muttered Rich. He was quick to follow the truck, although he chose his route carefully along the debris strewn pavement. Rain blurred his windshield between frenzied wipes, falling as soiled sheets vomited from the greenish sky. He was vaguely aware of Kali and Daniel driving behind him. He didn't bother to look for Maureen and Will.

The red truck bounced ahead of them onto the bridge. Rich followed. The filthy river was sloshing, pounding against the bridge now, slobbering over the lanes. Blackened trees and less recognizable debris slammed against the railings. The bridge swayed—once, twice. And then it fell.

Julie screamed as she felt their car tilting forward into the water.

The bridge cracked and tore into three pieces. The center piece surrendered to the current of the river, floated for a few feet, and dropped into the gun-metal water. A blue truck on the far side revved its engine, burning the rubber of its tires into acrid smoke, and scrambled up the incline as the edge behind them submerged.

Rich slammed his door open and leapt from the car, his face the color of the ash on his windshield. He was about to rush up the remainder of the bridge to safety when Julie's scream stopped him.

"RICH! HELP ME, RICH! I CAN'T GET OUT!" Her panicked face seemed painted on the inside of her window, a rain-streaked portrait of terror. "RICH!"

He froze with flashback fear. Mental images of fire blurred his sight. Daniel passed him, sloshing down the bridge on Julie's side of the car. She had her door unlatched, but the rush of water held the door and prevented her from exiting. He planted his feet against the car and pushed against the pressure. The movement shook Rich into awareness. He came splashing around the rear of the car and strained to help.

"ON THREE! ONE, TWO, THREE!" shouted Daniel. Together, they managed to force the door open far enough for Julie to squeeze out and into Rich's embrace. He pulled her to him, wrapping his arms around her. "Oh, Rich, I love you!" she wept into his shoulder. He held her tightly with one arm as he helped her climb the tilted bridge. Will extended a hand, and Julie took it, letting Will and Maureen tug her up and off the bridge to dry land where Kali stood, cradling Lila who was crying uncontrollably.

Below them all, the red truck was dipping lower and lower into the river. The muffled cries of the man and woman inside skittered on the wind. Soon they would submerge completely. Daniel waded toward them, brandishing a hammer he had brought from his car. He swung it as hard as he could, smashing the window beside the woman. Rich waded down to join him and together they dragged her lumpy body through the jagged space. Her dripping hair framed the screeching panic on her face. Rich helped her struggle up the incline where Will was extending his hand to tug her the rest of the way.

Meanwhile, Daniel half waded and half swam to the driver's side of the truck. He had barely enough room to smash the window above the charging current. He offered an arm to the man with the black cap who seized it and combined his strength with Daniel's to climb out. Rich helped tug him up the incline to safety.

The remainder of the bridge was sinking, taking the truck with it. Debris washed over the railings—an inanimate mob rushing, crushing from disaster. A huge scorched limb struck Daniel, knocking him into the river where his body rushed away with the current. The truck disappeared behind him. Kali's banshee scream pierced the roar of the water.

Rich glanced back at Julie once before he dove off the bank into the river.

Chapter 40

Boiling the Pot Down

"WHAT'S HE DOING?" yelled Julie frantically. "WHAT THE HELL IS RICH DOING?"

The heads of the two men bobbed erratically in the black river, often indistinguishable from the debris.

"Can they swim in that current?" Julie asked no one. "*What can we do? We have to do something!*"

"I'm calling for help," shouted Maureen around her cell phone. "But in this weather I don't know who can come." She grabbed a fistful of Julie's shirt, preventing her from following Rich into the river. "*They're on their own! You can't help! You aren't really a mermaid, you know. Don't make the situation worse!*"

The man with the black cap grabbed Will's arm. "There's a pontoon torn off one of those houseboats that's caught upstream there in the backwater. Must be from the lake. Maybe together we can send it down to them. They need something to hang onto."

Will shrugged. "It's worth a try. Better than nothing. I have rope in my trunk, but not enough to reach them." Maureen handed her cell to Kali, ran back to fetch the rope from the car, and scrambled down the muddy bank after them. Julie followed.

"We can make a human chain," said Maureen as she slid. "With the rope, we can make sure no one else gets washed away. Tie it to a tree that's still rooted." The woman with the dyed blonde hair who had been in the truck picked her way after Julie.

"I got good grip," she said, wiping the blood that was trickling from her elbow. "And I do good knots. My dad taught me."

"I'll go first," offered Will. "I'm a pretty good swimmer if it comes to that."

The man in the back cap nodded. "We'll make sure you don't go in that far, but I can't swim, so you're on."

"I can be next to Will," said Julie, setting her feet against a root in the dirt. "I swim well. *And my husband is out there!*"

"I'll go next," said Maureen. "I'm not a bad swimmer, either."

"Nobody can swim in this river," muttered Will, mostly to himself. "That's the point of the pontoon."

The woman with the dyed hair secured the rope to a tree that looked as sturdy as any and then they tied the rope around Will. "Okay." He gave his supporters a little smile. "I'll see if I can dislodge the pontoon and push it into the current, then you can pull me up."

He waded into the backwater.

On the highest part of the bank, Lila was clinging desperately to her mother. "Will they be okay, Mommy? Will they be okay? Is Daddy going to be alright?"

"I think so, Sweetheart." Kali was staring down the river, searching for Daniel's head in the maelstrom. It was time to be the stoic again. She sucked in a breath. "We're doing our best." She could feel Lila's heart pounding against her, a little girl who was enduring her fourth major trauma. Even for Daniel, Kali couldn't let go of her.

Will stumbled into the current a couple times before he was able to shove the pontoon hard enough to send it into the mainstream. Hopefully, it would travel close enough to the lost men. The human chain slowly hauled Julie and him up the bank where everyone stood panting, staring after the pontoon. Will spat out the water he had in his mouth, thinking of the myriad deadly poisons he had probably already swallowed.

"This water is revolting and it reeks," he said to no one in particular. The comment didn't help anything but it felt good to say it.

Kali was scanning the river. "The pontoon is shooting down the center of the river," she shouted. "BUT I CAN'T SEE THE GUYS ANYMORE!"

"Mommy! Mommy!" cried Lila. *"Where's Daddy?"*

Kali hugged her tighter. "It'll be okay, Baby."

"Quick! Untie the rope from the tree and give it to me!" ordered Will. "I'll run down the ridge. Maybe they'll come close enough for me to throw them a line and tow them in."

"I'll come with you!" shouted Julie.

"And me!" added Maureen at the same time the couple from the red truck said the same. Then all five headed down what was left of the bank.

"WATCH OUT FOR WEAK SPOTS IN THE BANK!" Kali yelled after them. "THE RIVER'S STILL RISING! I'LL STAY ON THE CELL!"

In the river, Rich had finally managed to reach Daniel who was doing what he could to raise his mouth above the water as often as possible. "I think the branch dislocated my shoulder," he muttered to Rich when he had a chance. Dark red blood colored the back of his shirt. Rich nodded, looking around for anything that could buoy them. He couldn't keep them both up indefinitely. The battered pontoon bobbed in place, slowly rotating before waves that were cresting over a sunken structure, waiting for an opportunity to break free. Rich struck out as powerfully as he could to swim to it. Sticks and bits of blackened debris pelted him as he swam—even the carcass of a burned cow. He thought of the lake and how he had failed to stay properly submerged. This was different. This was swimming and he was good at it. He could do this. He *would* do this. Once he had his arm around the pontoon, he swam for Daniel. He needed everything that was left of his stamina to direct the pontoon through the current, and he silently thanked God he had been working out—50 laps three days a week. He'd never let Julie down again.

"Can you hang on?" he asked Daniel who was fighting to catch a breath between times when he was pulled under. Daniel nodded, but Rich could see the pain and exhaustion in his face. Rich kept him afloat as best he could while Daniel reached an arm over the pontoon. "We'll just rest a minute," Rich told him as he gulped breaths, "and then we'll kick as hard as we can when we're closer to a bank. I'll tell you when."

"*Gracias, mi amigo.*" Daniel's voice was almost a whisper. "You didn't have to come for me."

"Like hell I didn't," replied Rich. "You helped me rescue Julie." He surveyed the landscape ahead of them. "It looks like there's a place up ahead where trees in the water break the flow. If we can kick over there, we might be able to grab a limb."

"*Amigo,* I don't have much strength left. I'll help you kick, then you go."

"You aren't getting out of this that easy. Now kick!"

They jetted past the trees Rich had targeted and smashed against protruding rocks but kept kicking, anyway. Inch by inch, they neared more trees that marked the old shoreline. Rich had no idea how he was going to reach a limb without letting go of the pontoon, but time was an enemy. Daniel's grip was loosening. Rich was desperate. An idea had to occur to him soon.

A shout went up from somewhere south of Heaven. "I SEE THEM! THEY'RE OVER HERE!" Rich didn't recognize the voice or the bearded man wearing a black cap who was on the ridge doing the shouting, but he kicked harder. Then he spotted Will running down the hill to the water. The bearded man was wrapping a rope around one of the trees. "YOU GO. WE'LL ALL PULL," he yelled to Will.

Will splashed into the water and began swimming toward the pontoon. "I HAVE A ROPE TIED TO ME," he shouted when he was close enough to Rich to be heard. "WE'LL DRAG YOU IN." He reached out to grasp Rich's hand. "THIS WAY TO EGRESS!"

Rich had no idea what he was talking about, but he locked his arm around Will's. "You okay, Daniel?" he asked, glancing backward.

Daniel nodded weakly.

"Take *him* in!" Rich ordered Will. "I can stay with the pontoon a little longer. His left shoulder's dislocated and he's bleeding. He's really hurting."

Will nodded his understanding and grasped Daniel in a lifesaving grip around his chest. "I've got you. Just relax."

"PULL THEM IN!" shouted Rich, and the chain of people along the rope strained to comply, matching their strength against the savagery of the river. His eyes locked with Julie's for a brief moment as she stood in the water and tugged hand over hand in front of Maureen. The distressed, raw love that teared in Julie's gaze was a physical gut wrench to him. He felt its power smash through his cells, upending his reality and sucking away what was left of his breath. Was he crying, too?

Meanwhile, hungry waves cascaded over both Daniel and Will, trying to tear them back into the flow, but Julie waded forward and, with Maureen to help her, seized Daniel around the chest and hauled him up and out. Will's eyes narrowed as he looked back toward Richard. He lunged toward the pontoon. While the others were occupied with Daniel, Will gave the pontoon a single, mighty shove back into the current, sending Rich downstream with it. Will could hear Julie's scream, *"RICHARD!"* as Rich was swept into the flood.

"I CAN'T REACH HIM!" shouted Will and fought his way ashore.

Rich hugged the ruptured pontoon, knowing it was beginning to take on water. Damn! He recoiled from a mental still photo of Will's expression as he pushed the pontoon, icy determination in his eyes. Everybody's nice guy Will wanted him to drown. He wanted him dead. Rich had never doubted Will didn't like him, but he'd never suspected he hated him that much. Who could despise anyone enough to watch him die? What had he done to ask to be murdered?

The current was fierce. Beneath the waves, a barrage of garbage pelted his legs, tearing his pants and assaulting his skin. He was losing strength. He should've done more stamina work in the gym. He closed his eyes for a moment, hoping to summon a second wind. He had a mental flash of Julie lying in his bed—beautiful Julie. He had wronged her. She was fighting to save him. He'd been wrong about so much. And Will wanted him dead. Will was a killer. The thought made him dizzy.

He reopened his eyes. The river seemed to sneer at him, taunting him, daring him to die. His mind heard an echo of Julie's voice from the lake: "Be calm." He needed to think smart. He needed to live. Will was a killer. He needed to protect Julie.

Ahead, the river was emptying into low farm land flooded into an immense, disgusting lake, swirling with destruction. If he could escape the current, he'd have a chance. The pontoon had become a liability as it sank lower and lower. He released it. He imagined he heard Maureen telling him not to quit...and Tutu's voice, her grandmotherly voice, telling him everything was going to be okay. He struck out across the current, using his aching upper body to compensate for his defeated legs.

He heard or perhaps felt the whirr of a motor. A boat. A spindly elderly man in an old wooden boat with a small outboard motor was heading toward him. The dark-skinned man was grinning underneath his tattered straw porkpie hat as he pulled alongside. "Come on aboard, Son. Got a place reserved for you."

Rich tried to pitch himself into the boat, but he couldn't command his body to do it. He had finally asked too much. The elderly man reached over and, with hands that seemed too frail to be so strong, helped haul him in as the boat rocked dangerously in the waves. A small brown-and-white dog and a tiny spotted fawn huddled in the bottom between the seats, seemingly taking comfort from one another as bilge water sloshed around them. They watched with wary eyes as Rich settled himself on the worn bench seat.

"Been picking up survivors," said the man. "Name's Ben."

"Rich Teller." Rich leaned over to pet the dog who seemed to appreciate the attention. The boat exuded a fishy/molding smell that overwhelmed the scent of wet fur. "You found me just in time. I didn't have much left."

"Got a notion I hadn't finished cruisin' around yet. More debris comin' down the river all the time. Gotta dodge some of the stuff. Didn't expect a man, though." The man wiped a hand on his denim overalls and offered Rich a dull green thermos. "Hot coffee. Made it myself. Looks like you could use a swig or two." He settled himself at the motor maneuvering the boat through the waves.

Rich gulped the coffee, letting the heat sear energy down his throat.

"They predicted this flood," admitted the man, "but you never know what that's gonna mean. I saw on TV the waters took some cars and folks who didn't expect so much of it. Lots of houses gonna need to tear out all the drywall they put in after the last flood. This ole earth is changing under our feet. Glad I got a boat."

"Do you live around here?" asked Rich.

"Naw. Too pricey these days. But I got a friend who lets me keep my boat at her place. I generally use it for fishing. Don't expect I'll be fishing in this goop for a while, though. Talk about your contamination! Hope you didn't swallow too much. Bad water can make you sick real quick."

Rich lowered the thermos from his mouth and handed it back. "Sorry. I didn't mean to drink it all."

"Looks to me like you needed it." The man accepted the dented, paint-chipped thermos that squeaked as he sealed it and made a hollow clink as he placed it against the pail by his feet. "How'd you come to be in the flood?"

"A friend of mine was knocked into the river and I went in after him."

The old man smiled, revealing teeth decorated with metal fillings. "We got gold-hearted people on this earth and a whole lot more that's confused about which way is up. Seems like you're one of the gold ones. How'd your friend do?"

"We got him out. Then I was caught in the current."

"Glad to hear about your friend. Always open to good news." He sighed and patted the fawn. "Purty, ain't she? Warms my heart to have her trust me like this." He looked up at Rich. "There's a Red Cross tent down the way a bit on the high ground by the highway. If you got no objections, I'll drop you off there. They'll be able to patch up those places where you got cut and get you connected to your people." He surveyed the horizon and urged the boat forward, his little outboard motor whirring with determination. His gravelly voice had no trouble rising above the sound. "Think I'll stay out here till suppertime or my fuel runs out—whichever comes first. You know, I ain't the only one cruisin' around with a boat—lots of folks havin' attacks of goodness in the floods. It's a glad sight. Don't get many chances to lend a hand when you don't have money. And some others takin' advantage. Shame. Life is ugly when you're shriveled inside."

Rich drew a long, weary breath and exhaled it. In the boat bouncing above the rapid flow of the river, time had slowed as though they were suspended in an alternate dimension. He wasn't sure he hadn't climbed into a slice from the past. "Thanks for picking me up. You're good people. To tell you the truth, I'm not so sure about me."

Ben chuckled, making his face into a happy raisin with a stubble of gray beard. "Got a case of confusion, huh? Me, I jus' walk the path that's in front of me."

Rich nodded. "I'm really tired—maybe more tired than I've ever been before. Everything's looking blurry to me right now." His mouth twisted into a crooked approximation of a smile. "You're going to think I'm losing it, but have you ever felt like you died and didn't know it?"

The old man pursed his lips. "I'm listening."

Rich dropped his gaze to the tiny fawn staring up at him with wide, forest eyes. "I don't know how to explain it. And I don't know why I'm trying to tell you…"

"Cuz I'm here."

His sigh made the dog cock his head as Rich continued. "It's like if I looked in a mirror right now, some stranger would be looking back at me. I half expect to see my body floating by, bloated and dead. This is the second time I've nearly drowned in the past few months. It doesn't get easier. I'm light-headed and unsure. I guess that's what exhaustion will do to you."

The old man stroked his face with his free hand. "Could be it ain't only exhaustion."

"What do you mean?"

"All I know for sure is bad times takes us places inside. Maybe better, maybe worse…we don't come out the same. I'm thinking we get to choose how we see things."

They were quiet for a few minutes, letting the whirr of the motor and the slap of the waves against the hull fill the silence. Finally, Rich spoke. "Do you believe in aliens?"

The old man's forehead squeezed together. "Believe. *Believe*? Jus' because I'm old, don't mean I got all the answers. Belief is precious. Only small-minded folk can go spreading beliefs around because they're sure they're right about everything. Folks like me, well, we hold our beliefs real close—don't depend on too many. Keep it simple. I don't spend no beliefs on aliens. But I've sure enough seen things I can't explain in my years. Do you think aliens put you in this river?"

Rich laughed. "No. Of course not." He shifted on his seat. "I don't know. One thing leads to another. I don't know anything right now."

Ben smiled a wide smile, his eyes sparkling. "That sounds healthy to me. Be stingy with your beliefs. Spend 'em on love. That's the only-est thing left in the bottom when you boil the pot down."

Rich nodded. "I know an old woman who talks like you."

Ben laughed. "Don't need a woman. Thanks, anyway."

Chapter 41

What's in Their Minds?

"OLD BEN? EVERYBODY around here has seen Old Ben. Some neighborhoods have heritage trees or historic mansions. We have Ben." The man driving the car wasn't much older than Rich. His sandy hair whipped his face in the wind from his open window. "I heard they drove him out one year, oh, a long time ago. You know, back when a dark face was enough to make you call the cops." He laughed. "Come to think of it, we haven't progressed much from then, have we?"

Rich stared out across the hillsides. "No. I guess not."

"I heard he was lucky he wasn't lynched back in the day. People thought he'd kidnapped a little white girl. He hadn't. He found her wandering around lost and was looking to take her home, but he was in a lot of danger for a time. I heard people were punching him out until the little girl finally got somebody to listen to her. Unfortunate."

"Yeah."

"Anyway, he's harmless. At least that's what people say now. Mostly people leave him alone because he's friends with the richest woman north of the bay. Some say they sleep together, but he looks way too old for that stuff to me. Maybe he's taking those pills that give you a four-hour hard-on, huh?" The driver laughed. "Or maybe his kind don't need pills."

Rich felt his stomach lurch. "He saved my life."

"Oh yeah?" The driver turned to look at Rich's expression. "You're serious. Well, that's something, isn't it? It looks like the tent medics did a good job fixing you up—except for those scars on your face. But they aren't new, are they? You collected your tax break in bandages."

"Yeah."

"No offense, but when people go into the river when it's flooding, I'm not sure it's worthwhile yanking them out. I mean, you set yourself up, didn't you? Why should I pay taxes to fix you up when you asked for it? No offense meant."

"The bridge collapsed."

"Oh yeah? Well, I don't imagine you could do much to avoid that."

"Not much."

They arrived at the incident command center, an abandoned restaurant that had been commandeered for the emergency. The driver pulled up in front. "There you go. Say, you didn't tell me your name. Are you from around here?"

Rich opened the door. He was already searching the people milling around for a familiar face. "Teller. My name is Richard Teller."

The driver leaned toward him. "Teller Real Estate?"

"Yes."

The driver whistled. "Used to be a big name around here."

Rich closed the car door. "Used to be. Thanks for the ride." He didn't look back as he walked toward the building, feeling his legs like wooden posts strung with frayed muscles.

"Rich! Rich!"

He felt her shout as much as heard it. The vibrations of it struck him like electrical impulses laid against his heart. He turned and she ran to him—a woman more beautiful than anyone he had ever seen. Her red hair still shone in the sun although it was streaked with mud. Her body wrapped around his as she held his face in bandaged hands and kissed his cheeks and then his lips. His weary arms embraced her, letting the pulse of her lend him fresh energy.

At last she pulled away far enough to be able to peer into his eyes. "Rich, are you okay? They said you were picked up. We've been searching every cot."

He nodded, staring at her, wondering how he hadn't remembered before how very much he adored her. "Old Ben rescued me in his boat. He didn't even know me, but he pulled me out—me, a dog, and a fawn. He saves things."

Tears were slipping down her cheeks in silver streams. "Oh, Rich. When the current took you, I was afraid. I was so afraid..."

He nodded. "I saw you." Somehow the three words stood alone, heavy with meaning. He repeated them. *"I saw you."* A revelation. "You're magnificent."

She kissed him again, lingering longer this time. And when she looked at him her gaze slid down through the core of his chest. "Rich, you look different."

He nodded. He was immeasurably weary and yet very young and new. In the filthy flood the world had slipped into a fresh dimension—something kinder than he had ever seen before. He suddenly realized the others were standing near—Kali and Maureen...and Will. He felt small and clean. "I don't know how I can ever thank you all," he told them in a voice that quavered just a bit. He avoided Will's gaze.

"Are you kidding?" Kali shook her head in mock amazement. "You saved Daniel's life. He's waiting in the car with Lila, but he told us what happened. You saved him, Rich. Pure and simple."

He shrugged. "And all of you saved me. We're even." He blew out a heavy exhalation. "How's Daniel doing?"

"The medics snapped his shoulder back and cleaned him up. They say with a good shower and a lot of sleep he'll be fine."

"I was worried," Rich told her. "He was bleeding and that water is so polluted."

"They gave him antibiotics." Kali came to plant a kiss on his cheek. "Thank you."

A stranger in a black baseball cap with a woman who had platinum blonde hair offered a handshake. Rich accepted automatically. "Bill Boynton. This here is my wife Shelly. We wanted to wait to meet you. You and your Mexican friend saved our bacon getting us out of our truck. We'll never forget it. Never. If you ever need mechanical work—either one of you, just pull in to Boynton's Body Work and we'll make your vehicle good as new—no charge." He pressed a soggy business card into Rich's hand.

"I seem to be without a vehicle for the moment, but thanks."

"You had a Mercedes, didn't you?" asked the man Bill.

"Yeah, but I think that's my last. I won't buy another. Bad luck."

The man grinned. "Try a Dodge truck. They can get through anything...but a river."

Everyone laughed. Exhaustion made them giddy.

The blonde-haired woman stepped forward to kiss his cheek. "We won't forget. You all are always welcome wherever we are. Now we gotta get home. We have kids waiting. Thanks to the lot of you, they'll have parents to tuck them in tonight." She took her husband's arm and they walked away.

"Maureen was right," said Kali staring at Rich as at an odd specimen. "She said you seem different—in a good way. It's so plain even I can see it. You don't talk the same. The look in your eyes is different. If I didn't know better, I'd think we found an alternative Rich. I guess we never saw this side of you before. You risked your life and preserved our family. It would be our honor to have you and Jules share our car to go home."

Rich smiled. "I feel weird—exhausted but good. Thank you."

Julie patted his chest, her eyes shining. "Kali, this is the man I fell in love with."

* * *

After they had left, Maureen sat in the passenger seat of Will's car and pulled the door closed with a thud. A million years had passed since they first arrived. She felt old and heavy.

"I guess Rich is a hero now," muttered Will as he drove behind Kali's car.

Maureen's words were clipped and even, devoid of emotion. "Yes. I'd say he is."

"Who would've thought. I wonder what his angle was. He has Jules ready to worship him. God, that woman is gullible. And now Daniel and Kali, too. Makes you ask yourself what's next." Maureen didn't reply. The turn signal clicked into the silence. After a while, he added. "We stink. That water was disgusting. I'll have to shampoo these seats."

Maureen stared through the windshield. "I think you were contaminated."

"I'd guess we all were." Will feigned a smile. "You were pretty fierce today. No wonder you win your court cases. You don't give up."

Maureen didn't turn. "I don't give up, but now and then I walk away."

He slid his hand back and forth on the steering wheel. "Prudence. I guess they call that prudence."

She exhaled audibly. "Will, I saw what you did to Rich."

He glanced over at her solidified face and back to the road. "What do you mean?"

"You know what I mean. I looked up at just the right moment... when you pushed him back into the river. If he had drowned, you'd be a murderer."

He licked his dry lips, tasting the river anew. "And you'd be a witness?"

She nodded. "Yes. I'd be a witness."

He pulled to the side of the road as an ambulance passed. When the piercing sound was distant, he turned his head to look at her. "So what are you going to do about it? It wouldn't be easy to prove."

She didn't blink. "The question is what are you going to do?"

He pulled the car back into traffic. "I'm going to drop you off and then I'm going home." He glowered for a while as he drove before he continued. "Don't tell me you buy that crap about Rich magically changing. Not you, the big-time attorney."

She stared at him. "I'm watching you change right now."

He laughed a hollow bitter laugh. "The *'e'epa*?"

"You tell me."

His face twisted into a scowl. "Bullshit. And I never saw any insect people, if that's your next question. I thought you were too intelligent to believe in invisible mind parasites. You need to stay away from Miss Kalani. She's rotting your brain."

Maureen's voice didn't change. "I don't need Tutu to tell me your energy is different. If there's a reason, I doubt you know it. I'm sorry, because I like you, Will."

"Don't you mean that in past tense?"

She sighed. "I suspect that's up to you."

His face fell into a pout. "You think pretty highly of yourself, don't you? Like I'd be stricken if you didn't like me anymore."

Maureen turned her attention to the side window. "You're good at letting go of the attainable. It's somebody who's married like Jules who has you snared."

"Jealous?"

She pivoted to face him. "Interpret this conversation any way you like. You will, anyway. But you were willing to kill a man for Jules. And I'd bet if you had succeeded, you would've found you don't want Jules, either. You've gone to a dark place, Will, someplace unworthy of you. Your friends can't save you from you, and right now you don't want them to try. Ask yourself why sometime when you're permitting yourself a bout of self-awareness—if you ever go there again."

They had arrived at her condo, and he pulled the car up in front. She had climbed out her door when he spoke. "I'm sure you'll tell them your story of what happened in the river."

She leaned down to pin him with her stare. "I don't know if I will. That should be your job. But rest assured, they'll notice the change in you even if they don't know about your attempt at homicide. It's not subtle."

She closed the door on his "Bullshit!"

* * *

Will considered not going to Tutu's house, but he had left Hermione there and while she was good company and well behaved for a dog, she was still a dog and needed attention from someone healthy enough to give it. Would Maureen call ahead to tell Miss Kalani what he had done—to warn her about having a potential murderer in her house? No. He couldn't believe she would. He wasn't a threat to Miss Kalani…if he was a threat to anyone. Hadn't he been the one to wade into the river to free the pontoon in the first place? They should realize he was…a hero. He was still damp and filthy and exhausted…because he was Julie's champion.

Who could think of him as a threat? All he had done was give one little push. It could've been an accident…or an illusion. Maybe it didn't happen at all. The current pulled; he didn't push. Maybe it was Maureen's overactive imagination. And maybe the dirt bag asked for it. Who else was going to save Julie?

He parked in front of the house and sat for a moment, staring at the porch where Julie had been shot. A shooter was a threat. He wasn't a shooter. He exited the car and went to the house to knock.

"Come in!" Miss Kalani's voice was weaker than usual. Shadowy pouches sagged beneath her eyes as she rocked slowly to and fro, watching him as intently as the dog was. "Sorry for not getting up. My knees been complaining something fierce today. But I'm glad to see you." Excited, Hermione hopped down from her position on the sofa and ran to him, circling, sniffing and examining as only a dog can. Will wondered what was going on in her canine brain. What did she learn from her examination? What made her look up at him with glazed-oak eyes that were suddenly sad?

"She says you got a story," interpreted Tutu.

He stood immobile, deciding if he should evade Miss Kalani and leave. He didn't owe the dog or this old woman anything…much. "I went into the river to save Richard and Daniel," he blurted, hoping to sketch the day for her in a rush and escape. "The flooding made the bridge collapse. Rich lost his car and so did some other people. Hermione probably smells the water. It was sickening." He sighed, wishing he had chosen to exit immediately.

Tutu was staring at him, her smile enigmatic as it often was. "Come. Sit. You gotta let yourself settle outside the excitement." She was addressing him and not the dog, but Hermione came to sit at her feet. "Kali called to say you was gonna be late. She said you had a day of disaster and miracle. She had to tend to Daniel and Lila, so she left the telling to you. She called you heroic."

Heroic? Kali called him heroic? Was she being sarcastic? Or did she mean it? Will waved a dismissive hand. "I can tell you all about it tomorrow. I need a shower. I'm tired and smelly and contaminated." He was reluctant to sit near her who could pull information from air. She was making him feel guilty and irritated—for no reason whatsoever. It wasn't her business, anyway.

"Tell me everything that happened now, Will, while the details is fresh. Please. Rest. This furniture ain't as old as me, but it's old. It ain't going to Hawaii—maybe to the animal shelter for dogs and cats to sleep on. Or maybe I'll leave it here for renters. Furniture should serve us. A little bad water won't matter." She struggled to her feet, suppressing the moan that was in her face. "Sit. I'll fetch you some whiskey and a sandwich. Then I gotta know everything or I gonna lose my busybody license."

He couldn't have said why he obeyed. Something in her presence—the thing that had been there all these years they had been neighbors.

He gobbled the sandwich and chugged the whiskey, although he had eaten a hot dog at the Red Cross tent. An emptiness inside him demanded to be filled. He'd make another sandwich when he got home…and maybe open a few beers. "Rain brought flooding earlier than anyone expected," he began, straining to remember the proper sequence of events. He wanted to tell the tale as close as possible to the way Kali would tell it, so he recounted the day, detail by detail, leaving out only what Maureen had said she saw. "And now I need to go home," he added in conclusion.

Tutu's gaze burned his flesh. She was as bad as the dog. She sensed things.

"You seem sad or frustrated or angry—like you lost something," she told him without turning away.

The whiskey urged him to have his say. Surely she would understand. She always did. And she didn't care much for Richard, did she? Hadn't she talked against him? "Frustrated, maybe," he said. "I don't know how long Richard can play hero, but he did it today. And Jules ate it right up."

There Miss Kalani was, smiling that smile again—the one that seeped inside you and probed—worse than a proctologist. She rocked as she talked. "Disaster can change a person, and I ain't surprised if it changed Richard for the good. But I'm pleased. I wasn't sure he'd make the choice. The pity is how many people was out there who ain't one bit better tonight and ain't likely to be better folks tomorrow, either."

He squirmed in his seat. "So you believe he's redeemed?"

"Do I think he earned angel wings? Not likely. He gonna still be Rich. But from what you say, I think he sloughed off a lot of what's been eating at him. Julie could tell because she loves him. She been watching for it all along. You don't agree."

He stood, broadcasting crumbs across the floor as he spoke. "I sure as hell don't! You're going to tell me he cleansed himself of those damned *'e'epas*, like any sane person believes in that crap. I'm sorry, Miss Kalani, but I think you need medication or something. Rich was a bad man, is a bad man, and will be one until he kills Jules. That's what I believe."

"I see you do. Sit down, Will. You need to unwind before you hurt yourself."

He perched on the edge of the sofa, scowling at Hermione who growled a soft warning for him to calm himself. "I need to go home. I'm tired and, yes, angry. I don't see we have any place to meet to talk. You're in crazy land."

Seemingly oblivious to his insult, Tutu scratched her chin where a determined stiff hair was trying to make a statement. "I been watching a TV show where they said aliens is a fact. They had pictures of things like big white magnesium pills zipping through up and down in the sky and into the ocean beyond the coast. They was nervous about it—figured they was looking at more enemies, and they didn't yet know how to fight them. People—especially some white folks--is naturally defensive, because they got this idea they on top of a heap and gotta scheme to stay there. They don't trust cooperation."

She rocked a few more times. "A nasty woman in the grocery told me she been horrified that scientists say in the future everybody gonna come in shades of brown. I looked hard at that woman. I wanted to see what kind of life she got that the worst she could imagine was having darker skin or using some other language."

Will threw his head back against the sofa cushions in disgust. "Why are we talking about racism? I'm talking about a dangerous man loose in society."

She shook her head. "And I'm saying the worst folks got to fear is what's in their minds. *'E'epas* build on what's there. If aliens want to wreck this human civilization, all they got to do is feed fear—like politicians and crooked business people do. Set us one on the other, until nobody got the sense God gave a cockroach."

She stopped rocking and leveled a rheumy stare at Will. "It don't make no matter if you got evidence of *'e'epas* or aliens, either. Fact is, they gonna do what they gonna do and we don't have the smarts to stop them. And it ain't about what you think or believe, because we none of us understand more than a speck of what's out there. It's about who we are inside."

He leaned forward over his knees. "Maureen told you I tried to kill Rich, didn't she? And now you think I'm infected or whatever."

Tutu didn't pause in her rocking. "I ain't talked to Maureen." Thump, thump, thump...her rhythm continued as she kept him pinned in her gaze.

He stood. "Keep Hermione. Give her back to Jules and her precious prince. Go to Hawaii or go to Hell. I'm finished with all of you." He strode from the room, feeling furious and miserable and more disoriented than he had ever been.

Chapter 42

Kissing Nightmares to Sleep

"MOMMY, MOMMY, MOM-MEEEE!" Lila's scream echoed through the house. Kali sat bolt upright, her heart pounding. She automatically grabbed for her military weapon that wasn't there. Daniel, too, was sitting, his eyes wide. They both threw back the covers and leapt from their respective sides of the bed. They reached Lila's room at the same time. Kali took Lila into her arms, feeling the racking sobs as much as hearing them, while Daniel sheltered them both in his long arms.

"It's okay, Baby," soothed Kali. "It was just a dream. Everything's okay."

"We're here for you, Lily Pad," added Daniel in his deep voice. "Nothing can hurt you."

Lila reached out to touch each parent in turn with her pudgy fingers, as though reassuring herself they were real. "They were after me! They were gonna get me! The big men! They were chasing me!"

"No, Baby, no one's here but us and Maureen. No one can get you. We're here." Kali looked toward Daniel. "It was just a bad dream."

"Mommy, they were hurting Daddy. He had blood on him—all over! They hurt him, Mommy! They threw him in the river and he washed away with the dead cow. And they pushed me in a cage with a zillion kids. They pushed me in and slammed the door...bang! And the cage was full of monsters! A monster grabbed me and touched me. He wanted to hurt me! He caught me in his hands and wouldn't let me go! He was gonna throw me in the dirty water. He was gonna shoot me!"

Daniel's eyes were moist. "No, *hija*. They can never get you or me again. We're far away from the cages now. We're safe here with

Maureen, and soon we'll be over the ocean in Hawaii in our new home. It's a wonderful, safe new home. The bad people aren't welcome there. We have good friends to protect us. We'll be safe."

Lila's chest was heaving beneath her pink dinosaur pajamas. She paused to draw a ragged breath as she looked from one parent to the other. "They can't come to Hawaii?"

Kali shook her head as she rocked the little girl, to and fro, to and fro. "No, Baby. They can't come. Patrick's friend Nainoa won't let them. Daddy and I won't let them."

Slowly, Lila's gasping deepened to more normal breaths. "I'm glad we're going to Hawaii. I don't ever ever want to see that other place again."

Daniel kissed the top of her head. "Me, either, my love. Me, either." He left Kali to rock Lila back into sleep.

"Think of beautiful things, Baby," Kali told her in a soft, rhythmic voice. "Think of the leis and Nainoa's pool. Think of the friends you met at Patrick's wedding. Good times are coming, Baby. Good, happy times. Beautiful flowers and friends and loving times."

"We'll go on a plane..." added Lila, gradually settling into Kali's arms as one settles into a down comforter. "We'll eat peanuts and go far, far away. I'll bring my dinosaur Maureen gave me. I like Hawaii."

When Lila had drifted deep into Kali's images, Kali gently laid her back into her bed, tucking her dinosaur beside her. She leaned over to kiss her daughter's damp forehead. Kali wanted to let herself weep, knowing the many frightening images fate had recently delivered to Lila's childish mind—the fires, Julie's shooting, the detention center, the flood. No little girl should have to see so much. But Kali didn't dare open the gates of her emotions, because she wasn't certain she could close them again. Old images from the war tumbled into her knowing—images that haunted her rest. Children all around the world were forced to endure hideous realities created by adults. She wanted to be able to kiss Lila's knowing away, but helpless to do that, she crept quietly from the room.

She found Daniel sitting in the living room, his head in his hands.

"Are you okay?" she asked him, wiping a stray tear from her own cheek.

"Yeah." He turned his face to her and she could see he had been crying. "I couldn't protect her, Kal. I couldn't protect my Lily Pad."

Kali sat beside him, slipping her arm around him and laying her head on his shoulder. "You did all anybody could. We got her out in time. We got her out."

He sniffed. "I read about a boy they kept for something like 23 days...23 days, Kal, and he had his birth certificate with him! He was an American-born citizen! But he was Hispanic so they didn't believe him. They didn't check for 23 days! It wasn't just me and Lila. We weren't the only ones. They didn't care that we were legal. There were white people in there, too—poor ones from Europe. They don't care, Kal. It's not about law."

She took his hand in hers. "I know. There's no morality in those detention centers or the authorities who run them. They're designed to be inhumane and disgusting. We were blessed to know Maureen and G.B."

More tears ran down his face. "I couldn't protect her! She could've died in there. Our baby girl could've died. We both could've."

Kali kissed the side of his face. "But you didn't."

He drew in a long breath and exhaled it in ragged bits. "They took my manhood. I don't feel like a whole man anymore. I feel beaten all the time. I feel small."

She turned his face to her with soft fingers. "No. They didn't take your manhood. They can't. Don't give them that power. You saved that couple—Bill and Shelly Boynton. They would've drowned without you. You helped save Julie. You're brave and selfless. You're a hero. The bullies at the border are strong behind their guns, but if you had a chance to meet them one-on-one, you'd defeat them. I know you would. Together we'll help defeat them, Daniel. There will be things we can do from Hawaii. We'll do everything we can. I swear."

He twisted enough to be able to kiss her fully on the mouth. "I love you, *mi corazon*. I'm married to a mighty warrior."

She kissed him soundly. "So am I."

Chapter 43
Galloping Off a Cliff

MORNING SUNLIGHT SLIPPED through an opening in the heavy damask curtains, creating a bright stripe down Richard's naked back and up onto his head where the new hair was less disciplined since it had been burned off. A few days had passed since the flood, and he was ready to explore his new energy. The brightness that came through the cream-colored sheers behind the curtains gave him an other-worldly aspect, as of a misplaced god come to claim his due. He wasn't smiling exactly, but the lustful twinkle in his eyes loaned him an air of both boyishness and manly desire combined. He extended his hand to stroke Julie's face, letting his fingers linger on her lips. "I hope you know how gorgeous you are, Mrs. Julia Scott Teller, and how beautiful you will always be to me."

She smiled and slid her naked body down beside his, caressing his skin with the length of her own, wrapping her legs around his. "Oh, Rich, I knew you weren't really an asshole, but the nastiness lasted so long! I was scared. The things you said to everybody! The things you said to me. It was like you were possessed or something. I tried to tell people it wasn't you, but they didn't believe me—except maybe Tutu. I think she suspected I was right. I knew you'd come back to me one day. All that love couldn't just disappear. Real love doesn't go away, does it? Does it? As long as we work to preserve it?" She pressed her ear to his chest. "And we will work to preserve it, won't we? Keep telling me I'm gorgeous. Try it again so I can feel the vibration."

He dropped his voice to an exaggerated low register, almost singing, and repeated, "I hope you know how gorgeous you are. I'll spend the rest of my life proving love is what we are together."

She laughed and licked his nipple, nibbling her way up his chest to his lips. "You make me gorgeous. And now you make me proud. Do you know how much I love you?"

He kissed her long and slow until she was breathless and her bones seemed to melt beneath his fingers. "Yes," he said in a tone that stroked her with soft, warm breath. "I do. It's the most magnificent sight I've ever seen—one I hadn't realized before. No one has loved me like that. Please forgive me for taking so long to wake up. It was some kind of crazy shit that got hold of me. I'm the most blessed guy in the world. And I'll never forget again." He lowered himself over her, caressing her as he kissed deeper and deeper, teasing her breasts as he massaged down her belly and between her legs until she released her moisture and moaned to his touch. By the time he entered her, she felt impatient and hungry and ready to climb on top of him and make it all happen again as soon as possible. So she did.

When they had exhausted themselves, they dozed briefly, entwined in each other's arms and legs and wetness, not thinking any longer, simply languishing in their being. And then they entered the shower together, playing in the artificial rain, soaping one another and teasing and wondering if they had enough energy to make love a third time. He lay across the bed and watched as she slowly tugged her bikini panties over her long bare legs and then added a tight pair of knit black pants. To please him, she skipped wearing a bra, instead letting the fabric of her tunic brush her nipples into alertness.

"I adore your breasts," he mumbled as he sat up. "They're a work of art."

"And when they finally droop with gravity?" she asked, grinning as she fondled them for his entertainment.

"Then I'll love them..." and he dropped his voice... "lower."

Julie was still laughing as she answered a knock at the door. Her face was bright with happiness. Her wet hair hung in tousled auburn curls over the shoulders of her white tunic, leading Will's eye over her nipples to her tight black pants and bare feet beneath.

"Hi," he said humorlessly, restraining Hermione as she pulled at her leash. "I brought your dog. She belongs with you—antiques or not. You adopted her."

"Come in." Julie didn't seem to notice his mood as she stepped back for them to enter and then sat on the stone tiled floor to cuddle Hermione. "Rich! Will and Hermione are here!" She laughed and winced simultaneously as Hermione stood with her nails on Julie's naked toes, licking her face, and wagging her doggie body.

"You should've called to say you were coming, and we would've made lunch." She laughed, thinking that if Will had called no one would have answered. In fact, with warning, she might not have answered the door. "It is lunch time, isn't it? I'm sure Rich and I could whip up something, anyway, if you're interested. Or we could order in. Gosh, do you think Miny's glad to see me? I didn't realize how much I missed her. Thanks so much for bringing her. Who gives a shit about a bunch of antiques I never liked in the first place? They aren't worth one good doggie kiss. Oh, good girl!"

Rich came from the rear hallway, barefoot, his plaid shirt hanging loose over the waistband of his jeans. "How ya doing, Will?" he asked, but his gaze was cold.

"Okay." Will hesitated, watching the woman and the dog. He hadn't missed the details of both Julie and Rich being pink-cheeked and barefoot. He thought he could smell their love-making. He could feel his own temperature smoldering with ill humor…hot coals anxious to flame. Deep breaths. He needed deep breaths to focus. "Could I talk to you privately, Rich?"

"Sure. We'll go down to my study. Jules, why don't you take Miny out back?"

Julie stood and clapped her hands. "Come on, Miny! Let's go play!" The two of them ran out the sliders at the rear of the house. Rich gestured for Will to follow him downstairs. He led him into a windowless dark-wood study, lined with bookshelves that held few books. The overhead chandelier burned yellow with tiny artificial candles. He took his place standing behind a huge mahogany desk with a padded black leather office chair tucked beneath it and turned to confront Will.

"Not much of a reader, I take it," commented Will looking around with a superior smirk.

Rich kept his voice even. "This was my dad's office—for drinking, arranging rendezvous with married women, and collecting real estate resources. I got rid of it all. This is what's left."

"So you're getting out of real estate?"

"Doing it differently."

The two men stood in the silence for a moment, feeling the shadowed atmosphere thickening all around them like quantum quicksand.

Will spoke first. "So, did you tell Jules about me pushing the pontoon?"

Rich's voice lost its sociability. "When you tried to drown me, you mean? Damn! I think you knew the answer to that when she let you in. She needs a break from bad news, so I didn't tell her. She likes you. That's one of us."

Will's scowl deepened. "Maureen says she's a witness, just so you know. Are you going to press charges?"

Rich pulled a semi-automatic pistol from the waistband at the back of his pants and aimed it at Will's chest. His jaw twitched against the power of his clenched teeth. His voice was flat and hard. "Charges? No. The law's too unpredictable. You could get off. This is self-defense. You came in here and drew a gun on me. Dad kept one that wasn't registered here in the drawer. Jules will be disappointed in you. I'm going to shoot you dead, Will Manning. Then we'll be even. You won't have a chance to terrorize Jules or me ever again."

Will didn't move. He was staring into the black bore of the gun barrel. The shot wouldn't hurt for long. He'd asked for it, but he wasn't sure why. He was beginning to calm. "Actually, you were on the right track. I did come here to kill you. I have my Mom's old derringer in my pocket. I was going to blast you before you knew what was coming. But when I saw Jules with you I knew she'd never understand and she'd never forgive me—if I ever got out of prison.

Maybe having you kill me is the best solution all around. You go to prison, I'm out of my misery, and she's free of you."

Rich held the gun steady. "You're that jealous? You're in love with my wife?"

Will challenged his gaze. "I want to protect her. I figure you'll kill her some day and abuse her in the meantime. I've heard the way you talk to her. I know you hired that hit. She deserves better."

"Shit." It was a comment more than an exclamation. "You're an idiot, Manning. I didn't hire a hit on her. I didn't know anything about it until the detective told me and then the Mob demanded the money they were missing—a shit pot full of money, by the way. I have no idea how much was part of the hit deal. And I had to pay. My family was an exhibit of mental illness gone bad. I got myself snipped when I met Jules so I'd never reproduce them." Rich lowered the gun and flicked the safety on. "I married Jules because I love her. She's been my lifeline out of the cesspool I grew up in. When I thought she abandoned me to the fire, I lost it for a while. I mean, I totally lost myself. I became my dad—my worst nightmare. I grew up terrified of him, hating him while I nearly destroyed myself trying to please him. I couldn't see my way free until the flood, and then Jules saved me again. I can't really explain it. I don't know how I'll make it up to her. It never occurred to me you thought you were protecting her." He laid the gun on the polished desk. "Here. If you still want to kill me, I guess you'll have to do it. But I hope you don't. You could never love her as much as I do."

Will shook his head slowly. "Well, hell. You take all the fun out of it." He felt himself draining. Precisely what was draining, he couldn't have said.

Rich began to laugh...the kind of unanticipated, nonsensical laugh that explodes tension and feeds on itself, swelling larger and stronger until it steals breath. Will gradually joined him, chuckling a little at first, but then drawn in by the vortex of relief and Rich's contagious guffaws.

"We're a pair," muttered Rich when he could talk again. "I thought you hated me."

Will shrugged. "I'm not crazy about you, if you want the truth, but…Jules aside…I don't hate you enough to kill you."

"Why hate me at all? What have I ever done to you?"

Will leaned forward over the desk. "You're a class A asshole, that's what. Bigoted, superior, and obnoxious. Jules deserves better."

Rich picked up his gun, dropped it into the desk drawer, and closed the drawer with a small thud. "Jules told me I've been acting like an asshole. She's been reminding me of things I've said, and I have to admit she has a point. If anyone should hate me, it's Daniel, but he says we're good. I don't get where you have the high ground, though, Manning. After all, you tried to drown me."

Will nodded. "I'm glad it didn't work, if it's any consolation."

"Yeah, well, I am relieved about that, now you mention it." A shadow crept over Rich's face. "Maybe I needed it—people trying to save me and you trying to drown me. Maybe that was the perspective, the balance, I needed to find myself. A person can get lost, you know. When you've been fed enough bullshit in your lifetime, you can choke on it and get lost."

"So you want to thank me?"

Rich grimaced. "I wouldn't go that far."

Will shook his head at some comment he had trapped in his mind. "I guess I owe you an apology. I don't normally try to drown people."

"And I don't know if I could've pulled the trigger."

Will's sigh was audible. "I guess that makes us even."

Rich headed for the door. "Not really, but apology accepted."

By the time Julie came downstairs, the men were searching the family room fridge for beer.

* * *

The afternoon had sunken into its final languorous hours when Maureen responded to a knock on her door. The boxes of Ramirez belongings had shipped, so the rooms felt oddly empty although her basic furniture was still there. She could imagine missing Lila's happy if tuneless singing and having not one but two sous chefs each time she prepared dinner. No wonder she had finally agreed to go with them--temporarily, probably. She needed the sense of family they gave her. After her disappointment in Will, she needed the predictability of Patrick and Norman. She was already packed.

She could see Will through the peep hole, so she opened the heavy door and remained behind the screen. "Will! What a surprise!" She tried to read whatever was hidden behind his eyes. Could she sense animosity? Revenge? Was he here to eliminate his only witness? He simply looked tired.

He sighed so heavily his shoulders rose and fell. "Maureen, I need to talk with you. Is there somewhere private we could go?" She could smell beer through the door, but he didn't seem inebriated, just overwhelmingly defeated.

"Come in." She would've scolded a client who did as she had just done by letting him enter, but she felt like doing it, and she had learned to pay attention to her instincts. "Kali and Daniel took Lila to the mall. We have a few minutes at least. Have a seat." She gestured toward the living room sofa. He obeyed.

"I talked to Rich," he said as he sat. "Just a few hours ago. I didn't need to tell him what happened with the pontoon. He already knew."

She nodded, squelching a sarcastic comeback. Already knew? How could Rich not notice someone pushing him into a flood? "… And?"

"I apologized. I didn't realize he loves Jules so much. I think she was responsible for the change in him, because she believes he's a good man underneath. I could see it all over her. She lights up beside him. It doesn't matter that I love her. I've gone gooey for someone I couldn't have before. You were right. Maybe I really don't want a relationship. Maybe I'm addicted to longing. I gave Hermione back to them. I've agreed to do more traveling for my job this year. It's time for me to climb out of my safe hole."

Maureen settled into her chair, curling her bare feet under her. "I'm sorry, Will. You must be hurting."

He stared at his shoes. "I'm supposed to be glad she's happy, and she is. You should see her."

"Yes. I've seen."

He looked up at Maureen with eyes that seemed to droop at the edges, a little boy whose best friend moved away. "I thought I should tell you, since you saw my worst. Rich forgives me. I told him I was only trying to protect Jules. I went to his house to kill him and he almost shot me. He thought he had to save her from me. We're square now—no hard feelings. He's not a bad guy."

She made a face. "Men don't know how truly nutty they are."

"Yes. We do. But what are we going do about it?" She laughed then, and he noticed how pretty she was when she laughed. "So give me some time and maybe you could go out for drink with me one day...if you haven't gotten too used to hating me by then." He paused a moment and added, "I'm sorry. That didn't sound good. Like you're a consolation prize or something and you're way too good for that." He paused to draw a long, uneven breath that he was careful to exhale away from Maureen. "If you haven't noticed, I had a quantity of beer with Rich. My thinking is skewed."

Her smile softened. "I'd go for a drink with you one day—especially if it's coffee, but I'm moving to Hawaii with Kali and Lani and Tutu next week. So much has changed since I talked to you."

"Damn, you're leaving, too? What about your place? You've worked so hard to make this nice. And I thought Lani and Dean were moving into Miss Kalani's house. I was looking forward to having them as neighbors. The neighborhood could use their energy."

"They might, after the baby arrives. But Lani wants to have their baby in Hawaii near family. Nainoa is paying for me and Lani and Dean to fly over. Because he can, I guess. He got Dean some gigs and a place for Lani and Dean to stay...in honor of Tutu, I expect. It turns out she really is descended from historically important Hawaiians...which makes the bloodlines of Kali and Lani high status, too. I think Lani's hoping the move can become permanent, but I'm not so sure about Dean. His attitude will depend on his career, I suppose."

Will shrugged. "A guy's gotta provide for his family. There are rules."

A tiny frown creased Maureen's forehead. "I guess so. Meanwhile, Kali and Daniel have a beautiful cottage waiting, thanks to Daniel's new job. There's even a pool. Lila's over the moon about it. Nainoa wants me to interview for the directorship of a nonprofit headquartered on both the big island and San Diego. I have mixed feelings. I don't know if I'm the director type. But I'll respect the favor enough to investigate. I'd love to live closer to Pat and Norman, and Hawaii wouldn't be hard to take. I'm going to rent this place out in the meantime. I think Lani and Dean are looking to rent out Tutu's place, too...until they know where they want to stay. Finding renters is easy. So many locals still need homes after the fire, and Lani and Dean can use extra cash for the baby."

Will's face fell yet further. "Nainoa. How could I forget him? He's stuffed full of helpfulness, isn't he? Oh yeah. He seems like a great guy—super well off, and he looked like he was into you when we were at his estate. You made a nice couple dancing. His mansion would be a helluva place to live."

"Live? Whoa! Slow your pony, Cowboy. You're galloping off a cliff again. Stay on the trail." She shook her head, recognizing that here-comes-another-party-with-no-date-for-me look on his face. "First, you and I are not a thing. We're friends. Don't go tragic on me. Second, I'm not going to Hawaii to date Nainoa, much less live with him. I'm pretty sure if he ever marries again, it'll be to a native Hawaiian. He believes in preserving the blood of the people, and who can blame him. Plus, I'm ready to experiment with who I want to be next. I'm not looking for somebody to define me—not Nainoa and not you. I'm looking for fresh perspectives. I want to feel young again. I want to do young things. Whether that has anything whatsoever to do with you, I haven't the foggiest idea. I rather hope it might. I told you I like you. You're more than you think. That's as far as I go right now."

He seemed to draw himself up taller and straighter, and his expression reverted to one that was more familiar to him. "I hope I haven't blown my chance with you by being incredibly stupid. I have a job coming up next month that'll take me back to Chicago for a few weeks. Hopefully, I'll get my head on straight while I'm there and we can see where we are when I get back. I have a crush on Jules right now; it's true. What guy doesn't want a fantasy—especially a guy whose closest relationships are with drawings. I'll recover. You're twice the woman Jules is. You're real." He sighed as he laid his head backward on the sofa. "I don't mean to sound pathetic, but right now I feel blindsided by everybody who acted like they were family to me jetting off to Hawaii without giving me a heads-up. I guess I asked for it, but damn. I've looked after Miss Kalani for years. I love that old lady. To be honest, it hurts to be left behind."

Maureen leaned forward. Her voice softened. "Then there's something you need to know. I'm sure no one meant to exclude you. I know I didn't. I haven't told Jules yet, either. We've been seriously overwhelmed by all the details of moving. It's about Tutu. She says she knows her time on Earth is ending...and so do I. I can feel her fading, Will. You'll be able to feel it, too. I'm sure she's waiting to be in Hawaii before she lets go. I don't doubt she's in control. We all want to be there for her when she dies. That's the rush about getting there. We want to be a part of her transition."

His self-pity dissolved, replaced by a palpable sadness. Maureen wasn't certain he wouldn't cry. "God. She's been my only family for years."

"You can come with us. I'll see if there's a seat left on our plane—maybe a cancellation or standby. If not, there'll be other planes. Lani and Dean are on a later flight. I'm sure we can find somewhere for you to stay on the island. Sadly, I don't think you'll need to be there long. Tutu loves you and so do the girls. I know they'll be glad to have you near when her time comes."

He nodded. "I'd like that."

* * *

As they all stood in the waiting area for their flight, Tutu hugged Will. "I'm thankful you was able to be here."

Will embraced her, holding her close for several minutes before releasing her. His eyes glistened. "I wanted to be with you. By the way, Rich and I talked out our differences. We're doing our best to grow up. He and Jules are coming later. In fact, they offered to pay for my ticket." He forced a chuckle. "Maybe they just wanted to see me delivered far away."

Tutu frowned. "Don't you joke about friendship, Will Manning. Feel the joy of it and be glad. I knew we been blessed when Maureen and Julie came to us from the fire. Think how much more our lives is than they was then. Think how much bigger our family is. And that's only a beginning. Family can be as big as you wanna stretch."

Kali chose a black plastic seat beside Maureen and dropped into it, bracketing Lila's pink backpack between her legs. Nearby, Daniel was watching Lila perform one of her impromptu dance interpretations, complete with tuneless singing. "I wish we could overwhelm the badness in the world with the kind of family feeling we've developed through our troubles," Kali said wistfully.

Maureen reached out to squeeze Kali's hand. "We've been doing the best we can with our corner," she said with a small smile.

Kali nodded then grinned. "I think we might have vanquished a quantity of *'e'epa*. Wait until you see, Tutu. Rich is a changed man."

Will helped Tutu lower herself into a seat. "So am I," he said just loudly enough for her to hear.

Tutu distracted everyone from her groan as she sat by launching into a fresh lecture. The others gave her rapt attention, thinking of when she wouldn't be there to scold them any longer, thinking of how the world would feel colder. "When you see darkness around you," she told them, "don't curl up and hide. Don't go feeling sorry for yourself or thinking life would be better if you was different. Give up wishing you could control everybody else. Remember you got sun stuff inside. Scientists say you, me, all of us is put together from leftover stars. So you can make light for you and anybody else, if you want, and you should because folks gotta hold light for each other. When people do that, they can be killed, but they can't be destroyed. Star stuff just moves on. Love don't die."

"Is that religion?" asked Will, baiting her.

Tutu smiled. "That's reality."

A forcefully cheerful attendant arrived with a wheelchair for Tutu. "Miss Kalani?" she asked.

"Yes, ma'am," replied Tutu. As the attendant fussed to secure her in the seat, Tutu looked around at her adopted family. "You see this girl come to see me safe on the plane? Her mama got cancer but this girl stand here, smiling and talking nice to me when all she want to do is go home and tend her mama. She doing her job and more because she got a good heart and she responsible for folks. She being real careful with my legs and feet. She giving me the care she want to give her mama."

The attendant stopped and stared. "How do you know all that?"

Tutu patted her hand. "You got your troubles in your eyes. We all do. When you help me, in a way, you helping your mama, too. And when I say thanks, that's her voice with mine. We ain't separate. None of us is. We got love tying us together. That's the magic, if you believe it."

"I believe," said Lila solemnly.

"So do I," affirmed Kali, leaning low to kiss her grandmother on the cheek.

"About time," muttered Tutu as the teary-eyed attendant rolled her away.

About the Author

Susan Adair Harris began writing novelettes in middle school. After winning a national persuasive speaking competition as an undergraduate at Ohio University, she was hired to teach high school outside Cleveland, Ohio. Her original children's one-act was successfully produced for the North Royalton elementary schools. During the summers, she recorded books for the Library of Congress Talking Books program through the Cleveland Society for the Blind. After directing high school plays and musicals, she left to attend graduate school and taught communication courses at the University of Denver as she finished her M.A. and a.b.d. She was recruited to teach for Denver Public Schools and was awarded Speech Coach of the Year. She then taught communication, reading, and English as a Second Language at Trinidad State Junior College while running a regional adult education resource library. Meanwhile, she taught TSJC courses at the Trinidad Correctional Facility and was elected president of the Colorado Adult Education Professional Association.

She has written several screenplays, most recently assisting with the biographical documentary *Lee Wulff: A Remarkable Life* as editorial consultant and associate writer. Her first novel *Death Lost Dominion* was published in 2015, followed by *The Woman Who Saw Souls* in 2017. While writing *They're in Your Mind*, she was also writing features for *New Legends Magazine* and the *World Journal*. She specializes in realistic characters, engaging dialogue, and unpredictable, suspenseful story lines that unwind over deeper themes.

She can be contacted at susanadairharris@gmail.com which accompanies her author website www.susanadairharris.com and she offers weekly blogs at personaljourneyswithgramma.com. She also maintains active Facebook pages that accompany her websites. She loves to hear feedback from fans.

www.ingramcontent.com/pod-product-compliance
Lightning Source LLC
Chambersburg PA
CBHW051947240626
47153CB00005B/1664